Not Exactly Godless

Margot Sinclair

BENYA PUBLISHING

Library of Congress Control Number: 2025941912

First published in 2025 by Benya Publishing

ISBN: 978-1-968455-09-5 (paperback)
ISBN: 978-1-968455-10-1 (ePDF)
ISBN: 978-1-968455-11-8 (ePUB)

Publication data:
Margot Sinclair
Not Exactly Godless
Volume 4 in the "Not Exactly" Series

Design and layout by Scribe Inc.

Benya Publishing
P.O. Box 799
Sullivan's Island, SC 29482

www.benyapublishing.com

Preface

Who remembers the '90s? The Clintons were in the White House. The SUV was the new thing. Martha Stewart was a household name. Cell phones were clunky things a few people carried in cars.

More important to our story Charleston, South Carolina, was still Charleston. Big patches of the city were shabby and ungentrified. The old families lived in the old houses and maintained the old rituals in their kingdom by the sea.

And there was and is an underbelly of the city of organized and disorganized crime that the visitors never see.

When the judge shoved into the aisle seat next to her on the airplane, Honor Revenue thought she was going to start screaming uncontrollably. After three months of him relentlessly stalking her, she had decided to give up New York and go home. Reclaim her sanity. Then he had gotten on the flight out of La Guardia, and now during the change in Atlanta he was making his move.

"We got to talk," he said. He was old and skinny with fluffy cotton hair. Skin like he had dry rot. Stank of cigar smoke.

"We've talked," Honor said back. "Too many times. You on the bench talking down to me. Back in your chambers, you drooling at me. Out in the street you yelling."

She tried to remind herself of all the things the shrink had told her about dealing with obsessive nuts. Remain calm. Converse in a normal tone. But don't give the slightest encouragement. That was right before he had asked to keep one of her shoes. The shrink had asked.

Honor's last name—Revenue—didn't mean money, but rather it was French for "returned" or "come back again." Her ancestors were Huguenots and had settled in Charleston, South Carolina early in its history.

Passengers were shoving huge suitcases into the overhead compartments. Ruthlessly scoffing two and three blankets like they were afraid of an arctic crash and battle for survival.

"My soul is on humming bird wings," Judge Reggio "Reggie" Lorenzo confided. He pressed both hands to his heart.

"Great," she said. "Flit or fly away."

What it was was since she was about three years old, men had been riveted by something in Honor's looks. Enchanted. Enthralled. Crazed. Ape-shit with desire. They'd just glom onto her. Propose marriage. Expose themselves.

Now she was a 22 year-old auburn haired cover girl with a deep luminosity to her eyes, and the curse was almost relentless.

"Come on up to first class with me," the judge urged. "I've reserved a seat. Drinks are free. I know you like mimosas."

"I guess you'd know. You've been stalking me without pause or let-up."

The judge gave a low throaty chuckle. "I'll go over your body like a Briggs & Stratton on a contour lawn."

Honor was getting rattled. She felt like a living paradigm of the plight of women. "What is that? Some kind of mower? You're saying I need mowing? A shave? What? I have a mustache? Unnatural body hair?"

"I don't know that yet. I'm not that good at stalking. I'm just a beginner with this obsessions thing."

That was when Beau-Jack St. Martin McCully said to

the judge he believed that was his seat. Said hey, it's Honor Revenue as I live and breathe. Still got those perfect eyebrows. What a heart-stopping, home-wrecking, race-horse beauty you are.

Honor looked up at a stranger in jeans and a denim shirt, necktie painted with a sunset. He was about her age, maybe a bit older. Early to mid twenties, somewhere in there. Tall. He had that black haired Elvis/Burt Reynolds/part Cherokee Indian look. She didn't know his name. Men remembered her. She seldom remembered them. If she did, it invariably was just the minimal encouragement they needed to trigger a testosterone avalanche.

The judge proposed how about they trade seats? Beau-Jack said no he wanted the one he'd paid for. Sit next to this finger-licking-good lady fair Delilah. The judge got obstreperous, told everyone on the plane that he was a judge of the state of New York and they'd mess with him at their peril. A stewardess began threading her way through the struggling mess of people in the aisle. Advancing on them with a look of grim purpose.

Beau-Jack said truth be known he was a college dropout, but he still had some kind of doubts on the judge's jurisdiction on an airplane. The judge said you go to New York don't you? Sure you do. Everyone visits the Big Apple.

Beau-Jack admitted this was true. He sold furniture to the antique dealers up there.

"Then you never know when you'll need a favor from me. Now disappear, you throw-up, barf-face, snot, phlegm, yuck."

Beau-Jack looked vaguely nauseated. "Jeez where'd you learn to talk like that? You got teenage kids or something?"

"Hey, do you think you're dealing with an amateur here? I put away sociopaths like you every day of the week."

Beau-Jack sounded intrigued. "No kidding? Have we got some common characteristics? Us sociopaths, I mean."

"Textbook. You're all good looking enough to have a way with low self-esteem women. Or old bags who can't find their mouths with the lipstick. For instance, one day my old bag wife Carmen was hanging around the bench. Nagging me about something. And this malfactor dude starts hitting on her. Here I'm getting ready to send him off to Attica. He's got his wrists in manacles and he's rubbing his crotch at her. And she's eating it up. Like it validates her as a woman or something."

The stewardess got involved at that point. Talking with her teeth together in a forced smile. Reminding the judge of the air piracy regulations. Taking him firmly by the arm. He went with her, but kept yelling back. The judge was screaming at Honor that she was a Godless woman. She had gotten inside his soul and was devouring it. The stewardess put him in a seat. He pulled out a green cigar, asked if it was the smoking section.

"Colorful guy," said Beau-Jack, snapping his seat belt.

"Very," said Honor.

"Does he need to be killed or something?"

■ ■ ■

"I want the church to have the furniture when I die," Grace Revenue instructed.

Noble "Rusty" Royall, the recently arrived Rector of St. Ambrose, looked at the hideous horsehair stuffed sofa

and chairs with loathing. The room was absolutely choking with cabbage rose wallpaper. The grotesque triple-
backed couch where they sat even had antimacassars.
He forced an insipid smile. "We have a lot of years before
we must worry about that." Patted her liver-spotted hand.

Rusty's companion Chandler Lovelace smirked. He
was feeling a bit woozy from the bottle of Chablis he had
swilled with his lunch. Still, he knew there wasn't a decent
stick of furniture in the house. Elaborate tufted upholstery
no one would have today. Cheap, machine made rubbish
of the Industrial Revolution crusted with fussy floral and
scroll decorations. Acorn trim. Quatrefoil rosettes. Cabri-
ole legs. All of it mass produced in Grand Rapids, Michigan and sent all over the country. It was a delight to go on
these little duty calls with the new Rector and watch him
squirm. Bored silly at the endless reminiscing and out-of-
date social views of his parishioners.

Chandler was squirming a bit too, needing badly to
take a whizz. He shifted his great, flabby bulk up out of
the chair. Said he'd leave the two of them to chat. Had to
spend a penny.

Grace sort of goggled at him through thick glasses. Old
fool, he thought. Riding about on a bicycle wearing a pith
helmet. Tourists snapping pictures of her like maybe she
was a famous local character.

Tourists. That outlander trash was permanently under
foot these days. Mayor had turned Charleston into a theme
park. There was no off-season.

Old Charlestonians—and Chandler felt himself thoroughly one of them—will tell you that the area South-of-
Broad Street is roughly the size of Monaco. Aside from

the growing invasion of modern day Yankee carpetbaggers, the old families pretty much regard it as their little kingdom by the sea. And the Revenue house at the foot of Legendre Street, although not of an ideal style in the history of American architecture, occupied one of the premier locations. With its view of the harbor and ancient oaks of Whitepoint Gardens, Chandler felt one could rise each day feeling utterly in harmony with the best life has to offer.

Chandler wouldn't own a great house until Mummy and step-Daddy went to their reward. But he was patient. Just as he knew patience would one day reward his divinity degree with the rectorship of St. Ambrose.

Chandler waddled out of the room, flat feet slapping the threadbare carpet. Decent enough digs on balance, he thought, if you cleaned out the furniture. Perfect example of steamboat gothic. Turrets and stained glass windows. Divide it into two condos, and they'd easily sell for a million apiece. He shuddered. To loathesome Yankees.

Ah. The lavatory. Just when he thought he couldn't hold it any longer.

Gad. His trousers were a bit tight. Putting on a trifle of weight. Need to cut down on the sherry and roast beef.

Whew. Utter relief. Bliss even. Be nice if he could swing back through the kitchen. Locate the liquor. Have a short pick-me-up.

Royall was certainly a seditious twit. Bringing his charismatics into the finest Episcopal church in Charleston. Waving their hands over their heads when they prayed. Disgraceful. Provoked a schism in the congregation. Brewing a religious war.

And all of his fanfaronade liberal causes run amok. A dismaying new surprise popping up every week. On Thursday, the old biddies book club had been stunned to find he had invited the author of *Gays in Gray* to address them on the topic of "outting" the Southern Confederacy.

Chandler knew the canny art of biding his time. Once Royall had stepped in it in a really big way, then it was Lovelace to the fore. He'd be rector of St. Ambrose. Return it to the true path.

The big bathroom was decorated as ghastly as the rest of the house. Over the toilet, an oleograph of John the Baptist's head being delivered on a silver salver by some grinning blackamoor. Out of date plumbing, exposed pipes painted over fourteen times with hospital pea-green. Probably wasn't originally a bathroom given the age of the house. Which was why the room was so large.

Good God almighty look at that.

A Tiverton Commode. Not as in sit-on-the pot commode. No, a moveable washstand with cabinet underneath. Walnut burl and floral marquetry. Almost French in inspiration.

Not a speck of paint on it. No restored feet. Impeccable. Chandler knew his antiques, and this was a true Colonial-era Tiverton from the Tiverton-Bewely cabinet shop in Tuckahoe, Virginia. You could always tell because Tiverton's work was both oversized and overweight. Nothing frail or dainty about it. The ornate walnut beast must weigh three hundred pounds.

Like all segments of the luxury economy, antiques were going through the roof lately, and Americana was red hot. Half a million for a Pennsylvania Dutch blanket chest.

Eight million for a Queen Anne secretary. Two hundred thousand for a Ward brothers duck decoy.

But a Tiverton. The one thing in the house of value just jammed into the bathroom. Forgotten in the detritus of neglect. Chandler ran his fingers over it lovingly. Exquisitely rare. Perhaps even unique. This certainly merited rave reviews and repeated standing ovations.

Chandler went back into the hall. Much to ponder here. Credulity was indeed strained. How on earth did Grace Revenue come to be in possession of such a gem?

Whups here was that blind old bat now. Wondering what he was up to for so long. With a sudden sense of alarm, Chandler realized he had his donger hanging out.

Dam' fool woman was totally nearsighted. Hadn't even noticed. No sudden moves now to draw her attention. Hands steady.

"My daughter is coming home from New York," announced Grace. "I want you to meet her. She needs to know the eligible young men in town."

2

"Move it, bitch. What happen? You hit a iceberg and the ship going down?" Luscious Decatur, the club owner was sweating from every pore, cracking open mini bottles three at a time, pouring them into three glasses on the rocks. His pot belly shaking as he moved in time to the music.

Talisha Mackey was tending bar at the Stallion Club up on upper Meeting Street. Which is to say she was pulling draft Millers, three taps at a time, jerk the mugs out, sling them down the bar. Put the ticks on the tab. She was sweating too. Caught up in the last call frenzy, morons thinking they about to be cut off the sauce. Last call usually lasted for an hour and a half.

She shouted above the ruckus. "Under the circumstances, I figure I'm moving pretty well."

"You stabbing me in the back, bitch. You costing me *mun-eee.*"

This was not her idea of the college-grad high life. Wearing leather fringe boots and red hot pants, a vinyl vest with no shirt, working til near dawn at a black stripper club so rough white bikers never even came in. Living at home watching her momma pop pills and hearing the same old stories til she needed hospital-grade Tylenol herself.

Most college grads have gotten over thinking their parents are crazy. In Talisha's case this was impossible because her parents really were crazy.

Her father had an obsession with the Kennedy's, gave her the middle name of John-John which was a real nuisance growing up. Living in his made-up world, he told everyone who would listen he had helped Rosy Grier tackle Sirhan-Sirhan after he shot Robert. This was tolerated at the waterworks where his job seemed to mainly be watching the fluoride register gauge to make sure Charleston wasn't poisoned.

Her momma's big ambition was to hypochondriac Blue Cross into canceling the city employee health policy and put them on Medicaid. She had her own medical encyclopedia set—fourteen volumes plus index—and selected a disease of the day. The only thing Talisha could do to help was never suggest she'd like to be married or leave town. Those two subjects always brought on a health attack.

The sound system was playing Rick James "Fire and Desire" while a strung-out-on-crank stripper with nothing but a g-string on her cooze was butt-grinding at the audience. The air was stiff with smoke and spilled beer and unwashed bodies.

A drunk dude was leaning across the bar telling Talisha he was full up with love for her. He had been doing it all night. Grabbing at her tits. Saying he was going to give her ass a reputation. Put it in a very personal relationship with him. Now he had spent all his money, Luscious yelled for the bouncers and they heaved him out into the street.

Talisha had gone to the academic magnet school when it was still attached to filthy old Burke High. She had been a straight-A student and taken the usual raft of shit. She was playing whitey's game. She had a corncob up her ass. Even girls threatened to whip up on her.

When it came time for college, Smith, Radcliffe, Stanford and Duke all got into a bidding contest for her enrollment. Her momma said all those sounded mighty too far from home and she had to go lie down. She was dizzy and seeing spots before her eyes.

"Rejuvenate yo ass!" shouted Luscious. "Move them buns at a jaunty angle!"

Talisha flung empty Colt Malt Liquor bottles into the bin with a shatter of glass. Jerked three chilled mugs out of the freezer and slapped them under the taps. Pulled the levers. Shit, the keg was dry. She yelled at Luscious.

"Keg's dry!"

Luscious wrestled the new keg in place. Muttering, cursing, shouting above the music. "You don't hustle them buns better, I'm gonna give your ass a no-ceremony leave-taking. You go work a cash register in a Piggly Wiggly. Say 'you want paper or plastic bags?'"

"How about you make nice?" said Talisha, wiping sweat off her face. "We're growing apart fast here." She took about five deep breaths which was all she was allowed and started chopping lemons and limes.

Off at Clemson, Talisha had made the mistake of partying one night with three football studs name of Leone, Dewone and Tierone. As football studs will do, it turned into a gang-rape in a dorm room. Her screams had done nothing but bring the other jock house animals in to watch the goings-on.

There was a whole fol-de-rol tug-of-war after that

between the interests of organized athletics and the women's rights movement. As will happen in these matters, athletics won out. The three rapists were allowed to remain enrolled and a lot of ugly rumors began floating about saying Talisha was a professional, doing tricks for money in the jock house. It had all been a fight over a fee.

Afternoons, Talisha kept sitting in the Dean's office demanding justice. Nights, phone callers to her dorm kept suggesting forcefully that she let it go to rest. Enjoy the football season. The Tigers were doing great. What was her problem? She had enjoyed it after all. Fifteen witnesses said so.

One day an assistant athletic director called her into his office and said she needed to see a psychiatrist to get her head straight. Right in front of her he wrote out a suicide note and said she ought to sign it and blow her brains out. Jump off a high-rise dorm or something. Because she sure wasn't offering the world nothing but grief.

Talisha snatched the note, scooted out of the office before he could stop her and went straight to the local TV station. She had imagined the TV folks would do a hard-copy exposé number on it. Hire fingerprint experts, polygraphs, you name it. Sherlock Holmes the thing. Instead they let the Clemson athletic assholes handle it and ruin the evidence. Then the note disappeared.

The athletic department issued a statement in which they said she was a "delusional and very sad young lady and their hearts went out to her."

Talisha's momma took to serious ill health, saying Talisha should never have left town. The College of Charleston was a perfectly fine place. She could live at home and look after her parents the way God intended.

The keg hooked up, Luscious pulled himself up by the bar top. Face as purple-black as an eggplant. Gold teeth gleaming. "Hey, bitch, I got my rush-hour going here. Affluent black males wanting to shed the long green. And the numbers is down."

Talisha slammed the three mugs under the taps. "Yeah and I'm in a conspiracy theory to impoverish you."

Talisha on her own hired the meanest lawyer in Charleston, a white bitch with flame red hair name of Rannie Ralston. Rannie was not your touchy-feely white liberal. She only hugged Talisha once and that was for the TV cameras. Otherwise she treated her like some poisonous mushroom. It wasn't hard when you were sitting with her to realize that Rannie's ancestors had owned a passel of slaves and enjoyed every moment of holding folks in bondage.

But Rannie sure delivered. The day she filed suit she went on TV saying castration was better than the electric chair for the animals on the Clemson squad. If the University didn't intend to cooperate, she'd have the boosters club in bankruptcy Chapter 11 reorganization trying to scrape together intramural touch football. Once her jury verdict came in, the big time gridiron stuff was gone to be history.

Within a month, Clemson settled for so much money that Talisha paid her way through four years at SC State, an all black college, and retired her parent's mortgage as well. And that was after Rannie had taken a full third as her fee plus expenses.

Rannie was all business. No sentiment. When they were cutting up the money, Rannie told Talisha to keep her business card for if she ever got gang-raped again.

And at this point in her life, Talisha was starting to think that was a more lucrative line of work.

"Shake them tail-feathers, baby," Luscious said.

She gave him a look. "Shake my tail-feathers," she snarled. "Put on my high-heel sneakers too maybe? Move my money-maker? My booty? You living in some kind of time-warp?"

He said, "Hey, ho-bitch. You can have all the college big talk you want. It don't cut no ice round here. Don't give you no air of mystery. No high management expertise. We in the beverage delivery bidness."

The drunk was back. Reeling through the door like a punchy boxer. Lop-sided face. One eye shut. Talisha was the first to see him walk in with the gun. Some kind of short barrel Saturday night special with tape on the grip. She could hear a voice. Her momma saying: "Honey, you get out of what you know, you gone end up in a universe that ain't got no God."

Ka-WHAM!

He had fired a shot into the ceiling.

The incident come to a sudden conclusion. Six dudes at the bar turned around and shot him to tatters.

BLAM WHAM Ka-DAM BA-DA DAM!

Everyone had come armed. It was that kind of club, that kind of night.

Talisha knew for sure she had to get into a safer line of work.

■ ■ ■

Chandler Lovelace was truly irritated at having to drive up to Flat Rock in the Oldsmobile with Mummy and her new husband. Roland was no happier with the state of affairs. His stepson was his most unfavorite person in the world. Damn philosophy ass-wipe he called him. Thirty years old and never held gainful employ. Chandler in turn spoke loudly to his friends of Roland's comic earthiness.

Flat Rock in the lower Blue Ridge Mountains of North Carolina was one of the sacred rituals of all true Charlestonians. They had been migrating there since the ante-bellum days of escaping the malaria season.

Nothing terribly fancy. Roughing it in little cabins that smelled of mildew and squirrels' nests. Let the *nouveau riche* build elaborate mansions around golf courses at Highlands and Linville. Quality would always tell.

All the same, Chandler detested the woods and the cold water and bugs. But it wouldn't be for long. They'd have to come right back with the body for a burial orgy. He must polish up looking bereft.

Perhaps Honor Revenue would be there. Honor of the innate sorcery. Honor of the Tiverton commode worth over one breathtaking million dollars.

Yes, Chandler had looked it up in a variety of antiques and auction house directories. The last known Tiverton commode had belonged to one Anna Gould, granddaughter of Yankee robber baron Jay Gould. She had bought it in the 1930s, current locale unknown. Chandler had estimated the million dollar price based on what Tiverton's were going for at Sothebys'. And he considered his estimate an extremely conservative and low one. Given a bidding war between two frenzied Tiverton collectors—who knew where the price might go.

He smiled at the memory of the gorgeous commode with sinuous burl skillfully planed and joined by those fine colonial craftsmen Tiverton and Bewely. The commode which Grace Revenue so very much wanted to give to the church upon her death. Serious ingenuity required there. So much potential for real gain.

Money either real or lost in the mists of the past always hovered politely around the fringe of social acceptance. Roland Lewy brought very real cash to his marriage with Chandler's mother Phyllis. A true hick from Abbeville, S.C., he had built and sold a carpet laying company for a larger fortune than he admitted to the IRS. "Let Lewy Lay You" emblazoned on the trucks. God. A regular rondo of vulgarity that man. At the dinner table he would relate ribald incidents of substituting cheaper grade of shag than what he was contracted to provide. Once had bilked an entire condo complex on Hilton Head.

Now in retirement, he spent his mornings searching for bargains in the newspaper. Laying in freezer loads of sale-priced Arby's roast beef sandwiches and then microwaving them. Boasting of his savings.

All of this miserliness was only symptomatic of greater ills. He refused to grant Chandler a respectable allowance. Or any allowance at all. Putting him in needlessly difficult circumstances. And consequently Chandler's life pretty much slid downhill into hostile terrain and social obloquy. Taking his meals at home. Made the butt-end of endless Roland-jibes and rebukes.

Absent Roland, Mummy would need little encouragement to return to her natural extravagance. Chandler would join her in a strategic combination for that purpose. And she'd have an inheritance plus insurance money to rip through. Delicious double-indemnity insurance for accidental death. Get rid of the *déclassé* Oldsmobile and acquire a Range Rover like everyone else. Yes indeedy. The Lewy estate would be an instrument of peace and prosperity.

And why put up with even one night of bats and cobwebs when so many lethal opportunities presented themselves *en route*? One thing you could rely on with Roland was bad plumbing. Since his prostate surgery he had to pee every hour or so. Typically wore an adult diaper. When Roland pulled off at the overlook, Chandler announced that nature was calling him as well.

"For God's sake don't stand in full view of every car that goes by," Phyllis carped.

"Righty-ho," Chandler agreed exuberantly. "Discretion is the better part of *et cetera*."

Sticking close to Roland, he chatted about prostate screening, whether he was too young to begin it. What were the danger signs. He worried inordinately about ill health. He wished only for a long and pleasant sojourn on earth.

They were on the edge of the overlook where trees met the stone wall, the mountains of the Blue Ridge spread out before them. A buzzard drifted symbolically on an updraft.

"Pleasant sojourn, my ass," scoffed Roland churlishly. "What you need is a dam' backbone instead of a wishbone."

"I'd say that begs the question," Chandler argued. "When the real issue is fiscal probity."

Roland was fighting his diaper now, trying to get his wee-wee man out. "Don't fancy talk me," he snorted. "Damn fool educrat."

Well, now seemed a perfectly adequate moment. Afterwards say I didn't do that. It was some look-alike of unknown identity. Here we go now. Stance. Poise. Shove.

"You dumb-ass . . . what the hail are you . . . ?"

The swine was fighting back! God he was strong!

Whups! There he goes.

"YIIIIiiiiiiiii!" Roland screamed in a diminishing note as he twisted and twirled, clawing at empty air in his descent. Down, down, down and down.

There was a faint crump when he hit the rocks at the bottom.

Roland was dead and gone. A bit of torn clothing fluttering from a bush. For Chandler, the sight held such a pleasant afterglow. Search one's person for any tell-tale marks of the struggle. No scratches or scrapes. In with the shirttail. Smooth the hair. Assume the stare of disbelief.

That was that. Really rather symbolic. Cronus castrates his father Uranus. Flings his testicles into the sea. And foam-born Aphrodite comes forth. The pagan goddess of love and sensuality.

In that regard, the highly decorative beauty Honor Revenue was waiting for him back in Charleston. Honor with the night-dark hair. Honor with her Tiverton commode. By which life would be cleansed and restored.

"Chandler!" Phyllis said sharply. "Where's Roland?"

He gave her the wide-eyed wonder look. "He's not with you?"

3

When Honor's agent learned she was leaving New York she started shrieking and beating on the walls, threatening mega-lawsuits, you'll never work in this town again, that kind of thing. She—the agent—had always been histrionic. It was New York. She had her neuroses. Lived on Seconal. Now that she had ditched her weekly sessions with a dominatrix guru—joined a Sex Addicts Anonymous group in its place—she was really on edge.

"Thanks for sharing your concerns," Honor told her.

It had seemed so simple. Go home for a while to the big old Victorian white elephant house on Legendre Street. Listen to her mother natter about preservative-free foods. Commune with familiar objects in her bedroom. Walk the streets of the old city and say hi to high school friends grown up. Coo over their babies, gossip about their marriages and divorces. New York left you nature deprived. She'd soak up a deep tan at the beach.

Everything seemed simple at first. Like being a big-time fashion model.

Modeling was a standard adolescent girl dream. You've got frisky colt skinny legs. Your teeth are cinched in by braces. Mail in a snapshot a friend had made. Take the call from a big agency. Whisked to New York and put up in the dorm with other bedazzled teenagers, none of whom would make the cut. Except in her case it all clicked into place. She was both a critical and popular success.

The initial joy faded fast into a blurred working world of manic-depressive supermodels fighting and bitching and sabotaging each other's clothes. All diet pills and vomiting and black speed taken too far. Most of them were intellectually stunted, had short attention spans and trouble reading big words. Worried incessantly about head colds, hives and pimples. Honor made gracious small talk and ignored them. She was a divinity professor's daughter after all. Oozing her way through confrontational episodes had been early training.

She took acid once, smoked pot twice, had an affair with a photographer. Then he got obsessive and threatened to decapitate her. Broke into her apartment and smeared what she first thought was toothpaste all over the walls. It turned out to be penis desensitizing cream.

And it wasn't just him. Wasn't just deep-pocket Wall-streeters or drug-head rock drummers or sad-sacks in supermarkets. Vagrants and voyeurs and pedophiles fell in love with her and swore they'd go straight if she'd love them back. A wino once pursued her through the streets acting out an episode from the *Love Boat*. One winter she thought she was paranoid, convinced she was being shadowed by cloaked figures. They turned out to be cloaked figures. A trio of nuts from a mime school who had seen her in a SoHo cafe and gone *folie à trois* bananas over her. They pleaded to scrub her bathroom while naked. Or wear fur g-strings if she was excessively modest.

Every man in the world didn't go crazy over her, but there was a steady unbroken, unrelenting stream. In the airport at La Guardia, a skinny stoner in a purple Mohawk had set off the metal detector with a scrotum ring of all things. You'd think he'd be embarrassed. In fact he was too intent on hitting on Honor. Unflinching. Staring at her with crazed eyes. It tended to rankle. Make her look through men, over their heads, around them like she was comatose. That accentuated her mystery and exacerbated the problem.

Skedaddling away from New York, Honor did not think of herself as a failure. In the few short years, she had cleared close to a half million dollars and invested it all in mutual funds. Problem was her owlishly bespectacled, married with five children broker became obsessed with her. He pestered her, plagued her, wouldn't leave her alone. When she complained to higher management, he used his moderate computer skills to completely erase her account.

Sure, she had the paper records, but there was absolute zip in the machine. Who could say whether the account had been liquidated as the broker claimed? She filed paperwork, sat in outer offices waiting for ambiguous conferences with stone-faced suits. The higher up the chain of management she went, the more lawyers moiled in wanting their pound of flesh, the more ludicrous her whodunit claim sounded.

She got a lawyer and sued. And then the judge—a bilious old weasel who dry smoked green cigars on the bench— had gone king-hell obsessive on her. "I got a need to be liked," he whispered nightly over the phone. "I want all of America to stand up and say, 'That's a man who knows how to love and be loved.'"

The police department had given him her unlisted number. He sent her dead white mice in the mail.

Lying stretched out on her familiar bed at home, Honor had the dreadful feeling that the judge was living in a motel in Charleston. All day she kept getting hang-up calls at the house. Heavy breathing. A tsunami of leering drool. Trying to reduce her to an emotional amputee.

She waited for the cover of darkness and went outside in the sticky heat to do aerobics. Under the interlaced branches of the oaks, she'd strain her body into something approaching angst-free.

She could remember as a little girl when the air pollution wasn't so bad and fireflies still appeared in the gardens on July nights. The other kids would gather them in jars, but she thought that was unbearably cruel to kill them like that.

All the lights were on across the street giving the huge Ralston mansion an air of brooding fantasy. The Ralstons were an ungodly jumble of personalities. Mother who drank like a fish, cursed, passed out face down trying to open the driveway gate. She had enough idle time and venom to make life a living hell for anyone who displeased her.

Sighing Moira was Honor's age. Not much of a playmate growing up. She'd stub her toe and you'd think she'd slammed her hand in a car door. She was usually hoarse from tantrums and allergies and crying jags.

The older one Rannie had become a lawyer and taken over the father's practice. She looked kind of fleshy voluptuous except for those eyes like the Gorgon Medusa. Hard-bitten male lawyers were terrified of her brute style. A nasty rumor had her murdering a bail bondsman in a fight over buried drug money.

Honor wondered if her stay in Charleston would become a Xerox of New York.

■ ■ ■

"I want that . . . *that man* . . . out of the church when I return," Mary Canty Ralston instructed lividly. She tossed down her drink and poured another from the silver shaker. Three caramel leather suitcases lay open on her bed in various stages of packing.

Moira was neatly folding things which her mother Mary Canty would then refold in some other way to be contrary. Moira was good at precision in small matters. Mary Canty excelled at contrariness.

The man in question was Noble "Rusty" Royall, Rector of St. Ambrose.

"Rannie" short for Randolph Ralston sat grimly watching her lush of a mother, tolerating her one last night before the trip to Italy. She was thinking, here I am one of the more successful attorneys in Charleston, and it's not enough I pay all the bills in the family. Maintain the great historic trust of No. 2 Legendre. Quash drunk driving charges against my mother. No, that's not sufficient. I have to babysit a 22 year-old virgin ding-bat sister.

If Moira had been a Barbie, that would have been one thing. The boys would like her. She'd get married. Become someone else's problem. Instead—picture-perfect pretty though she was—Moira was such a nincompoop that even the stereotypical "don't like brainy girls" type guys couldn't stomach her. Not even sex-starved Citadel cadets.

Drops out of college with no valid excuse. Says well it

just goes to show that college isn't for everyone. But what will she do? No one has shown any interest in marrying her. Work is incomprehensible to her.

Rannie knew what Moira would do. She'd sit at home and spend money. Help their mother lay on the fiscal squeeze. Announce, all these charge card bills have come in. They seem to be mounting alarmingly. Why aren't you doing something to reduce them?

"Ordaining these gay people!" Mary Canty ranted. "God, do we even dare take communion any more?"

Rannie looked at her own drink. Jim Beam in a short glass. On the rocks. Just like her daddy drank when he was alive. As a little girl she'd run into his arms and smell that familiar odor of pipe tobacco and bourbon. He drank because gentlemen drank and he drank to tolerate the evenings at home. His wife Mary Canty, a charter member of Alcoholics Unanimous. Soaking up money, soaking up booze. Her beverage of choice was a bizarre mix of blended scotch and crème de menthe. She carried a flask of it wherever she went. It was going to be a problem on the international flight.

Moira was into historical research. Ante-bellum South. Civil War. Whups, War for Southern Independence. She was genealogy officer for the Junior League. She read panting novels by Woodiweiss and Victoria Holt. Her idol was Charleston's own Drayton Mayrant who wrote romances in the 1940s.

"June is going to have a blue moon," said Moira. "Do you know about that? I don't know why it's called that. No one does. Because it's not blue. But it means there's two full moons in the same month. The second one's the blue one. Red really. Or orange. It comes every two to three years."

Outside was quiet, a realm of will o' the wisp lights among ancient trees. In an anarchic world of unrestrained growth, the old part of Charleston seemed resistant to change. But out beyond the historic district, the asphalt and plastic culture crouched like a hungry beast.

Meanwhile the mayor used them as a theme park for tourist dollars but gave no *quid pro quo*. Property taxes on the old mansions were reaching a Westchester, New York level. Motorhomes parked outside your house. Trash thrown in your yard. Rubberneck goons staring in the lower windows, pissing on your flower beds.

And the maintenance. Don't ever get Rannie started on that. She held back the level of physical deterioration in the house by massive infusions of cash. She sometimes thought she'd like to plant kudzu and let it smother the place. See how the Historic Charleston Society took to that.

Moira patted her daffodil blond hair, said, "I can't believe my eyes seeing Honor Revenue back home. I just know she's here to spy on me. See if there's a boyfriend she can steal. She makes me so angry. I swan I'm almost reduced to tears."

Rannie thought grimly, that's my sister. She's a slot machine. Pull the lever and you never know what three fruits are going to line up. So why my low repute around here? Why is the sweep of family history against me?

She looked out the window and saw Honor Revenue in her yard doing some kind of aerobics. Dressed in leotards. Breathing easily. Perfectly fit and supple. There were fireflies around her like she was a fairy princess. Rannie hadn't seen fireflies in years. She thought air pollution had done for them.

Honor and Moira were the same age, across-the-street neighbors since the sandbox days. Had been at Ashley Hall together. But never friends. Who could be friends with Moira? Honor was straight-As, volleyball and swimming. Moira was the dog ate my homework and I'm just such a dunce and oh silly clumsy me.

Honor was close to six feet and thin as a rail. Hip bones showing. Perfect dark hair and eyes. And then those ostentatious tits to complete the ensemble which announced that life was completely and utterly unfair and made Rannie want to heave her glass through the window. Scream "You cock sucking, bitch! Get your perfect tits and ass back to New York where we just have to look at you on magazine covers!" Be that blunt.

Rannie was 32. Never married. She had flame red hair like a Celtic queen. Lush bosoms and hips that made heads turn, but fighting a constant weight problem. She had nothing against cock-sucking per se. In fact she had done plenty of it as a teenager. That was the way she kept boys interested in her. Problem was, once she had the law degree even that ceased to work.

Some people called her the meanest lawyer in Charleston. Not to her face. They were scared to do that. Rannie would describe herself as not dodging the hard issues. Not overly averse to disturbing the sensibilities of sedate big firm lawyers. The men who thought they owned the practice of law.

She wasn't into dependency. Could go for the jugular with the best of the attack-dog tort lawyers, the criminal defense maestros. Wasn't one to freeze the inequities into place. No particular friend of the status quo. It had never offered her any money.

But like anyone else raised South-of-Broad she was loyal to the idea—to the myth—of timeless Charleston. The ritual and artifacts protected her from qualms about the future. Like her deceased daddy, she liked to go to church two or three times a year and feel she was a suitable Christian. And when she went, she wanted to find things predictable and the same. A big bit on the boring side. But the same.

So it was certainly a shock at Christmas to discover more than half the congregation were total strangers and they were raising their hands in the air, waving them when they prayed. And to find that twitty pretty boy Rector Rusty Royall leading the pack. What a pious prig.

Which was what made Mary Canty's strident demand seem more like a reasonable request. Rannie's daddy would have been outraged. Were he still alive, he would have done something about it.

"Good God! Is that that fool Roland Lewy? Has he gone and killed himself?"

Mary Canty was in kind of a wrestler's crouch above the small bedroom TV. A blurred still photo showed the former owner of Lewy's Carpets.

The news announced a Charleston man had fallen to his death from an overlook in the Blue Ridge Mountains. His wife and stepson were distraught.

"I think he got tangled in his diaper," said Chandler Lovelace, his fat face filling the screen. He was dabbing at his eyes with a handkerchief. He blew his nose into it loudly.

4

Honor's mother Grace said real loud that it was sure a curiosity that on average only 95 people a year died in plane crashes while some 6,000 choked to death. And Lord knows what the numbers were on falling accidents.

No one filing out of the St. Ambrose graveyard after the Lewy burial turned to stare. They were long accustomed to her persistent eccentricity, her belief that plague, flood and typhoon were positive blessings in a world of pain.

Years before, Honor had learned that more than a spirit of compromise required her to keep her mouth shut at such moments. Any effort to quiet her mother produced louder protestations of the exactitude of the data.

Grace said she was glad they had installed a sprinkler system in the church. The preservationists had been very upset over destruction of the ceiling plaster, but fires could sweep death far faster than most folks imagined.

The weather was a brief perfect before the dreadful heat of summer set in. It made the walk to the Lovelace—none could bring themselves to call it the Lewy house—quite bearable. The group strung out. Old men and women, many tottering with canes, shuffling with shiny metal walkers. Admiral and Mrs. Pellegrin (USN Ret.). The Millengen-Johnstons. The Cardys and the Delameres and the Pompions. Waites and Brewtons and Garretts. The old guard of the church, all secure in the certain knowledge that the old ways were best.

Within two days of her return Honor had received countless phone calls trying to line her up to combat the invasion of charismatics. Or from charismatics inviting her to their special prayer sessions so she could develop a personal relationship with Jesus Christ. A "charismatic" is a "spirit-filled" Christian, they explained. The word charisma means "gift." Our faith experiences include manifestations of one or more of the spectacular New Testament spiritual gifts such as speaking in tongues, prophecy, or spontaneous healing.

Bunch of flaming holy rollers, the old guard harrumphed with arch disapproval. Trifling with sacrilege where it runs over into blasphemy.

Honor's mother seemed oblivious to the internecine strife. For her, doom and gloom were the twin poles of the world's future. She always managed to combine an aggressive goodness with total pessimism in a way that Honor found unanswerable.

The mourners straggled down Church Street with its 18th century houses and the pavement broken and tilted in places by the roots of ancient oaks. Turned onto Bocquet Lane past the Chastain House with its two-tiered portico with Ionic columns and marble steps. The original Chastain had made a fortune in the slave trade. He went everywhere "fann'd by a Negro with peacock feathers."

Then the Villepontoux House, one of the first in the Palladian style in America. It was built from the proceeds of commerce with pirates. Blackbeard's siege of old

Charlestown had been caused by a spat with Francis Villepontoux over the division of spoils. And finally the 1750 Lovelace House with its Portland stone and pediment with a bull's-eye window.

The line bunched up as they mounted the steps into the house. Creeping along now. Through the central hall with its elliptical arch, up the stairs with the Venetian window on the landing. Each offering condolences as Phyllis Lewy greeted them in the second floor drawing room. Saying how lifelike Roland looked in the coffin.

Grace enjoyed savoring the subject of death. She said she was glad the Piggly Wiggly wasn't giving green stamps anymore. She was cleaning out her kitchen drawers, getting ready for the inevitable. By that, she meant her own demise.

Phyllis joined in. "I've given all of Roland's suits to the Salvation Army," she said with a sharp nod. Nothing emotionally feeble about her. Like most southern matriarchs, she was a match for any tragedy, certainly the death of an irascible husband. And she had now outlived two of them.

It was a lovely service everyone agreed. In truth the most memorable moments were Moira Ralston shrieking out loud that she had misplaced her handkerchief and just knew she had brought it but where on earth had it disappeared to? And Chandler Lovelace going "Oh *good God!*" with disgust at some moment in the eulogy. Twisting about in the pew and crossing his fat thighs.

The drawing room was fully paneled, mahogany doors, marble mantels at either end. The reception was a groaning banquet of food and drink. It was Charleston after all. Grace Revenue sniffed the salad dressing for off odors. She said good old mayonnaise was not as dangerous as people imagined. The salt and lemon juice made it resistant to spoilage.

She wasn't about to eat the three bean salad. Might break a tooth on a stone or some other rubbish. Wondered aloud if the chicken had been cooked within two days of purchase. She passed on the deviled eggs for fear of Salmonella.

When Honor was a little girl, her mother never let her eat eggs from an Easter egg hunt. They had been out of refrigeration for more than two hours.

"You must marry immediately," Grace pronounced. "I won't be around forever you know."

Honor objected. She didn't need a man to look after her.

Grace didn't hear. "Chandler seems like a perfectly nice young man."

Honor looked across the crowded room at him with deep foreboding. A greasy Trinity College necktie. Huge belly bulging out underneath with the shirt stretched open between buttons. He was murmuring in his mother's ear. Phyllis reared back and exclaimed indignantly, "No, of course I'm not changing my name back to Lovelace. Why on earth should I? Are you having one of your crazy spells?"

Chandler rolled his eyes, gave a long sigh. He was eating potato salad. He looked like someone who would always be ready to stay for supper.

Honor could hear the refrain in her head. Accentuate the positive. If life hands you a lemon make lemonade. If you can't say something nice . . . She said, "Mother, I really don't think so."

"He's suffered a great tragedy. I think you should be nice to him."

"What on earth does he do?"

"I believe he's a house sitter."

"A house sitter?"

"Yes. He watches people's houses for them when they're out of town."

As if to verify this, Chandler loudly announced to someone he'd soon be making the annual decampment to the Romneygate House while its owners were at Saratoga for the racing. It was a great trust, he pronounced dramatically, dropping his voice half an octave. The elliptical fanlight above the front door was one of only two in America. He was waving a scotch and soda. He seemed inebriated.

Honor backed into Moira Ralston, said excuse me. Moira let out a little shriek, said well Honor Revenue. Fancy seeing you here. It was just sooo nice to see Honor back in town even though they had always been in such competition.

Honor said, "Competition?"

"Men just always make such fools over me. It's my calling in life I guess. They're like moths to a flame. It always made you sooo jealous. Do you remember?"

Moira had flipped out. She had never had a date in her life to Honor's knowledge. Dropped out of Sweet Briar because the other girls made fun of her. Just came home and lived with that lush of a mother of hers in the big house on Legendre Street right across from the Revenues.

Because Honor was a divinity prof's daughter, she had to always be nice. Moira got invited to every birthday party and created a scene at every single one. When Honor was seven, her mother had gotten creative in a minor way in the kid's games. There was an egg toss where you chucked it back and forth with a partner, taking a step further apart each time. If the egg broke, you were out. Go wash your hands in the hose.

First toss, Moira caught hers square on top of the head splatch. Ran screaming home. The mother came boiling across the street drunk demanding that the party be broken up and everyone sent home. Mary Canty was big on lose-lose situations.

Chandler had rapidly turned into a loud drunk. "I can't believe the audacity of burying him at St. Ambrose! The man was a Baptist for God's sake!"

■ ■ ■

"Can I help you?" asked Talisha from behind the receptionist's desk with all the cigarette burns and vulgar graffitti carved on it. She had been working at radio WPST for three weeks now. She wore a blue-and-white striped cotton man style shirt with French cuffs, a gray nylon skirt to look like an executive secretary. What she was was a general dogsbody.

The two white dudes looked like they could move refrigerators without a dolly. Great big steroid arms. Short sleeve shirts rolled over their shoulders. Your basic Dixie Mafia enforcers. One seemed to be rolling a quid in his jaw. Maybe he needed a place to spit.

"We're like a bilateral commission," he slurped. "Come down here to these plush offices to accelerate your boss man paying up on some basketball wagers he made."

Talisha looked at the junky room with scratched plastic furniture. Pine paneling. Dusty framed civic awards. Stuffing coming out of the couch like a rat had got in it.

"You must have the wrong address," she said. "No plush about this place."

He leaned on the desk with both knuckles. "You know the human figure ain't but so pliable. Twist and bend it and you hear things crunch. Arms, legs end up at permanent odd angles."

"I don't need a bunch of heated rhetoric," she said. She sidled out of the room. They looked like they would flat-out alter your basic infrastructure.

She slid inside her boss' office and put her back to the door. Announced there were two white dudes outside who were a dire threat if she'd ever seen one.

Jackson Whaley McCully waved her to be quiet. He was on the phone with the bookie now. Big sweat stains spread under his armpits. Beer gut bulging over his sans-abelt white pants.

Jackson was a gambler on sports. He claimed he liked the onrush and emotional peaks. The problem was gambling is a zero sum game, and he tended to get the zeroes. After the Bulls-Knicks game he was $50,000 down and the vig had mounted it to 60 in less than a week.

Jackson told the voice at the other end of the phone his operating budget was currently committed but not to worry. He had a variety of irons in the fire. Visiting sites for potential industrial parks. Just flew back from a West coast venture-capital conference. He was developing a line of big-girl clothing outlets. Market research showed a third of American women were size 14 or over.

Some growling came out of the phone.

Jackson said, "You say you know I ain't been out of town? Well, cover stories will break down."

More growling.

"Hey, don't malign me, buddy-row. We been doing bid'ness over the years. You know I'm good for it. You at the top of debts-to-pay-pronto list. You got the eligibility criteria. I am on record here as saying you is the relevant group."

Growling.

"Well if you're gonna be an asshole about it I'll tell you just how it is. How it is is I been to a lawyer who tells me gambling contracts are just bald-ass illegal in this state. Sure you knew that. But the gist of it is you can't bring a lawsuit on one. The court leaves the parties where it finds them. Which is kind of a setback for you. You can caveat and cavil about it all you want, but there it stands."

Silence.

"Sure you don't tend to sue folks. But prong two of my two prong plan is to go public with my undercover investigative journalism on organized gambling in this state. I'll be broadcasting it any hour now in my Paul Harvey voice. You know how that would be. Widespread media coverage. Governor appointing a task force."

Silence.

"Well sure it's a calculated risk. High rates of return come out of high risk. And anyhow fuck you."

Jackson punched a button to change lines and called the 911 cop number. Told them two loonies with guns were threatening to shoot up his station. He needed a major security dimension. Like maybe a SWAT team p.d.q.

He poked his head in the outer office and told the hoods he hated to not be more interactive, but the cops were on their way and it was time for the byplay to end. "I ain't no porkchop to feast on," he added.

They gave him some sullen looks. The tobacco one spit a long stream on the floor. They walked out, shoulders wide enough to rip off the door frame.

Jackson McCully looked at his watch nervous, tapped at it like the second hand wasn't moving. He peeked through the blinds at the parking lot where the hoods were hanging around. Chain-smoked a few menthols. He said you got to deal with bookies in a meaningful manner. You try to feed a dam' predator and it just comes back with more appetite. Get all that increased salivation.

Here Talisha was all dressed up in a nice blend of blue and gray, working at a nothing station that played elevator music, and trouble had found her. There was no excitement. Middle-age call-in shows about gardening. Lounge bop. The DJ would fall asleep listening to it. Engelbert Humperdink music. Tom Jones. That was the strongest they did.

She said, "Can I just divert here a moment and remind you that it's Friday. Which is payday. What I'm trying to say is should I get the checkbook for you to sign?"

Jackson gave her a sour look and lit another menthol cigarette.

"I just thought it might fill the time," she persisted. "Since we're doing nothing."

"Come on, come on," he fumed looking out the window. Slamming his palms on the sill.

"Kind of an initiative on my part."

The hoods were talking into a cellular phone. They had plenty of time to dally. WPST was on the neck of the peninsula, a little run-down unincorporated pocket between the cities of Charleston and North Charleston. It had dirt streets, litter and a view of river water on both sides. The county police who patrolled it were spread thin and never set any records answering calls.

Jackson declared, "We got some glaring differences here, sweetheart. I'm staving off a knee-capping and you're thinking on Friday night partying. Now either you get an intelligent assessment of the situation or I'm gonna do an internal review and say bye-bye to your African ass."

A siren sounded in the distance. The two hoods perked up their ears and started drifting away. Trying to act casual.

"Well here comes the cavalry. Overturning the hell out of that verdict."

Real firm, Talisha said she needed her money. Her momma expected her to pay rent. And she was personally worried about the state of WPST's finances.

Jackson stopped at the door and looked her over. "We just ain't dancing to a common tune. Yeah, you outlived your usefulness. You're fired. Go cry to the Labor Commission about it. And you can't pull no Civil Rights shit. I got less than fourteen employees."

Well, it hadn't been much of a job. Answering the phone. Some low-level sexual harassment out of the boss. Jackson saying, "Sweetheart you one good looking, high-ass negress."

Outside, Jackson was talking to the cops. Hands spread apart showing how big the enforcer dudes were. Now he was getting into his Buick Regal. He started the engine. The whole roof of the car came off with a white roar.

GA-BA-DOOOOOOMMM!!!

The glass on the office window actually bulged inward with the explosion but didn't shatter.

Jackson's body flew up out of the car, did a centrifugal contortion and hit the wall of the building. Whap. Fell to the ground spread-eagled and singed blue-black. His eyes were wide open in death.

The cops were brushing glass and debris off their clothes. Ears ringing. Saying holy shit what was that?

5

"So you were a witness to the fatal carnage," yacked Alvin Teckler, chewing gum. He was WPST's attorney without much else in the way of a law practice. He had two suits—one summer, one winter—and had been walking since his Mercedes 190—your basic baby Benz—got repo'ed.

"It was a climatic scene all right," said Talisha, her voice flat, not really looking at him. She was cleaning out her desk. Throwing stuff in a cardboard box.

She hated the way the little white dweeb would go, "Yo, yo," at her or "Yo, whus'up?" playing homeboy gangsta. What she hated even more was he had represented one of the Clemson football dudes who raped her. Like everything he did, he was pure-T fuck-up and got fired pretty quick by his client. He didn't even remember her from that ugly shit event.

Neither of her parents had been interested in her near-death by car bomb experience. It was June 6 which in 1968 was when Robert Kennedy died in the Good Samaritan Hospital in LA. He had been shot on the 5th by Sirhan Bishara Sirhan. Talisha's father had candles lit all over the house.

She said, Daddy, you got kind of an unwillingness to do anything different. Stuck in a rut.

Her mother demanded who was going to shore up Social Security? Cost contain Medicare? That was a top priority in her book. Anyhow she thought she had lymphoma. Her armpits were hurting.

"I been down to the morgue to identify the body," said Alvin brightly. "It looked like something in a funhouse mirror. All distorted."

Talisha eyed him cautiously. He was young with curly hair that drooped down over his eyes. She thought maybe he had it done at a hairdresser. "Bombs will kind of get to the core of your being," she observed.

"Well he was a lackluster kind of guy. As an entrepreneur, I mean."

"He had a record of stonewalling when it came to paychecks."

"Hey, I hear you. I've been there and back. Being on hourly billings is no bed of roses. Jews and Afro-Americans both know the hard truth about slavery."

"Don't start on that 'Go Down Moses' shit," snorted Talisha. "I got a busy day of job hunting planned and laid out."

She was thinking she'd drag home this evening, out of work and footsore. Remind her momma Oneida she had near got blown to Kingdom Come. Her momma would say she thought she was coming down with spina bifida. Could Talisha drive her to the hospital?

Alvin took hold of her arm. Hey, there was no hurry. He had someone coming for her to meet. Give her the pitch. He said sit in the big chair behind the desk. Polish up your sales resistance but be warned. I do a strong close.

Talisha sat down. The chair still seemed warm from Jackson McCully's big ass.

Alvin was lecturing, "With Jackson McCully gone—now that that layer of management has vanished we can realign operations. Do some out-of-the-box thinking. You got a station so burdened with debt, that McCully junior, Beau-Jack McCully has got to sell out at least a major portion." He made a picture frame with his hands. "Think on it. Employee ownership. It's the coming thing."

Talisha said un-huh.

"Turning around a business is nothing. Actually owning the thing will prove to be the greatest challenge. And yet it's so easy when you got expertise on FCC regs the way I do. We create the hybrid of all federal license darlings—the black female owned station."

Talisha pointed to her chest with a finger going 'Me?'

"Fifty-one percent. It'll take you to the next level in your life. You'll be highly visible. Total authority to execute all decisions that come your way. Big staff reporting to you. What do you think?"

"So far I'm taking a mixed stance."

"Perks are always part of the package," he lured. "Company car. New wardrobe. Drinking Courvoisier and Perrier-Joüet."

"How much of it does Alvin Teckler get? And who else is involved?"

"Let's get RICH is kind of a nice rallying cry!" the Reverend Roscoe P. Morningstar boomed as he came through the door in his orange-rust suit and straightened hair. Big paunch. Skin the color of gingerbread. He talked with a lot of wide gesture hand movement. Talisha didn't know his name at the time, but she got real familiar with it over the following weeks.

"There are manifold EVILS in the world I done fought to a standstill stamping out root and branch. The growth of lotteries and Indian reservation gambling. Making folks think LUCK and CHANCE give them success in life instead of they own self-determination. Then you got air conditioning and modern appliances telling folks they got control, think they OUTGROWN God. I done wrestle with this like Jacob with the angel. I say to you HERE and NOW, play the requiem for Satan. For if you keep on in your foolish way, the true impact of all this is not knowing which way to jump in this world OR the next one."

"Is that free-wheeling energy or what?" gushed Alvin, all het-up with enthusiasm.

Talisha shook her head. "If you're trying to bamboozle me, you're doing a upstanding job."

Reverend Rosco raised both hands above his head, waving them in a palsied motion. "There's a storm warning out there on a horizon flickering with heat lightning. Atheism is just another word for Godlessness. We LIVE in the age of lowered budgets and heightened fears. Broken homes littered with estranged husbands. Highways littered with broken 18-wheelers. Housewives and shut-ins watching 'As the World Turns' 'stead of going to the fount to LEARN how the world turns."

He paced the room slashing the air with his hands. "God and personal faith lives in MY heart. I say my prayers on MY knees."

Talisha started to say something, but there was no break in the flow.

"And then I ask myself—am I just a workshop for the Lord? Or am I SOMETHING MORE? Am I ADAPTING to new markets or staying with underperforming product lines? Why should I be my bank account's worst enemy? I'm in a business like any man. I'm in the business of selling Jehova."

"I tell you he's visionary," Alvin beamed.

"You want to do a religious format on WPST," said Talisha.

"And sell blessed DOLLAR bills," said Reverend Roscoe, eyes glittering. "For five dollars each. Maybe ten once it gets going."

■ ■ ■

Honor fumed, "Mother, you never know when you might need a chair to sit on." She pulled mustard and pickles out of the refrigerator, slamming them on the counter, thoroughly disgusted.

Grace said nonsense. She was going to her reward any day now and this would save Honor the trouble during her period of grief. She fully intended to get rid of the furniture in the house. Chandler says the Rector is most grateful for it.

What would they eat off of?

She was keeping the kitchen table and chairs.

Where would they sleep?

Two bedrooms would be preserved.

"I never liked any of it anyhow," Grace said matter-of-factly. She had hated something she'd lived with all her life.

Honor had never given much thought to the furniture. While Charlestonians might feel it refined to know styles and marks of quality, she was taught that was an impermissible vanity. But it was part of her familiar landscape. If she went to New York, it was there waiting when she came back. Now this stable element of her world was about to evaporate.

As they spoke Chandler Lovelace of all people was making an inventory, estimating how big a van would be required. He was laying plans to cart away Honor's life. Her home environment. Every single stick of furniture. Leaving her with bare walls.

As a divinity professor's daughter, she had grown up with the constant culling, the incessant giving to those less fortunate. "You weren't using it" was always the justification for throwing out Honor's personal articles. But this was over the top.

Grace had spent much of her life planning for death and disaster. She would take moderately dire news and carry it out to some berserk conclusion that involved the end of time or at least a cataclysm on the scale of the fall of the Roman empire.

The Teamsters Union planned to strangle American commerce and rule the country through the threat of regional strikes. The oceans were nearly fished clean. World water shortages would bring starvation and plague. Nuclear waste would poison the aquifer and force the evacuation of Florida and Georgia. Charleston would become a dumping ground for violent and desperate refugees.

Grace had had Honor as a late-life baby and was positively delighted by the hysterectomy that followed so quickly afterwards. When her even more elderly husband died, she took it as a sign that she would soon follow. Otherwise she was hale and hearty. Strong as a horse. Bicycled for miles every day in any kind of weather. But death was ever on her mind.

This past winter she had taken the long planned trip to the Holy Land with a group tour. Now she felt she was prepared to be "called home." She had executed a living will and was very bothered about news accounts of doctors refusing to abide by them, dying elderly having to get guardian *ad litems* appointed to sue the medical profession.

Grace said don't use that peanut butter. There was no gasp when you opened it. The vacuum seal has been lost somehow. Throw it out immediately.

Chandler Lovelace entered the kitchen crowding it with his huge bulk, all bluff and hearty. Grace said they'd invite him to eat, but the luncheon meat was more than five days old and had lost its quality. She hoped he never left raw meat in a hot car. It could turn into a breeding ground for bacteria in under an hour in those circumstances.

Chandler looked appalled, said no of course he didn't. Then started right in jabbering at Honor. Saying it was always tumultuous to part with familiar objects. The sentiment. The shared memories. He applauded her courage.

He was wearing madras Bermuda shorts and white socks fallen over his ankles. Gunboat shoes. A striped college blazer that wouldn't button over his enormous gut. Handkerchief hanging out of his sleeve like another century. Some kind of pretentious *fin-de-siècle* aesthete. A mock Oscar Wilde fanning himself with a straw hat and telling her he was a Trinity man. Trinity College Dublin. Did his divinity there. Honor's father had been a professor of divinity had he not?

Yes. They came to Charleston after he retired. Chandler knew that. Everyone knew it.

Incredibly, he announced he was handpicked for the post of rector in the event Noble Royall came a cropper. And many expected this imminently. All those dreadful charismatics he had brought into the congregation. Their shared radical agenda. Reprehensible.

What on earth was he talking about? You didn't just "become" rector of St. Ambrose or any other Episcopal church. You weren't elected by the congregation.

"The ordination of gay ministers." Chandler raised a warning finger. There the battle lines were drawn. Split the church right down the middle. Many are unaware of these facts or else choose to ignore them. Disregard the unpleasant. He personally did not wish to tar it all with the same broad brush. Understood good folk can differ on these issues. Your mother's doubtless sincere in her tolerance of the newcomers. Honor really needed to become more acquainted with the deplorable situation. To aid her in this, he proposed a luncheon engagement. Honor and Chandler *à deux*. The two of them. In concert. Get her up to speed on the social discord.

Honor said she wasn't sure. She had barely gotten back in town. God he was like some distorted yuck out of a funhouse mirror.

"Of course she'll go," Grace insisted blithely. "She'd be delighted."

"No, really," Honor demurred. She felt like she was on the edge of an abyss.

"No need for gamesmanship," Chandler chided. "We'll settle on Tuesday. Noonish? Hmm? That's not really rushing things. Well-paced. Very well. Agreed."

He bade them good day with a big smile of satisfaction. Huge sweat stained buttocks shaking as he walked out. Handkerchief dangling from the sleeve.

"Ta-ta for now!" he called back, waggling his plump fingers. The hanky waggled with it.

6

The gluttonous Chandler Lovelace was not the only immediate nastiness in Honor's life. Judge Reggie Lorenzo was
still in town, calling the house almost hourly, giving off
his signature cigar hack. He said he was going to pierce his
chin, get a metal stud in it. Be hip. A fun boy. She'd dig
his lyric beauty. He used that word. Dig.

Then the haughty Browder Delamere ran into her at
St. Ambrose on a week day and instructed her to not stay
in the sanctuary alone. There were negroes carrying out
the pews for refinishing. You never knew what might happen. Crime of opportunity. His Porsche 944 Turbo was
right outside if she wanted a ride somewhere.

Honor looked around the sanctuary with its barrel
vaulted ceiling and galleries on the side and rear supported
by Tuscan pillars. There hadn't been a crime committed
there since it was first built in 1719 by Blanton Chassereau
and other Barbadoes planters come to the city to invent
the indigo industry.

Blue-blazer-and-rep-tie Browder ran the Charleston
office of Dombey & Trouche, the stock brokerage which
had "disappeared" her fortune in New York. It had kept
its local name even though devoured years ago by three
levels of financial conglomeration. He was in his thirties,

at least ten years her senior, but knew her because she was on so many magazine covers and as a result in local news a lot. His shoes were Gucci and his shirt had a monogrammed cuff.

Honor needed to go to work and had zero job skills. Fashion modeling tends to take you out of the mainstream training environment in the crucial young years. So when she saw the opening as bookkeeper for St. Ambrose she went right over to the church office. They had a budget of a couple hundred thousand a year. It wasn't a lot of money to manage. A dogsbody kind of job typically held by a distressed gentlewoman. And there she met Browder right next to the statue of William Pitt guided by the Archangel Michael.

Browder was a big mover and shaker on the Vestry of course. She broached the subject of her lost investments, and he oddly seemed both aware of it and ready for her. That was in the hands of the lawyers, he said masterfully. He was not at liberty to discuss it. Wouldn't be ethical now would it? However he was prepared to discuss in excruciating detail his divorce action against a nymphomaniac wife. Hint that he would soon be available. Long pause as though she was expected to whip out her calendar and pencil him in. He was thinking of buying a Ferrari Mondial. Metallic blue with black upholstery.

Honor said it was too bad his marriage wasn't doing well. Had he considered counseling?

Browder put up both hands. "Whoa. Let's back up here. I run the carriage-trade brokerage in town. No nickel and dime accounts. Do you think I don't understand negotiation? I have no client skills? I need some psychologist numbskull to tell me about offer and acceptance? The problem lies with my wife wanting to boff everything in pants. Initially she had the minimal good taste to restrict herself to our social set. But when she started branching out with lowlife, I had to put my foot down. She'll probably start on negroes next."

In the off chance Honor had lost track of just who he was, he reminded her. He wasn't just an extremely successful broker but also had family money. The plantation on the Cooper River—Bellefontaine—was a showpiece. The 1830 house on East Bay Street and his contemporary log mansion at Flat Rock had both been featured in *Architectural Digest*. And his wife was not going to get any of them. He had photos of her naked with a real low life. Boffing. Legs in the air. Disgusting.

"Great to run into you," Honor said. "But must run. Want to snag the bookkeeper's job."

He followed her closely. She needed work? He could get her the church job with a phone call. He'd provide something at Dombey & Trouche but that would be unethical—humph—given their snafu. And he wasn't going to leave her alone. Not even in the church. Not with these negroes hanging around.

He said the violence that has come to this town. And not just the murder-a-week problem. That was basically negroes up on Columbus and America Street. Line Street. Bogart. Those seedy negro places. But it was moving downtown with a vengeance. Just yesterday a negro was arrested in the middle of Meeting Street, loaded on drugs, blowing soap bubbles of all things. Had checked into the Mills Hotel if you can believe that. They have to take anyone who will pay. Civil Rights laws.

Then there was that bombing at a radio station up on the neck. Blew up the father of that lowlife Beau-Jack McCully. Beau-Jack now owned it. He was going into business with a negro. Or negress actually. Probably boffing her. What a lowlife.

Honor interjected, "You know I really would like for Dombey & Trouche to find my money and give it to me. I don't see what they get out of holding it."

Browder took a stern posture. "I thought I made it clear that was not a topic for discussion. Anyhow the New York judge on the case has vanished. So it's mired in his backlog."

"How did you know that?" Honor asked, surprised once more.

"I was briefed by New York. Now let's decamp. That lowlife McCully might show up. Can't stand that boy."

Something clicked. Honor asked sweetly, "Is he the one boffing your wife?"

Browder looked like she had used a hammer and chisel on one of his back molars.

■ ■ ■

A few blocks away on Broad Street, Rannie Ralston sat behind the big mahogany desk in her law office surveying the two clowns—one black, the other white—sitting there opposite her trying to play their cute games.

Leone Jones was saying, "The man be out in traffic on Meeting Street blowing soap bubbles was all. Why can't them cops leave black folks be? Quit all the hassling? Know what I mean?"

Rannie was painting her long nails a bright scarlet color. She nodded her head amused. She had first run into this particular turkey when he was a football player at Clemson, gang-raped some girl. Called himself Sierra Leone now like he was a man of mysterious origins. As ex-football players will do, he had put on a whole bunch of weight.

She finished the last nail and admired her glistening handiwork. "The MAC-10 that was sticking out of Booger's baggy pants might have caused the cops to treat him a little less than cordial. Then of course the felony load of cocaine in his luggage kind of cinched it and got the half-million dollar bond set."

She waved both hands to dry the nails and went on. "Booger-T—that's like his professional name—he gave me a phone number to call. You'll never guess who answered at the other end."

Leone and Beau-Jack McCully looked at each other. Beau-Jack said no they couldn't guess.

"Do the Blood Fingers mean anything to you two worldly lads?"

Leone ventured, "You mean as in Crips and Bloods? Blackstone Rangers?"

"And Blood Fingers," Rannie added. She said she was just guessing, but the cops didn't know who they had at this point. That's why there was any bail set at all. The man was wanted on so many fugitive murder warrants you could lay them side-by-side on I-95 and reach D.C. with them. He had been hired as out-of-town talent by Wayne's Wagering of Columbia, SC after the two white goons got heavy handed with McCully, Sr. and immediately arrested.

"Excuse my bluntness at your time of deep mourning," she nodded to Beau-Jack. She blew on her nails lightly.

Beau-Jack said his grieving for his Daddy had been short and to the point. It was behind him now. He'd regained his composure.

Rannie was thinking Beau-Jack was damn good looking. Buffed body. Couple years younger than her. Maybe 27, 28. She was so horny she could do a bedpost. Under different circumstances with him she could fall in love . . . No, the guy made reproduction antique furniture. Sat around waiting to inherit a loser of a musak radio station.

Well, he had the station now, but it was so mired in debt he was selling off most of it just to pay the debts. And he had additionally inherited his old man's gambling bill which was owed Wayne of Wayne's Wagering. And Wayne was her client.

Rannie didn't think highly of Booger-T and she said as much. "Despite Booger's body count as a recommendation, that boy is dumb and self-destructive, with the result he's now in the county slammer. He expects to be bonded out, however, and Wayne doesn't feel he owes it to him. So Booger's looking to our fat boy Leone here. Those were his exact words. Fat boy."

Leone put his long pale purple fingernails to his chest, did a 'who me'? "Me bail him out? With what money? And what does he mean 'fat boy'? That ain't nice."

Rannie gave him a bored look. Asked if he got through third grade before Clemson faked a college admission. Asked, haven't you put on a lot of weight since I last knew you?

Leone said well true, but he carried it well. But what was the man Booger going to do out on bail? Jackrabbit?

She said no shit, Shakespeare.

Beau-Jack drawled, "Rannie, you're a top-ranked bitch." There was admiration in his voice.

"Practicing law," she allowed, "is like anything. A matter of confidence. I've got a high-quality program. Integrity. I focus on the client. What I'm saying I guess is I provide a useful commercial service, kind of a supplement to the community."

Rannie said she had brought the two of them in together because their problems while different were not unrelated. And she had limited time. Wayne's Wagering was her client; ditto Wayne's independent contractor Booger-T.

Beau-Jack owed his father's gambling debts to the current tune of $70,000 and it was growing hourly. Leone, or whatever it was he called himself now, had to come up with $50,000—the fee, the juice—for Alonzo Freedom Bonding to bail the hit man out of jail.

And of course, when Booger got out, if Beau-Jack had yet to pay the $70-Gs, well . . .

Beau-Jack stared at her thoughtfully. Leone shucked and jived. He had found Booger-T in a single-car pink Cadillac accident. Loaded on some designer dope. Flipped over in the median on I-95 outside of Petersburg, Virginia. Give the man a ride down to Charleston was all. Favor to a brother.

Rannie gave him a wintry smile. "He sees your association and friendship as more meaningful than that. At the hotel he gave you $30,000 cash to go out and buy him a BMW. You helped him hump the luggage up to the room. The Samsonite bags with all the coke inside."

Leone got huffy. "You don't know none of that. That's like hearsay."

"True. But I believe it. Now put the money on the desk. I'm taking that as my fee."

"I ain't *gots* the money," Leone whined.

Rannie sighed kind of disgusted. "Don't start. There are telephones in the jail. Booger can make collect calls to D.C. Those charming Bloodfingers have the weapons of mass destruction, they've got the delivery system. When it comes to avenging some 'dis'—is that the right way to use the word?—they've got unwavering convictions."

Leone protested anyhow, saying he needed the money to help him through college or technical school. She listened a bit, tapped a long red nail on the desktop. He whined some more. And why couldn't it go towards the bail money? She tapped again. He laid the money out. Had brought it in in a little fannypack because he was afraid to leave it anywhere.

Even in hundreds, it was a nice thick wad. She licked her thumb, counted. It was three hundred dollars light. She caught his eye to let him know. But she let it slide. She could revisit that decision later on.

Rannie tossed the money in a drawer and said don't let me detain you two busy boys. Swiveled her chair to look out the window. The geography of the peninsula was pretty simple. Broad Street was lined with law offices. The federal and county courts were at the corner of Meeting and Broad. Above that came businesses and mixed quality housing to Calhoun Street and then above that the black ghetto.

Despite her enormous money-making ability, Rannie remained a solo practitioner. Some people said it was because she was so mean no firm would hire her, no hapless cluck out of law school would ever be her partner. The fact was her father had been solo, and Rannie did everything in her life in his memory. She kept the office as it had been when he died. The same seedy furniture, faded Declaration of Independence.

Beau-jack stood up and stretched, said he needed to go where there was a cold beer within easy reach. He had some heavy worries to resolve and things were seeming mighty defeatist at the moment.

Rannie advised, "That's life. You play the game or the game plays you."

7

"We're on the road to creative strategy," proclaimed a gray-suited Alvin Teckler as they walked out of the big bank on Broad Street. "Ever see those old Bob Hope/Bing Crosby movies on cable? 'On the Road to Hong Kong' and all of them?" He fiddled with his red necktie and did a little soft shoe.

Talisha allowed she was worried about how he had faked the income statement, saying they had $500,000 a year in cash flow. From what she could tell working around WPST it had maybe $80,000 at most and pretty much all of it grabbed immediately by creditors.

He told her not to sweat it. Banks were used to being lied to, and as a black female buyer, she had the whole thing guaranteed by the federal treasury, half a dozen state and federal agencies. Anyhow they were going to retire the bank loan *tout suite*. Round up non-institutional investment sources. Airline pilots. MDs.

"We'll lure in the normally gun-shy investors. Broad appeal? Of course. How could it be otherwise? Believe in me. My enthusiasm is infectious."

"I'm having trouble catching it," she said. She had just spent two hours borrowing a staggering one million dollars and then immediately signing it over to pay off every kind of mortgage, lien, confession of judgment and chattel mortgage known to man. All of it debts of the estate of Jackson McCully.

Alvin did his shuck. "Hey, the market movement stays hinged to interest rates. There are some sources I could quote that would . . . well, later for that, but when it comes, you'll greet it with high fives. I know I don't have to teach you a work ethic. You'll run a gospel station like a charm. But you've got to learn a larger playbook here.

"You know how kind of at the end of the day you're kicking back with the old glass of white Chablis and your defenses are down? The heartfelt fantasies start to flood your system? VIP parking passes. Hotel suite with a wet bar and panoramic view of the skyline."

His lips were whispering in her ear. "You are one sweet redemption for a life of sinful longings." She realized he was standing on tip-toe to reach her.

"You look as good as those Jamaican fashion models with the Chinese blood in them. What do they call them? Chigroes? Just distill the essence of sex appeal. We could be the best one-on-one match-up."

She moved his hand off her shoulder.

He looked wounded. "Hey, I'm trying to make some deft moves here. No need to bristle. We got a trend in its infancy."

She was thinking about that porky, bearded geek married up with Maria Carey. Stately Imam with that weird orange-haired Englishman. Then it struck her. Those white men were all, like, billionaires. That was what gave them sex appeal. Alvin was what? A one-client lawyer with a quick-fix method for everything that came up.

Alvin asked, "Hey you going to get some bets down on the NBA finals? The Rockets are about sure to sweep the Sonics. But the point spread is the challenge."

Talisha stared at him. "You know way back in Sunday school they taught me gambling was a godless sin. But if that weren't lesson enough, I got the close-at-hand example of my ex-boss Jackson McCully getting his ass blowed off."

Alvin fanned himself. "Whoo, don't sugarcoat your opinions. I like that. Make any little issue a defining struggle. You are my answer to adversity."

Talisha got her beat-up old Saturn out of the parking lot behind the bank and drove home to her family on Rondeau Street in the tree-shaded black *bourgeois* neighborhood on the edge of Hampton Park. Green-shuttered clapboard house with an iron scrolled front porch. White trellis with scuppernong grape vine all over it thick and leafy green.

She had thought it would be a delirious moment of breaking out champagne and toasting a big step up in life for the Mackeys. All clap hands. Little Talisha is going upwardly mobile at last. She learned real quick that success was no alternative to family reality.

She started out, "Hi, momma, I just bought 51% of a radio station. It's got a gospel format which seems like a double service to things. Make my living bringing Jesus into the community."

Her momma Oneida allowed she personally had frail health. She had spent a long day reading out of the medical dictionary. She knew for sure she had Otitis syndrome.

Talisha said "Otitis?" Her daddy was named Odis and for a moment she was confused.

Oneida listed on her fingers she had vertigo, ear pain and hearing loss.

Talisha said you can hear me perfectly.

Oneida cupped her ear, said, "What?"

"I know you can hear me!" Talisha yelled.

Oneida told her to not shout. Her otitis was both diffuse and localized. She needed local heat and antio-biotics. Talisha could skip work and drive her to the doctor in the morning and get them prescribed.

Talisha said that wasn't possible. Did she hear the big news? She *owned* WPST.

Oneida said she reckoned she'd reduce her discomfort by going to bed. Talisha could busy herself and make them dinner.

It was a stalemate of disinterest.

Out in the kitchen, Talisha opened the cupboard and an avalanche of plastic containers fell out on the floor. Her momma kept every container from every restaurant and fast-food take-out on earth. If you ever tried to throw one out, she was right there to snatch it back. This big heap of plastic mess was like a resounding denial of any change in her life.

Her daddy Odis came in showing off a pro forma letter from some branch of the Kennedy Clan thanking him for his services. The latest tabulation got him up to fifteen total. The first fourteen were all framed and hung in the living room.

Every day of his life he wore red alligator clip suspenders and a white shirt with the cuffs and collar buttoned. On Sundays, he put a black suit and maroon tie over it.

He said listen here to this and read aloud *". . . through the strong efforts of brave persons like yourself, progress in civil rights is irreversible."* Said dawgone if they don't know it's true I was there when Robert died. They just pretty much come right out and say there's a direct link.

Talisha goes, "What?"

Her daddy said all these new books coming out exposé-ing both Jackie and Jack Kennedy had extra-marital affairs. Well, you never heard any of that dirt on Ethel Kennedy.

Talisha got out the frozen catfish which her momma hadn't even bothered to thaw. She asked herself why is it you're not surprised? You grew up figuring the only escape from this house was marriage. Assuming her momma didn't check into the hospital and have her appendix out on the wedding day.

She had had a boyfriend in college until he chose to spend his senior year with a butane torch and a glass pipe freebasing cocaine. Around February, he finally blew up himself and his dorm room, got all his hair and eyebrows seared off. Questions of morality aside, just looking at it from a practical angle, she decided the romance had dimmed.

Talisha dumped the catfish into a pot and ran hot water over it out of the tap. She could sure give a warning to thrill seekers. Radio mogul status didn't make any big changes in your life. The ultimate impact was maybe she'd manage to pull in just enough money to move out to an apartment. After she'd done the every-month payment on a $1,000,000 loan, have $400 free and clear. Make for a life of unending sensationalism.

■ ■ ■

"Good lord, no," protested Noble "Rusty" Royall, rector of St. Ambrose. "I certainly don't covet your furniture. Your mother pressed it on us. I refused of course."

Honor told him that was strange because Chandler Lovelace had come by and measured it all for a truck.

Rusty vowed he would certainly get to the bottom of that. There were unruly elements in the church. Always doing something counterproductive. Critical of any failure to adhere strictly to traditional values.

As to Chandler he was nothing but a confounded nuisance. Not old Charleston at all really, much as he'd like to have you believe it. His father Alf Lovelace had come over from Liverpool in England during World War II when Charleston was a navy shipbuilding center. Some species of foreman at the yards. Very humble man. Hard to believe he had produced Chandler. Rusty tried his best to be polite to him, but it was difficult. Chandler imagined himself an *éminence grise* in the church. Truth be told, he had performed very poorly in divinity school. Couldn't get a church to save himself afterwards. Was a youth minister briefly in Northern Ireland.

"Bite my tongue," he said. "Temper gets the better of me sometimes. But Chandler is so open about what he calls my 'radical credo'."

Rusty's office was as fine a structure as the church itself. Ceiling decorations carved right into the ancient cypress wood. Round-headed windows with mullioned panes. Watercolors of the great Cathedrals of Europe.

He settled into his chair behind the big desk and scanned Honor's application for the treasurer's post. He was very suave and well groomed, half-moons showing above the cuticle on his fingernails. "I'm feeling unusually tentative," he said. "Sitting in judgment of others is not my strong suit."

Honor knew her role was to sit there and be attentive to male vanity and needs. Let him project a personality onto her, assume she was sexually attracted to him. She'd speculate on when the aggressiveness would appear. If it would turn to violence.

"Hmm," he mused, running his hand along the back of his neck. "Absolutely no experience at book keeping." He giggled nervously. "But then we all come here with different backgrounds and goals. Differently-abled."

That morning Honor's mother had been doing the weekly pantry check of the "use-by" dates on all the boxes and cans. The menu would be planned around those. Honor wondered if that counted as worldly experience with frugality.

Rusty described his job as challenging in all aspects. "Ever under the watchful eye of the Bishops. The congregation, all of them expecting miracles. You compete for the standard hierarchy of prizes. Most Sundays when I'm preaching I look out there and see pompom waving fans. I'm comfortable performing."

He read some more. Creased his brow. "You really have no experience at all. Hmm, well. Why don't we take this opportunity to explore mutual goals and opportunities. The typical Episcopal church seems to be on Novocain. Wouldn't you agree? Drowning in apathy. Lackluster preaching. Listless ministry. Saccharine. Madame Tussaud's waxworks. True or false?"

He looked at her expectantly, but didn't really wait for an answer. Launched off into his reform project.

He planned an emotional and exhausting comeback for this church. Build the model parish of the 21st century. Aggressively establish St. Ambrose at the very center of the warp and woof of a newly woven social fabric. Avoid the shop-worn formulas. Reinvigorate the vows of Christianity. Untapped power. Synergistic potential in the community. Blah blah.

Honor ventured tentatively, "What I guess you're telling me is you're in favor of ordaining gay ministers. Ultimately sanctioning same-sex marriages."

He choked. "Well, yes, um every person must be able to achieve his or her highest potential in the social contract. I am no more than an enabler in that arena. No church is a moral one that fails to abolish fragmentation among its worshippers. Capitalize on the power of diversity in group dynamics."

He was getting jittery and talking way too fast.

"The older members say I'm creating a coffeehouse atmosphere in the church. I say they must embrace new forms of worship. McDonalds was a new way of doing hamburgers when it burst upon the scene."

"I'm not sure that's the best analogy," Honor ventured.

"Fine. Sure. Then call it a shift out of low-yielding fixed-income securities into growth stocks. How's that? Episcopalian enough for you? Hmm?"

He lurched forward in his chair, elbows planted on

the desk. "I know. Let's try a bit of role-playing. Imagine I'm a practicing homosexual but in a long-term relationship. No, that won't do. Imagine this. I'm the rector, you're Honor Revenue. I'm a practicing, unmarried heterosexual, contrary to the church doctrine of marriage. And I . . . I make a pass at you."

He came around the desk, kind of hovered over her. His voice cracked a bit as he said, "You look so very polished. Is that the word? No, poised. Yes. Hmm. You're young and vivacious. I'm sure you have great skill in negotiation. And in . . . intimacy."

In a quick striking movement, he kissed her on the neck. A peck really. The merest little smeck.

"There. I did it. Now how do you react?"

Honor sat back, crossed her arms in a defensive posture. "I say lay off. Keep your lips to yourself."

He flopped back in his chair, giving her a broad smile. "Excellent. We've ended on an entertaining note. And your virtue's intact. Unyielding defense on your part. Didn't give in. Hmm? Well, that about wraps it up. You're hired. Welcome aboard. You'll receive an enthusiastic reception."

Honor was surprised it was so simple. And yet why shouldn't it be? It wasn't much of a job. "You don't mind I have to learn from scratch?"

"No. Of course not. And if it's of interest, Browder Delamere wants you to have the post. Some forceful clarity out of that man." He did a mock shudder, held up crossed hands like one warding off a vampire.

She should have seen it. Rusty's innate silliness. Insecurity. Afraid of the big donors to the church.

What Rusty reminded her of was her Sunday school teacher when she was thirteen, just hitting puberty. His favorite story was how Abraham went down into Egypt and had Sarah, his wife, tell everyone she was actually his sister. There was an ample amount of veiled language involved, but the upshot was Sarah was so beautiful the sons of Pharaoh would want to rack out with her. If they thought she was married, they'd have Abraham killed. Unmarried, they could bang her to their heart's content and Abe would remain unscathed. Which was how it worked out. Also, Abe got well rewarded by Pharaoh.

Her teacher really got off on that story and told it a lot. Once he caught her alone and asked if she was suffering the stigma of menstruation. Stood there panting and slavering at her mortification. If you judged by the TV talk shows, it should have thrown her into years of therapy and breast-beating.

Out in the sun-bleached street, Judge Reggie Lorenzo was leaning up against a tree, a plume of cigar smoke coming out of his mouth. He didn't seem to be wearing a shirt.

8

"What are those things?" asked the circuit court judge leaning over the bench for a better look. "Some kind of Samurai knives? Ninja stuff?"

"It's some kinda Jap bladed weapons," explained the assistant solicitor.

Rannie Ralston had had no luck in suppressing the evidence on an unlawful search and seizure theory. Her client had been wearing a winter coat in 90 degree weather. The knives he was concealing were each 24-inches long. The coat looked like it would be real comfortable in Greenland.

Her numbskull client said right there to the judge, "Yeah, I was looking for two dudes what dis' me. Yeah, I was gonna stick 'em."

Rannie had long since quit worrying about her client running off at the mouth. She had taken $6,000 from his parents. That was all they were good for. May as well plead the sap guilty and get it over with. Let him draw however many years the judge gave him. Tell him it was a special deal she had arranged.

It wasn't much of a fee, but there were worse humiliations in life. That dim-wit Alvin Teckler had just lost a jury trial in a civil suit where the defendant hadn't even bothered to show up. By five o'clock every lawyer in town would be laughing about that one. "Worthless douche-bag" was the phrase most frequently used on Broad Street to describe him.

Rannie had seen her mother off on a tour of Italy that morning. The only difficulty was the predicted fight at the airport security check over the booze she was trying to smuggle on board in her carry-on. Now Rannie was feeling free and good about things. Then she spotted Sierra Leone Jones signaling her from across the railing.

Leone announced he was doing some studying about Booger-T and how the $30,000 ought to go towards the man's bail. Expedite his getting out.

Rannie used a bored tone. "Well, I have to disagree."

"Hey, the man is one dangerous dude. You want to live with his ani-mo-sity?"

"Right now he's behind bars. Once you raise the bail, he gets out. What's he got to complain about?"

Leone argued, "Yeah but the car. The man will *want* his BMW."

Rannie said maybe she'd have to explain to Booger that if she wasn't his lawyer then there was no confidentiality. Asked a direct question by a cop, somebody in the Solicitor's office, she'd have to admit that yes indeed it was the infamous Booger-T they had locked up. Now if Leone was real insistent about the cash, she'd be happy to hand it over. But first, she'd drop by the jail and explain to Booger how Leone had fired her and just what that now meant. All the unforeseen occurrences.

Leone stared at her, trying to think it through. He said maybe he had to study on getting a job.

"You're going to have to do more than get a job," said Rannie. "You're going to have to come up with something mighty valuable. $50,000 worth of valuable."

"You telling me to boost cars? What?"

Rannie lapsed into a daze of indifference. "You know, I'm not really a consulting firm."

Out in the hall, Alvin Teckler was backed up against a wall by his client demanding the return of fees paid.

"Hey looka-here," said Leone. "There's my old lawyer. I *knows* that dude. He was, like, my attorney in that little disputation up at Clemson. Dumped me when I couldn't raise the fee. But he's okay. You know what I mean? We got like a history."

Rannie wasn't listening. She was rid of her mother Mary Canty for a brief vacation. Maybe she'd lock Moira in the root cellar and invite the Air base in for an orgy. With her. Not Moira.

■ ■ ■

Talisha Mackey was sharp and to the point. "Let's get one thing straight. My ass is my own."

Beau-Jack McCully, her new minority shareholder partner in WPST said, "I don't catch the drift. You're the one wants to buy into the station. If my old man's gambling creditors come looking for money from you, you got your eyes wide open."

"What I'm saying," explained Talisha, glaring at him, "is keep *your* cotton-picking *hands* off *my ass*. No patting or pinching or checking to see how it's doing. Your deceased daddy was into that kind of thing."

"We weren't real close," said Beau-Jack.

WPST was pretty active. Alvin Teckler had created a huge office for himself on the ground floor where he intended to practice law and handle the business of the station. Moving men were hauling in his ratty furniture and gray metal file cabinets. Next to him, Reverend Roscoe Morningstar had an office with a brass plaque that said "Conclave for Christ" whatever that was supposed to mean. His furniture was a fold-up card table and lawn chair.

Talisha had been put upstairs in Jackson McCully's old chief executive office with the waiting room and sound booth where the D.J.s worked. She was hammering nails in the wall for a picture of Jesus walking on water and a crewel-work "Jesus is Lord," really giving it a whack to emphasize her feelings. She stopped and looked at Beau-Jack carefully. He wasn't much older than her, maybe a year or two. She knew he was a college drop-out which made her intellectually over his head. She could say that about a lot of white people.

He was wearing jeans and a pearl snap cowboy shirt with red roses on the yoke front. Hand tooled belt with a Wells Fargo buckle. He said gospel sounded like a good format. "The demographics offer a whole bunch of potential. Up to now the station ain't been what you call a high-end business. Maybe that's too broad based a definition. Cause McCullys ain't high-end folks. We eat animals. Sit at bars with wet circles from the beer bottles."

Talisha was wondering when he'd get lost. Go home and wait for dividend checks that wouldn't come. Her momma Oneida had been calling all morning saying the pine pollen was so bad she needed an oxygen tank.

"We come out of the mill village up in North Charleston. Daddy ate pigskins. Drank Blues. Wore Ban-Lon shirts with those long pointey collars with the little plastic tabs in them. Problem was he never believed in rock'n roll, but he was a big believer in Lady Luck. He was fatally wrong on both counts. Other than the poker game where he won the first FCC license and got going. It led him to believe he had an edge on the human race. Thought he was richer'n six inches up a cow's ass.

"Daddy pretended to work hard, had a couple of heart bypasses. He always wanted to take the money and run. But there was never no money. Never knew the first thing about betting. Won the station playing an inside straight of all things. That convinced him there was not even minimum rules of sanity needed for this world."

Talisha let him talk. Studied him. She thought he had a kind of a keyed-up, poised looking body. Probably lifted weights. Repetitions with hand weights around his apartment to define his muscles. Not those huge barbells like you see in gyms, those brutes trying to squat them.

Talisha allowed she'd never felt quite at home in North Charleston.

"Yeah," Beau-Jack drawled. "Growin up, it was a nigger-don't-let-the sun-set-on-you kind of town all right."

Talisha couldn't believe what she just heard. Truth be known, she had never heard a white man say the word 'nigger'. You always knew they did. Grew up knowing they did. But never quite heard it. Liberalism had got driven in that deep. Like a stake half-way in a vampire's heart. But he was just saying it. Kind of relaxed. And like a metaphor or whatever the word was.

"Folks were right rough up there. Have an argument, they'd show you a knife. All those weird knives you can buy in the pawn shops near the Navy base. Try to loosen your brain on its stem with a sucker punch. Use a pool cue on you."

Digesting his jive, she suddenly realized what she was hearing. A country song off of WEZL, the hick station out of Monck's Corner. Or like an old cable TV movie. Burt Reynolds in "WW and the Dixie Dance Kings." "Smokey and the Bandit." The whole thing was an act like Beau-Jack thought she was some plumb fool.

"Me, I figured I'd move down to Charleston proper with the furniture shop. Mix with the gentry. They sure enough are different. They'll put tomato juice in a drink of liquor. Worcestershire. Salt and pepper. Stick of celery. Like it's food or something."

Talisha said human speech couldn't do an adequate job on how valuable his insights were, but she figured he was needed somewhere else.

He agreed that was true. "Good luck with the station. It's a virgin operation. Yours to bring birth to it. I've got to raise $70,000 and counting to pay off Wayne's Wagering. You can thank me once the job's done."

Talisha watched him leave from the second story office. He got into a VW bug with a Winston cigarette ad painted all over it. Make your car a billboard. Pick up money just driving around she guessed. The dude had no shame.

Talisha knew for sure. He was crooked as hell. Just like his daddy.

9

"I don't possibly have any more room on my social calendar," Browder Delamere stated flatly. Looked about at the church committee for acquiescence.

Honor stared at him. Hesitated. "This barbecue isn't planned for your benefit. We're trying to welcome new people to the church."

He gave her a significant look. "We don't need any new people in the church. All those charismatics flooding in like a bunch of immigrants. Just want to be a part of things they say. Then once they're here in big enough numbers they twist everything to suit them. They're all so pathetic and sweet until they've got enough numbers to win a vote. Then they tout the advantages of democracy."

"You agreed to serve on this committee," Honor protested weakly. And she wanted the use of his plantation. Bellefontaine was one of the last near the city that hadn't been chewed up for a subdivision.

She realized how little suited she was to running a newcomers committee or to mixing in the church schism. Browder proposing they screen all the addresses, reject any that didn't have a 29401 zip. That was the South-of-Broad area.

The others on the committee all murmured a muted approval. Saying they wouldn't underwrite further change. These modernistic hymns. One actually had the word "co-dependency" in it. Deliver us from co-dependency.

St. Ambrose was certainly going through culture shock. A falling off in cordiality had moved to open hostility. During the Sunday service, some man in a lime green suit had actually started talking in tongues.

Boolaboola-bup-bub-yalla-lalla-balla-wallah.

It went on and on until he fainted from exhaustion. The old guard was quite incensed. Just like the Pentecostals they said. Why don't these people go to the churches with the neon signs outside? Find a minister who wears a tuxedo with pink piping on the lapel and a frilly shirt? Will we have snake handling next? Colored people?

As the committee meeting broke up, everyone agreed they were glad to see Honor back in Charleston. Her late father's views on theology matched theirs. She was a worthy addition to the church staff. She could keep an eye on things.

"A character witness," observed Browder, "at the taproot of *his*"—he nodded significantly towards the minister's office—"conspiracies."

Browder whispered that dreadful Rector Royall was intent on participating in a program that involved churches as an alternative to prosecution in juvenile justice crime cases. Give him his way and there'd be hooligans inside the church itself. Black ones. Stealing the copper guttering. It was an unsquarable circle.

Outside in the night, the broad spreading oaks seemed to puff and breathe in the dense heat. The sky was clear and stars were out. The church offices lay on one side of St. Ambrose, the old burying ground on the other. The great steeple, taller than the church was long, presided majestically. With its St. George and the Dragon wind-vane, it had been a landmark for mariners long ago. The original bronze bells from England had been melted down during the Civil War.

Heels tapping on the pavement, Honor walked down Sheldon Street past 18th century row houses, two-story structures made of tabby, a cement of oyster shells and lime. At the corner, the church manse stood set back behind a spear topped iron fence, a tiny patch of grass and two black cypress trees. She went cold when she saw Judge Reggie Lorenzo lurking in the dark, his cigar a point of cherry light. He hadn't shaved in several days, leaving his face a mess of white bristles. Rumpled suit with no necktie. No shirt in fact. Ladder of breast bone on his sunken chest. A true loose thread from the lunatic fringe.

"You wearing a push-up bra?" he rasped. It was a great opener and it got better.

"Man, those tits are like transmogrified." Puffed on his stogie. "My heart's a ball of wax. You've heard that expression. A whole new ball of wax. Well mine is melting."

"That's a real touching profession of love," Honor said sarcastically. She picked up her pace, trying to walk away from him.

He came right behind her. "I'm talking about the heat. It's so freaking hot down here you could fry eggs on your car seat. Which leaves us with the larger question of when you're gonna spread those legs for me. Give me some fast-moving entertainment. Do you watch those women's porn movies? The ones where they go all gauzy when the gal takes a vibrator to herself?"

Honor stopped abruptly. Turned to confront him. "You know I'm starting to say to myself 'enough is enough'."

He jabbed his cigar at her. "Making threats are you? You figure you can decertify my ass? My wife thought that, and look what happened to her."

A bar of light spilled onto the street as Rusty Royall opened the front door of the manse. He stood there hesitantly under the little portico with its slender Tuscan columns.

Judge Lorenzo blinked his eyes at this new development and slinked away into the night. Stopped. Looked back at Rusty. Said, "Eat me raw." Gave a bronchial laugh and vanished.

Rusty laughed lightly. "Do we have a sophisticated mystery here? A bit of puzzle-solving called for?"

"Somebody who decided to know me," said Honor. "He's struggling emotionally with the fact he's a born loser."

Rusty said he'd let her remain in his protective custody until they were sure the interloper was truly gone. She shouldn't feel bad. His life was not controversy-free either. Did she want to come in for tea? Or something stronger? Sherry perhaps? Or even a vodka tonic?

No, she had to be home.

He looked up at the stars. "I feel like I'm some holy man who sits on a distant mountain top. People wait six days to hear my handful of parables. Sometimes I draw cheers from the crowd. Other days they're brutally candid about my liabilities.

"But now here you are to end my bland existence. I might be all the resources you need. Hmm? By way of providing a romantic interest I mean. Break my enforced . . . celibacy?"

Honor said no she was not the one for that role. Maybe he should consider Moira Ralston. Wonderful girl Moira. Pretty and sweet and a real potential bridge-builder with the older members of the congregation.

He didn't take the bait. "No, you are the original mandate. Young and vivacious. My pulsating temptress. I am bewitched, beguiled, bamboozled."

She used her brightest possible voice. "Sorry. I have to rule that out. We work together. *Esprit de corps.* Unity. All that." She felt like a re-run of Mary Tyler Moore.

"I come highly recommended," he pressed. "As either predator . . . or prey. You choose."

■ ■ ■

It had not started out as a good day for Talisha. She had fired the D.J. she had hired just the day before. Found him smoked up on weed, drooling into the microphone. He left full of dire threats about civil rights lawyers and "obverse" discrimination. Saying black-on-black crime was worse than ever with her around.

Her ad salesman told her to not expect to post any double-digit sales gains anytime soon. The ratings were lower than whale shit. No listening audience. Or the ones out there were old, didn't buy much more than pork necks and hemorrhoid medication.

Her momma Oneida saying, girl, you needs be plagued

with guilt, me sitting here in misery. Got me a slow-growing malignancy. Talisha answered what you got is auto-hypnosis. Leaving her to look that one up. See if it seemed attractive.

Talisha prayed silently for divine mercy. Sat there wondering if she was the world's worst sinner. Her awful yearnings for worldly success being jerked around by the latest turn of events. Greed and covetousness, vanity and pride all coming home to roost.

That was when the fat dude walked in, wearing the Tommy Hilfiger clothes, put the lid on everything. He said, "Talisha, baby, you in luck. Sierra Leone Jones done come to the rescue."

She said, *"Leone?"* Not believing what she was looking at. Pissed. I mean really pissed. The last she remembered him was saying "The bitch done love it. Done beg for more. Now she like unner the influence a' them radical fem'nists. Doan like the football program. Or the personnel."

Talisha was *pissed off*. "What unmitigated gall and nerve has brought your sorry self in here? Taking time off from street crime? Got your ass bounced by a welfare mother you shacking with?"

He turned a chair around, straddled it with his arms resting on the back. "I'm struggling with domestic performance. But internationally I'm doing good."

He handed her a business card that said he was a registered agent for the nation of Sierra Leone. She gestured impatiently, said you're what? A lobbyist? A diplomat? Was this official or some scam?

Leone explained he was expecting a big lobbying contract from the Sierra Leone government any day. Some generals had to be paid off once he got the funds liquid. Meanwhile he had been dispatched by Brother Farrakhan to head up a million man march through the streets of Charleston. Which had brought him to the communication center of WPST.

"We gonna banish crime. Justice nourish. Feed them chir'ren so sin won't fluorish."

He was really fat, big rolls hanging over his belt jiggling as he moved in his chair with the rhythm.

"You'd never make it as a rapper," said Talisha. "Get laughed out of the recording studio. And brother Jesse got the edge on you in the political rhyming game." She was keeping herself under control as best she could, the hatred burning so brightly.

He accused her of not wanting to help publicize events run by Muslims. She had anti-Muslim prejudice.

Talisha bit her tongue. Told him the FCC required they carry public service announcements. There was no problem with that. He said that led him to the issue of monetary contributions. Putting something back into the community. Not just taking out. How much would WPST donate to the march? He had all kinds of heavy expenses getting underway.

"We're a start-up business," she countered, "and in a cash flow drought. We don't need you to suck us drier."

"Then how bout you gimme a job? Straight salary? Plus maybe a incentive commission."

"No way."

He kind of chuckled. "I cannot properly contemplate that rejection. This is a bantering conversation I know.

But the idea you won't put your old friends and associates on the payroll when they come and express such a serious interest . . ."

She glowered at him. "You're beyond interested. You're self-interested. Not to mention gutter trash what ruined my young life. I'm looking at you thinking you're something from outer space and proof positive there ain't no intelligent life on Mars."

"So the inference is—the reality of this affliction is—you is reverting to bad old ways. Just like when you suing my ass."

"The inference is get your ass out. I got enough shit storms in my face for one day."

"You are possessed of *demons*, girl. All huffed up with combat readiness. I am greatly gifted. Got the communicability of truths. Have you been to Washington lately? The nation's capital? Man, it look like Liberia up there. Holes in the streets. Crooked cops. Jesse Jackson afraid to go out at night because the brothers such a pack of killers. *Besieged.*

"Listen here. My first proposed project is a WPST prison gospel ministry. Get over to the county jail and counsel the inmates. Maybe take up money for them what can't make bail. After a proper screening of course. Check 'em out for innocence. So thereby we lay out a scenario. I ain't one to wallow in cliché, but I'm pleading publicly here."

Talisha shook her head no.

He insisted, "Looka here. We need us a democratic mandate. I vote to hire. You agin it? Okay, duly recorded. There. Deadlock. So I'll be the tie-breaker."

"I don't think we need an election right now."

He said that's cool. He could wait to be a second-round draft pick.

She said until hell freezes over.

"Well that don't really matter. Waiting for cold weather. Because you see how it is, is Alvin Teckler done give me the nod. I was trying to make it less a poison pill for you. Let you think it was your idea."

Talisha got up from behind her desk. Shook a finger in his face. "You want some democracy? I outvote Alvin on all issues! I own over half the stock!"

He reached under his shirt, rubbed his fat belly. Whined, "Don't be so *Godless, girl.*"

10

The federal bankruptcy judge rubbed his jaw and asked, "Is this some kind of joke I need to be let in on?"

Luscious Decatur, owner/proprietor of the Stallion Club, was sitting there with three of his girls, two black and one white. All of them were dressed in matching purple, the girls in hotpants that showed the cheeks of their butts.

Rannie Ralston answered she believed her clients were trying to make a fashion statement. She was in a rotten mood. Her tits hurt from drinking coffee but she needed coffee to get her motor running in the morning. Now she had to make a minor fool of herself.

She shook her head despondently. She wouldn't stoop to handle such a trash case except the Stallion Club kept sending her an unbroken stream of assault-and-battery with deadly weapons clients. She had six of them from the last shoot-out.

Pin-striped lawyers for the creditors glowered at them. Landlord. Beer wholesalers. Frito-Lay folks. Electric and telephone companies. They had put Luscious into involuntary bankruptcy. Rannie had countered with a Chapter 11 plan of reorganization.

Rannie argued it was no problem really. Luscious had

been feeling the intensity of his debts. But he was coming over into the . . . black. She had hesitated. It was so hard to use that word anymore without someone flinching.

Luscious chimed in, "That's right. Ain't no need for them creditors to try to get physical with me. Try that rugged inside play."

Rannie told him to be quiet. She rolled her eyes as she said his Honor might wish to peruse the plan of reorganization. Luscious would be enhancing his club offering. Going to better even the exceptional standards he had set over the years.

The judge rested his head on his fist, said okay, he'd bite. What was it?

Lucious jumped up again. "What it be is a clean slate approach. Targeting the new multiracial lifestyle of the South. Take a look at these three fine gals. From a design standpoint, they complement each other. Once the word get out—go with brochures, flyers, catalogs . . ."

The judge sighed get to the point, his hemorrhoids were acting up.

"We kicking off with a topless carwash like has been proved so successful in Florida. Maybe go on-line with a web-site to reach the computer literate. Advice for the interracially lovelorn. Point and click friendliness."

The judge said topless car wash? Web site? All he foresaw was the water company and America OnLine sitting in with the creditors next.

Luscious insisted, "We gone ride that emotion. They's just a full pipeline of possibilities."

Rannie made a face. "Luscious, I'm advising you once

again to shut up." To the judge, "Your honor what we're prepared to do is give the creditors a lien on all cash register receipts until such time as the debts are paid."

The judge agreed that was about the only solution. Sold off, the club would bring zip. He looked over her head. "Next case."

Rannie's mother Mary Canty had phoned from Italy at monstrous expense wanting to know the Italian word for alligator.

Rannie said alligator? She said yes. Also belt, pocketbook and shoes. And she wanted to yack at Rannie about her progress in getting the charismatics out of the church. Rannie admitted she hadn't made any. Mary Canty vowed if Rannie didn't she was going to convert to Roman Catholicism although God knows she wouldn't know a soul at the cathedral.

As they walked out, everyone staring at them, Luscious told Rannie he was thinking of opening a booth at the Minority Career Fair. Go right to the high schools as a source for the best girls for the client service area. Maybe get a federal grant, provide summer jobs for teens.

■ ■ ■

Preparatory to his date with Honor Revenue, Chandler drove Mummy's Oldsmobile through the topless car wash at the Stallion Club. This brazen-tit innovation was a first for the Lowcountry, but apparently legal as long as the girls stayed behind the black plastic curtain out of the public gaze. And there they came with the soap and garden hoses. Little bikini bottoms. Bare boobies bobbing.

Ah yes, delectable sight. Now take out the old percival. Stroke it while they wag those coconuts. Whups, that one sees the extended member.

She was motioning for him to roll down the window. Very well.

What? Want to reach inside? Yes indeed. Take hold. Fondle as you will. Provocative white girl with some kind of Celtic tatoo on her arm. Appropriate for a man of his tastes. Trinity College background and all that. The whores on the quays of Dublin used to jerk him off for pints of Guinness.

What? The big spade with the gold teeth was motioning him to drive forward. Seems a bit fast for his $20. Scarcely value for money.

When Chandler protested, the blue-gum galoot told him to hit the road, Jack, come back tomorrow if he wanted more of that stuff.

More of that stuff. Gad.

At least he could report to Mummy he had washed the car.

Damn, they hadn't even adequately cleaned the rear window. But no, something was written there. He could read it in the rearview mirror as he drove into the sunlight. It was a telephone number. The little minx had written it backwards. Clever little bint.

He meditated upon this during the long drive in traffic back to familiar turf on the peninsula of Charleston. Chandler's father had frequented whores. It was not inappropriate for a gentleman. Relieve the visceral needs. There was a problem of cost naturally. Protecting the wallet from filchery while doing the old in-and-out with the tummy banana. Of dire necessity, Chandler devoted an increasing amount of his time to the indignity of financial worries.

When he had set off for divinity school, the $100,000 in trust he stood to inherit upon his marriage seemed more than adequate. It would supplement his ministerial salary. Put him above the common herd. But inflation had ticked away, raising prices on the necessities of life, diminishing the value of the corpus. And those duplicitous stockbrokers always had their transparent excuses for why it didn't grow. You'd be eaten up by taxes. Capital gains were murder. Need to be conservative with our investments. Low risks are the route to go. The market baffled him. All that tiresome reading you had to do about industrials.

And additionally the principal part of his game plan was to marry an heiress. One properly freighted down with bullion. That was appropriate for the clergy. Man to command. Woman with large bank account as helpmeet.

When the years slid by and marriage to a bank balance didn't pan out, he began to focus on girls of genteel but more straightened circumstances. Making note of valuable objects which they stood to inherit but weren't fully aware of. Paintings. Rare porcelain or silver. Furniture. He kept a notebook of these calculations.

This had led to something of an imbroglio when Weezie Dawkins found the book and an entry under her name. He had foolishly left it behind on her couch along with cake crumbs and dabs of jam after inviting himself to tea. Her family owned those lots on Sullivan's Island which even a decade ago were worth a half a million apiece. Thankfully that little brou-ha-ha had died down. How many years ago had it been? Gad, the whispering at the Yacht Club. Mummy had not been amused.

It was midday when he turned off I-26 onto Meeting Street and the shabby buildings of the black ghetto of Charleston. Litter in the street. Spicy fried chicken emporiums. Darkies with sweat rings under their arms. They were always so perfectly composed as they waited at bus stops. The jet-black little picaninnys motionless, never complaining in the filthy heat.

Meeting took him straight past Marion Square with its big monument to Francis Marion, through the corridor of grisly new bank buildings and into the old covered market with the hordes of tourists.

Ah what have we here? A sports bar. A good place to rinse a thirst and lay plans for his Honor Revenue campaign. And a fortuitous parking place opening up. Grotesque family of tourists from Ohio in a mini-van. Surely an omen. Chandler Lovelace displaces the dross to gain the good things of life.

Parallel park the big Oldsmobile carefully. It was nicely washed. Go inside the cool semi-darkness and settle in at the bar for some wistful imaginings. The little honeys in shorts chirping at him so gaily. Yes thank you, a whisky and soda to strengthen the pulse. Perhaps a draft beer as well. It's a warm day. Do you have Bass Ale?

Life had seemed so fundamental in Dublin. Frothy pints of Guinness in the pubs on the Liffey Quays. Champagne under the striped tents at Spring socials. Bottle of Jamison's whisky in the college room. No one had thought his habits intemperate. Here in Charleston one had to be wary of the teetotalers. Such creatures were scarce in St. Ambrose, thank God.

Curious though. He had never seen that Rusty Royall

touch a drop. Extremely suspect, that man. Would have been much happier as a foot-washing Pentecostal. Must take care. Couldn't have Rusty carrying malicious tales to Honor Revenue. True, Chandler had imbibed a bit at Roland's funeral. But the grief was so overwhelming.

Honor with her hefty Tiverton commode with its delicately nuanced marquetry in some fruitwood, perhaps apple or pear. Entrancing Honor of the dark tresses and sculpted lips. Her thighs awaiting the first stain of his semen. Yes indeed. Think upon her and not that nonsense on those largish TV screens. Was that baseball?

Chandler's only close-up experience with sports had come as youth minister for that wretched little parish in dreary Londonderry. It was a true low. After the fashion of mixed blessings, it only lasted until the dreadful day he was refereeing a hurling match and the Catholic louts had beaten him in the head with their sticks. Beastly, barbaric game. Gave him a severe concussion.

Sent him back to Mummy and his lengthy unemployment that she made so much over. Well, she couldn't live forever. The Lord had called Roland home unexpectedly after all.

11

"You just caught a break, baby. Sierra Leone is here."

Talisha had been eating lunch alone in Jasmine's, a swanky restaurant on East Bay Street, trying to convince herself that she had some faint aura of upward social mobility. Outside, a bicycle rickshaw went by with two tourists in it.

She looked up. "You must of pulled a quad muscle in your brain. I done close out that portion of my existence with you looming large in it."

Talisha had learned right quick that running a radio station was no cake walk. Everybody just sliding out when they felt like it. Saying hey cover for me. I gots to go to the dentist.

She had told Alvin she needed to understand how the money worked. He nodded toward these ten-fifteen bound up books. Said there's the records. It's all there. Check it out.

Folks from the neighborhood just drop in like it was a social club. Bring a squash they claim looks like Bill Clinton's head. Expect to be put on the air to discuss this wonder of agriculture.

Some crazy white woman—Grace Revenue—had called

up that morning wanting her to warn her listeners to not turn plastic bread bags inside out and use them to store food. There was lead paint used on the labels.

Now she had megamouth inviting himself to lunch, just sitting down opposite her and unfolding a napkin. No idea whether Alvin had really given him a job or not. Alvin was real vague on the subject. Claimed Leone had some sound ideas about a prison ministry. She told him that's because he belong in prison.

Leone signaled the waitress like he thought he was a major celebrity and she should recognize him right off. Told her to do something nice with the catch of the day. Blackened or reddened. Whatever was the in-thing. He turned back to Talisha, leaning towards her on his elbows, trying to take hold of both her hands.

"Ooo-man, love this alfresco dining."

She said alfresco meant out of doors. Best as she could tell there was a roof over their heads. He said he knew that.

She looked around wondering if she was being stared at, eating with this loud fool in a Hilfiger t-shirt. She had worn a multicolored sequin jacket, thinking it made her look classy. Now among all these fancy white folks and their grilled lobster and gazpacho she felt it looked like the Stallion Club.

"I got to appeal this suspension," Leone urged. "We had some good times, baby. Think of the joy and laughter."

Talisha eyed him like a bug that needed mashing. Tried to be dry. Keep her cool. Didn't want a major scene in this fancy restaurant. "I don't consider being gang-raped one of my more joyous experiences. You and them other fine young scholar-athletes."

"Hey, what about me? I didn't like being sued worth a shit. That red-haired bitch. Man, she was scary as something out of 'The Exorcist'. Kept expecting her to turn her head 360-degrees all around."

"She sure enough outdueled your ass."

"I got to give you credit, Talisha-baby. You can argue a man to the ground. Don't underplay them past history elements. Got me gasping for air. It's like, Go, girl. Hit that jugular."

He told her he had a whole business plan figured for his prison ministry. Man, that county jail was as bad as South Africa. Heat. Noise. Baloney sandwiches. They was folks in there got they ass jugged for blowing soap bubbles. It was that bad. Out in traffic blowing bubbles, you go to jail. I mean, is that fair? Is that American justice?

Talisha ate her shrimp salad.

"Sure. Ignore Sierra Leone. He's lower than a snake's belly. But I ain't put off. Ain't gone bow out. You my sentimental favorite. When the check comes, lemme handle it. Consider this our first date."

Talisha thought about how she should have taken accounting in college. Looking through those books made no sense at all. Alvin could be stealing the business blind and she wouldn't know it.

When the waitress brought the check, Leone told her he needed to talk with the marketing department about doing a trade. The waitress looked puzzled. She knew he was up to something and didn't want to take the heat. Went off looking for heavier artillery.

Talisha asked what the hell are you doing? And if he

didn't have the money for lunch then why didn't he come out in the open with his poverty and quit calling it a date?

Leone explained he was working a trade. This was what radio execs did. Give a radio ad spot in trade for lunch, new clothes, you name it. All off the books so the IRS couldn't keep track of the extent of the underground economy.

Talisha said what you talking about? Leone said ain't she noticed all them building supply ads they been running? Lumber. Plumbing stuff. Electric wiring. Alvin was building himself that big house over on the Ashley River. Getting all his materials for free. Or rather at the expense of the station in lieu of cash. That's the history that was involved.

Talisha said Alvin got no right to do that. To which Leone says he's a Jew ain't he? You know what brother Farrakhan says about Jews?

"Let's not get into that hate-speech shit."

"Well you know what he says about numbers?"

"Okay what?"

"Six and three is nine. Put three nines out there you got like a little row of commas. Turn them round you got three sixes. The mark of the Whore of Babylon."

"So?"

"So numbers got symbolism. They ain't harmless."

Talisha stood up furious, rummaging in her purse. "Yeah they got symbolism. They how I count out the dollar bills to pay for this hot date. They how I'm gonna count off the minutes on my watch to when I never see you no more."

"Baby, I'm busting my tail for WPST, spending hours in that sweat box jail bringing folks to Jesus, and you dashing all my hopes. They's serious finance wrapped up in the equation."

"I'll help you with the first part."

"What's that?"

"The tail-busting."

■ ■ ■

"The symbolism of the Whore of Babylon is certainly an interesting one," said Chandler loudly. "666. It was really the symbol of Aphrodite. She was an Asian goddess that came into Greece via Cyprus. She had a famous temple at Ephesus. When Paul preached to the Ephesians, he railed against the Babylonian Ishtar. He realized they were one and the same. Same tradition. All that."

"That's interesting," murmured Honor, not very interested at all. She looked around Jasmine's vaguely wondering if there was a back door she could slip out. They had just sat down, and she already had an impulse to flee.

Chandler wore a wrinkled white suit, the jacket stretched tight over his fat shoulders, ancient food stains on the lapels. He shook out his napkin and tucked it into his waist. Leaned forward confidentially. "Temple prostitution, you know."

She said no, she didn't know, then bit her tongue. Now she'd have to hear about it.

Chandler slathered butter on the bread and shoved it in his mouth, chewing ponderously, scattering crumbs. "They were courtesans in a way." Chewing. "Men paid for rituals in honor of goddesses." Chewing, swallowing. "Sexual intercourse was a sacred rite. Corinth was famous for it." More bread in his mouth. "The word Elohim which we translate as 'God' came from the Sumerian 'strong juice'—'water of fecundity, spermatozoa'. The cult-prostitute performed a vegetative function."

Across the room an attractive black girl slammed money down on the table and stalked out. Her date got clumsily up, scraping back his chair. Told the entire room, "I think she's on the rag," and followed her out.

Outside, he yelled after her, "What is this? A blaxploitation movie? I could make more money sucking dick than working for you!"

"Why don't you give it a try?" she screamed back.

"I'll have the albacore," said Chandler ponderously.

"The tuna?" asked the waitress.

"The albacore."

The lunch special was albacore tuna *à la* Wando. Every restaurant in Charleston had something *à la* Wando. It was meaningless. The name of a little creek that emptied into Charleston harbor. They tacked it on like it was a local culinary tradition that went back to the first boat.

Honor chose the pasta primavera, making a mental note that her mother would enquire as to whether it was whole grain, fresh or dried. Dried could get buggy. Whole grain on the other hand turned rancid if not refrigerated. And fresh was really dangerous because it was made from fresh eggs. Salmonella lurked.

Chandler was saying after doing divinity at Trinity College, he had suffered a serious injury on the hurling fields. It had required a lengthy convalescence. Fortunately he had his trust fund waiting. It was activated upon his marriage. He would come into the corpus at that time. He gave her a significant look.

And he was anticipating a high post any day. Rector of St. Ambrose. He paused as though expecting comment.

"That's nice," she said, staring at the ice in her water.

He told her St. Ambrose was the 4th century archbishop of Milan. He set the prayers of the mass to music and invented silent reading. She said she had learned that in Sunday school. He said excellent. Since she would be working for the church, they would have ample opportunity for theological discussion.

There was a little silence. A lifetime of practice at putting the wallflower and the misfit at ease and she could think of nothing to say. Nothing.

"What is your position on the Rococo Revival Style?" asked Chandler. He was tucking into his fish now. Chewing.

"Excuse me?"

"Your furniture. Which you're giving away. Rococo Revival Style. Some Neo-Grec. Laminated rosewood panels all glued together and steamed. Flower, fruit and vine motifs stuck on them. Applied medallions. Quite hideous really." He pulled a bone out of his mouth and stuck it on the edge of his plate. Sucked his teeth. "Some of it's merely *papier-mâché* with black lacquer over it. Machine-made rubbish. Tufting, buttons and fringes. And those Turkish frame chairs are nothing but spring bundles concealed by the upholstery. Wooden legs screwed on. Revolting."

"I don't really know anything about furniture."

"Yes, I rather thought you didn't."

What she thought was the lunch would never end.

At long last the waitress cleared away.

"I had the albacore," said Chandler.

"The tuna?" said the waitress. "Did you like it?"

"The albacore," said Chandler firmly.

Honor realized he was signaling the waitress to give them separate checks. She was paying for her own lunch.

She told Chandler she hoped he didn't get scomboid fish poisoning. If albacore isn't properly refrigerated, the histadine in it changes to histamine. Your blood pressure shoots up. Frantic pulse rate. Headache. Numbness. Vomiting. It's seldom fatal, but if you've already got high blood pressure you could be at risk.

He looked distinctly queasy.

12

"For goodness sake quit pestering me over that ratty furniture!" Rusty Royall shouted. It was night, and his voice echoed in the church office.

Chandler Lovelace said well. He'd certainly be pleased to convey Rusty's sentiments to Mrs. Revenue. The woman takes the lead in charitable giving and now must suffer egregious abuse. And her own daughter working right here for the vestry. It made him wonder what demeaning and hostile behavior she had to suffer daily.

The man looked hunted. Knew Chandler had him backed against the wall.

Chandler bored in saying he feared the congregation was going beyond mere discomfort with its current rector. Certain members had joined together and mandated Chandler to assess the effects of change in the church. They wanted him to report the facts as he saw them. It was an original grant of jurisdiction. Quite a novel undertaking really.

"Very well," Rusty muttered. Giving in gracelessly. Sulking. "I'll find a use for it."

"I am gratified you have ceased to be unresponsive on this simple matter of furniture. I can assume rationality then. This however subtracts only in the smallest way from the larger issues. New forms of worship are not imposed by fiat. We are not some church of Rome. These matters are far from frivolous. No dissembling on your part. The fact remains, they occur on your watch."

Well that had thoroughly intimidated the dreadful man. The old guard could take a page from his book. Look upon my works ye mighty and despair.

Chandler went out onto the night dark street with its puddles of light coming through the oaks. Well, he thought. Lie down with charismatics, get up with Jesus freaks. He liked the sound of that. A little play on the old lie down with dogs get up with fleas. Rather Oscar Wildean. He'd have to try it out on Browder Delamere. The man appreciated a good quip.

Chandler made the short walk across Broad Street and down Meeting. It was a weeknight with few people about. A faint hot breeze rustled the oak leaves, pale moonlight turning their tips to silver. He picked up the pace through LeBow's alley, the darkness hurrying him along uneasily. All those dreadful negro muggers plaguing the city. Now out of the alley and safely under a street lamp on Legendre.

Heaving for breath in that wash of yellow light. Bit more adventure than he was accustomed to. Chandler liked a world of soft tones and contours. No sharp edges. He gathered his faculties and walked down the street to the end. The trees cast huge interlocking shadows.

Honor Revenue's window was lit. Chandler adjusted the focus on his pocket opera glasses hoping to catch a glimpse of her. A *sine qua non* sort of creature really. He had watched her over the years and thought how ideal a companion she'd make. Woman of moon-glow.

Marriage, while fated, would present its difficulties. The commercial theme though muted in the beginning would come through eventually. She'd expect him to be of independent means.

Well, he'd soon have his hands on the Tiverton commode. Sell it in New York and his fortune would be secured. The provenance would be a sticky wicket. Something that valuable would need a history. But Charleston houses were filled with forgotten items of value. He could cover its tracks sufficiently. Providing that fool Grace Revenue didn't suddenly tune in her daffy brain and remember it.

Ah there was the matchless Miss Honor. Gad, is she semi-clothed? Stripped to the waist but for that lacy black brassiere. A little on the emaciated side, but what a set of ba-zooms. Delectable. To sup upon those in the crepuscular glow of evening. Sheer surfeit.

He'd need to shape up a bit for her. His stomach had become rather rounded. A certain slack effect invading the biceps. Perhaps reduce the evening cocktails. Calibrate his intake and correlate it to weight loss.

And relatedly, there was the sex performance problem. Something of a technical field exercise really. Elaborate preparation could be negated by one minor slip. He'd had severe difficulty in that area in the past. Some exceedingly unpleasant experiences. Still, a bit of tupping practice with this whore Cindi and he'd be rutting like a bull.

"Well you *naughty* boy," shrilled a female voice.

Chandler nearly jumped out of his skin. Whirled about to find Moira Ralston. Good God. You. For a moment I thought . . . He was shivering all over with fright.

"Spying on your *true love*?" she chirped. She wagged a finger. "Sneaky, sneaky."

"What? What?" Chandler blustered. He fought to get himself under control. Stop his shaking. Bit flighty that girl. Creeping up on people in the dark. Never did fully understand her. Still, an interesting little buttocks on her. Jiggling back and forth. Would like to cup those in two hands. Squeeze until she yelped. See that look of sudden surprise at the pain.

Moira said she understood he and Honor Revenue were becoming a number. Having a little tête-à-tête luncheon at Jasmines.

"Um yes," he allowed. "Delightful time. The albacore was quite sound."

"Well, all I can say is you're a naughty boy, Chandler Lovelace. Standing reverently beneath her window in the dark. I must say, when this gets around . . . well, people won't know what to think."

Chandler fingered his opera glasses, muttered about nighthawks. Purple martins. Updating his list of local birds. Doing a count. "What? What's that?" he started.

A stealthy figure was over in the darkness. Lurking near a giant wisteria that wrapped around an oak like a python.

"Who's there?" Chandler yelped.

"Call 911!" Moira urged, the panic infecting her. "Don't you have a cell phone?"

■ ■ ■

"No," Rannie told Browder Delamere over the phone. "You can't come over and play."

"Why?" he argued petulantly. "Here I am openly signaling my needs."

"Why? Because my idiot sister is here. The smell of fornication gives her the heebie-jeebies."

"Oh? Is that the problem? Yes, she might gossip. Tell my wife. We need to hold a strategy meeting."

Rannie thought about the portrait Browder had commissioned of himself in heraldic armor. "Did I mention you also can't come over because you've got a dick like a chipping sparrow?"

"What? What are you saying?"

Rannie hung up hard and poured herself a Jim Beam. She knew she shouldn't. It was more calories than she ate with a meal. She'd quit tomorrow. Or maybe next week. It was hard to get through a weekend without drinking.

Whacked-out drooling morons for clients. Bills due on something every day. She made a mental note to phone Beau-Jack McCully and lean on him on behalf of Wayne's Wagering. Remind him—notwithstanding Booger-T in the clink—he had limited time before the collectors put serious stress on him.

Rannie carried her drink out on the screened-in quarter of the upper piazza and sat down in a wicker chair in the hot breath of night. The piazzas with their Doric columns—long galleries or porches they would have been called somewhere else—had been added to the house in 1830 as part of the craze for Greek revival grandeur along with the decorative paneled balustrade that hid the hipped roof. The fashion had spread from Philadelphia, then still the cultural capital of the nation.

Thick greenery drooped heavily in the humid air.

Rannie remembered hot summer nights when you could play outside because it didn't get dark until nine and then the sky was so bright with rings around the moon. Nothing was the same anymore. Kids didn't play in the dark because there were so many tourists and perverts and drug meltdowns. She frequently thought about moving off the peninsula.

A girlfriend—also a lawyer, three-times divorced by age 32—lived over in Mt. Pleasant in one of the tract mansion developments. Oversized brand new houses on streets with names like Burnt Rum Punch Lane.

All the Martha Stewart wives hung out pineapple banners. At Christmas they lined the drives with little candles in white paper sacks. Her friend said she was getting into this lifestyle. It gave her an identity to coalesce around. Maybe she could make the next marriage work. Have children and carpool them in a van.

Rannie was aghast. This had once been an obsessively hands-on kind of attorney. Got in a screaming, kicking match with an assistant federal D.A. the first week out of law school. She was Rannie's only comrade amazon. Now she was broken by the suburbs and the ticking of a biological clock.

Across the street behind a wrought iron fence and thick azaleas the Revenue house winked a single lit window in a Victorian gingerbread tower. Honor's bedroom. It held a mysterious air, haunting and haunted looking. Just like Honor, the only offspring of parents old enough to be grandparents.

As a child, Honor wasn't a particularly good person. Nor a bad one. She just was. Her face held a dreamlike look, not vapid like Moira, but like she could see into distant places. Living in that big rattletrap of a house with old people and a black cocker spaniel and black guinea pig.

Cats and dogs seemed to follow her. Or if the dogs were chained up, they never barked when she walked by. And when she hit twelve, men followed her. Not just gawky adolescent boys, but grown men of all ages. Sportsmen and professional men. Yachtsmen, harbor pilots, doctors, lawyers, trust fund drones. Hordes of men dithering and stumbling dizzy around her.

They sent her notes and gifts and called her on the phone and accosted her on the street. She felt their desperation, the heat of their desire, but it slid past her like a hot breeze. She was not ruled by passion.

It was the colored servants in the Ralston mansion who first whispered of witchcraft. They studied the blackbirds flocking on the Revenue roof in unnatural numbers. Packing the trees in the yard until branches broke and the ground was white with bird dung. When the men began gathering like the birds, Mozella, the Ralston maid would say that girl done catch them boys' souls like birds in a net. Theys something unnatural doing there.

Rannie's romantic conquests had been less numerous. She had lost her virginity at 15 to Browder Delamere, then a senior at Porter-Gaud, the ritzy boy's school in town. He smelled of Brut cologne and was going off to college in Virginia. Cupid's arrow skewered her heart good.

She had wanted so badly to let love scorch every inch of her body. Like all of the ones who followed, he was inept, scared shitless, a premature ejaculator. She had showed him everything to do, then masturbated afterwards to get any pleasure at all. Mortified, he had called her a whore. Yelled at her for bleeding on the seat of his father's Lincoln Continental. Later bragged to his friends that his dick was so big she couldn't take it all.

He graduated from Washington & Lee and became a stock broker with Dombey & Trouche. Married a Kappa Kappa Gamma and had three boys Chip, Skipper and Tyson. Typical. Lately, she had beaten his firm in a stock churning case. Taken them for seriously big bucks. When the jury brought back the six-figure verdict with a whopping sum for punitives, he looked all shivery and sweat-stained. As shivery as the night she had wanted to control him with love and deep, wet sex freely given with no put-on sham of fear.

Growing up, Honor's mother dressed her in homely, shapeless clothes. No short skirts to tug down over those perfect thighs. No push-up bras that would accentuate what grew into the world's most perfect bosom. Honor always behaved. No wild streak. No sneaking out with guys to quaff beer or puff reefers. No motorcycle rides. She was reclusive. Didn't even date. But the spell was always cast just by her entering a landscape. And men self-destructed without the least encouragement from her.

By the time Rannie finished law school, Honor's looks were so potent that men wanted to marry her. She would have been 13 or 14 then. Rannie would come home on vacation to find entire grades of Porter-Gaud boys playing in the street desperately trying to get Honor's attention. Drunken old farts at the yacht club would make jokes about waiting for her to grow up, their wives kicking them violently under the tables.

Rannie's life was a lonely journey. Each day brought

less hope of a passionate romance. Now to top it off, she had this love goddess neighbor to taunt her with her aura.

Outside, the night spoke in inaudible whispers. No, those were real voices. Rannie had finished her drink and was getting up for another one when she spied movement across the street. Someone was lurking out there at the edge of the wisteria staring up at the one lighted window of the Revenue house. Talking to himself. Scumbag peeping-Tom, she thought. Subhuman fart-breath.

By the time Rannie had seized a golf club in the umbrella stand in the front hall and gotten out onto the street, two voices were arguing.

A skinny old man with a jacket and no shirt and the obese Chandler Lovelace were pushing and shoving like teenager guys afraid to fight but afraid to back down.

Suddenly the skinny geek kicked Chandler hard in the gut. It was a wicked, vicious blow that doubled Chandler up, put him to his knees weeping in pain.

"Ass-wipe!" the old man shouted in a New York yankee voice. "Goddammit, I'm a judge! Don't I get no respect from you inbred peckerwoods?" He gave off a stench of bad breath and b.o. and crazed menace.

Rannie took this as her cue to lash him violently with the golf club. This was the scum that invaded Charleston ten months out of the year. Everything pent up inside her came rushing out. She wanted to beat the hell and guts out of him. She wanted to get his head, crack it open like an egg. He hunched down and took the head blows, the kidney jabs on his shoulders and arms. Screamed and shrieked. She thought she heard bones breaking.

"You shit! You cunt!" he shouted. But he was in full

retreat into the darkness. Stumbling away wounded on his twisted psychological journey.

Rannie was breathing heavily. Each blow had been a beautiful expression of all her hatred of tourists. Retaliation for every time her car got stuck behind one of those horse-drawn wagons, one of the big buses full of rubbernecks. Robo-cop terminator for all who paid outlandish taxes so Yankees could gawk at their gardens.

Moira, rigid with fear up to this point, started screaming uncontrollably.

"Moira? What?" said Rannie, noticing her for the first time. "Shut up, will you?"

"Where are the police?" Chandler demanded. He was still down on his hands and knees gagging up bile. "Persistent failure of government to protect the citizen!" He had dropped a pair of brass opera glasses on the sidewalk, shattering a lens.

"It's hell isn't it?" said Rannie. "Today's level of carnage. We normalize remorseless, impulsive violence. Offload the blame in other directions. Society failed the hoodlum. The social net failed to catch him."

"I'm hurt, I'm hurt," Chandler whined. "Call 911."

"Why don't you carry a cell phone?" Moira cried helplessly.

13

Honor Revenue sat at the long oak table in the St. Ambrose library to scan the *New York Times*. Sure enough, the Metropolitan section had an article about Judge Lorenzo disappearing. Which meant if no one could find him, he had taken a flight under an assumed name and paid for the ticket in cash. It also noted his wife had been shot to death less than a year before.

Honor sighed deeply and stared at the bead-and-reel molding around the ceiling. Sprays of acanthus leaves at the corners. Despite an extensive periodicals collection, the library was seldom used. A few old duffers came in, fell asleep in an armchair with *Readers' Digest.* Questions had been raised at Vestry meetings as to whether they should have videos that could be taken home. Rusty Royall was in favor of a sex education series for the teenagers. That had evoked the usual outrage from the oldsters.

She quickly turned the page as Rusty walked in. He wore his gray shirt with the white clerical collar, a madras jacket over it like he was trying to look jazzy. He said in a world mired in contradictions a moment of quiet reading was restorative for the soul. No comment? Having an attack of expressive aphasia? He giggled inanely.

Composed himself. Cleared his throat. "We're shaped

by what we read. Especially childhood reading. Don't you agree?"

"Uh . . . of course." She was thinking about *National Velvet* and being horse crazy as a girl.

"I mean think about the formative books for a young girl. *Charlotte's Web.* It's got a whole earth mother view of life. Life as a cycle of nature. No closure. Just an unending round of birth, tragedy and death. Who are the men in it?"

"The father?" she suggested.

"Stern and punitive. His principal role is killing pigs. Then there's a bratty younger brother." He was counting them off on his fingers. "A rat that eats garbage. And a cowardly oinker named Wilbur who will do anything, debase himself in any way to stay alive.

"Charlotte is like a Greek chorus. She spins a mandala web. She grieves over the tragedy of life. She dies birthing little spiders. And the young girl heroine is transformed by her experiences. She knows the birth of the little pink pig. Love. Fulfillment. She fights to keep it alive. But will it grow into a strong male figure? Of course not. It's just a little yellow-backed wad of blubber that needs her mothering. Forever."

"Oo-kay," said Honor dubiously. His voice and eyes were real intense.

"Was there a daddy spider? Hmm? Of course not. Because Charlotte had killed and eaten him after sexual intercourse. Did your mother whisper that hidden lore to you in private? Hmm? Is that the secret doctrine that all girls grow up knowing?"

He was leaning across the table getting awfully close. "Uh, what's your point?" asked Honor.

"You've spun a web around me. I'm helpless. You can kill and eat me any time you want."

Honor confessed she had no real interest in that.

"There are always opportunistic attorneys waiting in the wings to take your case. I'm an aficionado of such matters."

She was saying wha . . . ? when the phone rang. She snatched it up like a sudden rescue.

"I can't live without you," went the voice on the other end. Puff on a cigar. It was Judge Lorenzo. "I want you to sit on my face. Kind of squirm around. Do a cunnilingus chin dance."

She got angry. "You know, my mother nags nonstop. I have to wash the rind of a cantaloupe because you can spread Salmonella by the knife as you cut through it. Apparently, the FDA recommends this."

He said, "Yeah, it's a bitch keeping up with that. You peel fruits and vegetables to get rid of pesticides, you lose your fiber. You can't win."

"You're missing my point. I've got enough annoyance in my life."

"You? What about me? I'm beyond disgruntled. I get beat to shit by some red haired bitch on the street. It's crazier than New York down here. They say forty-seven percent of victims know their assailants. Well I was in the victim-to-a-stranger category. A freaking golf club! Talk about lax law enforcement."

Rusty was saying something. Honor put her hand over the receiver, mouthed what?

"I was proposing we conduct an internal review of my misbehavior. Come up with an appropriate punishment."

■ ■ ■

Talisha drove her beat-up old Saturn out to the lot on the Ashley River where Alvin was watching the construction crew working on his new house. Big new houses lined the street. Hundreds of thousands of dollars apiece plus Lordy-knows-what for the riverfront real estate. Some very heavy money.

Alvin's was going to be no smaller than the others. The big pile of high-end copper pipes and bathroom fixtures represented big value. All week, ads had been running on WPST for Flow-Easy Plumbing Co.

Alvin came right up to her car without shame. Invited her come take the Cooke's tour. He was putting in a sprinkler system just like a commercial building. It would save the expense of retrofitting later on.

Talisha thought retrofitting? She got out, fought with the car door to get it closed over the bent part of the hinge. She said most folks make do with smoke-detectors.

Alvin never avoided direct eye contact. The man had no shame. He said being a radio magnate, he'd be out of town a lot. The house wouldn't have on-premises supervision.

Talisha didn't beat around the bush. "All this high-handed stealing shit has generated some public outrage here."

"Hey, I hear you. You're black. African-American. You've suffered from 200 years of oppression and injustice. But you've got to learn who your natural allies were. We were slaves too."

"In Egypt? I think that was a bit beyond living memory. And we got more immediate concerns like where all these pipes came from."

He said, hey, he had no secrets from her. He was learning about trades, testing the temperature of the water. He didn't know how the IRS would rule on the taxes. He wanted to be the one to take the heat if it went wrong. Spare her any hassle.

He said, "I'm all for progress, but we gotta be careful and circumspect about all this. I mean what's actually occurring, what's actually gone down, well you don't know all that. We need a strong dose of reality to temper any overreaction here. Base our response on verifiable conduct."

"You are a lying, thieving bastard!" she yelled at him. "One million dollars we owe the bank. One million. Count it."

He got huffy at that. "I'm tired of all this Alvin-bashing. Sure, I'll put on a renewed push for reform. Revamp the way we keep the books."

"What we gonna revamp is your key to the office. I changed the locks this morning. You don't come in without I'm there. And I call in to the phone company and cancelled your charge card."

Alvin was real put-out over the news. "Hey, hey, gimmie a level playing field here."

She went on defiantly. "No, I'm giving you some practical effects. You keep pushing at me, I'll call in an audit and maybe you'll need a get-out-of-jail-free card."

At that point, he went all reasonable on her. "I'm trying gamely here to comprehend the message. Look. I'm using those face muscles. That's a smile. Let's have a round of hugs. Get control of the dark side of our natures." He reached out for her.

She stepped back, clutched her shoulders to cover her breasts. "I've seen all your range of emotions. Snake-in-the-grass. Shithook. Tapeworm."

"The station has such real potential," he pleaded, giving her that mournful gaze. "I'll make some obvious concessions. What have I got to do to regain my status?"

"Start believing in reincarnation. Maybe in the next life you luck up and it happen to you."

Now he tried anger. "Sure have a tantrum. When in doubt, pout. Yeah, I know the shemale routine. Welcome to the reality sweepstakes."

He turned his back on her like he was expecting her to make amends. Talisha thought what a momma's boy he must have been growing up. Have a snit-fit; get his way. She stood there leaning against the car, arms crossed, saying nothing. He looked around, saw she wasn't about to budge. Tried out yet another routine. Although this one really floored her.

He toed the ground. Hunched his little round shoulders. "We need a kinder, gentler future. I wanted this house to be impressive because . . . well, because I'm in love with you."

"What?"

"Seven percent of America identifies itself as racially mixed. You're the mother of my unborn children."

"You need to get your brain a medical screening."

"It's my name, isn't it? That's the hang-up. Alvin. Girls hate my name. Is this my fault? My parents made a compromise. All those southern hicks named Calvin. Jews named Malvin. They wanted something in between. So I end up an Alvin. *Al*-vin. Can you believe such a fate? I feel like such a shlub."

Talisha drove back to WPST doing a laborious mental review of the sanity of the world. Leone Jones was waiting in her office to make the day even worse. His hair was shaved on both sides in the style that's called conked. Had on sweat pants with one leg pushed up below the knee like L.L. Cool-J.

He said look-a-here, he had himself a volume of Egyptian love poetry. Thought maybe he'd read some over the air once she gave him his own show. Did she know all about Afro-centric heritage? How the Egyptians invented Greek philosophy and all? Well listen to this.

"'*Would you depart my bed because of belly hunger?*'— This is a woman talking. Like a Egyptian queen or somebody. It's her voice.

'*Gently take my full breasts.*

Abundant for you is their milky offering.'"

He grunted, "Ooo-*unh*. Turn me on." Kind of shivered all over and did a little dance. Pumped his fist in the air. "I mean we can reach an audience by saying 'this is *art*. This *matters*. This makes a *difference*.'"

"No," said Talisha, sitting down heavily in her desk chair.

"No? Whatchew mean no? I gotta skew your judgment on this. Gotta speak some words of censure here. Get some ethical standards going."

She said her listening audience was mostly over the age of sixty. They didn't want to hear about sucking tit.

He said he done concluded a two week survey of his own and WPST got serious material deficiencies. They could pull in the young folks what all caught up in the distressing vogue for Midnight Basketball and cutting church on Sunday. There was no more urgent task laying out there. He could run an over-air Crisis Ministry. Talk to the young colored ladies for whom the rainbow is not enough. Take up collections for hunger relief organizations.

She said so far he had got the least valuable player award.

He answered, hey, respect is a two-way street, bitch.

That was when the phone call came in from Dubose Afro-Barber & Styling Salon saying Leone had been by selling ads and gotten them to pay him direct. Was that okay with Talisha? Leone had also gotten a haircut on trade.

14

Rannie Ralston told Honor's mother Grace, "Sure, I'll guarantee your death. If that's how you want it. I've got a niche business here. Service ethos prevails."

She sat behind her big law office desk patiently listening as Grace Revenue explained she had a living will, meant every word of it, and didn't want Honor getting cold feet at the end. No thoughtless compassion need be wasted on her thank you very much.

Honor had come with her mother to the old yellow brick People's Building on Broad Street. Stone lions flanking the main door. Tallest building on the street. Six floors of lawyers.

She crossed her long legs negligently, her beauty on prominent display. The girl was a knock-out even in blue jeans. Or maybe especially in blue jeans. It was like she was genetically engineered for chic.

Rannie thought of her own body as workmanlike. Built to take some solid licks. Good for a sound banging with any man who had the courage. No one did except Browder Delamere, and he had frail little ankles that looked like match sticks when he'd wear loafers with no socks. He thought he had power over her because he had taken her virginity lo these many years before.

Grace leaned forward and squinted at Rannie through thick glasses. She said she didn't believe in all this state medicine prolonging people's lives. She thought the death process could benefit from the discipline of the marketplace. Was Rannie certain she could exercise oversight?

Rannie said there was a world of creative legal work out there. Somebody dies in a plane crash, lawyers trying to sue the travel agencies for putting the victim on the flight. That kind of thing. She stayed on top of change. Navigating the minefields with flair. Generating top volume. She had to with a spendthrift mother and sister to support.

Grace smiled kindly. "I'm sure I can rely on you."

"There's no reciprocal arrangement. I get nothing out of them but abuse."

"It'll probably be alkyl benzene compounds that'll carry me off," Grace speculated. "Direct link with cancer. I used to drink a lot of sassafras tea. It's so concentrated there it was taken off the market by the FDA. Plus it's in basil, tarragon, cloves, even black pepper."

Rannie's mind drifted off. She had been in a squabble that morning that still rankled. Had some twit from the Preservation Society screaming eternal vigilance at her. Preserving historic Charleston occurred not by accident but by design. Charleston's beloved Ralston garden, he proclaimed, held mythic status. It was an anchor of the past in an unsettled present.

What had happened was her mother had ordered a transformation to an Italian garden. "Such as Edith Wharton would have enjoyed" were the words in her letter from Italy. Not that her mother had ever read Wharton or any book at all that Rannie could recall.

But it was to have symmetrical designs. Statues. Box hedges. She wanted fully grown yew trees planted. All of this in place by the time she returned. She called it long over-due.

Rannie knew it was just a wild hair she had got up her ass on the Italian tour. A garden clubber from Virginia or Connecticut had made her envious. Still, it was easier to go along than to fight it.

The landscape gardeners had shown up, everything ready to roll when the twit appeared. Rannie told him nobody raced ahead of her in stubborn resistance to change. But there was no storied timelessness about the garden. Her grandmother had created it. He said wrong. It was your great-great grandmother, and Rannie knew that very well. In the meantime she could stop her disruptive behavior or he'd get a court injunction to stop her.

Rannie told him she was searching the psychology of violence. Trying to figure out why she didn't smash a brick over his head. Or use the golf club like she had on that night-crawling pervert. That had been particularly satisfying.

Grace asked if from a lawyer's perspective it was a good idea to freeze a piece of any chopped beef you buy so if you got poisoned you would have evidence of the source.

Rannie agreed, yes, that seemed reasonable.

Grace said food-safety advocates recommended it. Bacterium was getting so strong the old touch, sight and smell techniques for detecting it were no longer adequate. And the temperature you had to cook it at was rising in a shocking fashion. We'd be vegetarians in no time at all at that rate.

Grace hoped Rannie was not eating more than four

eggs a week. And for goodness sake never use cracked eggs, and wash the counter tops where you've spilled egg.

Rannie was thinking about the old fart she had lashed with the golf club. He had a high place in the pantheon of sleaze-buckets, no small feat in a packed-out field of contenders. The ravishing Honor Revenue had fueled the drama just by being in her bedroom with the light on. He was one more turd in her devoted following. If past history was any indicator, it was a nascent epidemic.

"Oh my goodness it's just so hot out I could just die!" Moira Ralston came barging into the office unannounced in a well-scripted rudeness routine. She told Honor, "The town is certainly abuzz about you and Chandler Lovelace. I do believe that boy is sweet on you. Y'all have so much in common."

"What on earth would that be?" Honor answered in an unexcited tone.

"Well I'm told on good authority you both are just crazy about albacore."

"Chandler had the albacore," she said. "And yes, Mother, I warned him about scomboid fish poisoning."

"Well I'm sure he was grateful," said Grace. She was sitting ram-rod straight, purse on her lap with both hands resting on it.

Moira wasn't listening. She was lost in her own chatter. She said Chandler was certainly leading a public outcry about the ordination of these gays or whatever they called themselves now. They used to be queers didn't they? And know their place was in the closet.

Rannie made eye contact with Honor. Honor shook her head in dismay, marveling at the incomprehensible.

"Honestly, when I hear things like that my silly head just goes into a tailspin. All this undercutting the basic ground rules of society. It's like everything I believe in has gone obsolete. Honestly. Well I know we're supposed to support all this diversity in lifestyles now, but I'm sure Rusty is just a misguided little boy. He just needs a good talking to from a southern woman. Just needs to be taken in hand. That's all it would take."

Rannie advised, "Moira, you need to switch to decaf."

Grace Revenue looked alarmed. "Oh no, don't ever drink decaffeinated coffee. It's known to cause a rise in low-density lipoproteins—bad cholesterol."

Moira said, "I've always believed in a prudent diet."

■ ■ ■

Beau-Jack McCully told Chandler, "We're re-doing the pews at St. Ambrose. Otherwise business is a little slow. Kind of running at half-throttle. Nice of you to enquire, cuz."

In the ground floor of his big, long workshop on Queen Street, black men were running electric sanders over the pews. Pale light filtered through the dirty windows. The air was filled with the smell of sawdust and sweat.

Charleston has its inbred aspect and the old families seem to almost revel in it. Everyone proudly refers to everyone else as cousin this or that. For Chandler Lovelace, however, his cousinhood on Mummy's side with Beau-Jack McCully was not a subject of pride. The McCullys were distinctly North Charleston-ish and beneath contempt. Beau-Jack's moving to Queen Street in the heart of old Charleston and opening his furniture restoration business did not improve his status. It just created an unpleasant proximity.

Keeping to his good manners, Chandler said allow him to express his condolences for the recent bereavement. Trying to sound the right tone. In fact he loathed Jackson McCully, frequently describing him as deplorable, despicable and a few other d-words.

Beau-Jack looked up from the sports section of the paper and said he was sublimating his grief. Working through it that way. And since he had him here, who would Chandler pick for the U.S. Open? Last year this kid 25 years old won the first qualifying round record at Shinnecock Hills, then dropped back to last by the time it was all finished.

Chandler said he never followed sports. Didn't watch it. Didn't read about it. He personally thought it was outrageous to pay people to play a game so you could spectate.

Beau-Jack said, "You don't follow any pro sport whatsoever?" Sounding amazed.

Chandler scowled at him, disliking intensely this cross-examination. In a right ordered world, he said, sports would be for amateurs only. Before his unfortunate head injury, he had been an avid hurler. Liked the cut and thrust of it. The mad dashes. Brute impact. He had taken to all things Irish in his days at Trinity.

"In America, commercial television begat grotesque sums being spent for advertising which begat a revolting consumer society which in turn begat grotesquely overpaid celebrities. And people complain about the European royal families, say they're parasites. Could you imagine some basketball lout rallying the nation at a time of peril?"

Beau-Jack said he couldn't argue with all that. Still, if he had his Daddy's gambling disease, he reckoned he'd take the Bulls for a sweep over the Sonics—they got a bench better than most starting line-ups—and pick Editor's Note for the Belmont Stakes. And he'd take the Braves and maybe five over the Rockies. They had some real shut-out material in their pitching staff. Use the slider well. Don't let the little stuff bother them.

Say, was Chandler looking for work? He was needing sanders and refinishers at the moment. How old was Chandler? Thirty-two? Thirty-three? He ought to get going with something pretty soon.

Chandler viewed the prospect of working with his hands with extreme distaste. He described himself as a nationally known expert on the subject of rare books, *objets d'art* and furniture. Perhaps Beau-Jack needed him as an appraiser. Otherwise he was currently exploring options. Since the demise of his stepfather he was hopeful of a rise in income.

Beau-Jack said yeh that was a bitch, him taking that walk off a cliff. But whatever happened to your trust fund you always used to brag about?

Chandler explained he only got his hands on it upon his marriage. Although he was expecting that fairly soon.

No shit? Who was the lucky girl?

Chandler demurred. He was not at liberty to reveal this. Although she was of good family, and he expected her to give an exquisite account of herself in bed when the time came. Under his tutelage of course. Hence he needed a bit of practice with the old in-and-out. Which was the reason for his visit.

He had come by the phone number of a common

prostitute. Upon calling said number he got a recording. Hi, this is Cindi. What two words have the most letters in the world? Give up? Post Office. Rather purile actually. He was loath to leave his name and number as he was temporarily residing with Mummy on Bocquet Lane until the Romneygate House opened up.

What, he was wondering, was the proper protocol for girls such as that? Did one ask the price up front, or was there a standard scale in the community?

Beau-Jack allowed he'd be glad to check on it for him. Least he could do for his cousin Chan-boy.

Chandler cringed. Beau-jack used to call him Charlie Chan and Chinkie Chandler when they were boys. Chandler hated that with a passion. The catcalls on the playground. The mockery. And he didn't look the least bit Oriental.

That was when he looked under a drop-cloth and saw the Tiverton Commode. It almost made him dizzy like when he stood up too fast or had to walk in the direct sunlight.

"You like that, huh?" said Beau-Jack. "Well, it's more than just furniture. It's a piece of history."

Chandler went over it with his hands, nose down close to study the perfection of the floral marquetry. "You've forged one," he said bluntly. His eyes were still bulging in admiration.

"Well now, all reproduction is something of a forgery."

"Yes, but you intend to contravene the law. I know this because the Tiverton commode is a virtual one-of-a-kind item." Chandler rolled his tongue in his cheek. "And the original belongs to Grace Revenue. Of No. 1 Legendre Street."

Beau-Jack's eyes narrowed. He cocked his head to one side. "You are quick as a cat now aren't you?"

Chandler gave him a sly grin. "You can't figure how to make the switch. That's your hang-up." He sucked his cheeks in. Made a smacking noise. "But I know a way."

Beau-Jack did an aw-shucks. Rubbed the back of his neck. "Five, six years from now I'll look back and say, 'Damn, why'd I pass up that chance?' But right now I'm trying to be a good boy. Staying out of touch with controversy."

"We drive it to New York in a van," Chandler proposed eagerly. "Split a million dollars."

Beau-Jack picked up a tennis ball and threw it against the wall a couple of times. He looked thoughtful.

"How 'bout you outline your plan, and we'll deliberate the sum-bitch."

15

Chandler told the moving company to bill Grace Revenue but not until fifteen days after the job was done. He saw no reason why he should suffer out-of-pocket expenses. She was the one donating furniture to the church.

The movers came to No. 1 Legendre on a blazing hot day with mockingbirds in the yard and sprinklers playing rainbows over the grass. Chandler wore a panama straw hat and white linen jacket, carried a brass-headed cane as a mark of authority. Filling that huge van would require a lot of authority to get it done right.

Ugly looking redneck with a flat-top haircut in charge of the crew. He stood Chandler up against a tree and said, "Look here, buddy-row. You don't know jack-shit about this. So keep your fat ass out of our way."

Well, huffed Chandler. He stood back and allowed Grace Revenue to supervise it all. Women could get by with chivying these sweaty oafs. They'd take serious umbrage at him. Ah well, it was an age of the liberated woman. Let them contribute their share.

Besides, this was an opportunity to chat up the delectable Miss Honor. Such a picture with her herbal tea at the kitchen table. Yes, believe I'll have one of those. Thank you. Two sugars, please.

She was staring at him. Bit overwhelmed by his breezy confidence no doubt. Just taking this important church project in hand. Mummy had been so over-critical of late. Saying he had no adult skills.

So facile to make conversation with Honor. She hung on his every word. Awed by his insights into biblical language. Philology. The science of words. The Latin *magus* coming from Old Persian *magush* meaning "big-penis." A fascinating object to all, both male and female. Hence the Greek cognate *pharmakos*—enchanter or wizard. Our word "pharmacist" comes from that.

"It's odd you know," he mused. "The Song of Solomon with its multiple layers of symbolism. Young man telling his beloved about flowers, blossoms, turtledoves. The doves nest in cleft places you know. Rather obvious imagery. But then you get that odd bit:

'Catch us the foxes,
   the little foxes,
that spoil the vineyards
   for our vineyards are in blossom.'"

He raised and lowered his eyebrows meaningfully. "They want to enjoy the deeper sensual pleasures of love. What then do the foxes represent that could spoil that play? Could it be body lice? Crabs?"

"Look, I've got to go," said Honor. Standing up. Now walking away from him.

A bit skittish that girl. Like a young filly needing taming. He'd break her to being mounted.

Yes, there goes the commode all nicely wrapped in

quilts. Lifting it up. Now it was safely on the truck. A month from now, Chandler would deliver the reproduction to the Revenues. Say he was returning it. Realized its worth and felt he had to alert them to their folly. His honesty would make a firm foundation for the Lovelace-Revenue nuptials. Pop the question while Honor was gushing with gratitude.

Meanwhile, the genuine commode would be sold in New York. How propitious if Beau-Jack suffered a fatality there. A cruel sort of town. Bodies turning up daily. So many possibilities for a tragic accident. All those cement canyons. A fall from a great height.

■ ■ ■

Honor Revenue thought Chandler was the most loathsome, despicable slime she had ever known. And she was an expert on slime. She stood under the wisteria vine fuming as the men loaded her life onto a huge yellow van. Cabinets and desks and wardrobes. Tables and beds and settees.

When she was only six or seven, wherever she went, strangers would stop and stare. Comment to her mother how beautiful she was, how exquisite her hair. You'll have to beat the boys off her with a stick. Better keep her locked up.

Honor had done elementary school at Charleston Day, but by fifth grade the boys were getting into so many fights over her it was strongly suggested she transfer to Ashley Hall which was all girls. Not that that stopped anything. By then adults were saying the boys are like bees swarming around a hive. I swear that girl is totally oblivious of it. How can anyone be so ignorant of what she provokes? A little edge of jealousy was creeping into the voices of the mothers. Her presence created an unpleasant comparison with the homely, the gawky, the ungainly.

The males started thinking and talking openly about her in a sexual way. By the time she was fourteen, grown men were acting on their lust, getting her off in corners, rubbing their crotches against her and bathing her in their hot, fetid longings.

"Sweetheart, I'll give you two solid hours of non-stop action. Just say the word. Just crook that little finger in my direction and give a wink."

"I'll kiss yore purty laigs for a dollar even if you never do pay me."

"Honey, I'll give you a union of opposites like you never seen before. Ooo-mommah! You best believe it."

"Dah-lin', you the jail-bait of my wet dreams. Ooo-oo. San Quentin Quail. Unh."

With the men so blatantly obvious, female commentary got cranked up to a higher level of angry fervor, fear and distrust. She's going to be nothing but a home-wrecker. I wouldn't let that girl anywhere near a man of mine. All that put-on butter-won't-melt-in-her-mouth. She's scheming away the whole time she bats those long lashes.

Honor clamped her eyes shut to block out the moving men. She used to sit on spring nights under this wisteria, thick as her waist and coiled around an oak, and smother in its heavy purple perfume. She had wanted a boyfriend. Someone special to love her. Not an army of lustful demons. But if she wasn't just perfectly still, if anyone spotted her, within minutes neighborhood boys would be in the street showing off on skateboards.

In New York, Honor had gone to a Jungian analyst who told her she was a universal *anima* figure—a personification of the feminine needs in the psyche of men. Mythologically she was a siren, a dark fairy, a *femme fatale*. An erotic fantasy. The dream that lures men from reality. Projecting their emotional needs onto her great, enigmatic beauty caused them to become instantly, helplessly in love with her.

She asked what should she do about this? He said it was hard to say. Each of them had to realize that they were seeking not her, but something within themselves. She said *each of them*? There's no blanket solution? He said he knew it was against ethics, but he had been wondering for the past half-hour if she would allow him to lick the soles of her feet. She refused. He said, okay, can I keep one of your shoes?

"Well there you are hiding," cooed Moira Ralston coming out from behind the tree. "I've been watching this big old yellow van just wondering what you were up to. You're always up to something aren't you? Yes, you know you are. Everybody's just talking and talking about you and Chandler Lovelace. The poor man spends every night outside your window with binoculars hoping to catch a glimpse of you in the buff. I swan. He is just a hopeless case, isn't he though? You are just the little cherry tomato of his hot dreams."

"There's nothing between Chandler and me," Honor denied flatly. Thought, bite your tongue. Don't get ugly. When what you'd like to tell the daffy little bitch is go play with the squirrels.

Moira's smile was so crooked it looked deformed. "Marry in blue, you'll always be true."

16

Talisha said, "We always leave a welcome mat out for white folks."

What she'd like to of said was she didn't need this worth a shit. Gooey white liberal minister coming by with his "projects." She had projects right close at hand. It was called paying on a million dollar bank note. Dealing with fuck-up personnel was another.

On an odd impulse that morning previously she had called the State Board of Corrections. Found that one Leone Jones aka Streetboy, aka Hardtop, aka Powerdude had done five years at BroadRiver for statutory rape on a fourteen-year old. He was one superlover ladies' man. Getting him out of the radio station was an immediate project.

When she confronted Alvin about hiring the dude without a background check, he said, hey, American racism had young black men at risk. A fourth of them were in jail or on parole. And besides, statutory rape was a cultural thing, not some standard of science. White male society had selected these arbitrary ages for consent. A misplaced moral equivalence.

Talisha said yeah right, fourteen or forty-five, it's all

pink on the inside. He kind of hesitated like he wasn't sure if she was serious or not.

Sitting in a chair across from her desk, the Reverend Noble "call me Rusty" Royall gave her his smile all full of grace and God's love. He expressed concern that the most segregated time in America was 11 o'clock on Sunday morning.

Talisha said six o'clock every evening most folks tended to go home to segregated houses. But she got his point.

That threw him for a moment. Put that trace of dismay on his face. Then he asked about WPST and what it hoped to achieve.

She said they were working on infrastructure projects. Trying to make black enterprise an economic frontrunner. What she meant was they were straining to make the monthly bank note payment.

Rusty assured her she had a winning concept. It would spawn a flurry of imitations.

The word simper come into her head. That's what he was doing. Simpering.

Talisha didn't lay out the dirty laundry, but another project she had just got through with was firing her second D.J. for smoking weed. He looked at her, big spliff a fraction from his lips, said he believed he had glaucoma coming on. He needed it to relieve the pressure on his eyes. He and millions of senior citizens were being denied compassionate use by misguided government policy on reefer madness. A comprehensive reform was called for.

She said you're how old? Twenty-nine? That wasn't too senior in her book. And her comprehensive protocols didn't allow for cop drug busts. That tended to sacrifice your broadcasting license.

He called her a handkerchief-head negro. She said yeah? Then scalded him with a string of fuck you's and get the hell out's.

Now she had to work two shifts, and it was making her tired just thinking about it. By this time, she had expected to be stepping out of long limousines with flash cameras popping. Wearing dark glasses in the glare of publicity. Tugging her dress down to not show too much leg at that little awkward moment.

Instead she had this kumbaya liberal rector. And what was out of place was the drop-dead good looking white girl with him, her hair in a pony tail that fell between her shoulder blades. She belonged on the cover of *Vogue* or *Harper's Bazaar.* In fact studying her, Talisha wondered if she hadn't seen her there. The girl was designed to be noticed.

Rusty's eyes kept coming back to the white girl, looks which she didn't return. Side-long glances. But the girl was way too cool. Been there, done that kind of attitude. Or maybe she couldn't stand him. Which stood to reason. She wasn't part of the liberal routine. None of those sickly lovey-dove smiles at the colored folks. No desperation on her part to be accepted.

"Don't misconstrue this as judgmental," said Rusty, "but St. Ambrose is a moribund church. To turn this around, I've developed an open-window agenda. A modicum of integration now. More next year. I have something of a plan to accelerate the process. Be intentionally multiracial."

Talisha thought here it comes. Make me the token darkie. Put our picture in the paper, you giving me some old cast-off clothes from the white ladies, some beat-up old furniture. She said, "You're proposing . . . ?"

That launched him off. "Bible studies which stress the multicultural kingdom of God. Joint programs between ethnically diverse churches. Service projects. Volunteer work. Monthly praise services that emphasize uniting people from different backgrounds. Share success stories and resources to promote multiracial fellowship."

Talisha was thinking share resources. Maybe there was money in it. Get that bank off her back for a month or two. Instead, she said she was open to dialogue. Maybe some of his ideas would diminish the misery index a tad. End this culture of isolation of black and white.

She was thinking, man, St. Ambrose. Downtown Charleston. White high society. When this hits the fan, Rusty Royall's popularity is gone be driven through the floor. She asked how would the mechanics on it actually come to pass?

"We'll start off with a pulpit exchange."

Reverend Roscoe who had been listening at the door the whole time took this as his entrance cue. Grabbed Rusty's hand with both of his and didn't let go. Introduced himself as the Reverend Roscoe P. Morningstar and set into one of his memorable performances.

"Here I am CRYING up against a somber wailing wall. Got a megatonnage of regrets and fear. And now you done TURNED night into day. You a Hallelujah Chorus and a half."

"Yes yes," trilled Rusty with tremendous relief at being

accepted with such enthusiasm. Half-rising up out of his chair, Roscoe still hanging onto him. "It's a long overdue opportunity. Can you fit it in your schedule?"

Roscoe flung both his hands up in the air. "Oh, man, I got a whole lotta back-up in my system. But I am going to take care of bi'ness, lemme tell you. I ain't distancing myself from your GRAND DESIGN. You is top priority."

Rusty was all the way up on his feet now, a flush of color in his neck above that church dog collar. "Well as I often say, it all goes back to what we as a society are conveying to posterity in the realm of . . ."

They had quit listening to each other. "We don't NEED no Congressional oversight here," went Roscoe. "Don't NEED guidelines to give us objectivity. We ain't in the WRONG place at the WRONG time without a clue to our credit."

"There'll be resistance from the old moss-backs," predicted Rusty all feverish, slapping a fist into an open palm. He seemed to be looking forward to it. Eyes glittering. "Potential backlash. I hate to see the firestorm. I don't easily speak about my personal challenges. A bit of a mini-drama. Calling me an extremist liberal. But they won't dare raise their voices loud. The fear of being labeled racist will spike their guns in a hurry."

"They won't CANOODLE with that calamity!" proclaimed Roscoe.

"Yes yes," agreed Rusty. "Won't sail in harm's way. No draconian threats. Yes. Hmm. Not only prudent but wise."

Roscoe was strutting and striding about the room, doing everything but a cake walk. "We gonna draconian up they WAZOO!"

Talisha was thinking maybe this crazy white man was planning on the end of the world and doing what he could to hurry it up. Maybe she could unload Leone on them along with Roscoe. Let that pair steal the Episcopals blind for a change.

The white girl was wearing coral lipstick. She watched without any sign of emotion.

Roscoe said, "And I want to play my own home-version of that game too."

Talisha had missed something. She went what?

Rusty looked at her like he had forgotten she was present. Blinked. "You know, this place could use some sprucing up. Would you like some new furniture? A kind of funky, fun decor?"

"Sure," she said. "And I guess you got some old clothes to get rid of too."

■ ■ ■

The newcomers barbecue at Bellefontaine Plantation almost didn't come off. Browder Delamere resisted lending the use of it right up to the last minute which put the telephone committee to a lot of extra work and nearly wrecked the entire thing. He cited his disaffection with Rusty Royall. The new modes of worship. The turmoil over the civil standing of homosexuality.

Honor thought wait until you meet Roscoe Morningstar.

Like all of the old plantations, Bellefontaine lay on the bank of a slow moving river lined with marsh and willows that trailed their branches in the water. The original house had burned and been replaced by a designer deer hunting lodge with screened porches on three sides. This landscape-out-of-time was on the fringe of a rural world that was steadily being eaten up acre by acre as the city metastasized and spread.

Evening came with a flutter of bats and then a night spangled with stars. A faint swish of wind. Light brimmed over the treetops as the full moon rose, the first in a month of two moons. Men basted the pig in the big black cooker, grilled shrimp on a grate.

Honor's mother would have warned everyone against paralytic fish poisoning. When shellfish feed on blue-green algae they produce and concentrate saxitoxin. You lose muscular strength and coordination. Temporary blindness. Paralyzed limbs. If the muscles between the ribs seize up, you can't breathe. Die of asphyxiation.

Oh my god there was that dreadful Chandler Lovelace talking to someone. Beau-Jack McCully. What was he doing here?

Beau-Jack was saying, "Yeah it's a right cute answering machine recording all right. Why is a fish so easy to weigh? Because it's got its own scales. A real knee-slapper. Anyhow, I go by the Stallion Club. Find out her name is Cindi. You knew that. One of the more popular girls. A real home-grown product. Lavish set of hooters on her. Pre-leased for months in advance. But she cleared a slot and booked you in. No 'Mother, May I' game on this one."

Chandler saw Honor watching and raised his voice in a hearty way. He urged do come join them. They were discussing the qualifications of candidates for local political office. The county auditor's race was a hot one this year.

"Lavish hooters?" drawled Honor.

Chandler's face flushed beet red. He hailed someone loudly and rushed off.

She said to Beau-Jack, "Let the truth set you free. What are you doing even this close to a church?"

Beau-Jack said her attitude revealed a growing cynicism among American citizens. Here he was being a local businessman, getting into mainstream Charleston. He was as new to church as the next boy. Overcoming bad raisings. Since his daddy's sudden demise he was experiencing option shock.

That was when a voice out in the dark yelled yee-haw! Something hit the ground near them. Ker-plunk. What was it? A beer can?

Rain threats Honor had factored in. Mosquitoes. People getting lost on the way. Browder's obstreperousness. But she had forgotten the Charleston tradition of wastrel younger sons. They tend to live on plantations playing at landed gentry. Shooting things. Drinking a lot. Hassling the tenants who do the real work.

Boyce Delamere—Browder's younger brother—had decided to join the party with a gang of friends. They came over from the hunting lodge looking like a passel of bad omens. Five big boys in their twenties. Hunting pants and boots. T-shirts with billfish pictures. Caps turned backwards. Boyce said he thought they'd drop by and break the ice. Loosen up the party a little bit. Given their track records, things would get very loose in a hurry.

"I figured it was worth a dam'ole look-see. Huh? What say?" He spit on the ground. That long kind of drool that often comes just before men go into a vomiting mode.

Yes. He was drunk. What other state is there for a Boyce Delamere? He was swaying noticeably.

"They're going to try to provoke a fight aren't they?" Honor muttered.

Beau-Jack agreed the charm of the younger set would wear thin in a hurry.

"Ain't it worth a look?" Boyce said aggressively to a newcomer couple. *Ain't it?* It was hard to believe he had been to a private school.

"Um, we're the Flemings . . ." the husband said tentatively. Extending his hand.

"Flemings, huh? Like in Fleming ass-holes?"

"I beg your pardon?" said the wife icily.

"Jus' a little joke. Flaming asshole. Fleming. Get it?"

Honor groaned oh shit. Here we go big time.

Beau-Jack agreed there was sure enough a man-made disaster in the making here. He walked over to them. Told Boyce it was funny but their presence at a church function didn't exactly give him a warm and fuzzy feeling. Made him wonder about their intentions.

Boyce squinted at him in disbelief. "Say what?"

"Living out here in this kind of macho subculture. Seeking daily dominance over wild animals. I don't know your motivation exactly. I could speculate."

Boyce bellied up to him. "How 'bout I whup your dam' ass and throw it off my property? What say?"

Beau-Jack was cool. "Well, you know I'd have to resist that vigorously. Tell you what. Lemme propose a conciliatory action. Step over here behind these cars a minute. Maybe we can do an overhaul of your attitude."

As Honor watched from a distance, Beau-Jack slid something onto his hand. Good Lord it was brass knuckles. Wham! Smacked Boyce right in the face. Boyce went down hard, got to his hands and knees but couldn't get up.

Beau-Jack turned on the others and they backed up. Spread out in a scared little half-moon of spectators.

"You fuck-head! You bastard!" Boyce was screaming, weeping with pain. Blood drooled out.

"I'm afraid we differ sharply on that one. And anyhow you boys ought to stop drinking. Get you a case of alcohol dementia."

The others helped Boyce up, moved off muttering threats. Vowing their daddies would sue Beau-Jack's ass off. Litigation is always the last resort of the bully.

Beau-Jack came back to Honor. Told her he really hated these confrontational methods but sometimes it was all he had available. Don't worry about Boyce. He'd go back and go to sleep, drool on himself.

She said it was beautiful in its simplicity, she had to admit.

He said he liked to think he was with the times on women's issues. Didn't expect flight attendants to weigh the same at 40 they did at 21. But sometimes the old ways were best. Teaching by example. He was pretty much unapologetic about it.

He studied her in the growing dark. She could feel his eyes taking her measurements.

He gave her the boyish smile. "I've really got no qualms

about us taking up a dating posture. See where it leads. Depending on intangible influences, love, romance, that sort of thing."

Honor countered she was personally inclined to call her own shots. She'd had a lifetime of men who landed on the extrovert side of the Myers-Briggs Type Indicator. They had never worked out.

He said he knew she'd be predisposed that way. But his personality was no particular disgrace. King monkey has to show off now and again to impress the mate. In today's world it was economic survival. But he had his quiet side. Was into woodworking as a hobby. Made reproduction furniture. Didn't stay glued to a TV watching football.

She said maybe she'd consider standing and talking with him this evening. He could call it a date if he wanted.

"I like that hint at compromise," he grinned.

"Why do I feel this is some kind of a Faustian bargain?" she mused, more to herself than to him.

17

Chandler sat precariously in the rickety kitchen chair, his huge rump hanging off both sides, saying since she offered, he would have a glass of port. The house was now virtually bare of furniture. He had come by to see how she was getting along? Did she like living in a stark environment? It seemed very post-modern.

Honor hadn't offered him port, or anything else for that matter. She said she wasn't sure they had any. He said he feared he was a man of the past century. And to please not serve it to him in a claret glass.

Honor rummaged in the cabinet. There were dozens of bottles with dribs and drabs in them her mother hadn't tossed out. Normally she threw everything out after a month. She located the port. Then thought, why am I doing this?

"There is none, I'm afraid," she said, sitting back down.

He sniffed, "Oh. More's the pity."

Did she follow horse racing? He was thinking of placing a small wager on Editor's Note. Belmont Stakes were coming up. He had an inside tip.

Honor asked wasn't Belmont already over with? He

frowned, no, of course not. He kept up with racing in a minor way. Racing was the sport of kings as they say.

Honor had just hung up the phone on Judge Lorenzo. He had told her he was sitting there in the motel room without much to do. Watch daytime TV. Read the Gideon's Bible. And he had come across the part in Proverbs about the brash woman who seduces men into the delights of wickedness. It was making for an overheated atmosphere in the narrow room. Ordered her to get her ass over there without dodge or delay.

Honor had felt like tearing the phone out of the wall. And now she had this . . . this *thing*—sitting there.

Chandler said he had given an exclusive interview to the *Post & Courier* condemning the position of Noble Royall and of the Bishops. It was essential he reaffirm the traditional stance of the church. He had of course cited the pertinent parts of Leviticus—men lying with men as with women is an abomination.

"It's not a mere *divertissement*," he added. "It goes on to say they shall be put to death. Their blood is upon them."

He wondered aloud if Honor had noticed anything unusual while working at St. Ambrose. Why? Well of course all the usual suspicions arise.

Wearily, she asked what were those?

"That probably Rusty . . . is one. You know. Doing the wickedness of Sodom. The Genesis 19 bit."

Honor's mother had spent the morning lecturing her on the excess of salt in dehydrated soups and frozen dinners. Caffeine was certain to raise blood pressure. All the studies showed that. And smoking . . . God, don't get me started on that.

Honor insisted she had never smoked, but her mother wasn't listening.

Without knocking, Moira just walked in the kitchen door. "Yoo-hoo. Anybody home? Oh there y'all are, you silly couple you. I was just admiring your garden. Just festooned with roses. Is that the word? Festooned?"

Honor gritted her teeth. "Chandler and I are not a couple."

"Well of course you are. At least in spirit. I know the rest is hush-hush. But you're both all energetic. And enthusiastic. And I guess neither of you exactly *does anything*."

Honor was furious. She had worked, earned substantial money. She was working now. The idea she was being equated with this useless parasite was just too much. Or speaking of parasites, what on earth did Moira do?

Moira spoke to Chandler. "She's just lovely, isn't she, Chandler? You must agree."

He blushed. "Well yes. Indeed. She is quite visually arresting."

Moira sniffed the air. "What is that you're wearing, Honor? Chanel?"

"It's Eau de Ciel," said Honor.

"My, you've certainly put a lot on."

Moira wandered off into the dining room. Her tapping footsteps echoed a bit in the empty house. Her voice carried back.

"Well my my my. It certainly is interesting with no furniture. Your mother was always just so darling. All her zany ideas. Do you remember when she had that atrocious egg-throwing contest and the whole birthday party turned to a shambles? I guess you just breathed a sigh of relief when that was over. And now we have no furniture at all. Is it like a new fashion? Do you call it groundbreaking?"

She clapped her hands.

"Oh I just see it all with such clarity. Astonishing really. You've been furnishing a secret place. Some little love nest. What a darling little scandal to have right under our noses."

Honor fought to keep her temper. The phone was ringing. She knew for sure it was the judge. Moira would worm into that for the final humiliation. Spread it to everyone in town.

"Aren't you going to answer the phone?" asked Moira.

■ ■ ■

"In a world of lying and connivin' and deceit, WPST brings you the hope of salvation. Now let's sit back and enjoy 'Impulse to Good' by the 'Open Covenants'."

Talisha knew it was beyond human endurance for her to sound so wide awake. She was working double-shifts now, back-to-back.

She swivelled in her chair, rapped her knuckles on the desk. "Leone, I told you to put the money right here and then get out of here. And don't ever come around again unless you enjoy wearing handcuffs."

He shuffled in front of her in the sound booth whining he *needed* the cash from Dubose Afro-Barber & Styling Salon for walking around money. That was why he had kept it. No other reason than that.

Talisha told him most folks in town had forgot, but the

academic magnet school moved away from ratbag old Burke High because she had personally taken a Saturday night special away from some hoodlum and shot him in the leg with it. Did that sound familiar?

Leone argued violence never solves nothing. Just sows the seeds of future violence. He was counting out the money, going slower as he got to the last of the bills like he hoped some of it would stick to his fingers.

She said she had no nostalgia for that bygone era, but dismay all he wanted, the facts of that incident weren't going away. When somebody got in her face, she didn't run. If he needed remediation on that lesson, she was there to promote it.

Leone protested he wanted nothing but respect between police and community, boss and workers. Looking real pleased, he produced a gold chain for her, a cheer-up present. Said in the midst of all this hurt she was laying on him, his emphasis was on service to WPST and its top management.

She studied the chain, wondering if it was solid gold or plated.

He explained working around WPST had got him reading the Good Book a lot more than usual. Finding where it dove-tailed with the Koran. He found in Proverbs about a young man loving his own wife. Calling her a lovely hind, a graceful doe. He said, "That you, baby. You got the loveliest hind-end I ever did see."

She said a hind was a female deer. Then what was a doe he ask? She said there could be two words for the same thing. They're called synonyms. He said, oh yeh, like pussy and poon.

Talisha said he certainly raised the level of public discourse. She told him to get gone. She needed those sparse moments between songs to eat a sandwich, brush her teeth, sleep. Maybe take a deep breath.

He left.

The song was over, and Talisha whispered into the microphone, "That was sure enough the Lord's work there. Our cup runneth over here at WPST. And now the sounds of dusk in the garden with the Sweet Gethsemane Voices."

Talisha put her feet up on the desk wondering if you could train the human body to do without sleep. She was perusing the newspaper when she saw on the police report column:

A North Charleston pawn broker was severely beaten by a man with a tire iron who then stole more than $5,000 in cash plus some gold chains.

Police are seeking a black male of medium complexion, moderately to heavily overweight, in the 20-to 30-year-old range. The suspect was seen running in Nike tennis shoes down Spruill Avenue. He was gasping in the heat.

She looked at the chain again.

Damn she was surrounded by outlaws and thieves. Roscoe Morningstar just dancing around with the notion of ripping off the white Episcopalians. Saying at this point they were still just talking numbers, but he just knew he was cruising to victory. WPST got a big future bleeding them hand-wringers. Rich whities all eat up with guilt. Wanting to atone for segregation, Jim Crow laws.

Not a one of them—not Alvin, Leone nor Roscoe—had the slightest interest in doing any of the work. That white cracker act Beau-Jack McCully don't even drop in to say hi.

The little red light came on showing the phone was ringing. Her momma Oneida called up to say she was suffering irritable bowel syndrome and needed her to come right straight home. She had chronic abdominal pain, constipation moving into full-blown spastic colitis. Talisha said to go sit on the pot. The song was ending.

The machine ejected and she popped in a new CD. Leaned close into the microphone and purred:

"It's a lonely world full of pain. Everyone needs a sacred love. This is going out to that special someone. You know who you are. This is 'Jet Travel to Jesus' by the 'Mobile Soul Team'."

18

"Check it out," rasped Judge Lorenzo. "Calvin Klein." He tugged at his black t-shirt, a fat, green cigar in his hand. "All cotton. Sixty-five bucks."

"It's a black t-shirt," said Honor. "You can get one at Woolworth's for two-ninety-five."

"What? Two hundred? Yokels down here must be nutso. They better stick to nylon-polyester."

"That's two dollars and ninety-five cents," Honor corrected.

Honor sat across from him in the motel room on Meeting Street, her in a chair, him on the bed. He kept patting the mattress, encouraging her to sit next to him. An attaché case on his lap was snapped open, but the lid kept her from seeing what was inside it. She declined to join him.

"So what's your problem?" the judge demanded. "Hanging around that church, you figure you should keep off sexual intercourse before marriage? You being peer-pressured into celibacy?" He had a black eye and a big bruise on the side of his head. He was not wearing shoes or socks.

"The way I figure it," he said, "economic independence is enough. That's what I told my daughters. Delay until then. Then hump away. You living at home? Is that the problem?"

"Leave me alone," Honor insisted sternly. "I've come here to warn you. Afterwards I'm hiring a lawyer."

"I know how this business works, so don't give me a raft of shit."

"What business? Stalking? You've done this before?"

"And I want you to get a medical certificate. I'm not putting up with a damn case of herpes. I've already had a week long attack of asthma and fatigue. Damn pine pollen. Crazy peckerwood town. Everybody so inbred they got the same blood type. O.J. Simpson oughta come here. They'd never pin anything on him. Shit, my guts are killing me. I need some Tagamet."

Honor told him she couldn't take it any longer, him sitting in here at the phone issuing demands. Why didn't he go back to New York and rule on her case? Get her money out of the brokerage, then maybe they could meet, have a drink.

He berated her, "What is this? A revolt against the sexual revolution? You trying to turn back the clock? Whatever happened to casual sex? Where's your social cohesion? Let's get some bipartisan agreement here."

He was shouting now. Honor shouted back. "On what? On you being a plu-perfect asshole?"

"A lot of women have similar reactions," he snapped. It didn't seem to depress him. He was mad. Squint-eyed. Ground his cigar out in an ashtray.

"You've done this before? Stalked other women?"

"Just my wife. That don't really count." He reached into

the open attaché case, pulled out a revolver. Held it with both hands. Pointed at her.

She panicked. Her voice went squeaky. "You going to shoot me? Do you think your actions carry no consequences?"

"Look. For brevity's sake, I'll just get down to it. You've driven me over the edge of havoc. I can't take it any longer. I figure I'll go on from here to a better place. It's magic bullet time."

He rocked his hands upward, put the barrel in his mouth. Pulled the trigger.

BAM!

His brains splattered out all over the wall.

Honor never understood why she snatched up the gun and took it with her as she dashed out. Over the next month she would turn herself inside out and never arrive at a reason.

At the time though, all she was thinking was Moira Ralston was probably hovering outside the motel room. She wasn't in fact, but that didn't make the thought go away.

■ ■ ■

Standing in the sawdust in his Queen Street work shop, Beau-Jack McCully said, "You should've listened to me about Belmont. Much as I figured, Editor's Note came in first."

Chandler asked how he had picked the winner? Was there a system?

"Well, you got things you watch. The owner had won the last two Belmonts. This particular horse, Ed's Note was

16 in the Derby. But he came in third in the Preakness. A fast-closing third. He'll stalk the leaders, but he's known to play around at the end when he should close with a rush. But a jockey who knows how to use his whip could make him perform."

"He used the whip?"

"Naturally."

Chandler scrutinized him. Moistened his lips. "What are you leaving out?"

"He paid off five-eighty to the dollar."

Chandler asked five dollars and eighty cents for every dollars wagered? Beau-Jack said that was correct.

Chandler said Jesus wept. Take ten thousand dollars. Turn it into fifty-eight thousand. He could picture it stacked in hundred dollar bills. Bank straps binding them. Maybe some loose change spilled out to one side.

Beau-Jack was enthusiastic. With the Triple Crown behind them, it was time to start seriously thinking about golf. He could barely keep still in his seat. The anticipation was great. Just eating him up.

Chandler wanted to know about his pending date with Cindi. What would it cost? He was breathing heavily. The combination of sex and money had created a heightened atmosphere.

Beau-Jack reported Cindi up close had right sturdy looking thighs. Was Chan up to the rigor of those nutcrackers? Chandler brushed this thought away. The price, he insisted. How much?

Beau-Jack raised a cautioning hand. Don't get your

bowels in an uproar. It was no problem. A hundred-fifty. They usually expected a tip. Maybe ten bucks.

Chandler balked at that. Said why wasn't it *prix fixe*? He wasn't about to be diddled by some whore.

"It basically is," said Beau-Jack. "A hundred-fifty up front. You give her the ten as she leaves. Makes her feel good about herself."

19

Chandler yelled upstairs to his mother wanting to know where the gooseberry jam was? The little jars she always ordered from Pepperidge Farm!

He wore a silk dressing gown, his underwear on under it. Heavy, hairless legs showing.

A crew of moving men were shifting Grace Revenue's furniture into the Lovelace house on Bocquet Lane. It necessitated some restructuring within the rooms. Very tricky logistics. Shift objects about here and there. Squeeze this and that together. Stack that on top. He would have to sort it out later. Well, perhaps not. It wouldn't be there very long. And his back was bothering him. That nasty blow from the strange lunatic on Legendre Street that night.

The workmen sweated like animals. It got Chandler overheated just to watch them. He sat down heavily at the dining room table. The absence of jam was a real grievance. Symptomatic of a general decline in standards.

Then his mother floated down the stairs. Phyllis looked aghast. "Good Lord I pray."

He explained it was a project for the church. New area of responsibility for him. Mrs. Revenue was donating her furniture for a worthy cause. He had offered to store it until such time as the rector put it up for auction or gave it away. But where was the jam? She knew he couldn't eat his toast without it.

His mother looked at how he had laid out the table. Eight pieces of toast in a silver toast rack. Soft boiled egg in an eggcup. Earl Gray tea. *Post & Courier* neatly folded. The headline said:

NY Judge Found Dead in Motel
Owed half million in back taxes

Phyllis asked is this your little fiefdom? Somehow I thought it was my house. Chandler answered she knew he always ate a solid English breakfast. It was fuel for the day. Now they really had to do something about the absence of jam.

Phyllis said it would be nice to turn back the clock to grandmother's time. Deal with every problem in life at one remove. If you wanted to give orders to a servant, correct some dereliction on his part, you spoke to the higher class of servant. Let him do the actual unpleasant task.

Chandler agreed yes wouldn't it. He often dreamed of that. But Mummy had the Lewy legacy now. She wasn't cash-strapped. She could find out what Latin Americans wanted for their services. If they would wear white gloves. Wait at table.

She vowed she was suffering from an estate tax load like she had never imagined possible.

Chandler scoffed. That was the norm when you inherit a vast sum of money.

Phyllis looked balefully at the men bringing in one

worn-out monstrosity after the next. Stacking them one on top of the next. There wouldn't be room to move. Her home was now a warehouse.

She told Chandler this was not a new sermon she was preaching but it was high time he found what he was going to do in life. The ministry hadn't panned out.

Chandler airily replied he had a number of projects under consideration as well as a great deal of reading to do. Besides, he had been feeling somewhat under the weather. He thought he had a summer cold coming on. And his stomach was bothering him mightily. Some madman had attacked him on the street. Completely unprovoked. It had left him shaken. Given him flashbacks to the hurling assault.

She said getting a job would give him a natural increase in confidence. All that buying power of a regular paycheck would just perk him right up.

"I detect a bit of a polemical bite here, Mummy," lisped Chandler getting quite formal with her. Chilly even. "The costs of this sort of ill-treatment are rarely analyzed, or if analyzed, rarely acknowledged."

She told him don't evade the larger issue. And she wanted to go back over the points that needed clarifying. (a) He had to find a job p.d.q., and (b) failing in that, she was cutting off his allowance. So it was like a double-whammy.

Chandler kept arguing. He asked was this a parody of excess? Her angry tones reflected a fundamental misunderstanding. Come come now. No need for harshness. She knew he often got fainting spells. The hurling injury. Those brutes just laying on him with their cudgels.

She said was she missing something? If he didn't like

it, get married. That would activate his receiving the principal of his trust. $100,000. That might carry him as much as ten years if he were careful. Then maybe he could get a disability from the government.

He huffed that given this trend of thinking, he would have to react.

"You do that. Open the want-ads. Office clerk/cashier. Great opportunity for advancement. That sort of thing."

Chandler sat down heavily. That certainly dimmed the luster of the day. The toast suddenly looked most unappetizing. Work at some menial job? Termite exterminator? Hod carrier? She wanted him to sweat like these negroes. And now he was sweating. Perspiring freely. She had gotten him so upset. Mummy side-tracking him like this when his plans were progressing so nicely. Honor quite liked him. Everyone said so. Moira Ralston. Everyone really.

Beau-Jack kept talking to him about wagering. Chandler knew table gambling was for suckers. How could you beat the house with the odds in its favor? But horse racing—you had sentient beings at play there. Living horseflesh and jockeys.

If he had just gotten a bet down on Editor's Note, who knows how much money he would be rolling in now. Certainly enough to buy him the few small pleasures he required. Jam in little jars. Plymouth gin. Jamaican coffee. A subscription to the *Irish Times*.

"God be careful with that!" he shouted, exploding out of his chair.

They were bringing in the Tiverton. Gyrating about.

There was no excuse for that sort of clumsiness. The stupidity of these people simply astounded him.

■ ■ ■

Honor had a look of permanent anxiety on her face. She walked and moved in a haphazard way. Unkind people whispered she was drunk. After work, she closed herself in her smothering bedroom. Her mother wouldn't let her run the air conditioning because people were starving in Bangladesh. Even at night the air was so close. A drought dragged on. No wind blew from the harbor.

She kept thinking about Judge Lorenzo's gun snuggled under her underwear in the drawer. Afraid to throw it off a bridge into a river. Afraid to chuck it into the harbor. What if someone saw? She had no idea of the tenacity of fingerprints. Could you just rub them off like in the movies? What if there was some new test? Some fluorescent thing or other?

She wanted her old world back where she at least sort of knew the rules of the game. Her mother's standard advice when you had problems was take the lemon and make lemonade. It didn't seem applicable to this situation. Or was it? What did it really mean? Smile with equanimity at life's insults and reverses. Be a good girl.

Yes. She'd be a good girl. Do hair-shirt penance. Stake out the moral high ground.

In short order, she signed up for United Way and Red Cross. Volunteered to make sandwiches for the drifters at the homeless shelter on upper Meeting Street. Logged in extra hours at St. Ambrose updating membership lists, calling, cajoling for tithes. She totally organized the Camp Kanuga weekend and outlined preliminary plans for the autumn harvest *fête.*

And it was in his office at St. Ambrose that Rusty Royall found her on a hot morning when the air conditioning had broken down in the church offices and the fans barely stirred the heavy air. He hesitated just the least bit before entering the room, as though listening to make sure no one else was in the building.

Honor had spent the night visiting the sick in the area hospitals. She wanted rest and Darvons and absolution so bad that she was willing stigmata to appear on her hands and feet. She stood up, gathered the account books. Rusty said to not leave. Sat down behind his desk. He'd been needing to talk with her. About her behavior. And of course she had come to his office because she felt she needed the talk.

She stood there in front of him, apprehension playing up and down her spine like the notes of an xylophone. Or strings of a zither. Some image like that.

Rusty wore his ministerial collar and bedside expression. Unctuous. Healing. The rector who believed in laying on of hands.

He said the Christian faith is a faith in many things among which was miraculous events. Ezekiel was levitated in front of witnesses. Habbakuk flew from Judea to Babylon. Elijah was whirled up to heaven. After his resurrection, Jesus rose up into the clouds and disappeared. Once you accepted these stories, occult powers became likewise real. For example the ability of witches to cast spells and conjure powerful forces.

Honor said that was interesting. She wiped the perspiration from her upper lip.

August 1 was a bit more than a month away. Did she know the significance of that?

She hesitated. "Um . . . no."

He was watching the ceiling fan spin round. Then his eyes locked on hers. "The witches—the old religion that worshipped Diana as the moon goddess—called that night Lugnasadh. A Celtic word. The church laid its Lammas on top of it. But it remained . . . a fertility festival."

She glanced over her shoulder to verify the door was open.

Rusty continued his weird spiel. "You're like the mini-bar in a hotel room. I know the price is way out of line. But I can't keep my hands off it. It's just too tempting."

He motioned to her impatiently. "Come here. Let's kneel down and pray together. Side by side as it were."

"No," Honor protested, her voice a little too loud. Giving away the edge of panic.

"Be my fan dancer. My lissome Salome. You're a rhapsodic piece. Luring me. On the verge of seducing me."

With the sense of concentrated energy, his eyes seemed to be growing. They were enormous.

"Your clothes are so subtly provocative. You do it instinctively. You are a child of nature. I'd like to see you lick yourself delicately like a kitten." His lips grew purple, the color of ripe plums. "You're going to be vengeful aren't you? Leave me weeping. Prostrate with grief."

"No, no," said Honor hurriedly. "It's just that I volunteered for a bereavement support group. I'm on the suicide hotline. I'm tickled to death to help out." Realizing her verbal *faux pas*, she slapped both hands over her mouth and scuttled out the door. God, the guilt was insufferable.

And the gun was lying in her underwear drawer.

20

"When you're putting up walls, you don't need roadblocks," blared the recorded ad for Big Boy Lumber Town playing out over the airwaves from WPST.

Checking the books, Talisha had found no entries for that ad or any other building supply ad for the past month. A real clear picture had formed in her mind of a huge stack of lumber out at Alvin's new house. Heart-of-pine for the floors. Cedar paneling. Alvin was doing trades while actual ad sales weren't generating enough to pay the bills.

Wondering about the screwed up events that got her to this point in her life, she looked at the list of his numbers. Answering service. Pager. Home phone. Car phone. Cell phone. Like he thought he was a real big shot. She tried the car phone.

"I can't hear you!" he shouted. "Connection's bad. Are you showing displeasure?"

"You got some kind of a bidding war going on with the advertisers? See who will pay you the most to cheat me? The sum total of which I might add seems mighty-nigh flabbergasting."

Still shouting. "You're not being very lucid. What is this? More baseless allegations?"

"You sorry thieving son-of-a-bitch!" she yelled back.

"Do I get a chance to respond here? You think I've got dubious integrity? Have you led a life of utter perfection? You free from error? Hey, let him in the glass house throw the first stone. Right?"

She couldn't believe this brazen jive turkey. Try to get a grip on him and he slipped through your fingers like a wet bar of soap. "What I'm gonna do is think the unthinkable and put a bug up an IRS ass about you."

Alvin said to don't risk compounding their problems, not polarize some emotional divide between them. He allowed he'd be in the office tomorrow, they'd bridge those philosophic differences. They shared a common vision. Everything was cool.

She warned she'd better see him within a half hour depending on traffic. Otherwise she'd facilitate that IRS process with a couple more phone calls.

"What is your problem, girl? We're maintaining your existing wage. I've got plans to ramp it up at year-end. You've got your ownership interest. Co-producer credit for all the shows if you want to move on to bigger markets. New York, Hollywood maybe."

She was so exasperated. "We've got to pay the bank. Every month. Remember? And there are late charges tacked on if you get behind."

"I'm confident we can find a reasonable way to achieve your goals. Implement some innovative programs. Whatever. SCrrr-crrrRR. Hey I'm having trouble receiving you. Scriiittt."

Talisha knew he was making the noise, pretending it was static.

Leone stuck his head in the office. She snarled what do

you want, butt-face? And anyhow get out of this office and stay out.

He announced she had a visitor.

"You way exceed the industry average in being a blood-sucking, don't-take-a-hint hanger-on! You ain't part of the personnel here!"

That was when she caught how quiet and unnatural he was. Not the shucking and jiving sociopathic Leone she knew with his whole blubber body in motion. She peeked through the security eyehole in the door.

A wizened, stoop-shoulder old man sat out there thumbing through old copies of *Ebony*. He had long almond fingernails and turquoise rings on each finger. Black suit like a preacher. White shirt buttoned at his skinny neck but no necktie. And mirror lens sunglasses that reflected whatever he was looking at.

"That was the renowned Caravans," said the DJ. "And now let's do a little continuous movement further up to Jesus from traditional to contemporary with . . ."

She breathed, "Is that who I think it is?"

"He sure ain't no mirage."

Talisha thinking holy shit. Doctor Dread. The Root Doctor. Get away from me, man. I got Jesus hanging on my wall. Praying away in Gethsemane. You go on back out on John Island.

She said to tell the good doctor she was stepped out. Wouldn't be back anytime soon.

Leone agreed that had a superficial appeal. But what if the man just set there and wait? Wasn't on call. Didn't have no emergency rounds or nothing.

Talisha scrubbed at her tired eyes, her forehead, her neck. Here she was living through economic stagnation, this was not enhancing her performance for the day.

Leone was scared. No doubt about it. You could smell it on him. He was slack-jawed. Looked like he didn't know whether to shit or go blind.

Then it struck her. She was scared too. Just sitting out there, the doctor was sending a message. He had brought a dark corner into the room. Mumble the wrong words and he'd sure enough self-destruct your ass.

Talisha liked to live in that realm folks call reality. She didn't need no hocus-pokus, no ju-ju. Sure she was scared of the dark like everybody else. Darkness wasn't no friend like it was to an animal that needed to hide or hunt. Shadow go over the moon and set the dogs to howling, she wanted to be indoors with the lights on, TV showing something cheerful.

But worst of all she was raised on root stories. She couldn't discount it. All that pure chance in life had to be explained somehow, and magic seemed to fit the bill. Folks would hire them a doctor to chew root and get a man off innocent with a jury. Fall in love, fall out of love. Or do dirty stuff to somebody. Make bruises appear on your body when nobody had hit you. Choke up a hairball like a cat that spent its life licking fur.

What were those spider webs doing in the corners? She had cleaned the ceiling with a broom just yester-day. She checked herself all over but she was wearing nothing blue for protection. The sky was clear and blue. She had the sky on her side. Stand by me, sky. Jehovah. Elohim. Dear Jesus.

The nervous jitters just come all over her. Hands behind her back twisting her knuckles. Walking out tentative like a girl at the eighth grade dance afraid the boys will laugh at her skinny legs with the stockings falling down.

She couldn't see his eyes. Not even a hint of eyes. The mirror lenses showed two pictures of her not looking good at all.

"It's a day of happy reckoning," he said getting kind of creaky to his feet. "The meteorology is happy. Hot weather for we who are melanin enriched."

She said that was nice to know, but what could she do for him.

He gave her a sly smile. "I've come because you call."

"Say what?"

"This is going out," he recited, "to a special someone. He know who he be." The smile came back.

She could hear him breathing in and out. In and out. An old man's breath leaving a sour smell in the air.

■ ■ ■

Honor knew she needed her head examined for keeping the job at St. Ambrose. All morning, she had sneaked glances at a handwritten poem that had been slid into the account books for her to discover.

> *Your lips are a scarlet thread,*
> *and your mouth is lovely.*
> *Your cheeks are halves of a pomegranate*
> *behind your veil.*

It was biblical. The handwriting was no mystery. It was Rusty Royall's. Saying he wanted her and was watching her. Going to have what he wanted. Patience wearing thin.

She crossed the cloister with its bright green grass and gothic stonework. Having stepped up her good works to a feverish pace, her days and nights were a blur. She ran a Sunday night youth group, boiling hotdogs and putting up with snotty over-privileged teenagers. Organized the entire medical missionary expedition to Honduras. Ram-rodded the redeemer ministries for the mental health clinic, the unwed mother home and the drug half-way house. Set up two years worth of inspirational speakers for the Church Women. Lined up religion professors for the Wednesday night Bible study.

Still it failed to disengage her mind from the blood splashed motel wall, the gun in her underwear drawer. No way was she going to take the blame, she told herself fiercely. Lorenzo was a vitriolic old swine. Ranting at her like it was all her fault for existing. What was she supposed to do? Quote political philosophy at him? One man's need doesn't create a woman's obligation.

Beau-Jack McCully had a bunch of men replacing the pews that had been refinished. He whistled, "Mighty nice outfit. You're looking awful new-fashioned."

She said thanks. But she flinched at the compliment to her clothes. Rusty had said she dressed in a provocative way. Judge Lorenzo had admired her clothes in the moments when he wasn't complaining about his denture adhesive.

Beau-Jack asked you know anything about antique furniture? How to tell the priceless from the junk? She said she had zero knowledge on that subject. Just curious, he said.

He yacked, "I'm reading where we got a Texas virus in the shrimp crop. Ponds being closed down by DHEC. I swear you can't eat anything these days."

Honor told him he sounded like her mother. She was a food nut before being a food nut was cool. Was an original voice crying in the wilderness against French fries coated in beef tallow.

Beau-Jack said it was just the cultured shrimp that was at risk. Out in the wild they were okay. Problem was how could you tell the difference laid out there on ice in the fish market?

"We don't have to make small talk," said Honor. "I was just passing through. Rusty will have to okay your work. When he does that, I'll cut the check."

He said Rusty, huh? Y'all pretty tight?

Way too loud, Honor snapped there was NOTHING WHATSOEVER between them. And anyhow all shellfish carried the risk of algal poisoning. You could get mental depression, temporary blindness, lose limb coordination. Even be paralyzed. If it hit the muscles between the ribs you quit breathing. Asphyxiate.

He put both hands up palms out, said whoa. Cool down, Nellie. Nothing untoward meant. Nothing at all. No need to prosecute to the fullest extent of the law.

She mumbled she was sorry. In a church you had to be so, so careful about propriety. Brush up against him in front of someone and Moira Ralston would have it all over town.

Beau-Jack proposed his solution to the problem. Give him a spot on the active roster. To wit, start dating him. They could go out to a Blues club. Eat wings and drink beer out of paper cups. He said I tell you what, you got the looks that equal my extraordinary romantic passion. Them bee-stung lips, woo-eee. More rhythm and less blues.

She didn't crack a smile. "I do appreciate your theatrical personality, but thanks anyway."

"Do you know I write music? Always wanted Daddy to change to a Country & Western format. Then figured I'd get a shot to play my own songs. If I had my guitar I could do my latest. It's called 'Daddy Was a Dirtbag But Momma Had Dreams'. It's a real catchy little ditty."

He pantomimed strumming a guitar. The air around them felt like it was heating up. His ardor building as he talked and showed off. Tried to be the velvet-talking cute country boy. Said, "Lemme get my guitar and I'll do some heavy lobbying for your love. Man, I'm psyched."

"Toodle-oo," went Honor, waving her fingers lightly at him. He was one of the light-weight insistent ones. Not berserk. An artful dodger. Kind of like an annoying, bratty little brother.

"Hey, you're leaving me distraught," he called after her. "I thought you'd invite me home to drink lemonade. Let me eyeball what you got in the house that might need refinishing. When it comes to doing furniture, I got the hired-gun type mentality."

21

"Lie down with charismatics, jump up with Jesus freaks," intoned Chandler to his reflection in the massive pier glass mirror in the front hall. He downed his third vodka and tonic, checked his watch. Chandler was convinced he kept sober better with the company of vodka. And with the arrival of his guest any moment now he would need to exercise sobriety.

He was housesitting at the Romneygate House one of the true architectural monuments of Charleston. A planter's townhouse built in 1801, it was set back from Gaston Street by a large lawn with a sunken bowling green. Regal really. Adamesque oval rooms that projected into the garden facade. Noble. The stairhall ceiling with its parachute like dome. Imposing.

A sputtering choking noise came from the street. That odd mechanical mess of cars that won't shut off once the ignition is turned off. A creaking car door. Loud slam. A voice whooping holy shit what a motherfucker of a place.

Chandler cringed at that. Downed his drink. Braced himself for the ding-dong of the bell. He opened the door and gave her the smile of approval. "Ah, the ever-provocative Cindi," he said warmly, hands thrust in his jacket pockets like a squire of the manor.

She was wearing a neon pink tube top and white capri pants. A bright stud winked from her navel.

His original plan was to step outside to point out some of the salient architectural features. Massive fanlight window under the pediment balanced by a smaller more graceful one over the front door. Keystones above each window. Then perhaps a stroll in the yard to show her the entablature on the mammoth side piazzas. The twin 10-foot Labrador retriever topiary. Make her fully cognizant of the nobility of her surroundings.

Cindi gaped. This was sure something else. Most houses she went to got washing machines, junk, old tires in the yard.

Chandler brought her inside quickly. He did compliment her Celtic tattoo. Said it gave her a sense of touching the past. She beamed at the compliment. Yeah, it looked better than screaming skulls and shit you normally get in tattoo parlors. All those spiders. Or the dead things coming out of graves. Those were the worst. And you know what she really hated? The homemade jobs that men gave each other in prison.

Chandler raised and lowered his eyebrows. Shook his head dismissively. He ushered her into the dining room with its gray and white marble mantel supported by Ionic columns. The cornices he lectured are variations of anthemia, a Classical ornament using honeysuckle vine and flowers. She said that was cute cause she was here to suckle his honey.

He tittered at that. This trollop was making him damned uneasy. He outlined his planned light repast. A bite of the succulent Cranshaw seedless watermelon. A morsel of

Sharlyn. A taste of Yellow Doll. A scrumpetey-dump of Temptation honeydew. A delving of Sugar baby watermelon for a moment of roguish seed spitting here at table. And rounding off with *un petit gout de Charentais.*

She said she didn't speak Spanish, but did he know that watermelons originally came from Africa? That's probably why niggers like them so much. Part of their cultural heritage.

Chandler harumped no, he was unaware of that footnote of history.

She asked what do you think of those boys with the electronic keyboards? They're not real musicians are they?

Irritably, he said what? No, of course they weren't.

She said that's what I think too.

Cindi looked around with awe. Chandler sure seemed to have a big lead in the game of life. Living in this fine mansion. It kind of melds all your dreams together at once. It was nice enough working for Luscious Decatur. He didn't mind if you turned tricks on the side. Going out on deployment, he called it. That's funny ain't it? He sure got a way with words.

She said she was in the federal witness protection program. Chandler said what? She said it was okay. Her testimony had put her old boyfriend behind bars for life without parole. Man, he was a local crime pattern like you wouldn't believe. Knelt a federal agent down and blew his cotton-picking brains out.

After the trial, the feds had moved her to D.C. but she come down here with a new boyfriend who was on like a contract job. Her boyfriend was like the general manager of special operations for somebody else.

Chandler didn't understand that. The girl was a genuine specimen of rural retard. Right out of *Tobacco Road*.

It was awful up there in D.C. battling hours of rush-hour traffic. Nice getting back south although Charleston was more crowded than she expected. Her boyfriend got locked in the county jail on some bullshit and needed to make bail. At the rate she was going he wouldn't ever get out. Maybe Chandler would like to give her an extra big tip. Was there anything special he liked? Blow-jobs? Rim-jobs? She was into productivity. Didn't get hung up on inhibitions in the least way. She was like a compliance person.

Ignoring the melon, she stood up, started peeling out of her tube top. "You ready to do some bodysurfing? Come on. Get it out of your pants. Let's take a look at that bad boy." Her boobs were quite fulsome although they sagged severely.

Chandler chuckled nervously. "Well, perhaps a little selective disclosure here." Unzipped his trousers.

She took hold of him, cupped it with both hands like an incubator. "We need to upgrade this equipment, I tell you what. Come here to momma. You need a good lovin' home."

Chandler said nervously, "It will soon enlarge its dimensions."

"Hey, no problem-o. It's a relief for a change. Most men just come right at you with that big sticking-out thing. Want you to hold a yardstick up to it. Go oo-eee ain't that just about the biggest in creation."

She paused and looked at him. "What's the matter? You got like an on-going drug problem that needs attention?"

"I beg your pardon?"

"You got to shoot up?"

He said he was starting to wonder if he needed gynecological records on her.

She said well, you can't be too safe these days but all the same that's kind of on the insulting side. He said well, lie down with dogs, get up with fleas.

She asked what'd she do? Violate his civil rights or something? He said he was ready for her to leave. Walked to the door of the room like she was supposed to follow.

She declared well this was a nice surprise party. He was lucky she wasn't working for no pimp. What she'd have to do then was take her nails and claw the shit out of his face. That was so she'd have skin under her nails when she went to the cops and accused him of rape. Pimps made you do that or they'd beat the living dog-dookey out of you. Accuse you of stealing the money. Using it for a drug habit.

That put Chandler in a real wrath. He told her she was a dreadful cunt and if she even contemplated such a thing—if he required surgical closure of his cuts—if she made the slightest scratch on his person, he would choke the life out of her and bury her in quicklime in the cellar.

His voice rose. He was practically spluttering. By God he labored mightily in the vineyards of the Lord. He was sentinel and watchdog!

"Man, you gotchore unnerwear in yore crack."

"GET OUT GETOUTGETOUTGODDAMYOU!!"

She said well yeh sure. Okay. Whatever. She knew it was a tough world. Tobacco companies targeting minors with their Joe Camel advertising. Gives you a real pit-of-the-stomach feeling.

He watched her all the way down the walk and while she started her pathetic car and drove off. Take a strong hand with gutter snipes like that. It was the only way really. Else they'd walk all over you.

God what unremitting squalor. Sitting there trying to make sparkly dialogue with a harlot. Repellent. She made him think of a cur dog studying a wrist watch. Wondering what the ticking noise was.

He had had quite enough of what life had put on his plate. He was going to move his agenda forward. And no life was important that stood in his way. Pushing Roland off the cliff was an act of social justice.

High time for a radical departure from his past timidity. In a world of tax fraud, money laundering and public bribery, where was the sin? A world that permits Las Vegas with its hokey volcano explosions and staged pirate battles while life's losers throw their money on the tables of Mammon.

He poured out more vodka and settled into a deep chair to watch "The Best of British Spanking."

"You've been a bad boy," purred the sultry siren voice. It was a Soho tart accent. Chandler remembered them with relish.

"I'm going to have to give you a spanking."

■ ■ ■

Rannie Ralston stretched and yawned, "You know I got a client sitting in the county jail on cocaine charges. He's trying to file a civil rights action, says he has a right to satellite dish TV. I told him he was boring me mindless. To get a life. But then how can he? He's sitting in there with three roomates and that shiny metal commode with no seat."

Moira looked tense. She was always tense, like she felt her period was coming on. Every day of every month.

Outside the big house on Legendre Street, the glaring heat of the day was smoothing into the wet heat of night. Gray clouds of mosquitoes swarmed among the rich growth of the garden, wet from the sprinklers. The Italian garden project was deep-sixed. Too much red tape. Mary Canty would have to lump it.

Rannie poured herself a third Maker's Mark on the rocks. She was out of Jim Beam. This was something her mother drank. Although Mary Canty mixed it with Dr. Pepper.

"Human dreck. Thinks he can negotiate his fee. Like he's in a position of strength. The man's sitting there lost between incomprehension and stupidity. And he's highly critical of the way I'm handling things.

"Booger-T he calls himself. He's got some bitch in tow that the cops missed because she was out buying junk food that wasn't on the room service menu. Now she's on the street hustling her buns for money to make his bail."

Moira sat there looking none too thrilled. "You know I don't like to hear these sordid stories. I can't sleep afterwards. Mother would be irate if she knew you were doing this to me."

Rannie brushed off her objections. "Why? Crime is like this big trend. And yes, I'm feeding off it. It's like an ecosystem."

"I'm putting my hands over my ears until you stop!"

"Hang on, there's a moral coming."

"I'm not listening." She covered her ears and tightly closed her eyes as well.

"He says it's like a twelve-step program in there except you never get to go home. So I go well, your divorce from outside life is close to becoming final. I thought that was kind of funny myself."

"I'm not listening."

"I always thought you looked like rice pudding, Moira. Maybe tapioca. Remember how we used to be force-fed that muck? You were always a prodigy of priss-pottery. I'd kick your shins to make you yowl. Didn't take much. Even look at you cross-eyed, you'd hit the upper registers. You'd get worked up over nothing, start jabbering like a scat-harmony."

"Are you finished yet?"

"I don't expect you to take up fast-pitch softball. But you're twenty-two now. Still a virgin. Unquestionably. Why don't you just select some guy and bang him until you pass out from sheer surfeit? Do it till your nose bleeds?" She downed about half her drink. "Just think of this as vocational counseling."

"I am in love with a fine gentleman," Moira said rigidly, proving she had heard most of it. "My entire life has been pointed to this moment."

Rannie gave a short, barking laugh. "A fine gentleman? When it comes to ridiculous, you've got boundless creativity. Is this a line from a novel you're reading? Hello, planet earth?"

Moira didn't answer.

Moths banged against the screens. Over the roof tops, heat lightning flickered among the jumble of chimneys and wind vanes.

Rannie picked up the remote and started channel-surfing. Re-run of *The Six Million Dollar Man.* Re-run of *Wonder Woman.* Re-run of *The Dukes of Hazard. Jeopardy* re-run.

Whups. There it was. The Stallion Club. Lucious Decatur flashing those gold teeth. She had advised him to stay out of the ads. He'd scare off the white people. There was his inventory shown from the shoulders up. Afro-tresses. Big hair.

"Shit a brick, there she is. That's his bitch. Cindi something."

"What?" said Moira. "His what?"

"That trailer trash girl there. She's Booger-T's bitch."

22

Talisha stood tapping her foot, fuming in the shade of a tree outside her house on Rondeau Street waiting to be picked up and taken to the service at St. Ambrose where Roscoe was going to preach. Tight-lipped in her Sunday best pink outfit. A look of fury in her brown eyes.

The note at the bank was overdue and here came Alvin Teckler driving up in a Jaguar XJ12 he had gone out and gotten in the company name. Sticker price of $79,370 plus a $3,700 gas guzzler tax.

And that damn Root Doctor Dread sitting in the back with his arms folded like he was a tribal king or a guru or something. She couldn't take him into St. Ambrose.

Here he had been hanging around the station just setting there scaring the ever-loving piss of everybody who came in. Following her when she went across the road to get a sandwich and a coke. Telling her—can you believe it?—telling her he knew she wanted to marry him. Or if she didn't know, it was because she couldn't accept fate as revealed in the flight of birds. Now he wants to bring his heathen voo-doo into the classiest white church in town. And Alvin kissing up to him, bringing him along.

Alvin goes, "Check out this luxuriously appointed interior. Burled walnut on the doors and center console.

Wrinkled leather seats. Genuine lambswool carpets. Seat heaters. Can you believe that? You got your cigar lighter in the backseat. Cigar smoking is real big in Hollywood, New York City, class act places. Chicks are smoking them now. Tough as shit. Kind of sexually suggestive. Fellatio. That kind of thing."

Talisha jabbed an accusing finger into his chest. "You ain't radiating honesty."

He took hold of her finger and held onto it. "Quit being so morally indignant. You'll get to drive it some. It's a company car. This is high-level mystique. Can't you just see youself sitting up here posing and pouting? Just think of it as a dividend boost in your life. You'll look as rich as cheesecake."

He tried to take her whole hand. She jerked away, put both hands on her hips and leaned into his face. "You're waiting to give me the bad news."

"What?"

"We're talking about maybe three lifetimes of free advertising you gave away for this car."

He said he didn't think that was a reliable insight into the matter. He realized it was hard to talk across the races. He tried to respect sensitivities.

Her eyes narrowed to slits. She said she couldn't seem to monitor him close enough or quick enough to keep the station out of the high insolvency category. She probably wouldn't have his sorry ass killed, but she wasn't ruling it out.

Alvin looked disgusted. "I make no secret of my affection for you. I figured you'd break the color barrier. Be the first black chick to date me. Alvin, the world-class lover boy."

Talisha stuck her head in the back seat and said to the doctor. "You want to do something get into my good grace? Why don't you put a root on that fool? Give him fire ant bites all over his body. Broken toes and fingers. Leprosy. Tooth ache requiring root canals."

She left Alvin looking up at the sky. She would drive her junky old '92 Saturn to the church. Hope it didn't break down and have to be towed out of the parking lot.

■ ■ ■

The parishioners of St. Ambrose were not particularly pleased to see the Reverend Roscoe P. Morningstar sitting up in the front of the church on Sunday morning. A colored girl in shocking pink with a pillbox hat and veil beside him. Watching them all the way through the early phases of the service was like waiting for the other shoe to drop. Probably expecting a civil rights collection. Rebuild black churches burned by the Klan. Reparations for slavery. Then the shoe dropped.

Rusty Royall announced the Reverend would be delivering the sermon. Its subject—"True Love Waits"—would make a statement about a serious social issue—premarital sexual intercourse. Directed at the church youth, it proposed a resolution on sexual abstinence before marriage.

"Abstain, ABSTAIN, saith the LORD GOD ALMIGHTY JEHOVAH!" Roscoe began in a booming voice that would have been right at home in a black church.

Honor Revenue couldn't concentrate on what he was saying. Her mind whirled. Rusty leering at her. Judge Lorenzo splattered across a motel room wall. Her mother reading with relish a news account of new forms of water-borne bacteria that chlorine couldn't kill. Twelve hundred deaths last year from cryptosporidium that slipped through filters into the drinking water. Our pollution was catching up with us, Grace had observed cheerfully. Bacteria and parasites were multiplying in the lakes and rivers at an alarming rate. It was pretty much curtains for humanity.

"A world of nothing but sex, sex, SEX!" Morningstar was booming. "Women with saline balloons in their BA-zooms! Men seeking penile-enLARGEment surgery!"

Chandler Lovelace stood up like he expected everyone to join him in protest. When no one did, he stalked out loudly.

Morningstar dwelled on illicit sex during the year's separation before divorce. Called it a case of undenied access.

Feet nervously shuffled.

He said you try to legislate morality and you get a lot of finger pointing. The MIDDLE finger! Then gave a graphic demonstration with both hands.

Gasps. Stricken looks exchanged.

Fully wound up in the way only a black minister can be, Morningstar was sweating with exertion. Grinning. Leering really, like a caricature darkie. Pleased with the turmoil he was creating.

"Think of your personal BODY as a conservation trust! It's like a LAND BANK where you put up the soil for future fertility!"

They all stayed to the bitter end, but few of them liked it. After the benediction, the crowded aisles surged with muttering Episcopalians. Teenagers who had been dragged unwilling to church were the most sanctimonious. Voicing their disgust for adult behavior.

"And like that big *jig* standing up there going . . . I mean I couldn't *buh-lieve* what he was saying."

"I mean, *get real.*"

"Celibacy. Out of *them*?"

"And shooting us all the bird!"

Honor Revenue didn't want to be around it, see the sneers and contempt. She could feel the confusion and fear and anger flowing out of the people like storms on the surface of Mars.

Ducking into the choir robing room, she ran smack up against Rusty Royall. The choir hadn't come yet. But Rusty wasn't supposed to be there. He should be out in front of the church with Morningstar greeting the people. Smiling and saying thank you. Yes, such a moving sermon. We're so fortunate to have the Reverend with us.

Before she could back out again, he laid a big wet kiss on her mouth. "Your lips distil nectar. Honey and milk are under your tongue," he whispered passionately.

"I don't need this," she protested, forcefully shoving him away.

"What *do* you need? I've got the Ultimate Sex Guide on CD-ROM for the church library. Programs for better sex. Case Files. Sexopedia. You and I could do some serious interactive theater."

She gave him another strong push. "Didn't you listen to the sermon?"

"Oh God yes hit me!" he enthused. "I'm a wicked, abusive person! It's more than appropriate!"

A voice advanced toward the room gabbling at a loud pitch. "Give me gladiolas any day. They don't shed. They just stand up tall."

Rusty's face was overheated, berry red. He said he had memorized Honor's schedule, knew where she was every moment of the day. He had found a dead starling outside his windowsill. He knew she had put a curse on the bird as a sign to him. She burned black candles and incense.

He grabbed for her, grappled with her, jerked her clothes. She gave him another violent shove.

And he fell flat on his behind.

Bump.

Just as Moira Ralston came into the room. She wore a wide hat with cabbage roses around the brim as though riding a carrousel. Blue eyes saucer wide in surprise. Hands up in the air. Head rearing back.

Seeing Honor disheveled. Hair in her face. Blouse open. A fingernail scrape across her cheek oozing the faintest bit of blood.

"You've been . . . *petting*!" Moira shrieked.

23

"Liver cancer," Grace Revenue grimly predicted. "Get your humid weather and the aflatoxins soar in figs. Or drought can achieve the same reaction."

Chandler paused holding the fresh figs. The East Bay Harris Teeter was crowded in late afternoon. All the people in the world and this half-blind old bat had to come creeping up behind him as he shopped for Mummy. It was so difficult to imagine Grace spawning the delectable Honor. Indeed, he had been musing upon Honor as he selected the figs. They were, after all, an ancient fertility symbol.

Grace said, "Figs all are grown in sub-tropical countries where you get heavy humidity. Or else in dry climates. They get you coming and going."

Chandler put the figs back in the bin. His hands were shaking. It was nearing the cocktail hour and he badly needed a drink. White corn was six for a dollar. He reached out tentatively.

"Corn has it as well," she interjected. "If you see any mold at all I'd throw the entire ear away. Culinary surgery is not adequate."

She also gave dire warning of fungicides on tomatoes

and a pesticide called Captan on apples and peaches. Avocados had Lindane.

Grace's cart was nearly bare. She had selected cabbage and carrots. Seemed rather a dismal meal. He imagined her munching it like a myopic old rabbit out of Beatrix Potter. She had kale as well. He despised kale.

Although he normally delighted in grocery shopping, Chandler was not feeling his tip-top best. The horror of that negro preacher in St. Ambrose had caused him to sleep poorly. Woke at 3 AM with his heart pounding and a nightmare of Grace Revenue demanding the furniture back. In the dream he was dressed only in his jockey shorts and she chased him up and down the aisles of St. Ambrose shouting he had stolen the Tiverton commode. Now here she was intently studying the produce for disease. Groping at things with claw-like hands. Squinting with her weak eyes.

Then had come the 6 AM phone call from Moira Ralston warning that his turf was threatened, urging him to violent action against the philandering rector. With some aspersion he told her he knew from the get-go that Noble Royall was no gentleman. Calling himself some silly boy's nickname. Rusty. Well *Rusty*—if he so wished—had become an acolyte in the church of the with-it sybarites. The queer libido. The hep-cat theology. Rusty would rise or fall based on the courage of an assemblage of good people to take a stance. Draw a line in the sand. Say enough is enough. *Finis.*

Personally he was outraged over Moira Ralston spreading tales about Honor and Rusty Royall. Still one had to watch one's step around her. She was deranged that girl. And her sister Rannie was like a Chaos Monster out of a feminist Hades.

Everything in his operation was so delicate at this point. Beau-Jack's workmen had brought by the reproduction commode at seven just as he was dozing off once again and he had had to walk over to Bocquet Lane to let them in. They did look lovely standing side by side. The commodes. Utter perfection contrasted with the stacked up Victorian junk. With stage two, WPST would take all of the furniture but the commodes. And then would come New York.

"Is there a greenish tinge on those potatoes? Do you ever notice a burning sensation when you eat potatoes? A bitter taste? That's your Glycoalkaloids sure enough. They're produced as a defense against fungi. Not to worry. It gets flushed out by your urine pretty rapidly. It will inhibit muscle relaxation though. And there's some risk of birth defects."

Chandler had contemplated broaching the subject of her daughter with Grace. She was after all his future mother-in-law. With her free and easy New York ways, perhaps Honor was unconsciously doing something to provoke an anointed decadent like Rusty. A most delicate topic. The potential for damaging scandal. Hanging like a sword of Damocles. Yet the old fool was lecturing him on how the common commercial mushroom had hydrazines that gave mice stomach and lung tumors in lab tests.

The Harris Teeter was his venue, the shopping milieu for beneficiaries of ancient trust funds, the *bodega* for those prized speciality items that were stylish and not merely expensive. The shopping aisles were normally serene waters on which he guided the gondola of his cart. Was he inextricably bound with this woman on a liferaft? Had she turned into some nemesis, hunting him through the store? He felt as though he were starving to death and she kept snatching food from his mouth like a harpy in an ancient myth.

By the time he reached the meat counter his mind was running riot with the unalloyed delight of liver and onions, succulent veal and kidneys in a brown sauce, thick pork chops with apple sauce and brown sugar.

"Don't ever put meat on a grill until the charcoal is reduced to embers," Grace warned. "The aromatic hydro-carbons are at a minimum then. Stomach cancer, you know. Old bacon or in fact any fatty meat can get rancid. Carcin-ogens. Mutagens. Even minimal exposure can wreck your digestive tract."

Chandler had a splitting headache. He wanted to weep with the pain and frustration. What, he begged, do you recommend?

Grace looked thoughtful. "Well you could go with ground turkey, although you never know about the poul-try fat they put in it. Possibly a small piece of select grade beef. Small, I stress. A couple of mouthsfull. Don't make it the center of your meal. And you're still taking a risk. Cattle will carry all those pesticides and toxic things they eat along with their feed. It collects in the fat. That's where they get you is the fat."

Chandler thought of holiday dinners with this wretched health nut. He could not surrender those sacred times. The wassail bowl. The joint of beef dripping in juices. The roast potatoes and mint sauce that she'd find bacteria crawling on. He needed very badly to sit down. He felt as though he might be publicly sick.

"What are you—you personally—planning on eating?" Chandler practically shouted at her.

"Turkey wings. Without the skin of course. Tuna dogs. They're extremely low in fat and don't have all the oil."

■ ■ ■

"Shut up, Moira! I can't hear!" Rannie yelled. She had one finger in her ear trying to block out her sister's sobbing, the no-brain stretched out on the couch in terminal misery. Her mother on the phone from Italy yow-yowing at her.

"They've got a passel of Catholics over here!" shouted Mary Canty, drunk and loud as ever. "We wasted the whole morning waiting around for the Pope to poke his nose out on some balcony. All these women holding up rubbish for him to bless."

It had been a long day. Rannie had a manslaughter client, mashed some poor girl while driving drunk. Served one year, put out on probation. In a routine drug test he came up positive for cocaine. He'll go back in and serve four more years. Asshole says he wants her to challenge the validity of the state's drug screening. And while that's going on could he go in a community service program?

She told him all that might happen if he had about $40,000 which she knew he didn't.

He said yeah, but look at the long-term ramifications. This was a golden opportunity for South Carolina to show the whole country how to fight overreaching by police authority.

Rannie said overreaching? Where do dimwits like you pick up this vocabulary?

She didn't dare tell her mother the garden was stymied and St. Ambrose now had a black mountebank preaching on sexual abstinence. It kind of took away from her air of indomitability.

Mary Canty was saying, "I want you to buy that for me. She has no need of it. They're poor as church mice."

Rannie went, "What?" She had missed a lengthy part of the diatribe.

Mary Canty acted like Rannie was an idiot child, but she backed up and repeated how the tour had gone to a museum of American furniture in Rome given by some Newport type Yankee. She had seen a Tiverton commode. Asked the guide where you could buy things like that. He said any one piece was priceless. She said how much? He said over a million dollars American. Then he put it in some squillion-zillion lira. Their money was trash in Italy.

Rannie said, "OK, so what's the point?"

Mary Canty said, "Grace Revenue. She has one of those. It's sitting in her upstairs bathroom. You see it big as life whenever you go pee."

Rannie was acerbic. "I didn't know Grace was part of your drinking set."

"Of course not. Woman's got the preacher's wife restraint. Never more than one drink. Put a bourbon slush in front of her, she'll never lower it but a fraction. But don't you get it? That fool Grace has no idea how much it's worth."

Rannie thought why not? A little manipulating. A little cheating. It's a world of moral relativity.

Now she had one more chore. Build a new garden. Get

in a slugfest with Rusty Royall over the way he was running the church. Steal from the neighbors.

Rannie went and made herself a Jim Beam on the rocks. "Moira, what the hell is wrong with you?" she shouted from the kitchen.

Moira lifted her face out of the tear-soaked pillow. "You wouldn't understand! You've never been in love!"

That gave Rannie pause. She tried to think of some names. There had been . . . or maybe . . . well, it wasn't for lack of wanting to be in love. And she used to get laid with some regularity. Men were just such wimps. Confronted by a lawyer who wore a 40 D-cup they just fell apart.

Rannie leaned against the door frame and watched her sister snivel. "So who is this stud-in-a-tux? Do you peel grapes and feed them to him? Make frantic, passionate love on a tiger skin while dripping candles light the boudoir? Force feed him on cunnilingus?"

Moira's face was scrunched up and red, eyes squinting. "God you're disgusting! You're so . . . so stuck up! You fear ridicule! You're not willing to give, to share!"

"That's great. Moira the compendium on retaining virginity."

"What do you know?! You don't know anything about me!"

"Okay, enlighten me. Does your fine gentleman ram his prodigious extension up your twat or not?"

"Of course not! Our relationship is deeply spiritual! God you're filth!"

Spiritual? A light bulb came on. Rannie blurted, "It's Rusty Royall! Holy shit!" Then burst out laughing.

"I hate you I hate you!" Moira shrieked. "Daddy always loved me more than you! That's why you're so mean to me!"

Rannie poured herself another drink and sat there thinking. Yes, if Daddy had lived it would have been a real *King Lear* drama around here.

She twisted the end of her flame red hair around a finger.

Rusty Royall. God Bless America. Was this possible?

24

One of the spades from WPST moving the last pieces of Revenue furniture out of Phyllis Lewy's house on Bocquet Lane said, "Hey, check it out." Chandler stuck his head in the room, fearful he was about to steal something. They gave him sullen looks. It was 10 AM and the heat had turned brutal. Black skin glistening with sweat.

Beau-Jack McCully came through the front door, careful as he moved around the men working. He said he was happy to see stage two in progress. He was sorry the date hadn't worked out. Chandler said the girl was not very generous with her affections. Took a quaff out of his mid-morning Bloody Mary with the raw egg and celery stick.

At least it might calm Mummy down to clear the house. And praise God there had been no breakage. It would have sent her through the roof.

He had not allowed them to drive the truck into the yard. Would have ruined the grass and flower beds. Which meant they had to lug it a big bit farther, but that was why God put negroes on this earth. No reason for them to be so resentful.

Beau-Jack said Cindi had reported the date was not love's young dream for herself. But there had been the problem of the up-front money that was supposed to be paid. As well as the tip. She seemed to think Beau-Jack was like a guarantor. He had had to set her straight on that.

"I can't believe the scandal that surrounds that loathsome Noble Royall," said Chandler, evading the issue. "Pawing all over Honor Revenue right in the church before witnesses. As if that coon minister preaching there wasn't enough. That colored girl's pathetic car breaking down in the church parking lot. There's open talk of mutiny among the congregation, I tell you."

He hadn't bothered to lower his voice. The "coons" and "coloreds" were coming through loud and clear. The spades gave him glowering looks. Humping a big sofa out, turning it sideways to get through the door.

"Lie down with charismatics, jump up with Jesus freaks," said Chandler. Beau-Jack stared at him, not getting it at all.

Beau-Jack said he knew grief disoriented the grieving. The death of Roland Lewy. It was a hard thing being without a stepfather. Living in a world of darkness. Maybe it's hard to get it up under those circumstances. Hard to get hard. But your ladies of the night expect to be paid just for showing up. The rest is up to you.

Chandler argued he'd given little cause for complaint that he could see. A lot of overacting on Cindi's part to compensate for her lack of couth. Border-line hysteria. He'd had to ask her to leave. They had been, after all, in the Romneygate House. He couldn't have her breaking things. Alarming the neighbors.

Beau-Jack rubbed his chin. "The problem you got arises when she turns it over to collection. That big dude Luscious Decatur what runs the Stallion Club. I suspect he's got a vested interest in it, takes a percentage cut. He looks the type who'd maybe curtail some of the enjoyment you get in life."

Chandler snorted he wasn't going to be intimidated by some procurer. But the thought of that behemoth jungle bunny with the purple clothes and gold teeth was unsettling. They seemed to have no fear of the police these days.

The truck started up outside. They were driving off. Hadn't bothered to check with him. Typical. Low-quality sort of help one got today. And not about to say thank-you.

Beau-Jack said lucky day. I tell you what I'm gonna do. I'll lay us a little wager on the Belle Terre Golf Classic. You got Rich Weston, Brooks Blackburn, Steve Isley. Tough pick. If we win, you pay the girl off. Get her off your back. If we lose, you're out nothing. I'll cover it myself. Chandler asked what the catch was.

"Well it's complicated," allowed Beau-Jack. "It's like superstition. I swore on my daddy's grave to stay away from gambling. If I'm betting for you, it's like no sin. You know what I mean? You're kind of the stalking horse for my conscience. And that'll make lady luck run our way. Lay some dollar bills down on the table, they'll come back with friends."

Chandler pondered this no-risk offer, pronounced it rather exhilarating. How did one go about selecting a winner?

Beau-Jack explained there were a variety of systems. Mostly he figured what his old man would have done and bet the opposite. It paid off five-out-of-five. They'd test it on this little golf wager. Nothing major. A hundred dollars. Try to win two-fifty. See what happens.

Then he said something else funny had happened. Rannie Ralston had called him up wanting to know the value of a Tiverton commode. Did Chandler have any clue on what she was on to?

Something struck Chandler as being rather odd. The room seemed emptier than he'd imagined.

Good Lord . . .

The two commodes were gone.

Missing! Absent! The goddam spooks had taken them! He clamped his jaw shut, afraid to speak this outrage aloud.

He realized with dawning horror he should have been more involved in the furniture shift. What would Beau-Jack do if he found out? Did he dare tell him?

■ ■ ■

"Man, talk about your butt-wipe white man," griped Leone, directing the furniture into WPST. "No cold beer. No even glass of ice water. Do this. Don't touch that. Don't scrape the other. The boy lucky he ain't join a missing persons list."

Talisha was looking at the furniture thinking it wasn't too bad at all. Antique elegant looking. Kind her grandmomma used to lust after but could only afford pressed woodpulp and paying on time. She ran her fingers over it. Lot of wood swirls and curlicues. Claw and ball feet on the sofa and chairs. There was so much of it they were having to fill most of the downstairs from floor to ceiling.

Alvin Teckler came down the stairs, limping from

having fallen and hurt his ankle. Leone put up both hands, cringed away. "Man, get away from me. I don't want to be around when the bubonic plague strikes."

"My first reaction," said Alvin sourly, "is I don't need this shit. Everybody treating me like a leper. Should I ring a bell to warn you I'm coming? Unclean. Unclean."

The fact was, word had spread not just at the station but around the whole neighborhood. Alvin Teckler had the root on him and was expected to be dead or crippled in short order. Black folks, which was everybody thereabouts, crossed the street to avoid him. Alvin blamed Talisha for this ostracism. He said he had been firing on all cylinders for WPST, had a unique opportunity to make a difference, and suddenly it's like, 'Uh-oh. Get back and give him room.'

Talisha said she intended to stay in the eye of that storm. Maybe a good gris-gris cursing would curb his free-spending habits. Get both his hands burned where he couldn't write checks, he'd become cost-conscious.

"Hey, I gotta express some serious skepticism on this."

There was a smile in her eyes. "It's superstition, sure. The possibility of injury is remote. But who knows? You may get crushed under the load of bullshit you tote around."

He got into his version of sarcastic. "You know Talisha, sweetie, you ought to take up a hobby. Paint by numbers. Photography maybe. Get immersed in aperture, shutter speed, film speed. That kind of thing."

He drove off in the Jag leaving her in the middle of WPST's financially troubled program. Five pink phone messages from the bank loan officer sitting on her desk like a nest of snakes. "Call ASAP." "Must talk." "We're playing phone tag." "Urgent." And "Imperative."

Leone and some dudes, undershirts and do-rags on their heads, humped in the last of the furniture. He said, "Get some red flock wallpaper, look as good as a New Orleans cathouse. Voolee-voo couchez avec mwa? Ooo. Momma Marmalade."

Talisha said when they had the bankruptcy auction it might bring a few thousand.

Leone said be at ease, baby. He had finally gotten the upper hand on their debt worries. All those phone calls were from the bank congratulating her on paying off the nut. Wondering since her credit rating so good, maybe she wanted to borrow more.

He bowed at the waist, said no applause please. The Funk-meister, the Gangsta of Love himself, Sierra Leone Jones had done paid off the bank loan. Was she listening? Flat out paid that mother off. Every penny. He said he wanted to end his exile. Get out of the deep freeze. Become a member of the WPST action team.

Talisha looked at him sharp like. "Where'd you get one million dollars?"

"From some spiritual friends."

"You ain't got them kind of friends. Where'd it come from? Loan sharks? Some dope dealer? What?"

"Friends in Washington. The D.C. Washington that is."

Her mouth drew up tight. "You expect me to believe that? You got a connect with Congress? Some federal give-away agency?" He said, "Well, not exactly."

A big silence kind of sat there. Then the light bulb came on.

"Oh my God," she gasped. "The Muslims."

Leone spread his hands expansively. It was a globalizing world. They had to be broad minded about credit sources. It was an essential move mandated by the cash-starved circumstance. He had his own stake in managing the growth and development of WPST. He had been a longtime friend of both her and her family.

She said what?

Talisha started talking in a whisper like the walls had ears. She ask what kind of vig was there on the loan. He admit he hadn't ask. But that's okay. He could deal with it. Brother Farrakhan was a close personal friend. Many's the night they sit doing numerology studies. The brother good at math.

Talisha told him he was the king of all dumb-asses.

He screwed up his face, said there weren't no need to go negative.

"No need? Them Muslims . . . they the biggest bunch of wide-ranging hard asses you'd ever hope to meet. They got more violence than a Kung Fu movie."

She said she felt like she was hearing a lonely locomotive whistle and feeling all alone herself. With that Muslim money in the business they were flat-out owned.

"It won't stay long," he soothed. "Just til we get some logistical and technical issues resolved. Get geared up into full retail competition with the other stations in town."

She spluttered with anger. "You giving me paranoia . . . high-handed duplicity . . . stupid-shit male moron . . ."

"There you go. Just can't pass up a opportunity to score points against me. Here we got a world of personal and economic challenge, and you into this gender-conflict thing. Girls are smarter than boys. Girls can take more pain."

Talisha jerked open the door screaming at him to get out. She hesitated. Stopped silent.

Sitting in the waiting room on the new antique couch were two wide-shoulder, short-haircut dudes in little narrow bow ties and short sleeve white shirts. Stone faces. Shades. Just sitting there with their arms crossed.

"It's cool," said Leone. "Brother Farrakhan always send a couple boys to watchdog the investment. It's like a security force. No extra charge. Now how about you loosen up and pay me a finder's fee? I got to have some incentives for all the players on the team here. Design a growth formula."

25

"Of course she goes weak in the knees around him!" Moira ranted. "Honor Revenue. The girl's practically double-jointed she does it with men so much! New York model! You know what that means! She's nothing but a common tramp! A slut!"

Rannie had never heard such violent language out of her sister before. Moira paced up and down the law office in an endless diatribe. She and Rusty were meant to be. Now this whore of Babylon comes sashaying along with her side-long glances. Making the ice tea. Being all sugar sweet and helpful while she worms her way into his affections. Some little deviled egg just wanting to be nibbled on. Have the creamy mayonnaise yolk part eaten first.

That whole scene in the robing room was deliberate. Honor Revenue wanted to be caught in the act. She had no soul that girl. No conscience. No milk of human decency. What did she care about Rusty's reputation as long as she had him trapped.

And he was such a fool. Men were all fools. Damn animals really. No thought of consequences. Just going all slobber mouth over a cheap tramp like she was some little bunch of fiery bright red radishes from the Harris Teeter with the green tops still on.

"A stiff dick has no brain," Rannie agreed. Wondering about the radish image.

Moira wasn't shocked by the dick cliché. Maybe she didn't hear. She lifted the back of her hair up and fanned herself with a handkerchief. Flopped down in a chair.

"I swear the heat is just frightful. Can't sleep at night. Leave a glass of water beside the bed and it evaporates. Bedclothes sticking to my thighs. Frogs out croaking in the fountain keeping me up. It makes me feel things in the dark. Things I shouldn't feel. Driving me crazy."

Rannie said what? But Moira wasn't really listening. Her jabber had gotten her into a private world. Through the looking glass. She closed her eyes and rested the back of her neck against the chair back. Her voice went low and eerie.

"A man's body lying on top of mine. An incubus. And it touches me in private places. Lifts me up and takes me way across town to the church. I feel like I was there in her place. Like he had me against the wall and had his hands up under my skirt. Tugging down my panties. Unwilling to wait. Unable to stop himself. Talking dirty to me. Trash talk. Filthy. Going to suck my nipples like scuppernong grapes. Suck out the sweetness. Whispering he was as horny as a convict let out of prison and needed a strong fuck so deep that every inch went inside me."

"Holy shit," gasped Rannie amazed.

Moira's eyes snapped open. She stared in horror. Edged up out of the chair. Handkerchief clutched in her hand. "I didn't say that," she yelped. "None of it. Not one word. You repeat it and I'll take a pair of scissors to your eyeballs! I swear I will!" She backed out the door and ran for the stairwell, not willing to wait for an elevator.

Rannie stared in wonder. Rusty Royall. Dear God. It might actually work.

■ ■ ■

"Honestly, I had no inkling," gabbled Grace Revenue at the kitchen table eating lunch. "You and Rusty Royall. Land sake. When I heard it you could have knocked me down with a feather."

Honor was exhausted from a late night of working in a senior citizens literacy program. She said, "I go off to New York at sixteen. Put up with that toxic hole. Come back to this little hick town Gomorrah by the sea. It's funny. I'm sitting here remarkably free of cynicism."

No reaction from Grace. She just went on nattering. "Here I thought you were without a suitor. Well it just goes to show you. I certainly hope you and that young man marry. It's part of attaining emotional and spiritual adulthood."

Exasperated, Honor was thinking you can run but you can't hide. First the pernicious story of her and Chandler. Now Rusty Royall. Totally repulsive Moira's little viper tongue wagging away. She had called Honor up three times just to hang up the phone on her. Honor would like to eviscerate the cow.

Then the even greater indignity of Browder Delamere, the up-front lascivious toad. He called hinting he could make her a better offer than Rusty. Proposing a weekend together down at Hilton Head. He was going to a broker conference. He'd tell people she was his administrative assistant. They'd go wink wink yeh right. Then he actually laughed. Like she should savor the joke of being his squeeze, exciting the envy of Board of Director old farts.

In a tight voice, Honor said if he'd straighten out her lost money maybe they could negotiate something. He said no, she had to "get to know him" first. "Pick up the tempo of their mutual attraction." "Kick up a rumpus." He actually said that. "Act out some lush clichés of lust to a background of knock 'em dead musical score." He said that mouthful too. That one had to be rehearsed.

She said impassively, "You'll have to excuse me. I'm afraid I cope with jerk-offs very poorly."

Honor crunched ice even though she knew it was the worst thing in the world for your teeth. Men looking at her like a steak tartare. A mound of livid ground up beef. Telling her she was Circe. A siren of the *demimonde*. A sphinx. A jungle-throb Sheena with a panther at her heel.

You smile at them, try to be nice, and they waste no time abusing their power. Let me take a peek at that mischievous vagina, those sprightly tits. Or worse they attribute you with powers as dark as Sprüngli chocolate. Want to put a diamond collar around your neck and act out the *Story of O.*

Be self-effacing, they hardly notice. The sex thing is too potent. Trying to explain to them graciously that you weren't up for their kinky games, didn't want to sit enthralled as they talked of monster ambitions, the heavy bread they pulled down. So then they get all violent aggrieved. Take my emeralds from Buccellati, the suede gloves with pleated cuffs—or I'll kill you. Hire a street hood to take a razor blade to that gorgeous face of yours.

The phone rang.

Rannie Ralston's secretary said Honor was expected in

Rannie's office at 2 PM tomorrow. Just like that. Imperial command.

"What for?" asked Honor puzzled.

"Well," said the secretary, "her exact words were 'to discuss your volcanic union'."

26

"I suppose it's all part of the new openness on the part of the clergy," began Rannie Ralston. "The modern *zeitgeist* or whatever."

"I confess," said Rusty Royall, "to finding myself bewildered. You're referring to . . . ?"

Honor Revenue thought Rannie was almost mesmerizing, the embodiment of the empowered female. Rannie had actually summoned them to her office. Had a secretary call and state a time they were expected. And Honor had shown up like little Bo Peep. Although she hadn't realized Rusty would be there. Nor he her.

"This move to ordain gay ministers," said Rannie. "You seem to mention it at least once a Sunday."

Honor was amazed at how Rannie could keep her face devoid of all expression. Lazy, half-lidded eyes. Give away nothing. The perfect poker face.

Rusty cleared his throat. "The church should be a unifying and stabilizing force for the community," he huffed. "And that means it must be inclusive."

"Granted," she said dryly. "However, I think there's sufficient butt-fucking among the clergy without your encouragement."

Rusty gaped at her, no doubt wondering when female modesty had gone all straight to hell.

She rocked back in her chair. "Do ministers ever banter among themselves? You know like cops and lawyers and other guys? Their gallows humor. Telling raunchy adventures?"

He stammered, "We . . . we have a certain breezy wit."

She nodded good. Then he'd enjoy what was about to follow. She handed him a scrapbook filled with newsclippings. Moira had asked her to return it to him.

Rusty held it cautiously. "Return it?"

"Well, whatever. She doesn't want it anymore. She's taken the scandal of you and Honor Revenue rather personally."

Honor was still watching, saying nothing. Wondering what exactly was happening.

Dumbfounded, Rusty leafed through a series of small news articles about himself. His arrival at St. Ambrose. The autumn harvest *fête*. A christening performed here, a wedding there. Slowly it sunk in that Moira had put it together. That she was infatuated with him.

Honor was every bit as startled. Rusty did not look happy as the object of an obsession. He was breathing through his mouth.

"Is this supposed to be humorous?"

Rannie said that depended on your point of view. Her sister wanted to sue Rusty for breach of promise. Rannie was restraining her from this course of action. Temporarily. She emphasized the last point.

Rusty was spluttering now. Saying temporarily? Did Rannie imagine she could force him into an unwilling marriage? Or was she after money? Which was it? Was this some kind of blackmail?

Rannie flicked a piece of lint off her linen jacket. "Call it what you will. The coming-of-age story of a ding-bat. Moira is convinced you were in love with her. Signaled in a variety of ways that you wished to marry her. And that Miss Bombshell here stole you away. The emotional damage has been enormous. There are remedies available at common law. I'm laying them out for you."

Rusty protested she couldn't possibly believe such a thing. It was outrageous! Nearly obscene!

Rannie shrugged. She was hired to vigorously present her client's case. Not to believe it one way or the other. Everybody in the church believed it anyhow. So he was pretty much convicted in the court of public opinion. So let's make this a peace summit and arrive at a treaty.

Rusty just sat there like he had suffered a brain aneurysm. Rannie shifted gears a bit. Her voice became almost drowsy.

"Being a single minister seems rather dreary. You're not stuck in a stifling marriage, and yet there's not a lot of sex, drugs and rock 'n roll. No falling in and out of bed with nubile honeys. You're longing for substance. You start a dalliance with Moira. Then along comes Honor Revenue with the thrusting nipples. The *haute cuisine* of libido boosters. This really adds a bit of zest."

"I'm not at fault," Rusty squeaked defensively. "Surely Moira can see that. Can feel some pity."

"Go on," Rannie urged, still in a low key.

Rusty's eyes darted from side to side. He licked his dry lips. He was moving gingerly. "Honor Revenue has some twisted, thwarted passion for me. The addictive, obsessive side of love."

"What?" said Honor sitting bolt upright in her chair.

He wouldn't look at her. "Deeply infatuated. Almost a clinical case really."

"How engrossing," Rannie mused.

"It began with a pastoral visit. She asked questions about fertility, contraception, STDs. It frankly made me uncomfortable. I tried to address her concerns with a common sense style. Yet show some compassion. I referred her to the health collection in the church library. Succinct information there. She selected a volume on breast cancer. Again, I reiterate, I felt distinct discomfort. She asked me to give her . . . give her a breast examination. To feel for lumps."

"You were naive," led Rannie sympathetically. "It's painfully obvious."

Rusty vigorously shook his head yes. Wiped a tear from his eye. "She was on a quest for her lost father. Trying to find his identity. I tried to help her face this emotional issue. Work through the intricacies of past failed relationships. Get her thoughts better clarified." He clasped his hands, hunched his shoulders as though making a painful confession. "We had . . . intercourse," he choked.

Honor jumped to her feet. "You lying son-of-a . . . !"

Rannie waved her to sit back down. Be patient.

Still Rusty wouldn't look at her. "I resisted. Told her I could not perform the sex act with a disengaged heart. She was impatient. Relentless really. Ravenous. There are some spectacular color photographs of us . . . 'doing it'. She insisted on taking them. She was the 600 pound gorilla. I felt like a dormouse. She had no understanding of boundaries. What is the proverb? Like a gold ring in a swine's snout is a beautiful woman lacking all discretion."

Rannie smiled maternally. "But you tried to help her?"

"I suggested support groups, treatment options."

"You proposed psychotherapy?"

"Of course."

"But she can't get over you?"

"She's myopic. I can't rule out the possibility of a hormonal disorder, of vitamin deficiencies. Fashion models often suffer from this."

"You should give me a short reading list on these topics."

He brightened. "I'd be only too glad to."

Rannie tapped her front teeth with a long red nail. "Horseshit," she said.

Rusty blinked. "I beg your pardon?"

"Do I need a doctorate in speech communication to get through to you?" She laughed. "I'm saying I don't believe a goddamn word of it."

"Wh . . . why is that?"

"Honor Revenue has had her choice of every man in the world since she was ten years old. And you look like you've got a dick like that baby corn you get at salad bars."

Honor sat back down, really wanting now to see where this was going.

"My idiot sister is a twenty-two year old virgin. It's time for her to explore new possibilities. Make a change for the positive. And to get out of the house. I've got enough trouble supporting a dipsomaniac mother. Together they make for an oppressive household."

"St. Ambrose has a singles group," Rusty suggested hopefully. One of his quick little elusive pirouettes. "It offers a variety of recreational activities. Many wholesome marriages grow out of it. I can personally . . . vouch for . . ." His voice trailed off when he saw Rannie's malign smile.

"My thoughts exactly. You'll take her to dinner at the Mills Hotel. I recommend the Steak Diane. Make light conversation. Try to keep your asininity to a manageable minimum. You'll take a room under an assumed name. Am I telegraphing the ending? You will have unprotected sex."

"N-no," he pleaded, twisting his fingers.

"It's not for the squeamish, I grant you. We may let the plan evolve, but that's where I am currently."

"Why are you doing this to me?"

"I want you under my power. I like having people there. It's kind of a mania for control."

As the full horror of it sunk in, Rusty started to get angry. Asked what if he refused? Rannie said she'd proceed with the breach of promise suit. He got huffy, said that was absurd. There were no engagement announcements. No witnesses.

Rannie looked him straight in the eye. Laughed. "Under ordinary circumstances, I really don't have a lot of trouble producing witnesses when I need them. But you've got so many enemies in the church, I could probably find two hundred folks who'd swear they saw you on one knee holding out a diamond ring to her."

As he stumbled out of the office, Rannie added, "Oh, one more thing."

He stopped, head sunk, back to her.

"This little pivotal battle for the soul of the church. I want you to lose it."

Honor watched him leave in wide wonder. Rannie had played Rusty like a fish the entire time. She made eye contact. "Can you take on a new client?" she asked. "I have this problem with Dombey & Trouche."

■ ■ ■

Winning the golf wager on the Belleterre Classic, a hundred dollars turning into two hundred-fifty caused Chandler Lovelace to celebrate with two bottles of Hermitage for lunch at the Carolina Yacht Club. The excellent Rhône burgundy in turn made him feel so good that he decided to go over and murder Honor Revenue's mother.

It was important Grace be absent from the picture of his pending marriage. He liked his meals deeply flavorful. Grilled squab with wild mushrooms. Sautéed black bass with saffron-mussel sauce. He wouldn't have his sybaritic pleasures put under the microbe-hunting microscope of Grace Revenue.

No fanfare and hype or particular sense of theatre about it. Nothing he felt was insidious. Just a simple strategy to alter his personal landscape for the better. Yes indeedy, he thought. Square the circle and move forward with his agenda.

He wore a blue blazer, bit tight across the middle and

under the arms. His Trinity tie. Nothing flamboyant. Appropriate regalia for a social call.

Just as he had expected, the front door was open.

"I am never disagreeable, never quarrelsome," he assured himself. "I conserve hot water. Write my bread and butter letters."

He pulled on plastic surgical gloves. It would be a simple enough matter to choke the life out of the old biddy.

The house had enormous possibilities. Garden was on a much smaller scale than it ought to be. He'd require English-style borders. Delphiniums. And there'd be no Grace Revenue underfoot to interfere with any of it.

"Helloooo! Anybody home?"

Odd. No one seemed to be around.

He tromped heavily upstairs. Ah, this must be Honor's room with the furniture still in it. Floral crest chair. Disgusting. Chest of drawers with that tedious nine-lobed shell—*coquille*—decoration across the top. The drawer fronts a riot of cornucopia, lotus and acanthus. The whole thing Japanned in an imitation of Oriental lacquer. Quite beyond the pale. A serious travesty of good taste. Ought to be burned with old automobile tires.

But while we're here, might as well go through her underwear drawer. Intriguing. Such skimpy little things. And black lace panels lending a peek-a-boo effect. Sniff the crotch. Drat. Freshly laundered. And look at the enormous cups of her bra.

What's this? A revolver?

Chandler weighed it in his hand. You knew where you stood with such a weapon. Just release this little . . .

there, opens right up. Here's where the bullets go in. Simple, really. With an automatic it was so difficult to know if there was a bullet in the chamber.

Yes, he might need this in dealing with Beau-Jack McCully. Critical short-comings in the man. No reason to share the loot with him. Sit by idly and let him profit from your labor. But he wouldn't die with a little push or a bit of a choke hold. Mid to large size sort of person. All that work with his arms. Scraping. Planing. Shaving. Lifting. Made him quite muscular.

It was odd Beau-Jack hadn't enquired about the commodes. Well, Chandler had an appointment with Rannie Ralston. She'd get them back for him and Beau-Jack none the wiser.

Yes, along with the gun let's take a pair of these black undies. Perhaps two. Seems the intimate thing to do. He and Honor would soon announce plans for their wedding. And once married, perhaps they'd recline on this very bed. He'd do a strip search of that delectable body of hers. Those larger than life bosoms. He'd claim the attention of those right early. Perhaps spank that pert little bottom of hers. Just a light birching to get her juices flowing.

He paused affronted. The bed was hideous. A gothic monstrosity with arches and crocketts in the head and foot boards. Looked like a Sir Walter Scott chapel. Sleeping in that must have seriously marred her emotional development. Such a ghastly picture above the bed. Oleographic print of a religious scene. What was it exactly? Judith of Bethulia holding aloft the dripping head of Holofernes.

Ick. Blood dripping down.

Well, he would overrule their bad taste later on. The

Revenues really needed his intellectual credentials, the Lovelace background, the aesthetics, to lend respectability to their somewhat shabby origins.

Chandler wandered out of the room and back down the stairs. Into the kitchen wondering if there was liquor there. Bit of a nip to keep the old pulse hammering. He wanted to have lemongrass chicken for dinner that evening. Perhaps a sorbet for dessert.

Newspapers were stacked in a blue plastic recycling tub. Chandler sat down heavily at the table and pulled one off the top.

He had so many things on his mind. The possibility of enlarging his income through judicious wagering. He looked at the sports page. Riverdogs edge Crawdads. LSU jars Miami. Tigers sting Yankees. Incomprehensible. And all of those giant jigaboos playing basketball. He couldn't possibly understand that.

Golf was different. It was still basically a gentleman's game. Chandler would perhaps take up golf when his life had stabilized. Maybe play the courses in Scotland and western Ireland.

Rich Weston had won the Powerbilt Belle Terre Classic. Warm glow there. Put $250 in Chandler's pocket.

Then he noticed something odd. The paper announcing the win said Tuesday, June 11.

He rubbed his nose. Today was Thursday, he was certain it was.

And wasn't it only the day before when Beau-Jack put down the bet? That would be Wednesday the 12th. Chandler looked about for a calendar. There was one hanging next to the phone.

The phone rang. He answered it. Seemed only polite. It was a policeman.

Startled, Chandler looked at the gun he had laid on the table. Nearly wet his pants. He settled down when he learned it was an official call. Took several deep breaths.

Grace Revenue's bicycle and sun helmet had been found on the middle span of the Cooper River Bridge. It was feared that she had jumped.

Chandler grunted in acknowledgement. Hung up the phone. Examined his plastic gloved hands.

He said well she's gone. Rode a bike onto the bridge and didn't come back. Simple as that. And I remain unscathed. All wrought up over nothing. Life was a higgledy-piggledy affair.

■ ■ ■

Rannie Ralston told Honor, "It's not easy to earn a living in a town with a jerk you gave a teenage blowjob."

Honor shifted a little uneasily. "I wouldn't think so," she allowed.

"You flex some muscles in public, win a good jury verdict, you feel like he's got the rumor mill going. Rannie went down on me. Rannie swallows. You'll have to forgive me for hating the guy. His hair slicked back with brilliantine like he thinks he's a Wall Street heavy hitter. 'Asshole' is the word that comes most quickly to mind. 'Toad-dick' perhaps."

Honor said she just wanted Rannie to sue Dombey & Trouche. Not hunt Browder Delamere into the grave.

Rannie snorted. "Trust me. I know how to go about this.

The practice of law is very little book knowledge. You learn with your hands. It's a world of feral beasts. Sometimes you can kill from a distance. Mostly you have to reach into the fur and choke the life out of them. A real ripsnorter with blood on the walls. You do it often enough, you get a following. Clients come in for you to sort out their tangled affairs. I'm their alter ego. I wield the club they're afraid to use. Dig the pit with the punji stakes in it."

"You charge me a third of what's mine just to get it back?"

Rannie said it was the standard fee. The difference was she got results. Anybody else would give her a load of legal bullshit, delays, feeble excuses, hidden costs.

"It just doesn't seem fair."

Rannie looked at her with mild interest. "Fair is an exalted sentiment. You meet and mingle with the wrong sort, they steal from you. No, it's not fair."

"It was a stock brokerage for God's sake."

Rannie shrugged, nonchalant. "I rest my case."

27

"Stop that atrocious gum-popping!" Chandler shouted into the phone. That harlot Cindi kept calling him, demanding money. Somehow she had figured out his number at the Romneygate House.

He had won the $250 bet. Beau-Jack had given him the money in cash. He could pay off the dreadful girl. But that seemed such a waste.

American Gladiators was on TV with the sound off. Just watching those big-thigh women battling with padded cudgels. Take the old Percival out and stroke it. There it was standing up nicely. Imagine entering them from the rear. Ram them vigorously. Make their knockers shake under them like a cow's udders.

Mummy was on his case as usual. When would he have a job? He told her he had no frivolity in his life. None whatsoever.

"I got to react with frustration here," Cindi whined over the phone. "Gettin' stiffed by you . . . it's typical of my life. Three digit deals. Clients that need a detox servicing. I got a life like a salvage sale. I'm sitting here with the question of how to face the future pressing down on me harder each day. Where's my break in life? Where's the slot machine that pays out more often than average? Ain't there some statue of limitations on bad luck?"

Yes, she called it 'statue'.

Chandler sneered, said he was sure she deserved accolades for her courage. Even if she was a boorish pig.

"Well fuck you very much, you dam' sumbitch icehole!"

He warned if she called again he'd have the law on her.

Cindi sassed she was talking to her boss man about finding a lawyer herself.

He snorted that's rich. Sue on a prostitution debt. He hung up firmly. That was that.

He flipped channels on the TV and saw the ad for a topless car wash at the Stallion Club. Perky black girls told the camera it was just good clean fun for all concerned so y'all come on out.

God there was that Cindi. He shuddered all the way down to his toes. It was like she was following him.

He almost didn't answer the phone when it rang.

"Five hunnerd smacker-roos," announced Beau-Jack all burbling cheery. "I rang the bell for you, Channy-cuz. The Hooters Pro Classic out in Louisville, Kentucky. You know the restaurant chain with the full-chested gals? You'd have loved it. You didn't have your best golfers in the world there, the purse being so small. But I got the bet down on your behalf and now Wayne's Wagering has handed over your five big ones."

Chandler faltered. "Five hundred dollars? You didn't tell me you were doing this."

"Well, you're not the most active participant in all this. Just chalk it up to cousinhood loyalty."

■ ■ ■

Talisha dragged home from the bus stop in the orange, dusty heat with her feet heavy as concrete, her nice teal-blue outfit all sweat soaked. The sophisticated urban lady. Right.

Her beat-up old Saturn had broke down right in the Episcopal parking lot as everyone was driving out on Sunday. Talk about feeling lower than a snake. Every kind of Mercedes and Lexus and Jaguar and Range Rover going past her. Saabs. Even a Rolls Royce.

Now it was ride the bus to work each day, having to change twice. Sticky seats and grimy windows. Hoodlum men trying to pick her up. Faces all shiny with sweat. Saying yeah, baby, lemme give you some cheerful abandon.

The realities of her labor market were two mean dudes in clip-on bow ties sitting out there in the waiting room. You could see the ankle holsters when they hiked up their black pants.

She owed the Muslims money that had just been owed to a honkey bank before. The ratings were low so she couldn't get the ad revenue she needed to make the thing go. Everybody stealing from her. Alvin, Roscoe, Leone. That white boy Beau-Jack wasn't around but that just meant he was up to something.

Just as she was getting ready to go home, some nut had called the station wanting her to warn the listening audience about white folks going into tanning salons without being aware of the dangers. She always tried to be polite. These were her listeners. So she listened and listened.

The white girl Honor's momma had jumped off the

Cooper River Bridge and this made her feel real bad for her. Talisha had gotten a letter from the woman two days before warning again about the lead danger in bread labels. She tried to focus on the problem. Yeah, her momma had used the bags to pack school lunches. But she'd never turned them inside out. Why would you do that?

Going up her front walk she got that "oohhhh-shit, here we go" feeling. Here come Doctor Dread getting out of a Safety Cab all stately and grand wearing a white mandarin-collar shirt and formal white jacket accessorized with a big Rolex and a bunch of gold chains. Little wizzened man with a head on him like a bird ready to peck at seed. He had come formally courting, he announced. Like some-body out of the last century. Maybe he was that old.

Talisha said she really couldn't ask him in to visit. She thought the house was slated for demolition or something.

The doctor said he tried to avoid acting overly possessive of loved ones, but he figured they were but a few formali-ties away from Holy Matrimony. Talisha was just reluctant to acknowledge the course of true love. She should not let stubborn pride stand in way of him being the answer to her concerns in life.

Trying to get past him to the door, she said, "I've got to call that idea a non-starter."

Oneida came out, pursed her lips, and said such rude-ness. Talisha wasn't too old for her transgressions to get visited with a rod on her butt.

The doctor solemnly took off his straw hat, said he had come in an effort to persuade her daughter to resume negotiations towards a marriage union of two supreme souls.

Oneida nodded yassuh. It was high time the girl got married off. Parents today couldn't do nothing with their children. The influence of television and rap music. Spoiled rotten by her daddy. Had her own telephone when she was fifteen.

Talisha yelped, "High time? I even say the word 'boyfriend' you get sick!"

Doctor Dread told her mother he generally viewed Talisha as resisting the inevitable. Given a chance, he figured to generate some momentum and once the baby was conceived she'd be all filled up with exhilaration. The phone would start ringing with congratulations. Avalanche of good will and joy.

"I presume you've an established business," asked her daddy Odis, coming out to join them on the porch. Edging in to put out the welcome mat. Sustaining male authority.

The doctor said it's alleged that he dealt in the left-hand path. Critics could claim all manner of falsehood, but there was always two sides of every bitter battle. True, he did his work when the moon was looking through tree limbs turning the gravestones white as salt. But he didn't hold with the whining and proclaiming of media-based protest politicians. If that meant no inter-state cut-offs would be named for him then so be it. He otherwise led a normal life, earned an honest living.

Talisha said she was sure his obituary would make for interesting reading.

Before Talisha knew what was going down, the doctor was in the living room sitting there with a Colt Malt Liquor in his hand and Oneida had got out the photo album. Showing him pictures of baby Talisha nekkid on a rug. Little buns up in the air. Hair tied off with ribbons like a bush of kite tails.

Oneida moaned it had been years of uphill work raising an ungrateful, tantrum-throwing child. Did he have some method to make her straighten up and fly right?

Talisha interjected that her life wasn't a cakewalk neither. Her momma would break out in hives from eating a bucket of strawberries. Decide she was dying of Dioxin and Agent Orange.

Oneida said her health was on a subsistence level. Talisha said her own personal mental health was about gone to hell and back. Her momma said to never again use profanity in her house. Talisha was about as thoroughly alienating as a daughter could get. Oneida intended on embarking on her own crusade for good health without daughterly assistance.

The three of them looked at Talisha like a puppy dog caught chewing up a furniture cushion. Shook their heads. Clucked their tongues. Needed a good swat with a rolled up newspaper. Straighten her right out.

The doctor avowed no parent should be surprised when a wild-child disappointed. Talking about her like she wasn't there. Then told them about a recent satisfied client. Family had a abusive son. Kicking holes in walls. Tearing doors off the frame. They hired some hands-on know-how from the doctor.

Oneida leaned forward all fascinated. "Did you get closure?"

He smiled, squinted with one eye. "The boy got his wake-up call. Three weeks of diarrhea so bad he had to carry a bucket around with him. Taught him he had to share his living space with a dose of blunt reality."

Oneida asked the Doc if he was good at foretelling the future? He allowed he had a small talent in that area. Indeed he had recently in a nightlong session learned from the innards of a roadkill 'possum that Talisha had an object of vast value in her possession all unknown to her. The message just kind of whispered darkly to him and he thought he would oblige by delivering it in person.

"That's so sweet," gushed Oneida, all oily. "You talking about your love for her."

Talisha went, *"What?"* Fuming and flexing her shoulder muscles. Ready to pitch a fit.

The doctor said no, this was a physical thing, best he could tell made out of wood. His love was another altruistic situation altogether. Love was ether that floated on wings that no solids could stop. Just pierced right through the other dimensions.

"Well *excuse me,*" said Talisha "while I go in my room and spread salt on the window sills."

Eyes shut, she sat on the maple bed thinking the sons-a-bitches are ransacking my life and future. Come to tell me about a treasure right under my nose. I'm supposed to ask and wheedle and beg to know what it is. Say pretty-please go grub in some other dead beast and find out the answer. Let me get just all wet in the crotch with selling my soul to Satan.

She could hear her parents talking, sounding off on their favorite themes. Oneida had lower back pain. Odis wondered if the doctor would be interested in some observations on possible conspiracies in the death of Robert Kennedy.

The phone call that came in from the station told her that Alvin Teckler had been beat to shit and the Jaguar stolen by parties unknown. He was in full traction at Roper Hospital.

Talisha stormed back out in the living room and accused the doctor of trying to get Alvin killed. How had he laid it on him? Burned a wax doll? Boiled a lock of his hair in toad oil?

The doctor said he was not lacking in natural gifts. He didn't want to be negatively in the news but there were profound aspects of his work that had to be known. Results that spell out that theme.

He had had to be right harsh with the Alvin boy. Talisha had asked that the root be applied after all. It was important that customers have confidence in the system. Mess with the doctor, you're going to get hit with something sooner or later.

"I don't want you dealing him a death blow!" Talisha shrieked. "I don't want no blood on my hands!"

"I'm just a fool in love," said Doctor Dread, smiling broadly. A big gold tooth winked at her.

28

Grace Revenue's bicycle and sun helmet had been found on the little pull-over space on the old Cooper River Bridge. No motorist came forward. The river was dragged, but at high tide, the current went out like a mill race.

The police came by to see Honor several times. They were deferential, sympathetic. They were widening their search.

The only note to Honor was a reminder to always remove the outer leaves of cabbage and lettuce. Pesticide residue collects heavily there. It was undated. Not what you'd call a suicide note. But there was something permanent about it, as if it were the last time she could remind Honor of this important safety precaution.

Rannie Ralston received a letter postmarked two days earlier warning her against the avidin in raw egg white. It binds with biotin which is a necessary vitamin, giving you a deficiency. And the salmonella risk from raw egg was monstrous.

In Honor's life, everything was put on hold. The battered women shelter. Serving sandwiches to derelicts and listening to them drool over her openly. All the hair shirt activity.

Honor could barely concentrate. The loss of a mother was like an extra sauce poured over a heap of guilt and all served up for dinner. She was drawn to the underwear drawer like the murderer in Poe's *Telltale Heart*. The gun hidden there underlined the fact that her face and body had driven a man to suicide. She had blood on her hands. She could take the veil, finish her life working in a leper colony, but the stain of guilt would remain.

Then she found the gun was gone.

Vanished into thin air.

She looked under the bed, tore everything out of the closet, dumped the dresser drawers. It was just gone.

Except for the kitchen, the downstairs of the house was devoid of furniture. Still holding the multilayered odors of soap and cleansers and detergents and wood polish and wax.

Grace Revenue had cleaned out the house, then vanished right behind her furniture, leaving Honor with no need to execute the funeral plans because there was no body. The organization seemed characteristic.

Had the gun ever existed?

Or was it just gone up in smoke?

A mysterious disappearance as the insurance companies would call it.

And like that, the self-inflicted flagellation stopped. It was over. Emotionally, she had gotten off scot-free.

Honor stayed alone in the empty house listening to the quiet. The drip of a faucet. The creak of the walls spreading in the heat.

She set willow pattern china against the baseboards to bring color to the bare house. Polished green apples. Deep green avocados. Bright yellow bananas.

There were no surprises in her life other than small acts of nature. A dead palmetto bug on the doorstep with ants swarming about it. A frog sitting still in the grass waiting to snake out its tongue at some flying thing. A watery rainbow hovering in the air when she turned on the sprinkler.

She found her camera on a closet shelf, bought film from old Mr. Burbage's wood frame little grocery on Savage Street. Solitary in the white hot light of day she photographed the houses on Legendre Street at odd jutting angles and developed them herself so she could hang the dripping blow-ups like laundry from lines of twine. Then stick them to the bare walls with tacks. Fill the rooms with the personalities of other structures.

With the downstairs of the house locked and shuttered she went naked in the hot afternoons. Sat on the second floor piazza behind the lattice screens melting slowly like butter left on a drainboard. The air conditioning she left off in respect for her mother's frugality.

She drank lemonade and iced tea and put the sweating glasses against her breasts, shivering at the deep cold on her nipples. She crushed mint leaves and smeared their sweet smell all over her thighs.

At dusk the moths seemed unduly thick in the yard although Honor left no lights on. Swifts were attracted to the bugs. And little flittering bats.

Cats began coming into the yard, attracted by the mice and birds and bats, and Honor told them to go away. Not loud. No shooing motion. Just a whisper in the dark.

And they went away. She could hear them yowling in heat two streets over.

The hot still night washed into the house and filled it

seamlessly. Her mother was in another dimension. Out there somewhere transparent and intangible. Except for the merest brushing like cobwebs.

She thought of twenty-two years of being in bed on time and up at the bust of dawn to diligently do chores. Clean sheets every week. Do good works. Save half her allowance for the offering plate on Sunday. Scrub in all the creases and don't ever touch yourself between the legs. Good girls didn't do such a thing.

But Honor had given up on being a good girl. She had granted herself permission to be a bad girl.

She lay on her back in the empty dining room feeling the wide heart of pine boards. They came from trees so old and huge that the two center cut boards were broader than human shoulders.

She lay on her back and spread her legs, dreamed of making love until her whole body ached. Pussy dripping honey. To say sweet baby don't stop and mean it so much she'd bite the blood out of his shoulder. Or the heel of his hand. Or his lips.

And then sprawl there exhausted. The smile of the well fucked on her lips. With a tiny droplet of red blood. That she would touch with the tiny pointed tip of her tongue.

But best of all, her man would be elusive in his emotions. A prodigy of cool. Moody. Distant. His eyes on far horizons and not on her.

■ ■ ■

Drinking whisky always made Rannie wake up around one or two AM, lie there thinking things over for an hour, pissed off about this or that setback in the day, until she finally fell back asleep.

That human fiasco Alvin Teckler had called her from Roper Hospital his head all swaddled in bandages that muffled his voice. He wanted her to file an uninsured motorist's claim for him against his radio station's insurance policy. She told him the necessary facts for that seemed to be absent. He insisted he had been hit by another car and that was how he got the injuries. When he woke up the car had been stolen. That was separate.

Rannie said, "You don't have health insurance at WPST. Is that what you're telling me?"

What she was thinking was well, Leone's been busy raising bail money for Booger-T. Sell the Jaguar for parts, he can probably realize thirty, maybe thirty-five thousand. He's nearing his goal.

Something was stirring in the house. A bar of light under the bathroom door in the hall. Moira was up. Probably throwing up with fear over her pending date with the rector.

It had required a little muscle application on Rannie's part. But Rusty was doing what he promised. The dinner date was set for Saturday.

What Moira was doing was washing her hands frantically with herbal soap. Sink full of suds. Water slopping all over the floor and wetting her nightgown with the little pink bows on it.

Moira always brushed her hair fifty strokes and laid out her underwear the night before. Once when they were little, Rannie had smeared anchovy paste in the underpants. Moira had sprung out of bed all chirrupy and slid into them. Then spent the next week scrubbing herself raw trying to get the stink off. Terrified that her crotch would draw cats. Died of embarrassment when she had to go to a doctor for ointment for the abrasions.

Their eyes met in the mirror. Moira's bright blue and hyper-alert. Her lemony hair fluffed in a mess like a fuzzy aura.

"Honestly, it's so hot I ought to lie in a tub of ice cubes."

Rannie pointed out there's such a thing as air conditioning.

Moira said that just gave her head colds. She kept washing, now all up her arms to her elbows.

"Life is just so unpredictable. One moment Rusty Royall's rutting like an animal with Honor Revenue. The next he's practically crawling on his hands and knees to me. I always knew he was crazy about me. All dreamy-eyed around me. Like a little boy really. Those Honor Revenue women are just a diversion because I was being difficult. Which is the only way to handle a man really. I can tell you I'm an expert on that subject.

"Soon everyone in town will be talking about us. Whispering at the Yacht Club. Saying we're such a number and aren't they just a perfect couple. Made to order. Won't Moira be just perfect helping him with all that church work?

"He'll have a lot of trouble keeping his hands off me. He wants me so bad. Can't stand to wait for the wedding night. Men are all like that. It's like scientific fact. Biology."

Rannie asked why she was washing.

Moira vigorously used the nail brush. "You know those

frogs? The ones out in the fountain that just keep up that burping urping croaking? Awful, hideous noise. Up and down. Up and down in a register of three. Daddy, momma and baby. Burr-up. Ree-gup. Eeep."

"Yeah."

"Burr-up. Ree-gup. Eeep."

"Okay, I get it."

"Well I put them over the wall. Tossed them. Flung them really. Kind of rough. Told them to find another home. But they just came right back. I was barely in bed before they had started up again."

"Yeh?"

"Well, it just got me all hot and bothered. You know I haven't been sleeping well."

"What did you do?"

"I squished them."

Rannie's eyebrows went up. "All three?"

29

"Stop calling here!" Chandler yelled boozily into the phone at the majestic Romneygate House.

He was sitting quietly watching the triple-x "Love Slaves of Cairo," savoring a single malt scotch, and this tart has to interrupt him.

"I ain't trying to fan matters up," said Cindi. "But look. I got this ungrateful boyfriend gets smoked up on crack and plays in traffic. Then wants to blame me he's in the jail house. But I was reading Ann Landers. You know, in the newspaper? And she had this little test. She said ask yourself are you better off with him or without him? It was so simple I just thought whoa! where have you been?

"Where has who been?" said Chandler suspiciously. The action of the video was terrific. Flogging the bejesus out of that Arab bitch. Look at her writhe. Buttocks like the rounded bottom of a hookah. And her pussy was shaved clean of hair. How salacious.

"Don't you get it? I thought, here's that handsome Chandler Lovelace in this great big ol' house. A model of big-ass success. So I told myself, Cindi, why don't you marry that man?"

Chandler gasped for breath. "That's absurd."

"No, I thought that. Really. I mean think about it. What does a girl do? She bangs a guy's brains out right up till after you've tied the knot. He's all dizzy with fever. Then he's cut off. No more recreational pussy.

"It's true ain't it? A man wants full frontal nudity. A cunt like a hospitality suite. He wants celebrity worship for his dick. Sex is the glue that holds marriage together. And licking the sweat off each other when we do it."

"That certainly sounds romantic."

She didn't catch his sarcasm. "And in our case, we'd be working at the thing backwards. Trying to get you set up with a hard-on. So it just makes sense don't it?"

"You're after money aren't you?" said Chandler bluntly.

"Well I expect you to let me go on buying sprees."

"You won't get a dime out of me!"

"I got a set of traffic-stopping jugs on me. I know you'd like to play telephone with them."

"No. I wouldn't."

Her voice turned cajoling. "Come awwwn now. I'm as goooo-ood as it gets."

His contempt dripped. "If that were true, I'd castrate myself."

"Well I figured you might raise objections. So I just decided we were common law married."

Chandler slammed down the phone. Common law marriage. What in the name of holy Jesus?!

The phone rang again. Chandler snatched it up. "You fucking cunt! You call here again I'll rip your tits off!"

"Don't blow a head gasket, big guy," drawled Beau-Jack McCully.

"Sorry," muttered Chandler. "I'm under a bit of pressure here lately. Money worries as usual."

"I tell you what, this US Open is where a man ought to be putting his money. You got big greens, big par fours. And all that rain up in Michigan, man, it's a bitch I tell you what. They doing the qualifying rounds and it is something else."

What Beau-Jack predicted was Fran Parkinson would be like a elevator. He'd be up and down. Fred Couples would drop out suffering back pains although unrelated to his disc problems. These would be different. He'd have a freak injury doing a chip shot. Probably Joey Gullion was the top pick. Yes, he was certain of that. On the qualifying round, mind you.

"You can predict this? You're omniscient?"

"Watch me. I'll phone up Wayne's Wagering in Columbia. Tell you the result tomorrow."

In fact, Beau-Jack said, as confidence in his system grew, he'd wager a couple of thousand. They'd need a mini-van or sport utility vehicle to move the commode to New York. Something used and in the $5,000 range. He vowed by bet number four or five he'd win that much for them.

But just now they were going for a thousand dollar win. They'd get that on Gullion.

■ ■ ■

Grace Revenue had said she wanted to be cremated and her ashes spread on the Blueridge Mountains of Virginia.

Dust to blow about and settle with dead leaves and humus at the base of trees. Sprout rhododendron. But there was no *corpus delicti*.

On the subject of corpses, the *Post & Courier* carried a peculiar story about the bullets in Judge Lorenzo being from the same gun that killed his wife back in New York. Honor thought good Lord. He had murdered the poor woman.

A week ago, a month ago, it might have driven her into black despair. His passion for her had caused him to murder? It was an obvious diagnosis.

But somehow the disappearance of the gun had lifted the blood guilt, the unremitting state of sin. The jinx was gone. Black cloud lifted.

The big Victorian house at No. 1 Legendre seemed quieter than ever. Lace curtains whispering in a faint breeze off the harbor.

Wanting the feel of green—symbol of earth, nature, life—Honor brewed a blender of lime daiquiri mix without the rum and crunched glass after glass of the tiny ice crystals and sugar. She cut open the avocadoes and scooped out the wet glistening nut. Spooned the creamy green flesh into her mouth. Tongued it until it mashed into liquid.

She was at a crossroads but it didn't matter which path she took. Each led to other forks in the road and there was no point in worrying about the road not taken.

At six one evening she dressed in ivory-colored linen which made her tanned skin look almost olive like a Greek or Italian. She thought about her personal appearance too much she knew. It didn't come from being a model on a runway. She had been a model long before. The divinity professor's daughter. Taught that she was always on display to the community eye.

Can't have you looking like a ragamuffin, her mother would say. And brush Honor's hair so violently she cried.

A faint sliver of moon was already visible in the sky. When the city lights came on, they would blot the stars.

Beau-Jack McCully's workshop was on a ratty section of Queen Street, an old cinderblock building that stretched out in back. A small walled courtyard choked with bamboo and banana plants. He lived upstairs above the work room. It was an enormous space, like a loft in the manufacturing area of an old city. You reached it by metal fire stairs on the side of the building.

She didn't really expect him to be there. It was beer drinking time. Hang out in bars with guys with ponytails and sweaty clothes. But he answered the door wearing white boxer shorts and holding a rum and coke. Just out of the shower.

"I was in the neighborhood," she said uncertainly. Then added, "No, I'm lying. I came over here on purpose."

"Hey, I'm a colossal optimist at heart," he said, standing back to usher her in. He didn't rush to cover up, say let me get my pants.

The room was long without any dividers. Little clusters of furniture to show each function. The living room area was marked by a threadbare Karastan carpet.

It was messy and filled with the eclectic oddball stuff that men tend to collect. She studied it as though it could be woven together by the eye, might have some coherent message, something to teach her about his soul.

An old moosehead. Raccoon skull. Deer antlers. Indian arrow heads. Framed box of butterflies. A Budweiser print of Custer's Last Stand. Tin signs advertising Drink Moxie and Remington firearms. An SC license plate from 1927. The Iodine State.

Beau-Jack said South Carolina vegetables had a higher iodine content than those grown in most states. In an age of goiter, it seemed like a point of civic pride. It was later they started putting iodine in salt.

There was nothing to really learn there. It was just idiosyncratic junk. And a major problem for whatever woman married him.

Except for the furniture. Which she suddenly noticed for the first time.

She knew next to nothing about it, except she knew it was exquisite. A serious, house-obsessed Junior Leaguer would go wet with lust.

"Is all this genuine?" She was really amazed.

"Reproduction."

"Get out of here."

He said some old boys played a mean game of pool, went bass fishing, hunted whitetail deer. He was into woodworking.

He gave her a short tour. Windsor chair, side chair and arm chair. High boy, low boy and serpentine chest of drawers. Adam, Hepplewhite and Sheraton. Red bay, cypress and cedar. He was very casual like it was nothing. Honor said they looked like they belonged in a museum.

Beau-Jack explained he used no electric tools. All the joints were cut, braced and pegged by hand the way they would have been done in Colonial times. He liked the aroma of wood, getting just the right tension on a cabinet door. The old designs tended to show the natural beauty of the material the best. Kind of let the wood have its say.

But enough of that. He was getting ready to boil blue crabs in a huge pot of seasoned water. Going to pull off the claws and eat them on newspaper spread on the wooden table.

She had a drink with him, filling hers with lime to cut the sickly sweet of the cola. One by one he tossed the squirming crabs into the pot, watched them struggle and then be still. Turn a bright red.

Beau-Jack told her his interest in woodworking was an outgrowth of South Carolina's public schools being among the last to ban corporal punishment. We're traditionalists down here. Know the eternal verities.

Anyhow he was a right rough boy in high school up in North Charleston. Get in fist fights in the hall, two hoodlums duking it out, with the teachers too scared to break it up. Gutless weasel of a principal cowering in his office. Blame the teachers later for not having a better grip on things.

Well there was one teacher who did have a whale of a grip. Old Mister T.C. Wyrick who taught shop and had been an army m.p. which all the guys thought was cool. Shop was dangerous as heck with all the sharp objects and buzz saws and stuff so Wyrick carried a cut-down canoe paddle and didn't hesitate to use it to maintain order. And he had biceps on him the size of smoked hams.

One day he got pissed at Beau-Jack and did his usual routine which was to bend you over a work table and lay into you until you cried. Reduce you to blubbering in front of your peers and you were pretty much tame from there on out. It was amazing psychology in its own way.

"So this made you an honest, upstanding citizen?"

"Well not entirely. But I was so anxious to please him after that that I took an interest in woodworking and it kind of stuck with me. Gave me something to do with idle hands that as you know are the devil's workshop."

Honor's clothes were too fine for the greasy meal. She looked at his boxer shorts. Without much thought, peeled down to her underwear. Following instinct.

As a child she had tea parties on a bedspread under the dogwood tree in the yard. She thought boys were creatures with dirty faces you had to boss and banish when they acted ugly and broke things. Dolls and teddy bears and her cocker spaniel were so much more malleable. She had no idea how delicious it would be one day to watch a set of white boxer shorts and wonder if there was movement under there. If a hard-on was rearing its head.

Honor knew her way around crabs. Knew how put a knife under the belly apron and pull off the back. Scrape out the viscera. Break the body in half and pick out the lump. Crack the claws and suck them clean.

The whole time they ate she felt the tug of temptation, the need for full spectrum-sexual intercourse. Screwing. Banging. Bouncing off the walls fucking. An act of defiance against her absence of sadness.

She tossed her hair, wondered what exactly it was women did when they wanted to be seductive. Men always said she did it without effort. She had never had to consciously try before.

He didn't react. She couldn't believe it.

"Are you having an affair with Browder Delamere's wife?" she asked.

He didn't skip a beat. "I sold her some furniture. Big chest-on-chest. That's a chest-of-drawers with the top chunk set back a bitty step from the bottom. Original was made in Connecticut around 1800. Conical finials. Carved swirl and heart-shaped cutouts. It was a nice piece of work. I'm quietly proud of it."

"Anything else?"

"New England high post bedstead. Eastern Virginia cupboard. Eastlake style library table. They've got a lot of houses. I guess you know that."

"You're not answering my question."

He wiped his hand on a towel and then slid it up her thigh. His eyes clicked on hers.

"Do you want to make love?" she asked.

"Do you?"

They both considered the joint proposition.

"Let's not beat around the bush," she said, unsnapping the front of her bra. Letting those omnibus hooters flop out into full view. Nipples flat in becoming modesty.

The bed was Honduras mahogany with nine-foot posts carved with rice plants. Honor climbed up on it and waited.

There was no menace in his nakedness. She knew how she felt inside. Knew she wanted it. That it would be easy and slow and good. That she had long legs and a long pelvis and could take every inch of him. And yes there it went all the way in just as she had expected. And she bucked and rode up against it. Milking each stroke of all its pure sensation.

Right in the middle she found herself thinking that freezing meat does not purge it of Salmonella. It only stops the growth. And room temperature was perfect for triggering it off again.

She forced herself to concentrate. She could fake an orgasm with the best of them. Be a wind-up sex toy. But no, it was taking hold. God yes there it was.

Her loins were on fire. She thrashed and twisted beneath his weight. She was too keyed up to take it slowly.

When she came she saw a collision of moon and stars and planets with other moons in orbit. She lay there gasping and damp, her body squeezed out like a sponge. Drained of all emotion.

He lay limp and heavy on top of her. Heart pounding.

"I've got a full warranty," he wheezed. "If you want to buy me. Or I'll give myself away for free. But don't rush. You've got plenty of time to decide. I'll give you a ninety-day option. Or one-twenty if you want."

Passion had evaporated and now sleep came like an arbitrary end to their languid affection. It lasted for several hours until Honor woke up with a start in the grayish blue light of the night.

Beau-Jack was sleeping peacefully.

Her mother's face had waked her. A memory of Grace Revenue and minister's wife decorum. Honor believed that ghosts were visions of the dead that our subconscious wills to return. We need their comfort or their blessing or forgiveness.

Dried semen lay on Honor's belly like the powder of a moth. Or sugar from a glazed doughnut. She brushed it away.

She got up and went into the living room area, turned on a light looking for something to read.

A newspaper article said the Japanese were at high risk from cancer of the esophagus and bone marrow damage due to a heavy consumption of bracken ferns.

It brought her to the verge of tears.

30

Rannie watched Chandler Lovelace waddle grandly into her inner office, accept the offered chair. Dressed in his version of full fig. Trinity College necktie that ended at the bulge of his huge gut. Seersucker suit that might split at the seams at any moment. He was sweating and smelled of morning booze. The heat outside was like wet wool.

She gave him only a fraction of her attention, her brain mainly working on the problem of her mother's outlandish expenses in Italy. Mary Canty had shipped home a *trompe l'oeil* topiary tree painted on wood, a wrought iron table festooned with birds, and 15—yes, she counted them—15 gold-leaf frames to put God-knows-what in. And all at God-knows-what cost.

She wondered how much Chandler's trust fund was worth. He used to brag about it a lot when he was younger. Act like he was some junior Croesus in the making. Well, she had a plan for getting her hands on a goodly piece of it. Get him up against the ropes and slap him around good.

She had gone to the Day School with this sodden buffoon. All the boys bullied him, ducking his head in the commode. He'd have intense conversations with himself. Would try to pull his sweater on over his book bag. He was her age and had never held a job.

Chandler observed aloud that the office could be in a forty year ago time-warp. He seemed to be approving. Not that Rannie gave a rat's ass what he thought. But she left that unspoken.

Rannie said she kept it the way it had been when her Daddy practiced law. Mawkish sentiment aside, it kind of spoke to her spiritual longings. Her Daddy belonged to a lost world. Everyone living on well understood terms. The old rituals still intact.

"It's a vanishing world, our traditional Charleston," she observed sagely. "The eccentric personalities. The crooked politics. Family hatreds as intense as Montagues and Capulets."

Chandler agreed fully. "Even the habitat is going. Yankees bidding the best houses up to a million bucks, a million-five. The small places going for three hundred as *pied-à-terres*. Frightful. Where are Charlestonians expected to live? The brick suburbs of West Ashley?" He shuddered.

It was tacky, Rannie nodded. All the change for the worse. Subdivisions named for the old plantations. The oak bowered road to Summerville chewed up, the trees cut one by one.

Chandler said he despised wire coat hangers from the dry cleaners. He would only hang his trousers on proper wooden ones. It was in small ways that continuity with the past was maintained.

He gazed out the window smugly. Acting like he had better places to be. Better worlds to live in. Said he was obliged to make an unprecedented personal disclosure. He had an object of modest value that needed to be retrieved from some colored people. He wanted the law on his side to minimize the acrimony.

Rannie asked what it was. He said a family heirloom. Been with the Lovelaces for centuries.

She said those were always full of sentiment. Heirloom was a nice word.

"We need a strong model of the family," he moralized. "No man is an island and all that."

Rannie seconded the emotion. Was he thinking of getting married?

That startled him. But his eyes really bulged when Cindi came in and sat down looking anxious and excited. The ambush was sprung. He was in a box canyon with the Comanches up on the ridge.

"This young lady needs to satisfy a grievance," Rannie announced. "Came to me all upset about her treatment at your hands. Her story bothers me a lot. I ask myself, 'what is it I can do to help? How can I make a difference?' I try to think in terms of Total Quality Management even in my personal life."

Cindi fidgeted. Chandler did a slow boil.

"Very well," he said truculently. "I'll pay her wretched bill. What is the total? A hundred-fifty dollars?"

"Yew tole me we was married," Cindi insisted. "Yew tole ever-body at the car wash."

Shock jerked him to his feet. "You're out of your damned gourd!" he squawked.

Rannie put an emery board to her perfect nails. "In South Carolina, common law marriage is established by a couple merely holding themselves out as being married. That's it. *Tout court* to use some French. You know French don't you?"

He was spluttering. She raised a hand to silence him. "You're asking what is she willing to do to accomplish her goals? The answer's simple. Whatever it takes."

"They're lying!" he wailed. "Pack of cheap harlots! Wagging their lascivious tits at a negro car wash!"

Rannie's face was devoid of expression as she pointed out that's why we have courts and juries. To determine who's telling the truth. But should he want to avoid the unpleasantness of a lawsuit, he could officially marry Cindi before a minister of whatever organized religion he chose. Well, not whatever. No Scientology. No Moonies. But something mainstream. Although Cindi's preference was Episcopalian. She wished to rise in life.

Chandler flopped back into the chair. Kind of a squeak came out of his open mouth. Flecks of spittle on his lips.

Rannie asked what had she left out? Did she need to make use of graphics?

Cindi said for Chandler to not worry about his pecker not standing up. She was going to make it the focus of a fitness program. Strength training. It didn't need to go into some kind of backlash.

Chandler gagged, "Some kind of . . . ?" His face flushed beet red. He began doing his best to rip the arms off the chair. "What is this rank insanity? I get a few reverses and now everyone piles on? Is there blood in the water?"

"I can be real submissive," purred Cindi. "You can boss me around, be the man of the house. Really. I'm a low self-esteem person. In heavy traffic I get scared to change lanes."

"I'll tell you what you are! You are . . . you are . . . you are an *acute embarrassment!!*"

"There's no need to verbally assault me," said Cindi, a little miffed. She crossed her legs and rotated an ankle. Her slave bracelet twinkled.

What Rannie was thinking with half her mind was Rusty Royall would sign into the Mills with Moira under an assumed name. But as man and wife. It would be the leverage she needed. They'd be common law married.

Chandler's eyes had gone blank. Voice whining with a stunned self-pity. "I lead a blameless quiet existence. I think that I can opt out of the filth of life."

Rannie gave a short laugh. "You know something, Chan? You're really a sack of shit."

■ ■ ■

"Country fresh poultry LAIG quarters, thirty-nine cents a pound!" resonated the Reverend Roscoe B. Morningstar from the pulpit of St. Ambrose. "Lemme proclaim that again. LAIG quarters . . . thirty-nine cents a pound!" He waved his arms, flapping his gown like a big purple bat.

The white congregation watched him cautiously. Sickly smiles. Straining to show how polite they were. Then he launched into what totally mystified them.

"Lemme SPEAK my mind
on MO-rality mankind.

Steps not taken,
EGGS unbreaken.
Need a ACTION agenda
Fo' Tom and Belinda.
Don't put NO price tag
On lost kids with a DOPE bag."

Most of the congregation had heard of rap music but never actually listened to it. Other than the thudding boom-boom-boom of the base out of some stereo in a car loaded down with negroes when they were trapped next to them at a red light. Afraid to look over and make eye contact. Saying come on come on light. Change dammit.

But Roscoe was sure enough throwing himself into it. Impassioned. Swatting at the air like he was battling demons.

What frankly disturbed the old guard was how the charismatic element began waving their hands over their heads and swaying with the rhythm. Getting into their ecstatic mode.

Roscoe hit a peak performance. Oblivious of the mixed effect. Stentorian tones thundering. And, well . . . cavorting. Doing jerks and leaps. Now sticking in a little chorus as an exclamation mark.

"Don't bury me DEEP,
Beneath that HEAP.
Glory to God!
Gonna CLIMB that mountain,
DRINK the Lord's fountain.
Glory to God!"

The charismatics started chanting it along with him. Glory to God. Glory to God. The church echoed with them.

Every once in a while a young black woman—Talisha Mackey—in a raspberry choir robe would come forward and mop Roscoe's head with a large handkerchief like he was James Brown with the Fabulous Flames. Although that image would have been lost on the congregation as well.

At these moments, he'd take a semi-breather from the rhyming verse but never really shut up.

"I got my primary (gasp) and my back-up systems (whuff) going here," he proclaimed, giving it those gospel gasps. Fighting for breath. He said deviation from the Lord (gasp) would bring a hard response (whuff). And then it was back into the swing.

"School breakfast PRO-gram,
Go down like EGGS and ham.
Praise the Lord!
Fam'bly and eddication
Make a good relation.
Praise the Lord!
Bless his name!"

At least half the church squirmed uncomfortably in their seats. The other half were swimming like fishes in the sea.

Suddenly he stopped. Whump. Silent.

Voice down low and prayerful. Head bowed.

"Lemme evoke some reverence here."

Pause. Snap head back. Look around solemnly. His face

streamed with sweat. The black girl fanned him with her robe.

"LEG quarters . . . thirty-nine cents a pound."

Pause.

"Chuck roast . . . dollar nineteen a pound. LIMIT two packages please."

Pregnant pause. Muscles swelling in his neck. Nostrils flaring like he was on the verge of breathing fire. Both fists up beside his head. Now shouting:

"Sex ain't some CHOICE like going between sirloin beef tips and chicken ENTRÉE!"

Well. That certainly got their attention.

General astonishment.

Incredibly, this led him into St. Paul's admonition against homosexuality. He quoted from Romans about men abandoning the NATURAL function of the woman, getting INFLAMED with desire for one another and com-mittting the shameless deed. He said space ain't LIM-ITED in heaven but the way folks ACTING today you'd sure believe there was competition for only a few spots left in hell.

He paused and fixed the congregation with a baleful eye. Pointed a finger at the front row which shrank inside themselves. "They will receive IN THEMSELVES . . . the PENALTY . . . which their PERVERSION . . . DESERVES!"

Underline. Full stop.

An approving murmur broke out in the congregation. AIDs they whispered. Well, of course. We should have known it was all predicted in scripture. Thank goodness someone still has the courage to take a stand.

Arms thrust into the air with an explosive movement. "I won't be made HOSTAGE to the WHIMS of the time!"

Pause. Glare.

"Won't bow down to SIT-U-ATION MO-RALITY!"

Pause. Glare some more.

"Won't KNEEL to the so-called agenda of GAY HOLLYWOOD!"

Well. To say that they ate it up would be an understatement. A considerable number gave serious thought to inviting Roscoe to preach for the full month of August when Rusty took his annual vacation. He seemed ideal really.

During the offering Roscoe told them to "GIVE! Give in defiance of sin and the DEVIL'S work!" He said they were "going for the full service gas here so y'all pay up according! High test soo-preme with an oil change and going through the car wash afterward!"

Money poured into the plates. People simply emptied out their wallets. Many wrote checks. Roscoe kept the metaphors flowing.

"You hear about flexible terms and low, low rates. Well a first class ticket to HELL comes absolutely FREE of charge! No loan terms or debt consolidation to mess round with! Easy and INSTANT approval!"

Honor emptied loaded offeratory plates into a grocery bag and sent them back. They kept being filled to overflowing like Roscoe had them all hypnotised.

"The fields of the Lord ain't ADJACENT! They ain't CONTIGUOUS! They right under yo' FEET! So let's keep 'em GREEN!"

When she carted the bags and plates off to the office, Honor was simply flabbergasted at the piles of cash she had to count. There had never been such a collection before.

She heard Roscoe's voice booming: "Now lemme retire amidst the GLORIOUS pomp of y'all singing that spirited Hymn 293 . . ."

Rusty came in and gathered up a wad of money and stuck it in his pocket. It would have been pretty obvious even without the problem of getting his robe hiked up to do it.

The church echoed with the loudest singing Honor had ever heard.

"Um . . . I'm responsible for the count," Honor said tentatively.

He looked at her vaguely. "I hear your concerns," he said. It wasn't his snooty voice. He seemed fuzzy and even disoriented. "I think I can compromise on most issues. Hmm? Abortion rights but no government funding of abortion. That kind of thing. But it doesn't really work out. Nobody wants to let me have my half a loaf. So I start demanding all of it in self-defense."

Honor said if he wouldn't mind too much how about putting the money back? Or if he was determined to take it, tell her how much so she could record it as coming out of the petty cash fund.

Their conversation was like two circles that overlapped in part.

"It's vivid preaching. Yes. But they're gaping at him like hicks at the county fair. They've given all this . . . all this money. And I have to finance a date with Moira Ralston. It won't be cheap." He gave Honor a round-eyed look. "Sure, you're saying I've got free will. But Rannie says I don't. That's not a compromise. It's an armed truce."

"Rusty, not to contradict whatever in heck it is you're saying, just getting back to the issue at hand—you have to put the money back."

He gave her that shy, boyish smile she remembered from the first time they met. Just a trace of dimples showing.

His slim fingers snaked around her throat. Tightened. "Love is stronger than death," he hissed.

She smacked his hands away. Said he must be having trouble with depth perception. Not knowing where his hands belong.

"You're not being very agreeable," he said. He giggled. Then grimaced.

"What are you being? Yourself? If so, you need a personality transplant."

He said he resented her tone. He wouldn't stand for it. Sounded real petulant. Like he was about to stamp his foot.

Honor reminded him they shouldn't be alone together. Their last personal encounter got him jammed up with Moira. This time it might escalate to the mother. He'd have to marry Mary Canty Ralston when she came back from Italy. And maybe adopt Moira.

This hit home in a visceral way. "I'm very confused," he lisped as he scuttled out. He left, however, without giving her any hard numbers on how much money he took.

31

Rusty Royall used his best Episcopal voice. "My sermon today *deals* with the creator as *fecundator* of the earth." He wore half-glasses, kind of looking down his nose at some notes, then up at the small sea of black faces.

After the rip-roaring success of Reverend Roscoe at St. Ambrose, Rusty was exchange preaching at St. Memphis Church of Synagogue AME up on Darnelle Street in the really poor black quarter of Charleston that runs unbroken along the railroad tracks to the neck of the peninsula.

Talisha had joined with him in arranging this and had all her equipment set up next to the choir stall to broadcast it live for WPST. It was a new dimension for the station. She didn't realize just how new, but she soon found out.

"God as *husband* . . . to the *land* and people."

Amen, someone said out in the crowded pews. Throats cleared. Feet shuffled.

"The sun's orb . . . as *divine* penis."

Talisha took off her earphones going what? What did he say?

Her parents were on a nearby row, nodding and tapping their feet. They considered St. Memphis an extremely socially inferior church—poor as dirt, tarpaper brick on the outside walls, naugahyde upholstery buttoned on the pews—but had come as a marvelous opportunity to criticize everything she was doing. Oneida was sitting very stiff in a new girdle she had bought special for the event.

"The *church*, much as the *temple* of Baal in the East, is divided into *three* parts. The *porch* which symbolizes the labia and vagina up to the hymen. The *Veil* which is in truth the hymen. Then the *Hall*, which is the vagina proper."

Folks looked around with wide open wondrous eyes. They were used to ministers using big words they couldn't understand. Fecundator had slid past them. But they knew penis and vagina.

"The *priest* with his mitred hat, or foreskin, or drill, or head of penis, whichever . . . *penetrates* the hymen . . . *advances* to the womb . . . spreading magic oils or incense. Semen as it were. The Word as *fructifying* seed."

Talisha realized at the same time as everyone else that the man done flip out. There was loud talk. Some Oh Lawdy what is this? Some watch yo' mouf', preacher man. They's ladies and chirrun here.

The five deacons locked eyes, and without a word exchanged, made a moral decision. They strode up the center aisle in a black suited mass to forcefully lead him outside. He resisted. They started to scuffle. Had to haul him out bodily, carrying him by arms and legs. Dump him out there on the dusty ground wearing that white cassock as milk white as the man's face.

"Jerusalem means 'city of the heavenly womb'!" he proclaimed, lying on his back. "The sexual imagery is so powerful! It was seen as holding up the sky in the way that the axle-shaft of the penis divides the splayed out legs of a woman groaning in sexual intercourse!"

Those who had family history of mental illness, involuntary commitments and such were saying he needed to mainline some lithium. Maybe get a shock treatment. Stop being an embarrassment.

Up on his feet, smeared with red dust, Rusty was shouting. "Two valleys came together like the open and inviting legs of a woman! The mount of Zion was the *mons veneris.* The Temple of Solomon was the womb!"

"Oh man they got problems wid him," said Odis shaking his head sadly. "Things is definitely not percolating well. Nossir. Might as well tell traveling salesman jokes."

Talisha held her eyes closed thinking business. Bank debt. Muslim debt. Advertisers. They had no show. There went the ratings. Lord knows who out there had heard the penis and vagina part. Busting the hymen with a mitre hat. FCC complaints. Total shut down. What to do? God help me what to do!

Clenching her fists against an urge to scream, she told her daddy to come congregate over in the corner with her. She told him if she shut down for an hour the sponsors would be furious and refuse to pay up.

He said well after this fol-de-rol that white man was sure not very likely to be invited socially into too many homes of the St. Memphis folks. He'd have to get his own fried chicken and biscuits. Stop by Col. Sanders.

Talisha said listen to me. Her only hope was to capitalize on his memory of the night Robert Kennedy was shot. She said that's the area where they're looking at things now at this point. Him playing a public service role.

He allowed he could do it. Down at the city water works he was accustomed to working without a net. She said open them valves. Let the microphone be a clearing house for your memories.

As ususal, Odis didn't need a whole lot of prompting. Just stuck his thumbs in the armholes of his suit vest and kind of launched right in.

He began June in L.A., California is much like May or January for that matter. It was always pretty warm. Always a bunch of sunlight. But the story begin at night at the Ambassador Hotel, a fine place then and now. A place of fancy cars and palm trees and a *maitre d'* of *hotel* in a tuxedo what would snap his fingers to signal a team of waiters come hopping, swish things off the table smooth as silk.

The Resurrection's Children Choir started singing to fill the time until the regular preacher could get his act together. Talisha adjusted her dials and let the choir bleed in to provide a musical fabric.

Talisha didn't dare call it a modest success. But she was filling the air time. She wouldn't have some mess of FCC forms to fill out explaining how a high class white minister started talking about God's wet dick and hairy balls and she had to shut down the station.

Figuring Talisha needed some more problems heaped on, her momma Oneida then took her aside and said her systolic blood pressure was acting up and she needed to get home. Let's go and no dawdling.

Talisha insisted she was busy trying to save her future and had to be exempt from this nonsense for at least an hour. Just one hour was all she asked. Look at the watch. Sixty minutes. Sit back and enjoy the choir.

Oneida said she wasn't hearing-impaired. She knew a rude daughter when she heard one. She was familiar with that situation. Uh-huh sure enough. Thinking about they ownselves all the time. Wanting Godless material objects. Well she had to deride that attitude.

Talisha counted one, two, three, four, five. Said this year to date . . . six, seven, eight, nine, ten . . . this year to date, she got no Ferrari, no fur coats, no diamond Rolex watch.

Oneida wasn't listening to that argument. She said don't look at her like she got two heads. It's a early warning signal of being locked off in the county home. Ungrateful children get you to sign everything over to them so you in poverty and can live on the government for free. Don't want to provide the systemic support a child owes a parent. Got you going and coming.

Talisha's Daddy was now in the kitchen making apple Waldorf salad while Robert Kennedy was finishing up his speech and about to cut through to avoid the big mob of photographers and well-wishers. Work was going on usual in the kitchen, nobody realizing Death was lurking there.

Odis said, "Now Miguel he wasn't much on chopping cabbage for your cole slaw. Would tear it apart with his hands. But I ask you. Who is beyond reproach?"

■ ■ ■

Cindi was crunching ice from her tea saying, "I don't use drugs or alcohol although ever-body around me has always been involved in what some used to call the drug scene. I go to church whenever possible."

Chandler was only half listening. He stared with horror

at her picture in the newspaper advertising the Stallion Club. She was thrusting out her chest with pasties on the nipples. "Showtime for Boys & Girls" trumpeted the ad. "Let Cindi Do You Right."

Rannie Ralston was forcing him into a *mésalliance* with this monstrosity to avoid being sued for common law marriage.

He had agreed to meet Cindi in a sleazy café over on the Savannah Highway to discuss their nuptials. Kept flinching, fearing he knew people although that was patently impossible in this dive. But he'd whip open the newspaper to hide behind it, and that was how the ad jumped out at him.

God the harsh reality coming screaming at him in broad daylight. His head was splitting open. He needed aspirin. He needed several drinks of any grade or proof of liquor. He wanted to lie down in a canopied bed in the Romneygate House. Let its massive walls shelter him from this vile creature.

Hot sunlight glared through the plate glass front window, the green lettering casting a slanted shadow on the wall. Cindi was devouring a fried pork chop sandwich which was the Sunday lunch special along with the hyper-sweet ice tea. Talking with her mouth full. "Well, I didn't have the best home environment. Paw-paw was always trying to wet his willie in me."

"Wet . . . his willie . . ."

"Well, that's what he called it. I didn't graduate with my high school class. Later on, I got a equivalent whatever they call it. Bought that diploma down in Mobile, Alabama for thirty-five dollars. I'm thinking of attending community college, maybe with the aim and goal of becoming a cosmetologist."

She leaned in across the café table real close, huge breasts mashing down on the Formica. "And I'm real good at CPR."

"CPR?" Chandler asked.

"Yew know. Swapping spit? Tongue and groove work?" She sat back and took a huge bite of sandwich. Chewed thoughtfully. "No, I got that wrong. That's you going down on me. But you get the idea."

Chandler knew he wasn't thinking clearly. That evil bitch Rannie Ralston. The threats. The ramifications of the threats. Mind boggling. He was supposed to marry this trash creature and then blithely hand over half of his trust fund. Out of which Rannie would take a hefty fee. It was monstrous. Beyond belief.

Now Cindi was demanding to meet his mummy. He had to create a plausible cover story. Something to minimize the hideous humiliation in some way no matter how minor.

Cindi would be in college. That was it. Reed College in Oregon. Experimental curriculum. All manner of zany oddballs there. Eccentrics. All the college girls seem to have tattoos now. And she's from the West Coast. Hence no one in Charleston knows her. And her major? Yes. Sociology. It would explain her interest in all the trash she talked. If anyone sees the club ads, he'd say she was doing research for her master's thesis. Girls do that sort of thing nowadays. Work as hookers even and then write dissertations on it.

He presented his plan to Cindi in reasonable tones. Said

this would be for the best. He had a position in Charleston to think of. She must respect that. Surely.

His hands were shaking. Didn't they at least have a beer license in this common-as-muck place?

Cindi balked initially. Said what's wrong with being herself? If folks couldn't accept her, that was their problem, not hers. She ate the side orders of potato salad *and* baked beans which cost extra. Tea refills were *gratis* at least. Chandler had planned on a truffle vinaigrette with his evening meal and now this cunt was going to cost him close to ten dollars.

He said it was an opportunity for her to stretch as an actress. Wouldn't that be fun? To be an actress? She had to play it this way. Trust him. His mummy was a very difficult personality. Exceedingly. Cindi wanted to have a good relationship with her didn't she?

She grumbled well okay. But she was going on record as saying it was a mistake.

And then she started cracking her knuckles. One slow painful finger at a time. It made Chandler squirm.

He had to get a winning bet down on golf. He had to retrieve the commode. The bet. That was the first thing. He needed liquidity desperately. He needed his trust fund. Lash all that together and he'd have enough cash to take off. Hide where Rannie Ralston couldn't find him. Wait for mummy to kick off. Come into the larger inheritance. New Zealand might work. Tasmania.

Frantically he went to the pay phone, dinged in a quarter and dialed Beau-Jack and in a garbled rush told him he needed to get a wager down on golf. Beau-Jack said, "Hey, man, you just won a thousand bucks on Gullion on the qualifying round. I got it here in long green waiting for you."

"It's not enough," Chandler wailed. "I need more." He danced up and down like he needed to pee.

Beau-Jack said, "Well shit man you're welcome for what I'm doing for you. Busting my ass. Taking all the risk. You're going to have to put up some capital of your own. Don't really have to lay it on the table. Just open a bank account with both our names on it. Wayne's Wagering would be content with that level of security."

Chandler protested he didn't have any money. Use the thousand he had just won. Beau-Jack said shucks that wouldn't do much good. If he wanted a real win, he had to bet some real money. Four-five thousand dollars. Or did he want to risk ten? Really bet the farm?

"Who's that?" said Cindi coming up behind him. She had followed him. God she was picking her teeth.

"Quiet," Chandler hissed at her. "It's my cousin Beau-Jack."

"Oh yeh. I know him. He's kind of how we met in the first place. I'm real grateful to him. Hey, Beau-Jack! Yoo-hoo from Cindi."

Chandler roared at her. "WILL YOU PLEASE SHUT UP?"

Heads swivelled in the café.

"Well shore," said Cindi. "If that's the way you want it. You gotchore unnerware stuck in your ass-crack?"

The phone fell to the floor. Chandler put his head in his hands, his whole body shaking with frustration and rage. He couldn't think. Said aloud, "Things cannot get any worse."

"Well, I guess that depends on your perspective," said Cindi. "I just figured out I'm pregnant. We'll have a little instant addition to our fambly."

He hadn't touched the bitch. Hadn't laid a pecker on her. He wouldn't be responsible for this. There was no way he would assume paternity. It wasn't part of his deal with Rannie.

Then an awful thought struck him. That grinning gold-toothed jig that owned the Stallion Club . . . Cindi's negress friends . . .

"What *color*," he said very carefully, ". . . is . . . your boyfriend?"

"He's black," said Cindi. "How come? Yew prejudice?"

On the floor, the telephone receiver was saying, "Listen, Chan-cuz. What's the story on that trust fund of yours? Why don't you dip into that?"

32

"You ain't restoring my faith in mankind," Luscious Decatur declared. "I don't run no string of hoes. I'm a night club what features freedom-of-expression nude dancing. Got a door-to-door marketing effort out there trying to turn around bankruptcy. Getting with the era of accelerated growth."

Chandler had paid $20 to go through the topless car wash in an attempt to persuade Luscious Decatur to get Cindi off his back. Now standing next to Mummy's shiny clean Oldsmobile, having their business chat, Luscious was not being cooperative.

"You figure I own them gals? Sheee-it. What you must think of my valued employees. It's just a whole world of widespread denial of human dignity.

"You think I glean them gals from leftovers down at the bus station? Walking the street up there on Spruill Avenue? You think they got handicap disabilities? We got testing and evaluation here. We got rehabilitation programs for them what into drug use."

"I told you I'd pay your price," Chandler insisted. "Within reason of course."

"Man, we gonna have some awkward repercussions

when my foot get connected with your fat honkey ass. This ain't a risk-free situation in your case. What I recommend is you make like Harry Houdini and disappear."

Acutely conscious of the loss of his twenty dollars, Chandler drove to WPST, a dreadful hole of a place in the unincorporated no-man's-land between Charleston and North Charleston. Bouncing over abandoned railroad tracks. Past burned-out buildings, weed and garbage filled lots. Smoke stacks and maze of utility poles against the sky. The huge Cooper River bridges showing across the water in the distance.

Chandler disliked dealing with negroes—always sullen or else outright violent—but having to do it twice in one day was over the top. He thought he'd go barking mad.

Cement bunker of a building with the big radio tower. Spray paint graffitti all over it. Weeds around the base of the walls. Litter everywhere. With deep foreboding, he went in the front door. There was the furniture stacked at random.

He was shown up to a second floor office by the ugly brute coon who had carried it away from his mother's house. Leone something. A half-way presentable colored girl sitting there behind a desk.

And there were the twin commodes. No sudden moves to give away his interest. But it was certainly odd they were here while the rest of the furniture was heaped downstairs. Had they guessed at their value?

A simple direct style was the best approach, he decided. The girl whatever her name was—Talisha-something— seemed half way civilized when he described the mix-up over the commodes. He took the story slowly so as to not confuse their simple brains. Saying they were indispensable items in his household. He really must have them back. He'd bring a truck this afternoon if that was convenient.

He gave them his genteel smile. Settled back in the chair to wait their agreement.

They stared at him like he was some curiosity. Her and that other big nig-nog Leone slouched against the wall cracking his knuckles like walnuts.

Talisha grimaced, "Commodes?"

"Yes."

"Like as in 'sit on the pot' commodes?"

Chandler shook his head, simpered. "It's a French word." He gestured to the twin Tivertons.

Talisha said these commode things were on the roster of furniture that came in. She was keeping them.

Mild consternation. "They're mine," Chandler insisted. He tugged at his shirt, lifting the sweat soaked cloth off his skin.

"Says who?"

Chandler was furious. He was thinking you sorry thieving jigaboos. Give you the slightest edge and . . . What he said was, "We don't have to make this a matter for lawyers. That's so expensive after all. I'm here to negotiate. I'm using honied tones. I'm reticent. Very nearly obsequious."

Leone put in, "You know in a world of drug-related violence, you'd hardly expect to find it in a gospel station. But it's kind of like an aspect of my persona. Wanting to whup up on annoyances. Wanting to beat they ass."

The girl Talisha interjected she was serving notice right

here and now there were no drugs in the station. Not a felony amount. Not a misdemeanor.

Leone said he was focusing only on the violence part of that statement. And he was ready to put Chandler on the disabled list if he didn't get his fat, chicken-white ass out of the station.

Talisha said okay, she had no objections to that. Settled back in her chair and crossed her arms.

It was the second time in one day Chandler had been called fat by some low-grade blackamoor. "Overweight am I?" he huffed. "I'll show you some nimble dexterity. I'll set my attorney on you. Cry havoc and unleash the dogs of war." He stood up, slapped his Panama hat on his head and stormed out.

"Yeah, you take a leave of absence, buckra-boy," Leone called after him.

Chandler stood in the outer office waiting room heaving for breath. Sweat was running out of his hatband. He felt clammy and dizzy like he had heat exhaustion. He could hear their voices back inside.

"You can leave now your own self," said Talisha.

"Meaning what?" said Leone.

"Meaning take a hike."

Leone said yeah, he'd take a respite from her abuse. Maybe she could work on her intolerance while he was out.

In the waiting room, two negroes in sunglasses and bow ties were staring at Chandler. They looked like cannibals ready to pounce ravenously on him. Shivering, he stumbled down the stairs.

Outside the station in the heat, Chandler leaned up

against the wall. He didn't think he could stagger the short distance to his car. He needed a drink. Why hadn't he brought a flask?

Leone came out behind him and asked if he had a smoke. No? Well, what about the time? Chandler hesitated, then peeked at his watch warily, figuring Leone was going to hit him the second he was distracted. He said it was 11:15.

Leone said he'd figured it was about sometime around there. Was Chandler wondering about what he just heard? He said him and Talisha had a relationship went back to early days. He was reticent to criticize, but she tended to take him for granted.

"Not your cup of tea?" said Chandler, still wary.

"Yeah it's tough around here, this Jesus music. No Boyz II Men. No Chaka Khan. She won't even go Brazilian capoeira or West African rhythms. I'm getting a clearer perspective on things. Maybe see my way through to some collaboration elsewhere."

Chandler waited, sensing he was about to receive a proposition. They were always up to some low shenanigans, the coloreds.

Leone said he had hated how the two of them got out of synch back in there. What he was wondering was how much that commode thing was worth. He didn't mean to show any great interest. Just curious was all. Talisha was not real open with information.

Chandler stroked his chin putting on a thoughtful look. He said maybe $20,000 out of which there could be an allotment of $1,000 for Leone should his assistance in recovery prove adequate.

The big nig-nog gave him a wink and a thumbs-up sign. "Hey, Sierra Leone Jones to the rescue. I think there's a message coming out here. That I can make a difference in your life."

■ ■ ■

Talisha was still working so many grueling shifts at WPST she didn't have time to think much on some fat white man coming by saying he wanted furniture back. It wasn't his anyhow. Rusty Royall had given it to her.

What Talisha thought was funny was that after her Daddy Odis taking over the Sunday show—doing his Robert Kennedy thing—the ratings had done a little blip up. Then somebody from state Educational TV had called wanting a tape, played it on a week night right after the Lake Woebegon rerun.

This in its turn got all kinds of egghead reviews, all of them positive. They called it "immediately riveting," "full of airy space and enveloping depth," and "uncannily postmodern." "An eloquent variation on oral history." Said it "balanced a sense of enormous tragedy with a fertile insight into humanity."

Talisha asked her Daddy if he'd like to work up some other routines for the station. Become an affiliation. He said it might satisfy a restless need.

Talisha also got on the lead paint in plastic bread bag labels and began making a big issue out of it over the air. Here black children were already at abnormal risk for lead poisoning. Every kind of pesticide and carcinogen being dumped in the black community. And you can't even trust bread. It brought in a lot of concerned phone calls.

In other news, Alvin Teckler was still in a full body cast but he seemed to be recovering. He'd call Talisha and say hey baby my hands are bandaged up like catchers' mitts but come down here and hold my pecker. It's the only thing that's loose. Wah-hah, just kidding.

Meanwhile at home her momma Oneida was convinced Doctor Dread had gotten mixed up in his spells and layed a major curse on her, the future mother-in-law.

"My arthritis be throbbing and my head be aching. I see the world through a bitter yellow haze. I need me a massage rehabilitation. Some alternative healthcare."

By that she meant she was hoping Doctor Dread would come back and straighten things out before marrying her daughter. She swore he was a perfect gentleman and companion, could charm the birds out of the trees. He was more like a scientist or a professor or something. She gave Talisha long lectures on African folk medicine and how modern medical science was starting to realize there was really something valuable there. Books being written on herbal cures.

"No marriage," said Talisha, giving her a scalding look. "Lemme highlight that. None. Not a one. The man look like a stick'a old moldy beef jerky left in a country store window for a century. Smell like it too."

Next Oneida started leaving and coming back in the house by the downstairs windows. Had a stepladder set up next to the house. She said they always bury the root at your doorstep so you tread on it as many times as possible. Acquire momentum.

The neighbors were all rich in detail about what was coming up. They dip back in memory of close loved ones what fall victim to that evil root. Choking on chicken bones. Run over drunk on the street. Snakes crawling out of their throats when they lying on the autopsy table.

They had never known a root doctor to marry although there were tales from way, way back before cars and electricity. Usually the girl turn into a black cat on the wedding night or go up in a puff of smoke and ash. Or they hear her voice crying way far off in the air. He'p me. He'p me.

Oneida took added comfort in her home medical dictionary. She declared she had something she couldn't pronounce and put her finger on peripheral neuropathy on the page. Right down below it was prostate cancer. Talisha said why don't you get a sex change and catch that too?

"Sure, you go all vibrant and vocal on me," sniped Oneida. "I know sarcasm when I hears it. I done spent my life being anti-cynical. Well, you do well to be aware of your African heritage. Maybe protect this house from . . . from *them*."

Talisha blew out her breath. "Spirits? Haints? I don't need to acquire that forbidden knowledge. Burning candles made of human fat and saying the Lord's Prayer bass-ackwards. I got spiritual heritage that will see me through the Valley of the Shadow."

Her momma looked hard into Talisha's face. "You always easy to locate even when squinting in the dark. Right smack in the middle of self-interest. Always got to be upwardly mobile. Partnering up with common low greed is what it is. Getting stuff and having stuff is like a mandated subject with you."

"Lay offa me, momma," Talisha shouted.

"You ain't no unspoiled nature. That's based on my own

personal experience and observation. It's like you always gotta have some sense of difference about you. You hear me, Miss College Book Smart Sassy-mouth?"

Talisha shook her head with exasperation, said she was serving God, giving space to new voices of the gospel on WPST.

"You more like a by-product of Satan," snapped Oneida.

Talisha said, "When you're finally on your deathbed for sure about a hundred years from now, I'll give you an introductory reference to him."

The two had never so thoroughly hated each other.

33

"You look outside the window," said Rannie Ralston gesturing down at Broad Street, "you feel like you're in time outside of time. You've got the sun and the harbor, the open sea beyond the barrier islands. Houses like wedding cakes. A sanctuary from the horror of modernity. Tranquil. You'd think it would be fashionable. Genteel. Mannered.

"Instead you've got a street of basic money grubbers. You've got your unbridled excess among the tort lawyers. Occasional outright feeding frenzy of an airline crash, a silicone tit class action. Insurance defense lawyers as weird and robot-like as galactic monsters. Not a lot of stopping and smelling the flowers. Know what I mean?"

Honor said she didn't need sympathy over the loss of her mother. Condolences were difficult for her too. She had come for practical advice. Rannie said that's what she was there for. Unmask the realities.

Rannie examined the wills. They were what is called mirror-image wills. Husband gives everything to wife. Wife everything to husband. If no survivor it goes to Honor.

The problem was no body. Grace had vanished without a trace. That meant seven years had to pass before there was a presumption of her death.

Rannie speculated the house must be worth a lot, but Honor would basically have to hold it in trust for the seven years before she could claim it. She made her eyes go distant, abstracted, not overly interested in what she would say next.

It would be okay, she proposed, to sell furniture maybe and use the return to pay taxes, maintain the integrity of the structure. Maybe she could sell the Tiverton commode. Probably not good to seal an attorney/client deal, but Rannie was ready to give her a few thousand for it.

Honor didn't react particularly. "Commode? It was given away with the rest of the furniture." She shrugged. "Mother was almost phobic about not keeping things that could go to the poor."

Rannie's ears perked up. "Come again?"

Honor explained it went to St. Ambrose which in turn gave it to WPST. All of the furniture. The whole kit and kaboodle. She still wasn't reacting. Had no idea of the value of the thing.

Rannie looked up the WPST phone number and dialed it. While she waited she said, "Godawful slum up there on the neck. Like some Frankenstein monster stitched together from dead body parts."

Talisha came on the line saying she was Talisha Mackey. Rannie asked did she handle routine management problems? Talisha said she handled all management problems. She was owner, CEO, D.J., V.S.O.P., you name it. Rannie said about that furniture that got loaned to you. Talisha butted in and said it was a gift. No loan about it.

Rannie demurred well there were two views on that one. But for the sake of argument, okay, say it was a gift.

Maybe disillusion was setting in. Maybe Talisha would like to get rid of the old junk. To be perfectly candid, her client would go a token sum of money. Help her redecorate to new specifications. Something upbeat. Contemporary.

Talisha said, "You're after that commode thing, right? Well you got to get in line. Anyhow there's something funny. There's two of them."

"Two?" said Rannie.

"Spitting image. Can't tell them apart."

■ ■ ■

"I've got to go lie down," groaned Chandler's mother Phyllis. The news that Chandler intended to marry this creature within the week was not well received. She couldn't seem to take her eyes off the tattoo on Cindi's arm.

Cindi was saying she had always wanted to have a big church wedding and did Episcopals wear funny costumes like them Catholics did? She was a Baptist herself. Little bitty ole church. So small you could smell the pinto beans and onions on the preacher's breath. She didn't know how she'd take to all this finery but she was willing to give it a go.

"Yew know what they always say. Let's see if the dogs'll eat the dogfood."

Phyllis' eyes were glazed as marble. "Is that what they say?" she whimpered.

Chandler said yes, Mummy, you go lie down. You need your beauty rest. Sudden shock and all that. When he got her alone he whispered frantically that Cindi was an aspiring actress. Come to Charleston to try her hand at theatre.

It was all a big put-on, this hick routine. Pulling her leg. Little joke. Girl was a notorious prankster. She really came from a very fine family in Mississippi. Long line of barristers. Father was a federal judge. Passed away a year ago, poor man. Terrible alcoholic.

Phyllis said yes, she knew a put-on when she saw one. This was some cheap trick of Chandler's to get at his trust fund. Well he could squander his patrimony if he wished. But he'd never get another dime out of her. His allowance was stopped as of this moment. And tomorrow she was going to the lawyer to change her will.

"It's not as sordid as it appears at first blush," Chandler protested. Pause a beat as it sunk in. "Change your will . . . ?"

She smiled wanly. "I know a woman of dubious virtue when I see one."

Once she had gone, Chandler poured himself a big glass of scotch and downed it in two gulps. As it hit his system, he decided he needed another. It eased the sting. By midmorning, he was seriously drunk.

Cindi said she was tired of watching good-morning shows and why didn't they go out on a shopping spree? Maybe look for baby clothes.

"He that is wounded in the stones," slurred Chandler, "or hath his privy member cut off, shall not enter into the congregation of the Lord."

"Huh?"

"That's Deuteronomy, you ignorant slut."

Cindi pressed her fat breasts together with her arms, the cleavage filmed with perspiration. "If you're going to be verbally abusive, I'm going to have to consult my attorney. She'll straighten your ass out."

Chandler stiffened. This bovine creature imagined he was a marionette she could jerk about. Summon Rannie Ralston like an avenging Furie to terrorize him. Much as it pained him to admit it, she was correct, and he had no snappy rejoinder. He was not a happy man.

Beau-Jack phoned to interrupt Chandler's melancholy and inform him the US Open was open. Day one. After the ferocious rain, the course had dried out and was playable. But as conventional wisdom had it, Bloomfield Hills was a monster. Greens so fast they were like billiard tables. You got the best players in golf four-putting. Woody Austin was the leader at three under par. Then Stewart, Janzen and Morse.

Chandler propped himself against a door frame. "What about that whoever-it-was who won the qualifying round?"

"Gullion? Yeah, there's him. Of course Greg Norman is your sentimental favorite. He's Australian. You should like that with all your Dublin Irish re-bop. We got Fred Couples and Nick Price pulled out with sore muscles just like I predicted. We got Davis Love. Nick Faldo. What do you think of Colin Montgomerie?"

Beau-Jack was jabbering at him like some flood of energy invading his life. He listened dumbly. Slack-jawed. Drooling a bit. Stress and scotch whisky was taking a terrible toll on his brain.

Beau-Jack told him Wayne's Wagering was pretty casual about security. All they wanted was to see a bank account with the cash in it and his and Chandler's names on the account. So he'd have authority to cut the check in the event of a loss.

Chandler insisted he could not get at the trust fund until he was married.

"Well find somebody and get hitched. It's no big deal. Everybody does it sooner or later."

Good Christ, Chandler thought. Everyone was shoving Cindi at him. Railroading him into matrimony.

"If we lose," he said grimly, "I have to kill myself. Or some other people. I've got quite a lengthy list."

"No negativity now. But just to be on the safe side, we're only going to lay down $2,000. That's your downside risk. Your worst-case scenario. Once we win, though, you'll get your courage up and we'll start making bigger bets."

Drunk and near schizophrenic, Chandler gripped the rolls of excess flesh about his waist like he wanted to tear them off. He was thinking seriously about strangling his mother before she could get her will changed. Drown her in the bath? Or perhaps shove her out of an upstairs window. So many variables to weigh.

"O'Meara was cruising until he four-putted the ninth and . . ."

34

While the song was playing, Talisha sat in the sound booth thumbing through the *Clarion Arise*, little newspaper, really not much more than a rag, but still the communication hub of black Charleston. The editorial page was a rambling gossip column that repeated stories everybody already knew but with the names deleted because they couldn't afford a libel suit. It would get chuckled over in every black barber shop and hair dresser shop in town.

Honky Rector Physically Estranged from Church

While this column would normally applaud the integration of area churches as a meeting of the right minds, things do go hell-bent awry from time to time. A certain white right reverend who will go nameless is one serious casualty of an era. Like a man who lost some brain neurons, he took to discoursing off at his mouth on the topic of sex symbols in old Jerusalem. In a psychodrama worthy of a roughneck saloon, the able-bodied deacons of the church trajectoried his white ass straight into the parking lot. Was the man blissed-out on Mad Dog 20/20? Or is he the fancy white church high cardinal of lunatic behavior? Stay tuned to WPST and *Clarion Arise* for the inside scoop answer to these two questions.

Whew. The editor could do censorious. Talisha had skated on thin ice and survived. Hanging on with fingernails and American optimism.

She changed the CD and wondered if she would make it through the shift without falling face down asleep. No hedonistic self-indulgence in her life. Nobody but dumbasses and cheap crooks eager to say hello to her.

Those two identical commode things sat in the big second floor waiting room. A real unsolved mystery why everybody was sniffing round them. Sure, they looked nice. Lot of fancy woodwork on them. So they had to be worth money. Maybe make the Muslim payment for a month. Maybe two months. If the red bitch Rannie Ralston wanted them, you could be sure they were pretty valuable.

Which was why Talisha had got an ADT system put in by an itinerant methamphetamine freak whose usual trade was burglary. For years, he had worked as a cooker, brewing up crank for a biker gang, breathing the fumes, finally fried his brain. Eyes and hands twitched like bedbugs jumping around, his mind off in some secret topography of his own. He had wired in the craziest net of electric eyes she had ever seen. But he worked cheap. She sold off Alvin's law office furniture to a wholesale warehouse to raise the dough. He wouldn't need it while he was in the hospital, and they had plenty of stuff from Grace Revenue.

When the song ended, Talisha did a plug for Shandy-Lea's Sandwich Shop, one of her few paying ad customers, then segued into "Take Me Cross That River of Broken Dreams" by the "Soul-Bank Check-Cashers." Sat back and rubbed her eyes thinking about commodes.

When the monster homes in downtown Charleston got

sold they often seemed to be handled by an outfit called Christies Great Estates. Talisha knew this was a branch of a fancy art auction house. Through information she located a phone number in New York and called them up. Some dink in a strangled voice kept her holding forever until she finally got hold of the furniture department. Finally another dink came on.

"And how may I be of service?" he lisped.

She described what she had as best she could. It seemed to make him clutch up there for a moment.

"And would these belong to you or someone who employs you?" he asked.

Condescending little shit. Once she was a major broadcast celebrity she'd marry Shaquille O'Neal, buy Christies and fire his little fairy ass. No compromise. No begging his way out.

She told him oh lawsy de yankees done come and run off ole massa and de Johnny rebels and jes leave 'dese here t'ings on her do'step and das how she done got 'em sho' nuff honey-chile dats de trufe.

And anyhow if he wasn't particularly interested, if he was too busy sniffing champagne corks or whatever he did in his high-life, then there were other art auction places in the Yellow Pages.

There was kind of a quaver in his voice when he told her to send him a snapshot. He said he was very excited about the possibility that these were Tivertons.

Doctor Dread stuck his head in the sound booth and enquired, "Will you be making it home for dinner repast? It'll be on the table at six. Join us in the indulgence of some macaroni and cheese, barbecued chicken, fresh collards?"

Talisha blew air out of her nose, lips pinched tight together. The evil old son-of-a-bitch had table-hopped into her house. Her momma was jumping her sorry ass out of the sick bed and laying out banquet spreads. Bring out candlelight and Napa wine next. Him sitting up at the head of the table like a presiding voo-doo king. Turn their home into a for real haunted house.

"No," she sulked. "I'm scuffling on here."

"Your absence will be apparent, my love." With the pink palm of his hand, he made a heart-shaped symbol in the air.

After he went out, front door clicking locked, Talisha used the remote control to aim down the stairs and turn on the crazy maze of photoelectric beams. It sealed her up for the long night shift.

"This is a new release from 'Saint Luxure & the Masters of Heaven Stairway'," she said into the microphone. "It's called 'Synthesize My Soul Clean and Pure'. Listen up close and you'll notice it's kind of a remix of 'Desert Storm of Sin' on their 'Orbital Choir' album."

Sometimes she thought she'd like to just shove in Louie Bellson doing "Skin Deep" or Little Richard screeching "Tutti Frutti." See what kind of reaction she got. See if anybody would even notice. She figured half her audience had their teeth out, snoring in La-z-boy armchairs come nightfall. Weren't even listening.

■ ■ ■

"We're stymied," fumed Chandler Lovelace.

It was past midnight, and he and Leone stood outside

WPST confronted by the ADT stickers on the windows. The station was shut down, everyone gone home. They had driven up there in mummy's Oldsmobile, Chandler having to stop by some wretched shack on Line Street where Leone seemed to stay.

Leone said, "Naw, man, they just put them alarm stickers up. Think it's a world full of mo-rons."

Chandler went from window to window, nose mashed against the glass peering inside. There were no blinds on the ground floor, but it was stacked full of Grace Revenue's furniture.

"You are a total fool," he huffed. "You can see the photoelectric eyes in the wall inside. A series of beams cross the floor." It was the one mechanical thing he vaguely understood because so many homes South-of-Broad had the same protection.

Leone said not to get personal and insulting.

Chandler was sweating heavily in the sticky, humid night. He studied the laser layout more closely. Scores of beams criss-crossed like a mare's nest at all levels of the room. The system seemed to be have been put together by a madman or a genius.

His voice rose. "Do we get what we deserve on this earth? Can I possibly be evil enough to deserve this?" Now he was waving his gun around. He wasn't going to be intimidated like the last time.

Turning on Leone, "What will you do if I remain personal and insulting? Attack me physically? Try to rough me up?"

Leone urged be cool. Hands in a placating gesture. He'd allow him some latitude this time. But just watch it? Okay?

"Assaulting me would be a major mistake!" Chandler spewed. "My anger is born of frustration! And I would squeee-eeze the trigger with carefully calibrated pressure."

"Shit man, put it away. Thing could go off." Leone was whining now. Hunched back, hands in front of his face warding off the pending bullet.

"I am a man of moderate habits. Abstinence is a virtue. I had no carnal knowledge of the damned cunt! Millions and billions in government funds going to benefit special interests while I stand here dying of disease and malnutrition! Tired and bruised."

Leone kept telling him to hush up. It was a rough neighborhood. You never knew what would come out of the dark. And sure enough two black dudes sauntered out wearing long baggy shorts over the knees. Gigantic sneakers. One of them with dreadlocks stuffed under a tam o'shanter. They showed off their knives. Actually one was a box cutter.

"Mind if we squeeze in here, white toast? Check out the status of yo' wallets."

"Armed hoodlum recidivists!" Chandler shouted, fists raised beside his head. "Social decay runs unabated!

"I'm gone cut his ass," said the one in the wool tam o'shanter, black, yellow and green.

Leone cajoled them, "It's cool. It's cool. We got us a deal going down here. Come on. Leave us be. Do it for a brother."

Chandler tugged his revolver out again. "I'll give you a wake-up call, America! I'll make my voice heard! I hold in my hand a weapon of mass destruction! Unrestricted access to the trigger I tell you! I will use it! I swear to God almighty I will use it!"

The two dudes took off running, and he emptied the gun at them.

GA-BA-BLAM-BLAM-BLAM-BLAM!!!

"Get out of here YOU SWINE! YOU DAMNABLE SWINE!!"

Click. Click.

The gun was empty.

Chandler bent over, throwing up his guts in the street, his whole system racked by fear and exhaustion and outrage.

"Listen here, m'man," ventured Leone. "I need like the use of your wheels for a short while. Gimme some traction there and I'll figure a way to get us inside. But I need at least a week without you bugging me for the car back. You hear what I'm saying?"

Chandler was still spitting as he handed over the keys.

Leone said, "Man, you do smell nasty. You gotta do something about that problem perspiration. Say now, is that a last year model Oldsmobile? What you figure the book value is on it?"

35

"Feeding our drinking habit are we? Hmm?" said Rusty Royall.

Chandler jumped and nearly dropped his green bottle of Cutty Sark in the brown paper bag. Rusty Royall had caught him coming out of the tiny hole-in-the wall liquor store at the end of Broad Street. It was the gentry-class store like every place that he patronized. He needed his scotch. It lent a measure of stability to his desperate existence. And this rectorial prick was spying on him. Trying to hint at slander. He went right to the offensive. Squared his shoulders back. Get the right posture for this.

"Stretched a bit thin are we in our work, Rector? That debacle at the negro church. Some murky waters there, but I've heard rumors. No, not rumors, details. Firm details. You'll be the object of official scrutiny for that one I daresay."

Rusty was staring at him in a disconcerting way. Thoroughly unintimidated. He responded lazily. "My we're in a cranky and critical frame of mind. You'll pardon my being dismissive of your customary rudeness. I guess you're under strain. Your impending hurry-up marriage. The confirmed bachelor embarking on *terra incognita*. Hmm?

I suppose you've even forgotten to schedule the church. We're nearly fully booked you know."

Chandler gagged, "How did . . . ?"

The swine was smiling broader now. "Your mother. She's quite voluble on the topic. How I envy you your good fortune. Although eyebrows are being raised at its rushed aspect."

He tried to recover. "Yes it's been a bit of a whirlwind thing. I wanted her to finish college. Reed College you know. She's in sociology. But she wouldn't hear of it. A person of wit and high spirits my Cindi."

"And where will you dwell? Surely you can't expect her to spend a life housesitting."

Chandler said he'd find an appropriate residence. He had realtors looking for an intimate property. He let his gaze go down the 18th century Rainbow Row, some of the most expensive historic houses in the city.

"Will you put one of those mirrored balls on a pedestal in your yard? Hmm?"

"What?"

"Isn't that her level of decorative taste? There is a magnetic charm about her. She bears a strong resemblance to a TV advertising personality I've noticed lately. Does she lack front teeth or is that a trick of the photography? She seems to breathe through her mouth which makes it quite noticeable."

Chandler was blustering now. "How dare you . . . ?!!"

Rusty took off his extremely new straw fedora and ran a finger around the band. "The Stallion Club car wash that one sees on TV ads? Hmm? Is that the lucky girl? It is the white one isn't it? And how will you support your future bride? Furniture distribution? Hmm? Seems like an adequate occupation for you. Perhaps they would take you on at Goodwill."

In a total wrath, Chandler roared that he came into the corpus of his trust fund upon marriage. It was more than adequate for their needs. Rusty said yes if you don't take a belly-flop in the stock market. It's a world of sudden collapses out there.

"You should know that well!" Chandler nearly shrieked. "Thrown out of a coon church on your ass! Pure evidence of the decline of Western Civilization. You're finished at St. Ambrose, Royall! Finished!"

"Do I detect a bit of spite? My, my." Unruffled, Rusty strutted away, calling back over his shoulder. "I'm sure your deft touch will bring her to perfection. With her on your arm, you'll only frequent the best houses."

Chandler was near tears. It was sizzling hot and he staggered, feeling faint. Leone had the Oldsmobile, and he was forced to walk wherever he went. The swine Royall was laughing at him. The swine! Mummy had turned on him as though the ordinary rules of decent behavior didn't apply. Gossiping about him like a common scold. Misery and fear of the gutter and death clutched at his throat. Cindi and Rannie Ralston were a doomsday cult that had taken him prisoner.

He stepped behind a diminutive tree and twisted the cap off the Cutty Sark. Drank deeply. He didn't care who saw. He drank again. It burned him like a torch.

God help him, this was his city. On good days he liked to step down Broad Street to the liquor store as though he were a clubbable chap on Pall Mall in London. He drank again. It was going down better.

He was going to get at his trust fund and win a big wager on golf to cover his immediate expenses. He was going to carry a Tiverton commode to New York and translate it into one million dollars.

Just gone over one of the little speed bumps of life. That was all. He had a mission to accomplish. Everything would be resolved. Bellyflop, Rusty said. Well if need be, Rusty would take a swan dive. Maybe from the bell tower of St. Ambrose. That would be appropriate.

■ ■ ■

At WPST, Talisha had stepped up her editorial commentary, mentioning with disapproval the adult video business with its sexually-oriented material. She condemned the latest drive-by shooting and noted the irony of the police saying they didn't believe it was related to the one the day before or the five the previous month.

She rounded out by urging keep an eye on the Weather Channel. The Lord works in not so mysterious ways.

Leone vowed he needed his own show. Reach out to the young ladies and warn them against substance abuse. They closing the gender gap fast on smoking. Both tobacco *and* dope. Getting all the related diseases. Doing hidden drinking. Smoking to suppress appetite 'cause all obsessed with their weight. And say, how did this new alarm system work?

Talisha told him no way every way. The alarm operated on a need-to-know basis. And no way to him being around girls under color of WPST's mantle.

He stiffened. "Don't lock into a steadfast position. What if there's a fire and I got to get furniture and stuff out? See what I'm saying? And as to girls, I'm tired of you holding that error in judgment back in college against me."

Talisha said she was reaffirming her stance. He wasn't getting anywhere near young girls. Not in person nor electronically.

"You in such *denial, girl.*"

She said he could put the remote control for the alarm system back on her desk and get on out. She'd seen him trying to boost it.

He dropped his chin in a sulk. "Awww man, you shore can harden your stance in a cursory second."

"And where did you thief that new model Oldsmobile you're driving around in?"

"It ain't mine," he said. "I'm selling it for a friend. He asked me to explore it as a cash source."

Around midnight, Talisha dragged home to find a frog cut open and spread out on the kitchen table like 10th grade biology, her momma and the doctor setting there poking in it with straightened out paper clips. And two long-necked bottles of Miller beer setting there, the both of them drinking.

Her momma Oneida said they were having a fine time. Doctor Dread was doing a combination of foretelling the future and curing her lumbago. He had pretty much erased her pain. She was seeking a permanent fix and a way to get away from cost-conscious managed-care programs.

Talisha stood and stared. The doctor had come right into the house. Him wearing that straw hat looked like an angry dog chewed it. Cosied up to her Born-again-in-Jesus momma and won her over to total black magic sorcery in what—an hour? an afternoon?

Talisha opened her own beer, held it away as the foam dripped on the linoleum. She said while there was a huge void in her love life she had made it pretty clear the Doctor wasn't about to fill it. It was against her upbringing and romantic common sense. And no clandestine voo-doo with a dead frog was going to change her mind.

The Doctor give her a look, said you ain't the target here. This frog was divining the future. We got some unclear visions, but some things in focus.

Talisha got drawn in despite herself. "You're a card-carrying trickster and liar," she declared. But she sat down at the table.

He poked at the frog and looked solemn. Said hmmm. She was worried about her business. She said tell me something I don't already know.

He took a swig of beer, said her upcoming show at St. Ambrose would give a lift and a surge to the ratings acclaim but a high-profile person would take off with cash leaving her in limbo.

This was unsettling and Talisha thought hard on it. Church money like any other kind of money always acted as a magnet for less than desirable elements.

She asked was that high-profile personality named Leone Jones? The doctor poked in the frog some and said it wasn't clear but he thought no. That name didn't appear.

She said she'd laud any improvement in her momma's whining and complaining, but he'd have to pardon her for keeping a healthy measure of skepticism about fortune-telling.

He put his hand over hers, and she jerked away.

He said, girl, you look as good as butter-rich dinner rolls. She said she never took to food comparisons, and they weren't about to achieve any consensus on romance.

He said there was one more thing coming out of the frog. Some *big* problems about to *leave* her life in a hail of gunfire. Two different hails.

36

"I thought it would be instructive if the court would take a gander at the plaintiff, your Honor," said Rannie Ralston. She swept her left arm down towards Honor Revenue as though unveiling a new statue in a public square.

Honor had never been in a courtroom in her life. Sure, you saw plenty on TV, in movies. But this was the real thing. Rannie had told her to dress like *Harper's Bazaar*. She said we're going to be wading through the testosterone in hip boots. We need full armor. So spend four hours at Elvita's being perfectly, exquisitely made up like for a photo shoot. Preternatural beauty that acts as a blank slate for the male ego to project its desires on.

Defense counsel was a silver-haired old partner, one of the heavy hitters from a big firm. An eloquent ogre in navy blue pinstripe and a yellow power tie. They were taking all this seriously. Dombey & Trouche was an important account. A big, big account.

Immediately after filing suit, Rannie had made a motion for expedited discovery. Fifteen days to put up or shut up by Dombey & Trouche. Now they were arguing it orally. Rannie cited unconscionable foot-dragging in New York by the Dombey & Trouche parent company, profiteering by unscrupulous *New York* attorneys, sleazy *New York* sense of values, total *New York* lack of candor, decency or humanity.

"So ordered," said the judge.

Defense counsel jumped up like an automaton. His mouth had opened but no words were out yet. The judge looked over his half-glasses. "Do I feel some mounting resentment of my ruling? Got a few vehement objections you want to raise?"

Defense counsel's jaw was hanging down to his chest. The judge staring at him like a hellhound with indigestion.

"Well you can quell that horse pookey in the bud," the judge drawled.

Rannie continued. "Your Honor, we know how much money these scoundrels have pilfered. We understand their claim it has been lost in the ninth circle of cyberspace, and we discount that as a bunch of lying twaddle. What I'm not quite at ease with in my own mind is what the amount of the punitives should be. But that's all speculative and down the road of course. When we get in front of twelve folks good and true."

The judge planted his jaw in his hand kind of fatigued, said to the defense lawyer, "You know what the problem with your case is? Shore, you're always interested when I put it like that. A plaintiff like that sweet-meat young thing over there . . . well, she's like a walking version of the Seven Cities of Gold. She's a mandate to any ordinary bunch of twelve slobs to bring in a bell-ringing verdict.

"Now what I'm doing here, I'm writing a figure down on paper. Liquidating my best guess. Turning it over face down. Sliding it to you like a hymn-sheet. It's my personal assessment of the settlement worth of this case. But don't be influenced by it. It's not some manifesto. Nothing you have to pay a lick of attention to should you choose to behave like a dam' fool and jeopardize your firm's entire account not only with Dombey & Trouche but also with the parent company."

The defense lawyer reached out like it was a snake. Turned up just a corner. Grimaced nervously. Turned up some more. Turned it up all the way. Slapped it back down and held his hand on it. He laughed nervously.

"Think that's exorbitant?" said the judge. "Well you don't need to seek my counsel. Go ahead. Be the partner who lost the Dombey & Trouche account by not settling when the settling was good."

Driven by curiosity, Rannie tugged the paper out from under his hand. Took a look. Went wee-ew. Did a pumping victory motion with her fist, elbow into her body. Aw-right.

■ ■ ■

"I thought I'd update you on my dinner plans," simpered Rusty Royall. He had his knees clapped together, sitting on the edge of the chair across from Rannie's desk like some kind of prisspot.

"I've laid it out rather well. Soup to nuts. I'm both amused and bemused. A bit of alcoholic refreshment to loosen the passions. Some raw oysters to heighten them."

Rannie glowered at him. She had that fool Grace Revenue giving away a million dollar commode. Along with death and taxes, she had this board-certified twerp Rusty

Royall taking up her time because he was the only sap she could think to shove her sister off on. "Did you have your teeth capped? You look different."

Self-consciously, he slid his hand over his mouth. "Dear me no. I am feeling exceptionally clear-headed. Bright-eyed. This pending romance is working rather like a health tonic. A rejuvenation clinic."

"What I was thinking was you look kind of bloodless."

His head snapped back startled. Dismissed the notion from his mind. Smiled. "It will be something of a theatrical debut for Moira. Virgin and all that. If I am to believe your testimony."

"Believe it."

"As a preliminary, I intend to slather her body with vaseline."

"Don't tell me any more," Rannie grimaced with disgust. She was thinking yuck. Men. No wonder she was single. She had big knockers on her that for sheer showmanship were unrivaled. Where was the troupe of men with heavy hitter dicks and big lines of credit? Radiating power and clout. High-profile studs who long to ravish an attorney on her desk top.

"I'll be quite candid with Moira about my aims," said Rusty. "As we're having coffee. High time she was deflowered and all that. Frank and open language. Won't slide into dissonance. I'll confess I'm tentative on actual technique. Heretofore my only love affair was with humanity."

"Sure," said Rannie dryly. Why was he suddenly so agreeable? He had to be up to something. His eyes were giving it away.

"My ministry contains no element of hucksterism. It's a high end design really. Is that too vain? Okay, vanity aside, at the very worst the golden midrange. May I be direct with you? About a personal matter?"

Rannie tipped back in her chair uncomfortably. Episcopalians have a confessional but never use it. It's considered bad form. She certainly wasn't ready for what came next.

"Man has always sought to connect with the earth's fertility. Rituals were created that imitated nature. Rain was translated as semen that made the earth fruitful. So the sky must contain an almighty penis. Religious sex acts—orgiastic ritual, the act of mass copulation—would incite the sky to do its duty. And sacred spermatozoa would seep into the labia of Womb Earth.

"Mystic religions—and all religions have their mystic branch—indeed all are mystic at heart—mystics believe that mortals can for brief, fleeting moments know what it is to be God—to be the gigantic, omnipotent . . . ahem, cock as it were."

His voice dropped to a whisper. "Drugs have always been used to achieve these transcendent states. The peyote of the American Indian is familiar. Less well known—because of centuries of repression by the established church—is that early Christians used the *amanita muscaria*—the Fly-Agaric mushroom for the same purpose. This practice was common in the Middle East. Sumer. Babylonia. Assyria. Judaea. It was kept alive in Europe through the witch cults."

Rannie probed, "You're older than you look, aren't you? When did you finish college? The late 60s?"

With her background in the gritty reality of life, she should have foreseen what was coming. Instead she was distracted, thinking she ought to put a private detective on him. See what kind of scut she could dig up. Something really humiliating and degrading.

37

Birds chirped in the water oaks outside the enormous Romneygate House. Having his breakfast Bloody Mary—Plymouth gin, a big dash of Worcestershire, liberal pinch of pepper—Chandler sat staring at the sports page with little comprehension. The headlines read:

Sonics won't die.

Seattle SuperSonics shucked and jived their way past an orange-haired Dennis Rodman to win Game 5 with an 89–78 margin. The series now stands at 3–2 and the once unbeatable Bulls are staggering.

A photo showed a large negro swinging from the basket. Chandler hadn't realized this was allowed.

Something was nagging at his brain. Beau-Jack had said—back when they were first talking about gambling—something about a sweep.

"What's a sweep?" he asked Cindi across the huge mahogany dining table.

She was painting her toenails a cherry color. Had little wads of cotton between each toe. A can of Diet Pepsi leaving a nasty ring on the table. "You mean like a broom?"

Chandler raised a disgusted eyebrow. "No. In basketball."

"Do you think maybe you ought to enter rehab for alcoholism?"

Chandler looked at the Bloody Mary in his hand. "I certainly do not." He had lowered his voice trying to not explode at her, but a razor's edge had crept into it.

"Well can I have some money to go get a bikini wax? I need to look sexy for our weddin' night."

He widened his eyes so the white showed all around the pupils. "No," he refused. "And don't ask again."

She pushed at her hair on both sides. "Somebody sure got up on the wrong side of the bed."

At night, Chandler locked his door and jammed a chair under the handle. The thought of Cindi gaining access to his bed filled him with horror. Trashy bitch with her thighs akimbo waving her painted toenails in the air to dry them. God, she belonged in a trailer park. Overhead hung a massive chandelier, its many arms reaching a 10-foot span. He'd love to bring it crashing down on her skull.

He punched viciously at the numbers as he phoned Beau-Jack McCully to demand a straight answer on this sweep business.

Beau-Jack sounded puzzled. "I don't recall predicting much of anything about a sweep. Anyhow that's pro basketball. Game's probably fixed. We're into golf and those greens up at Bloomfield are quickening fast as the ground dries out. Payne Stewart is two under and Greg Norman one under for the second round. Anybody shooting under 70 is doing just great. It's tough as hell making a pick. You can't know it until it just suddenly appears in your head with a light bulb over it. Well sometimes you can know it before that."

"Make up your goddamned mind!" Chandler bellowed at him. "I don't know what genes of white trash ancestors are buried in you—laziness, hookworm induced sloth, vitamin deficiency retardation . . . !" He was spluttering with anger.

"Hey, slow that tempo down, boy. You need some stress relief. Nothing secret about what I'm doing. This isn't going on inside a closet. You want to pick the big winner, go ahead. Whatever strategy resources I got will be made available to you. You make the call. Win us enough for a van to get to New York."

Chandler was still furious. He said Beau-Jack knew full well he hadn't the slightest notion how to do that.

"Well then you'll have to pretty much semi-rely on me. But mind you when I come up with it, you don't have to agree with me. Just listen. And you decide if it's right or not."

Chandler grumbled okay okay goddammit get on with it.

"I've got it," said Beau-Jack. "Payne Stewart."

"Payne Stewart? How did you just pull that out of the air?"

"It's a natural, the man wears knickers. Is that a good omen or what? I tell you."

In parting, Beau-Jack spoke to him in an obnoxiously familiar way. Like they were bosom buddies. Called him cousin Chan. Said the next free minute he got, he ought to get out of that big gloomy Romneygate house and have him some fun. Quoted what sounded like a country music song. Dress in style, go hog wild.

Chandler wanted another drink. The magic of the first one was failing him. Familiar certainties were vanishing left and right. Topsy-turvy this and that. Head filled with booze and unreason. Hand seized with sudden spasms that caused him to drop his glass.

He steadied himself. Said, be firm, my resolution. Mixed his drink. Got it down without mishap. Yes, perhaps just one more. He vacillated, then poured it. Couldn't hurt.

Lending the Oldsmobile to Leone had hampered his mobility in a drastic way not to mention the endless grief from mummy demanding its return. She didn't take well at all to his suggestion she buy a Range Rover. Leone dawdling along, saying he was studying on the problem of breaking into WPST. Like he was some kind of math researcher.

God the liquor tasted vile. Like eating turkey hash after Thanksgiving. And look at that slatternly Cindi. Putting on lipstick and then blotting her lips with a big wad of kleenex. Loathsome.

I sense I am being badly used, he told himself. If either Leone or Beau-Jack was lying to him, leading him on, mocking him . . .

—his mind fixed on the pistol he had taken from Honor Revenue's underwear drawer—

. . . somebody was going to die on the operating table.

■ ■ ■

A lot of folks thought it was the heat that caused Rusty Royall to go around the bend the way he did. And the heat was sure enough bad. A Bermuda high-pressure system squatted right down over the Lowcountry and shoved the heat index up to 105. Normally it oscillates and lets in some cool ocean air, you get some thundershowers. But this one just sat dead still.

Pets and old folks were dropping like flies along with those who worked with restrictive clothing or had heavy alcohol intake. Night brought no relief.

Rannie wasn't giving this much thought when the emergency broke. She was at home on Legendre Street with her feet up, a Jim Beam at hand perusing a private eye report on Rusty Royall.

Just as she had thought, the man was a lot older than his boyish looks indicated. In his late forties, which made him part of the draft-dodger generation that had gone to divinity school as an alternative to the selective service which was selecting American youth for a war in southeast Asia.

Yes, there were all the predictable earmarks. Arrest for throwing sheep blood on files in a draft office. Arrest for some kind of brawl with ROTC louts at a showing of the John Lennon, Yoko Ono film "Give Peace a Chance." Couple of drug arrests. For mushrooms. Very Tim Leary our boy. A champion of the non-medically-supervised psychedelic journey. The "turn on, tune in, drop out," era. Quite an interesting little rap sheet. Rannie's daddy would have hated him with a passion.

She was packing more ice in her drink when the front desk of the Mills Hotel called her and a very nervous man said, "We have an urgent problem."

"Can you be more specific?" She was well into the Jim Beam and didn't want any more problems.

He dithered. Exasperated, she told him to get to the damn point. Carefully, like his throat muscles were seized up, he pronounced certain key words and phrases. Rector of St. Ambrose. Her sister Moira. Certain scandal. Out of control. Out of their heads. Out of their clothes. Out of their room.

Well, that got Rannie to her feet with a new vitality. Virtually sprinting up the streets to where the classic Robert Mills hotel sat with richly glowing lights, palmetto fronds brushing courtyard walls in a hot breeze. Moira's night of joyous abandon had turned to shit.

Rusty and Moira had come traipsing down in the elevator buck naked except for their shoes. Climbed up onto the big lustrous mahogany bar that adjoined the restaurant. Shrieking and yelping and scampering about. Along the bar top, leaping out onto table tops. There was a lot of broken glass. Rannie wondered if they had somehow anticipated that, wearing their shoes like they did.

A frantic management had shut down the lights to camouflage the exuberant game of grab-ass. The late customers were huddled outside expressing a mix of outrage, incredulity, mirth.

The house security force, black men in tan cop uniforms, black doormen in green coats with frogging, had penned Rusty under the grand piano. He did not react to the flashlight they shined in his eyes. Just twitched rhythmically.

"Hundreds of orgasms," he was babbling. "Cosmic answers. Psychedelic peace and love."

"The dude believe in his own perspective," said a doorman.

"Well," said Rannie. "He certainly leads a couple of dramatically different lives."

For a lawyer of Rannie's skills—spending her life rattling cages, jerking chains, busting chops—it was child's play to intimidate a big hotel. Innkeeper's liability was a wide-open field with new law being made almost daily. Creative lawsuits claiming hotels owed a duty of safety in every berserk situation were a contagion.

Rannie was upfront about her position. She'd take her sister home. Rusty Royall, the nonpareil asshole, they could boot out into the street although it wasn't in their best interest that he remain naked, however delightful that might seem. There was no agonizing moral choice. Stuff him in his clothes and send him packing.

"You mean . . . ?"

"No lawsuit. No public outcry. I guarantee it. Sealed deal."

The nervous, sweating night manager seemed tempted to kiss her feet. "What's wrong with them?" he tittered.

"They're tripping," said Rannie. "Other than some potential for flash-backs, they'll both survive. Unfortunately."

The rent-a-cops wrapped a nude Moira in a tablecloth. Her eyes were sunk deep in the sockets like they were trying to crawl inside her head. She could only nod yes or no because her voice had failed her.

"You know come to think of it, I've never seen my sister naked before. It'd probably be a whole lot easier if she had one of those insidious eating disorders you hear so much about. Bony sternum. Stick-like arms and legs. Throwing up. Laxative purges.

"But look at her. She's fleshy and pink. Reasonably turgid. Kind of like ripe produce at the supermarket. Her veins are probably filled with white sugar, her brain's a bag of saccharine."

Rannie wanted to get gone. She wrapped her fist in the tablecloth and led Moira out of the hotel like a heartless housemother busting a boarding school girl for a bed-check violation.

She said to her, "You read that heavy TV watching compromises the neurological integrity of American kids in plague level proportions. But that's not you. To you, television was always uncouth. So maybe it's the love novels. All that old-South romantic gobbledy-gook you routinely store in your subconscious."

She looked at her sister. Moira was bubbling saliva. Mental fog. Derangement. *Non compos mentis.* Gaga.

"I guess you don't have any abstract thinking skills. Or maybe all your thinking is abstract."

Without warning, Moira sat down on the sidewalk. Rannie rolled her eyes, sighed in resignation. Steeled herself and jerked Moira upright. Dragged her on.

"Okay, so I've been shopping you around. This was the best I could come up with. You're going to get married and out of my hair if it kills us both."

38

Chandler's mother refused to come downstairs in the house on Bocquet Lane for the wedding which he figured was just as well. Her searing contempt was incompatible with his deep, dismal misery. The ordeal he was facing. The half a bottle of Plymouth gin inside him. Staggering as he walked. Barely able to stand upright.

He had been drunk for the past week pretty much straight. The liquor spawned a certain muddle-headed confusion, but it was the only way he could face the horror of matrimony. The stifling heat lay on Charleston unstirred by the slightest sea breeze.

Mummy had actually told people he was getting married to white trash. Or else that bitch Rannie Ralston had. Or Rusty Royall. Wherever he went there were whispers and sniggers. Word had preceded him to Dombey & Trouchc and a vicious squabble with the broker ensued. That toad Browder Delamere actually refused to release the money to Chandler's control before the wedding. Accused him of perpetrating a fraud. Spouting Mummy's party line.

"Are you beyond accountability?" he had screamed at the man. Called him dunderhead and charlatan. Excoriated the tendentious swine.

After heated argument, they had settled on a compromise. The marriage would be on Monday so the banks would be open. The stocks would be sold and the money would flow into a new account right at nine AM. Chandler would tie the knot at mid-day. Rannie Ralston would lend her moral suasion to make certain the marriage went through. Browder seemed properly frightened of her.

Vigilance. Eternal vigilance in dealing with pinstriped miserly pettifoggers.

Chandler slugged down another drink before making his unsteady way downstairs. Holding tight to the banister so as to not pitch head-first. His suit trousers pinched him viciously. If he sat down they would split.

As of three hours ago he was $100,000 liquid. Bank account in his and Beau-Jack's name. The first of what would be many happy wagers had gone down. He'd soon be in Calgary or Halifax.

Rannie Ralston waited in a gray suit. Supervising. Looking like some multi-headed Hydra.

Beau-Jack McCully was absent. Notoriously unreliable that boy. Perhaps he was placing the bet. Surely he wouldn't neglect that duty.

Otherwise Chandler could invite no one of any standing in Charleston. He was socially castigated. Demonized by events he dared not explain to anyone.

He glanced at Cindi standing beside him and closed his eyes in horror. Purple eyeshadow. A teased hairdo she had designed specially for the occasion. The sheer, unadulterated trashiness. And dressed in white as though virginous, the bodice of the dress strained to bursting with the swelling of her mulatto love child.

She said, "At the end of the ceremony, I'm gonna hold out my arms and you walk into them."

It didn't matter, he kept telling himself. He was going to take off. She'd just wander away and die of a drug overdose. He'd never see her again. The marriage was meaningless. It would not stem his exodus. He'd find his fleet-footed way to Canada. Vancouver would be nice. Or Banff. Get out of this stinking Lowcountry heat. Write Mummy tearful, pleading letters and try to turn her around. Tell her the dire truth of his tragic plight.

Cindi looped her arm through his and clamped onto him with an iron grip. Chandler cringed at her touch, feeling he was walking towards a scaffold.

He had hired some jerk-water notary public to marry them. You could do that in South Carolina. This chaw-bacon looking person sold aluminum siding. Or plumbing supplies. A few minor lies to Cindi. She had no earthly idea what an Episcopal minister looked like.

Noble Royall, the smug bastard. Sitting in his cozy church study thinking he's won. That he holds St. Ambrose in his autocratic fist.

"Dearly beloved we are gathered here today . . ." the notary began. But got no further.

A gigantic negro walked right through the front door dressed in black shirt and some kind of orange zoot suit over it. About fifteen gold chains. For no reason ever explained, he was carrying a six-pack of toilet paper under his arm. He seemed to know Cindi.

"Hop in the car, bitch. We're blowing town."

Cindi argued with him the way Cindi tended to do. Said she had a vested interest in this wedding and in trying to refine herself. He should get gone and quit embarrassing her.

He smacked her head back and forth a few times. Said his was a modest and reasonable request and "you ain't got immunity from it."

They got into a pale blue '96 Honda Passport DX which was later determined to be recently stolen and drove off.

Chandler stared drunkenly out the open door. This large darkie had brought glad tidings. Philanthropy. Enlightened social thought.

Rannie said, "Well that certainly takes the cake for *deus ex machina*." Then left in disgust.

"Well lemme just convey all kinds of amazement," said the notary public before departing himself.

Sunlight was dazzling. Radiant even. Showing a certain sharp disparity between his life only moments before and what it was now. The banquet of life had turned into a potluck supper. And yet he had supped. He'd been brought to the brink of disaster and then pulled back at the eleventh hour. Bowed down by tragedy. Now buoyed up. A marvel really.

He had his money. But was unmarried. That seemed just. He was a well-intentioned man. He need offer no apologias for his behavior.

Well. He'd have a sitdown. And a neat scotch. That would be good.

Stagger to the liquor cabinet. Whups dropped the glass. Still, he could take a swig straight from the bottle. Ahh. That was good. Gad, were those his pants rippping?

Sitting down helped him regain his composure. A

newspaper lay beside his chair. Sports section. Portentous headline.

Jones by one on 18th.

What?

The Open was . . . finished? Over?

Jones putted for par on the 18th. Took a one-stroke victory over Lehman and Love.

Where was Payne Stewart?

This was today's paper. The tournament was finished, won by this Jones person . . . on Sunday.

Something was wrong.

■ ■ ■

Talisha had just finished taking a strong on-air stance against the new BellSouth 185-foot cellular phone tower being put in the Seven Mile Community. She said it was an ugly blight and could fall over on the homes. Disadvantaged communities always got the short end of the stick so rich folks in BMWs could talk into mobile phones about nothing of importance.

Afterwards she played a recording of it back and liked the way it sounded. The word 'exhortation' came to mind. She had done a first-rate job. A voice crying for justice out of the gloom. It was a nice self-image, and mixing in the phone tower dispute was not really outside her jurisdiction. She hoped it would get attention with her listening audience. Maybe provoke some call-ins.

She got a call, but not what she was expecting. Beau-Jack

McCully told her, "Listen, if some dude named Booger-T shows up, tell him everything's cool. Wayne has been paid off. The station's free and clear of all that gambling debt that Daddy was so bad about amassing. So Booger shouldn't jump the gun to any wrong conclusions."

She hung up on him. Fool. Don't bother her with his nonsense. She was feeling too good—just totally juiced—and wanted approving calls. Folks telling her to keep up the good fight.

What she got was a walk-in instead, a change of mood that walked in off the street. Great big dude with that smell all over him said he had just spent some time in the county jail. For those who know it, it's a mix of sweat, over-flowed toilets and pinto beans.

With him was a white trash girl in a white dress with a little bouquet of flowers like she had been in a wedding as bride or bridesmaid. The dude wanted to know where Beau-Jack McCully was. Said how about boosting some cooperation? He was in a hurry.

Talisha told him Beau-Jack had nothing to do with day-to-day management of the station. Normally she screened who came just busting in and maybe he'd like to state his name and occupation for the record.

Dude threw his head back at that, said 'hunhf'. He said who was she? He had carte blanche authority to deal with WPST management. And performance was pretty much the bottom line in his business. He had to find and connect to someone.

She said he looked like a good argument for a three-strikes you're-out law.

He said answer up or he'd unload a raft of shit like she wouldn't believe.

She said she probably could believe it. She had been a lightning rod for critics, taken irate and obscene calls, although nobody had come in with guns yet. He said well that circumstance done just change, and pulled out what the cops later described as a .38 SIG-Sauer P220 automatic. They said it was a popular weapon in Latin America because typically, by law, private citizens couldn't own more than a .38 calibre with a magazine capacity of nine. This information came later when things were being talked about in a more academic way.

Right now, the gun had that jump all over you ability to transmit major fear.

The white girl said put it away, Booger. This seemed to be his name, not some racial insult she was calling him. Added she didn't want to be a witness to any more killing than she had already logged in in the past. It was a real bitch and just sent her life all to hell.

"Lemme hasten to add that you're making a major mistake," said Talisha.

Booger didn't take this well. "You having an identity crisis, bitch? You in management or not?" He racked the slide on his weapon.

At that point, voice communication kind of froze up from sticking in Talisha's throat.

At the next point, maybe three seconds later, the two Muslims came through the door with an armed response. Guns slid out. Pointed. Little snicks of safeties going off. Then doing their business.

BAM-BAM-BAM!

The guns bucked in their hands.

Booger went down hard and lay there with some minor convulsive heaving and gurgling. He might have had a mouth full of snuff. In point of fact, it was blood.

They stood over him, guns pointing down. It was a position of extreme dominance for many reasons, but mainly because he was dead. As was their habit, they didn't have much to say. The white girl wasn't saying much either. She just looked kind of sick.

So Talisha broke the ice. "Lemme state the obvious. That was pretty impressive. You boys could maybe do a defensive-shooting video. But it's time to get gone."

The Muslims agreed their presence was not a sustainable one.

Then took off. Just vanished like smoke.

With the aftermath seeping in, Talisha was dripping sweat and fear. She cried her life was just a compendium of bad shit. Then she remembered the predictions of Doctor Dread. Some major problems would leave her life in a hail of gunfire.

Talisha went to studying, thinking hard on all this. It made no sense. Who was this Booger person? Why had he come? How did his death help her out?

Then it struck her. The Muslims were gone.

The white girl in the white wedding dress was still hanging around whining she thought she was going to be sick. All this blood was just a real gross-out and her day so far had been nothing but shit and shenanigans. She had set out to get married and was now struggling with this change of plans. Booger had the car keys in his pocket and she didn't want to touch a corpse to get them. She didn't like dead bodies. Never had.

Trying to motivate her, Talisha said it was about to be a real frigid climate when the cops showed up. She knew this interracial love thing was big in some quarters, but white cops had tended to frown on it in the past, and far as she knew, still did. They were, after all, in the county of Charleston where minority representation on the force was low.

The white girl said that was okay. She was in the federal witness protection program and she needed to use the phone to call her handler. Get him to coordinate with the local fuzz. Pull rank on their ass if there was trouble.

Talisha asked was it a local call?

She said no, but it was an 800- number.

■ ■ ■

"Yeah, but I had the bet down on Saturday," insisted Beau-Jack over the phone.

"And we lost?" said Chandler stupidly. Staring into his glass of scotch. He could have sworn Beau-Jack had been talking to him about the bet only the day before. On Sunday. Saying Payne Stewart was the definite pick because he wore knickers.

"Shit happens. Who would have picked Jones? He's been off the tour three years. Had a dirt bike accident. Injured the ring finger on his left hand. Apparently he read a book by Ben Hogan and got all fired up. How was I supposed to know what was on his inspirational reading list?"

Well, Chandler figured he was $2,000 poorer. His trust fund reduced to $98,000. The phone rang the second he put it down.

"Are you married yet?" barked Browder Delamere.

Chandler could scarcely believe the impudence of the man. And to think they had once been allies against Rusty Royall and his ilk.

"It's a fascinating story," trilled Chandler. "A mix of irony and message in the events that have transpired."

"That better not mean 'no'," Browder threatened. "Because if so, I want your account restored by closing time this afternoon. I've got a fiduciary duty here, and the way that whole hundred grand was whisked out is a red flag signal. If you're up to some fraud you could be looking at jail time."

"You really need a wider field of vision," Chandler chided. Then as it sunk in, "What do you mean 'whisked out'? 'Hundred grand?'"

39

Rannie sat behind her office desk saying, "You convinced that chump Chandler Lovelace to lay down a huge losing bet on the U.S. Open? That's how you squared your father's gambling debts?"

"Daddy always had the will to be a con artist," said Beau-Jack. "He just didn't have a franchise on brain power. All his artfully concocted plans would go south in a skinny minute."

Rannie said they were talking about Chandler and his trust fund. He escapes marriage and then finds he's still got his ass in a sling. How did Beau-Jack get him to do it?

"I lied a fair bit," Beau-Jack admitted.

Rannie watched his face. It was matter-of-fact. Almost passive. Not smug or pleased with himself.

She said, "All that fake Anglo-Irish routine, Chandler always sounds a bit daft. And he's got that kind of wet grin of the career alcoholic. It must help him suspend disbelief."

Beau-Jack inspected the toes of his cowboy boots. "I guess the message here is human frailty."

She kept watching him closely. "Yeah, Booger-T shot dead tends to remind us all flesh is grass. And then you've got Chandler Lovelace who should know what he's doing, the value of furniture and all, handing not one but two Tiverton commodes to WPST."

"Well, that was pretty much by accident. He didn't mean to do that."

Rannie looked thoughtful. "I'm sure he didn't. Something so rare there's probably not but one of it in the world. But somehow a duplicate appears. And you with all those wood working skills."

"It's true I'm pretty much into early American. Thomas Elfe. Chippendale. But a Tiverton's over my head. All those little inlaid bits. Drive a man crazy."

"And you've got a part ownership in the station where the commodes now reside. Yet you're just hanging out all disarmingly blithe. Kind of makes me wonder."

Beau-Jack shrugged. "Don't look at me. I'm on hiatus from crime."

Rannie had decided he was more of a character than a clown. And he looked good. Probably a washboard stomach. She was so horny she'd like to hike her skirt up and show him her red-haired pussy. See what he'd do. Trying to calculate whether he'd take his time, give her what she needed. She could feel her body pulsating with desire.

She said, "Are you racking out with Honor Revenue? What's it like to get both big tits and long legs? I mean they are big *and* long. By any credible measure."

"Excuse me?"

"Seems like as tall as she is, when you're inside her, your head's at the level of her tits. But maybe that's useful."

Beau-Jack told her, you know what, the other day he put

a watermelon in the freezer, figuring to get it cold, then forgot about it. Was a bitch to cut, but the flesh was like a frozen popsicle. Rannie ought to try it some time.

Rannie cocked an eyebrow. "What? Is there some image there I'm missing? Or are you just changing the subject?"

He said he was changing the subject.

That was galling. Here she was openly talking sex with him. Offering him a chance to mount the lady lawyer.

He got up slowly out of the chair like his body hurt. Said while lots of folks thought chivalry was dead, his romance with Honor Revenue was moving high-profile.

He paused at the door and looked back. "If you see me around socially, I'll be the one with a ring through my nose."

■ ■ ■

Talisha told the uniformed cops to don't accuse her of holding back information. She was the definition of the word integrity and community spirit. It infused her spirit and lifted her work up above the ordinary.

They asked how could two strangers just be hanging around a radio station with guns and shoot to death another stranger come in off the street? She said she shared their honest concerns, but there was a fair level of random unexplained mysteries in life. Did they watch that TV show? Unexplained Mysteries? And what about Bible miracles? Did they believe the story of the loaves and fishes or not?

The cop scratched his head. "You see this as a miracle?"

"I see it as him leaving a message to his loved ones. Don't play around with guns."

The cop made a sound of disgust, said how about if she quit jerking their chains?

Talisha peeled a stick of gum, stuck it in her mouth. Chewed. She said if they wanted her to go negative—lay blame somewhere—she'd be obliged to state it didn't speak highly of public security in Charleston County. She herself didn't want to do that because she was aware of what all that constant second guessing by the press did to police officers emotionally. She thought maybe the presence of more cop vehicles within the community would work as a deterrent against these kind of goings-on.

The cops agreed that more police presence could be helpful, but they would really like to hear her innermost thoughts on the recent homicide.

Talisha said these were just the moments when she was grateful for simple things in life. Mocking bird sitting on a limb outside her house singing away. A grape popsicle on a hot day. Being alive and out of the line of fire when folks got killed. She'd raise her hands above her head in praise, say yes, Lord, I am free.

The cop sitting on the edge of her desk looked at his partner, looked back at her. Swung his leg awhile.

He said unless they got a personality change out of her they weren't going to get very far in the pursuit of justice. And he himself personally thought she was covering for somebody.

She shook her head firmly. "You can say all the ugly stuff you want, but you ain't substantiated that none of it's true."

On the way out he looked at the furniture, said weird. The station looked like one of those old Vincent Price horror movies you get on cable. "Fall of the House of Usher" or something. Then he gave her his card.

Talisha thought everybody's into professionalism these days. Cops got business cards. Probably have a bumper sticker next. How's my sleuthing? Call 1–800-Cop-Pals.

Like every day, she was feeling weary, frazzled, and beat to crap.

The next call she took veered her life onto a very different course. It was the little furniture fruit from Christies. He enquired how she was.

She smiled faintly. "Rich, spoiled and self-absorbed. Sitting here watching the clock pass on enchanted hours. How 'bout yourself?"

"I'm holding this bit of celluloid in my hand. The photo you sent us. Well, I must say I'm experiencing some extremely heightened emotions. I'm a bit agitated. If we are correct, and I'm fairly certain we are . . . if we are correct, you possess two Tiverton-Bewely commodes."

"Okay, I'll bite. What do you figure they're worth?"

"Given that there is only one other verified Tiverton commode, I'm using a reverential tone here. I'm presuming you want to sell them."

"Do you think you could cut to the heart of this?"

"We'd conservatively estimate one million dollars each. It could go much higher."

"Are you being flip? On amyls? What?"

"We're bringing a bottle of Roederer Cristal champagne to open with you."

"Yeh. That's cool. That's cool. I'll fit you in my busy schedule. Got a lot of broadcast industry lunches I take.

Nominated for press awards." She wondered if her voice sounded normal.

"Do you own other objects of value?"

"No, that's like my crowning possession. These deluxe commodes just kind of set here in my office. Makes the room into a loving environment."

She hung up with resolve in her heart and two million dollars ringing in her ears. Pay off the Muslims. Be a pampered lady. Act out love scenes with movie star quality men.

The rays of sunlight gave it a golden sheen.

Then she thought St. Ambrose. Powerful white people. The minute they knew what she had, they'd try to grab it back and probably succeed. Rannie Ralston calling up. The wheels were probably already in motion to whip up on her but good.

Then she thought—pre-emptive strike.

40

"Put it on Mummy's tab," Chandler directed the bartender in the Carolina Yacht Club.

It was a nice line that had begun many pleasant afternoons soaking in the amber glow of single malt scotch. Sitting surrounded by ship models and prints he had often imagined himself vacationing in Bermuda. Wearing shorts with jacket and tie, knee-socks. Quaffing a long gin while spinnakers decorated the horizon. Or downing a shandy while watching golfers hole out on the 18th green.

Golf. Chandler shuddered.

Now all was wormwood and gall. He was in deepest mourning for that which was lost in his life. Fallen afoul of curses let rip by vile fate. Hapless. Well and truly fucked.

True, he had escaped a marriage worse than death, but word of his humiliation was everywhere. Jigaboo in the orange suit shot dead in a radio station. Cindi had had the gall to tell him that with his trust fund gone she was going off to greener pastures of the witness protection program.

Yes, his trust fund had been plucked clean. Beau-Jack McCully had proven himself a common thief. His commode locked up at WPST, Chandler was penniless and without prospect.

To top it off, that damned Leone claimed the Oldsmobile had been stolen from him. Said to put in an insurance claim on it.

He rolled the short glass against his forehead to cool it. Scotch bringing a woozy fuzz to objects.

Laying in front of him on the bar was a *Post & Courier* story about Grace Revenue and St. Ambrose generously giving furniture to WPST. Talisha Mackey was quoted as saying, "Land sakes, I'm so happy that white folks this giving and open. Law-dee, I feel like a hot day in grade school and you find the water in the water fountain is ice cold and good."

The black bitch was trying to stake her claim first. Somehow she had gotten wind the commodes were valuable. Managed to engineer this story in the paper.

After a few belts settled into his blood stream, objects began to take on a zig-zag effect. He ate a handful of mixed nuts, chewing carefully so as to not choke.

A jaunty Rusty Royall was exiting with Browder Delamere and some heavyweight attorney with one of the big firms in town. The lawyer was not a communicant of St. Ambrose but of the equally august St. Philips. They looked conspiratorial.

Rusty spotted Chandler, hesitated like he wanted to stop and talk, changed his mind, changed it again and did indeed turn back. The other two went on out into the raw midday sun.

The adversaries confronted each other, eyes locked for a

moment. Preparing insults. Getting them letter-perfect. A gentleman is never unintentionally rude.

Chandler was about to say you're looking very smug, Rector Royall. Must have lunched on communion wafers. A side order of crown of thorns.

But Rusty made the first move. The sickly haughty smile. "In our cups are we? I suppose I'd feel the same after such a grave blunder."

"Having a preprandial," Chandler spluttered. "No harm in that. What? What do you mean blunder?"

"The WPST article. It's open there beside you is it not? Fascinating photo. I've gotten abreast of an odd detail. Those are Tiverton commodes in the photo. Obviously never intended to be given to that radio station.

"But then fools rush in where angels fear to tread. Our dear Chandler Lovelace hustles it out of my possession and causes that black girl to mistakenly believe it's hers. I've been consulting legal counsel. He's quite in agreement. More than gross negligence on your part. Must have been an intentional act. A conversion he called it. You'll be served promptly with legal papers as well as the girl."

"The commodes are mine," Chandler protested fiercely. "Damn your lawyer and his legalized thievery."

Rusty looked about the room wonderously as though hearing voices. "Yours? Why on earth should you think that? All those lengthy talks I had with Grace Revenue before her demise. Her intentions were perfectly clear and straightforward. One she gave to the church. The other to me. Wanted me to have it personally."

■ ■ ■

If there was one thing old Charlestonians had a nose for it was valuable artifacts. With property taxes steadily rising to the level of the confiscatory, many of them held onto their homes by selling off heirlooms one by one. The news photo seized their attention and held it.

Well-thumbed antique furniture compendiums were consulted. Field Guides to American Antiques. Magnifying glasses were put to the blurred photo to study the curlicues. It aroused the predictable talk. Two of them. Must be valuable. Faith in money is never misplaced.

The wife of an M.D. who played at running an antiques shop on King Street first thought of Tiverton-Bewely. It seemed so out of place in Charleston, but when she looked in the right reference source, there it was. She got on the phone and told everyone.

Their voices were melting, reverential as they speculated on the worth. Easily a million dollars, she vowed. One sold at Sotheby's in London for three-quarters that two years ago. Since then the market has gone through the roof.

A million. Tidy sum, that. Two of them means two million. Rather puts the "fine" back in fine arts.

The voices gathered with particular force as they condemned Grace Revenue's folly in giving them away to negroes.

Give the coloreds old clothes naturally. Let the maid take home the left-overs from a party. Heck-fire, give them lawn furniture if you wish. But antiques? They'd chop them up and burn them in the fireplace.

Grew in vigor the more they thought on it.

Dreadful fool that woman. Always was deranged. Generic lunatic really. Must have been. Jumped off the Cooper River Bridge.

But when Rusty Royall leaked that St. Ambrose had had its hands on these priceless objects and Chandler Lovelace had let them squirt away, they became positively shrill.

Might have known this would happen on his watch! Fat, blundering buffoon! He breaks the land-speed record for idiotic gestures one right after the next!

Red-faced and quivering with wrath, old Admiral Pellegrin (USN Ret.) pursued Chandler all the way down Tradd Street and into Bocquet Lane. "You brain-dead, scrofulous, lapis lazuli sodomite!" he raged. "Ought to squash your skull with a cinder block! If you ever dare chide me about my tithing . . . !"

Chandler pounded helplessly on the door of his home, but his mother refused him admission. "You've humiliated me for the final time," she said severely through the door.

He sat on the doorstep tear-ducts flowing. Given the shove. Everyone on the street saw it.

Working around the church, Honor Revenue heard all this. Caught their pitying glances. Poor little orphan girl. Such an innocent. Mother gave away your inheritance. Left you a house you can't sell for seven years. An eerie perfection to her insanity.

Honor gave them saccharine smiles and went about her business. She had been brought up on a life of conflict avoidance. She was to negotiate and mediate. Inspire others to seek perfection. Don't listen to detractors. Don't criticize. Always say something positive and charitable and kind.

Now she had hired the rough-and-tumble ball-buster Rannie Ralston to wrest her lawsuit away from her New York attorney and sue Dombey & Trouche. That had gone full-force to an unbelievably rapid conclusion.

And there was something odd about Beau-Jack McCully's prodigious output of reproduction furniture . . . plus his ability to resist going frenzied over her . . . something that was causing her to put two and two together.

41

Chandler's fragile mental condition was deteriorating rapidly. All his plans, his meticulous lifestyle gone bust. Trust fund stolen from him. Execrated by the members of St. Ambrose. Admiral Pellegrin baying at him like a bloodhound the length of Tradd Street and Bocquet Lane. There he had found the door barred against him. Mummy refused him admission.

"You've shamed me before the entire community," she said through the door. "I can never hold my head up again. Not to mention you've finagled something with my car."

His mummy had changed her will. He had seen her coming out of Buist, Moore, Smythe & McGee, the old establishment lawyers on Broad Street. And the conspiracy against him spread. The owners of the Romneygate House had phoned from Saratoga and strongly suggested he look elsewhere to house-sit.

Lost in the echoing silence of the great house, liquor seemed to magically appear before him. He drank it immediately. Valuable objects were mysteriously hurled through the windows. Afterwards, he would examine his hands wondering if they possessed a will of their own.

He prepared his favorite cream of mussel soup and then

dumped it on his head. He was startled to realize he was conversing with himself in baby talk.

Beau-Jack McCully had wagered and lost his entire $100,000 trust. Claimed he was only trying to up-grade Chandler's fiscal position. That jigaboo Leone had run off with his car. Said they'd work things out to get into WPST. He was coming up with a plan.

Work things out!

The reality of poverty chased Chandler like screaming furies all the way to the eight-acre gun store in North Charleston. Chandler had ridden the bus with negroes and hunch-backs and retarded children. Truly, he was plumbing the depths of depravity.

The store was marked by a gigantic American flag. A big sign proclaimed:

GROVER'S GUN'S GALORE
Home of the cutting-edge
on 2nd A. Rts.

Grover himself was grimly telling Chandler there was a lot of desperate eleventh hour tactics coming out of gun-control liberals in Congress. But it was an election year and them pussies was under the microscope of the American voter.

"I mean shit-fire there's folks think an ad with Chi Chi Rodriguez hitting golf balls in a motel room is too violent. Roadrunner cartoons is too violent."

Chandler had been looking at the Sen. Diane Feinstein target posters.

"I'm out of bullets," he said, proffering his empty revolver.

Grover gave him kind of a slow inquiring look. Raising an eyebrow. He said, "You're acting the role of a distraught man. I presume this weapon is in compliance with the Brady Bill and all applicable laws and ordinances."

Chandler reared up at him. "Are you questioning my motivation?"

Grover said whoa there, hoss, making haste to smooth the waters, disengage himself from any particular concern with Chandler's emotional state. Said not in the least. He just had the customer's welfare in mind. The psychological aftereffects of federal gun regulation still lingered.

"I'm a relative newcomer at all this," Chandler admitted, settling down. Accepting the apology. His fat shoulders sagged.

"Well, lemme address this empty gun issue here," said a right malleable Grover.

Chandler looked around. A sign declared: "'Before a standing army can rule, the people must be disarmed.' Noah Webster." He said yeah, he guessed the magnum hollow-points would be jim-dandy. Whatever Grover recommended.

Grover had gone all poetic. "I tell you in twenty years of gun sales, I've never seen finer styling than the Smith & Wesson. It's . . . well, it's just hauntingly beautiful."

He said in a world of gross deviance out there a man needed a good piece. It gives you an authentic voice in the Second Amendment debate. I mean, if you're as disturbed by the pattern out there on our streets as I am.

Chandler broke open the box and loaded the revolver in front of him.

"You, uh, you have to buy the whole box," said Grover. "It's like a store policy."

Chandler gave him a fixed stare. With his cracker voice, Grover was eerily reminiscent of Beau-Jack McCully.

"I ain't trying to be contrarian. Think of it as consumer protection. We don't want you in danger of an empty gun. If you see it in that context."

"You're right," Chandler said firmly. "That's first priority."

"I see a man with only six chambers, well it triggers a concern."

"Good policy blueprint," Chandler agreed. Then he bought a second box. Thought on it some more. Bought three.

Grover wondered out loud whether he was going to be doing any night shooting. If so, he had a Beamshot Laser Sight on sale for $79.95. Just attach it to the trigger guard and barrel. Point and shoot. He'd throw in some safety lenses with elastic back for snug, no-slip fit. They were shatter proof and enhanced visibility.

Yes, thought Chandler. An excellent idea. And a bargain at twice the price. He was able to afford it by pawning priceless objects from the Romneygate House for a fraction of their worth. Damn the swine with their race horses and Saratoga home. Think they could evict him like some common deadbeat.

Beau-Jack McCully laughing at him behind a poker face. Saying they needed to start out with small wagers to practice their skills and build confidence. Cousin Chan.

Just like Grover was saying. The handgun speaks plain and means what it says.

"How about some targets? I got Diane Feinstein. Got Brady in his wheelchair. And here's the Supreme Court."

■ ■ ■

Honor let loose and screamed when she climaxed. Afterwards, Beau-Jack, lying there, the pair of them naked, held her like she needed to be consoled for enjoying pleasure. She listened to her heart pounding, felt sensation return slowly to her hands and feet. She said he had certainly put her through a full range of extreme emotion. Sex with him was pure theater.

"Ardent courtship is like a kind of revelation," he agreed.

"Yes," she breathed heavily. "But it's like I'm the one getting wrung out. You're all relaxed. Or at least borderline cool. Haven't slashed my clothes with a razor blade yet. Left dead cats on my doorstep saying it was a sign of your affection."

The single vast cluttered room of his apartment was dark in the night. She was starting to learn something about furniture. Could distinguish satinwood from sweet gum. Identify Queen Anne style.

She stretched her long legs, her arms over her head. "I'm just lying here thinking. What a piece of work is man."

"Is that Shakespeare?"

"Ten points."

"I'm an erudite boy. If that's the right word."

"What else is on your personality profile?"

"I like to think I'm a boy of thought, care and concern. I understand commitment. I'm eager to commit."

"I'm not."

"Well, nothing's set in concrete. But you're pretty much guaranteed a rapturous reception any time you want to take your clothes off. Or if you don't. Just want to drop by and shoot the breeze. Talk about international relations or which way the Dow Jones went today."

Honor laced her hands behind her head and looked at the ceiling. "I've never had a man give me an outright rejection. That doesn't sound right. I don't mean for sex. I mean like I put out a feeler. Are you interested in me? They always lunge for it. What I've never experienced even once is to love a man and have him be indifferent to me. My mother would have told me I was vain and sinful to even have such a thought."

"Well, I can't say I agree with her on that. And I've eaten the apple. Know the difference between good and evil. Except for gray areas of which there are a gracious plenty. Those you work around. Your ill-gotten gains sometimes work out for the best. Sort of create your own justice system. Daddy taught me that."

She touched her cheeks. They were still flushed with color. "Do you miss your father?"

"I've pretty much put closure to him. Except for some loose ends here and there I had to wrap up. The old man had incurred some debts with folks who feel the sins of the forefathers should be visited upon later generations. Had to straighten that out. I've still got a small equity stake in the station. It's like a living memorial to his loud lifetime of mess-ups and fuck-ups. Failure became like a habit with him. He'd brush off the warnings."

"You participate in management?"

"No, Talisha Mackey does all that. Every day I'm right downstairs here on Queen Street with the sawdust and shellac."

"What I'm wondering is, these reproductions you make . . . ? And how there are suddenly two Tiverton commodes at WPST. Maybe you can shed some light on that?"

Beau-Jack's voice rose an octave. He said you know I always wanted you to hear me play the guitar. I've written a new song. "I Want to be your Bagboy in the Grocery Store of Life."

She said don't change the subject.

The doorbell rang. Someone was out on the wooden stairs.

Beau-Jack pulled his boxers on and told her to not move. Stay exactly as she was. Some kind of naked maja. Class remains in session. He'd get rid of whoever it was. And then he'd come back and start working on being indifferent towards her. See where that carried them. Frankly, m'dear I don't give a damn. That kind of thing.

As he walked to the door, Honor was idly looking around thinking the whole place was in desperate need of tidying up. Typical female. Or at least typical of Honor raised by Grace Revenue. It was like an inner direction inhabiting her skin.

A little dot of light played across the floor, then disappeared. She could see Beau-Jack's back. A voice mumbling at him that rose to a near shriek.

"Feeling inarticulate are we?"

BLAM BLAM BLAM!!!

She crossed the long distance in three racing steps. Long legs scissoring.

The door yawned open, black night outside. A clatter of footsteps had reached the bottom, now faded into distance on the cement of the sidewalk. A funny little dot of light was moving with the sound. Like a pinpoint flash light.

Beau-Jack lay in a welter of blood. Soundless. His eyes held a hint of guilty knowledge, then faded into a blur. Some dubious agenda had come back and bitten him in the vitals.

She touched him gently on the forehead with her fingertips, stifled a shriek.

She knew the number of EMS by heart. It was the legacy of Grace Revenue to have memorized emergency numbers. She held her voice calm with difficulty.

Afterwards, she knelt beside him unaware of her nudity. Held his face.

He was trying to talk, gasping. "Talk about mean-spirited. Underhanded. Vindictive."

She told him to shut up, and he did.

It seemed as though his soul was hovering above them. A puff of silver dust.

Time seemed to run in reverse. She was willing it backwards to make him live.

Finally she heard the scream of the ambulance cutting the silence.

42

"We get some real verisimilitude here. Your boy waiting anxiously on his front porch. Rooting around inside his pants. Scratching his nuts. 'Scuse my French."

Rannie Ralston was sitting in the office of the Solicitor which was what they called the prosecutor in South Carolina with the top dog himself. Him running a video the cops had made of one of her clients. Describing it with an informed dispassion. He always handled her personally. His assistants were terrified of being alone in a room with her.

"Here he's coming out to the curb waving down the FedEx truck. Driver's apologizing for being late. Hands over the delivery. Three tightly wrapped bricks of marijuana from Pensacola, Florida. Twelve pounds."

"What does that make the street value?" said Rannie. "$20,000? Around in there?"

"On the nose. Now look there. He's signing for it. Getting down his John Hancock. Rendering himself infamous. There goes the truck. Now here come our boys out of the surveillance van taking center stage."

"Freeze, mother-fucker," said Rannie drily, making her index finger into a gun and pointing at the screen. "Jeez, look at his face. He is the pratfall boy of the rogue's gallery."

The Solicitor laughed. "In the house we turned up fifteen more pounds, scales, a box of cash. $5,679 to be precise. We seized an Audi 5000. There's supposed to be a Mazda sports car somewhere. We can't locate it."

Rannie didn't mention she had already sold it in North Charleston, one of the lots near the Air base. Took the money as part of her fee. She also had a mortgage on the dirtbag's house.

When the general public decried light sentences for hardened criminals, wailed the justice system was too soft, what they overlooked was the unofficial fine—the lawyer's fee. Which was typically everything the simpleton scumbags had in this world. Rannie was almost legendary on Broad Street for wringing every last dime out of them.

Rannie said, "Not exactly a high-living, champagne-and-gold-chain lifestyle, that boy. Little junky frame house. Driving an Audi."

"No, but reasonably worth our trouble all the same."

Rannie sat there reflecting on the video, her career, an uncomplex relationship with her client. The video camera had led to a kind of environmental degradation for the hoodlum class. Turned even the garden variety of arrest into a ritual killing. She had pretty much plucked the turkey. Smart management of the account dictated expediting him into the slammer, moving on to new pastures.

She said, "A veteran lawman like yourself zealously pursuing my client, I'd say he's in great danger."

"You got a penchant for the apt turn of phrase."

"Thanks. I guess I can be a surrogate mother here.

Speak for my client and say he'll take whatever plea you offer."

"Forgiveness has its place in my vocabulary. Long as he does his time. Flies right afterwards. Course none of them seem to."

Rannie said she always enjoyed courthouse banter, but she had a living to earn. The Solicitor said don't do anything he wouldn't do.

She left the courthouse and walked down Broad street in the murderous southern heat. Rode the elevator up to her corner office in the People's Building with its view of the harbor panorama.

The ratty decor gave her the old familiar feelings. Safe like her daddy was still there and Charleston had kept its old ways. Two o'clock midday dinner. Courts closing in August because of the heat and everyone riding the train up to Flat Rock.

She kicked off her shoes and put her feet up on the desk. Lace black stockings. Crotch of her panty hose wet with sweat. Her pussy a pocket of frustration.

She had spent an hour on the phone that morning explaining to an asshole New York lawyer he wasn't going to share the Honor Revenue fee because he didn't do jackshit on a no-brainer of a case against Dombey & Trouche. He yelled and cussed and postured. New York yankee cussing. Using "fucking" as an adjective for every noun. Said he was going to the fucking Ethics fucking Committee about her.

She told him you do that. Go down that landmine-strewn road. But make sure you never come to South Carolina because she'd find some reason to have him put in jail. Late on a Friday after the judges were all gone home. See if he could get his ass through to Monday and the bond hearing.

"And I do mean ass. Literally. No metaphor intended."

Rannie got out the desk bourbon and poured a straight shot into a short glass. Drank it down.

Well Beau-Jack McCully was shot up amid gossip he was the target of the same bookie who detonated his father. Rannie Ralston knew better. That infectious grin hid the mind of a Class-A bandit. Deserved every copper-jacketed bullet. Bugger him. Women in menopause have to put up with hot flashes. That would even the score a bit.

Rannie had used Beau-Jack as a kind of stiff-dick litmus test and he had flipped her off. Given her a goddam look of disdain. Gone slavering after Honor Revenue like every other dildo brain man she had ever known in Charleston.

What was their freaking, dinky-dick problem? In a world swarming with passive-aggressive, dependent, big-hair bimbos, her feelings were uncomplicated. She didn't whine or sit around and soul-search. Didn't trampoline between wide-eyed cheeriness and morbid depression. It wasn't like she tried to deceive. She let her motives all hang out. Men could formulate their own point of view.

She despised charity events, loathed the Junior League. Used a personal shopper because malls made her break out in hives. She was healthily infused with good old fash-ioned animal lust. A moderate will to power. Some con-trolled greed. And why not? Without the profit motive, there was no way to measure success. She didn't think herself excessively opportunistic. But the main chance was after all the main chance. No point in not popping Browder Delamere where it hurt, taking a million dollar commode off people who had no appreciation for the finer things.

Besides, she had her moral responsibility to a motor-mouth mother and bubbly, bouncing doodlebug sister. Big economic sinkhole of a house on Legendre. Supporting all that made her feel like that painting of the Volga boatmen dragging a barge with a rope tied around her waist.

For shit's sake, she never whined at men about sharing household duties or getting in touch with their inner child. Didn't give a big goddam whether the toilet seat was left up or the toothpaste got squeezed out of the middle of the tube. She put in her diaphragm without any big fuss, didn't view a hard cock as an outmoded force in the information age.

Rannie poured herself another straight shot. Held it under her nose enjoying the sour mash odor. It helped her do a little honest introspection.

Goddamned Honor Revenue had always been man-bait. Sumptuous tits on that girl. So what? Rannie had big tits too. Splash of freckles across them. Ochre nipples big as saucers. They hung down pretty heavily, but that's what big tits did. It wasn't like Honor's could stand at attention.

But that wasn't the whole picture. There was something sultry there. Or torrid. Whatever the word was. Drop-dead knockout. Irresistibly alluring. Saying, "You want me?" Check into Heartbreak Hotel. It's right down there at the end of Lonely Street.

For the first time in her life, Rannie had a brief thought of her biological clock. Tick-tick-tick it went faintly.

She poured another shot of liquor, downed it, and flung the glass violently against the wall.

Well, no comment on that. Ya gotta play hurt, the football jocks always said.

■ ■ ■

Beau-Jack kept trying to talk around the tube that went down his throat. He said they might have saved him, but he was dying spiritually with all this plastic crap stuck in him. It was not an easy punch to roll with. Lying here in a hospital gown, his life in disarray.

Honor said it was a turbulent night for all concerned. Had the police asked him for the identity of the gunman? They had sure been on her case about it.

Beau-Jack said he had two bullets lodged so close to his heart the doctors were just going to leave them there. He'd set off airport alarms whenever he flew.

Honor said this truth-is-not-in-you routine sure reduces whatever leverage he had. So at the risk of bruising his ego, maybe racking up his over-inflated sense of self-worth, she thought she'd leave.

He took hold of her hand, said how about an outreach program? He thought their hearts were integrally bound up together.

"Are you into fishing?" Honor asked. "Sure. A macho guy like you. Well just think of this as a tag-and-release program. I'm chucking you back in the water."

Beau-Jack protested he knew his history was dismal, but he was working on changing values. Did she know you could put all of Emily Dickinson's poetry to the tune of the "Gilligan's Island" theme song? He sang her a couple of lines.

"Because I could not stop for death
He kindly stopped for me."

Honor said he was probably wondering if his little boy charm would win her over. Well he wouldn't wonder for long because she was going *a-dios*, m-effer, good-bye.

He yelled after her, "Hey, do you like homemade ice cream?"

Well not really yelled. More like a croak.

43

"I'm sure you'll want to abide by your mother's wishes," simpered Rusty Royall. He leaned back in his office chair. Made a steeple of his fingers.

Honor said well actually no she wouldn't. Or what she meant was her mother hadn't intended to give the commode to St. Ambrose. It hadn't belonged to Grace to give anyway. It was Honor's. Always had been.

For the first time in her life it didn't bother her to tell a lie.

Rusty was real snooty. He said she was violating the norms of charity and good taste.

Honor said she couldn't see why getting things in line with his version of events was some automatic good taste.

Rusty allowed he was very busy bringing in a diverse music program and enhancing statewide communication between the races. These demands on his time had obliged him to hire an established law firm to represent his interest in the commode. He named one of the more pompous attorneys in town.

"Well, that's going to make things very tense around here," said Honor.

He got flip. "That's easily resolved. You're fired."

She said what?

He grimaced slightly. "Sacked. Discharged. Whatever you wish to call it. Browder Delamere is solid with me on this one. You lawsuit against Dombey & Trouche is totally inappropriate for an employee of St. Ambrose."

"Inappropriate? They took my money."

"Well, there are two sides to that one. Anyhow, freeing up your slot will streamline procedures. It was inevitable really. Despite your little machinations."

"My what?"

His eyes slid away, then moved back to meet hers. "Sure, you know you're visually pleasing. And you use it to your advantage. All the little body language. Moving into the man's space with oozy fluidity. The gentle touch of fingertips on his arm."

Honor's mouth snapped shut, fury surging through her. She couldn't get out all the ugly words she wanted to say. "I want my final paycheck," she finally stammered. "Or I'll go to the Labor Department."

"Of course," he replied. "I'll write it out myself. You can cuddle up with my signature. Go girlish romantic over it."

■ ■ ■

Talisha answered the phone at the station when a white man called saying Roscoe Morningstar had missed his monthly visit. WPST was listed as his employer.

Talisha said, "And you are?"

"His parole officer."

Talisha thought oh shit. I'm sitting here all full of purity of purpose. Got floor-to-ceiling problems. Do I need this on top of everything else? What she said was she didn't think Roscoe was willfully lost because they had a big church service coming up she knew he didn't want to miss.

The white man said he was being nice, taking the time to call when he might have been sleeping late. But he was getting old, less tolerant of dissent. And if Roscoe didn't like their little monthly chats, didn't see any moral value in them, then maybe he'd violate him.

Talisha asked did that mean what she thought it did? He said yes. Just take it as a word of heavy caution.

Outside, a hot orange sun had the creaky old window air conditioner straining hard. All she needed was for the compressor to blow out.

Roscoe came through the door dressed in a parachute silk shirt open to the navel, his hair, glistening, slicked with Let's Jam gel.

She asked where you been? Your parole officer is getting lonely. Called up wanting me to commiserate with him.

Rosco answered lazily, hey, in my Father's house be many mansions.

"What does that mean? You got a bunch of girl friends? Place to shack up?"

He asked if she wanted a weighty report? An in-depth review? There were so many diversion in Charleston which was why the city was attracting out-of-state retirees.

Talisha said she didn't want his bullshit and gave him a stern lecture about what they're up to raising the ratings to get up ad revenues and keep the station out of bankruptcy. Shoulder to the wheel, nose to the grindstone, eye on the ball. She said how often we hear old folks saying here they did all these tests and the doctors still don't know what's wrong with me. Well she had no problem with the diagnosis. Roscoe was a con artist. And anyhow, what had he been behind bars for exactly?

Roscoe never lacked for a line of bullshit. He said for being a victim of the circumstance where he lacked the money to hire a top-flight legal talent and had to plead guilty. Any courtroom jury would have exonerated him. He was a man of proven style in the innocence arena. And anyhow there was corruption in that arresting cop force that went high, deep and wide. He could sure enough attest to that. Them crooked schemes and patterns cops get up to were a sight to behold.

Talisha was thinking do I need this shit? Whitey will give you forty acres and a mule, but he finds there's oil on it, he wants it back. She was about ready to have Rannie Ralston and now a second big law firm on her case about the commodes. It was like feeling the edge of a switchblade on her throat.

She said injustice was a shameful thing and she was all tore up weepy over Roscoe's version of it. Could he hear her voice catching at the thought of him being so wronged? But be that as it may, if he didn't keep his sorry ass out of trouble, she'd personally take the gloves off and call his parole officer to come out swinging.

He gave her a paternal pat. "Lord, honey, where's that turn-the-other-cheek philosophy? All the work I been doing ought to prompt some kudos and not all this nay-saying."

"We ain't been together long enough for this relationship to be trust-based."

"Evah-thang is cool. With my preaching leadership—and your back-up assistance—you'll get you a top-rated radio program. We going to do more than just swap greetings with those white church goers. We'll give 'em the moral certainty along with the finest lineup of gospel choirs in the Lowcountry. A musical feast for the ears. Hally-loo-ya. Lemme add emphasis to that. HALLY-LOOOO-YAH!"

Talisha's eyes puckered into a hard squint. "I been warned all my life to look out for what monsters I create. But lemme warn you. That last scene in Frankenstein, the village folks chase the monster over the cliff. In your case that translates—you fuck up—do something premeditated criminal—I won't wait for a parole officer to act. You're gonna suffer a permanent nervous breakdown when I bust something over your punkin' head. I'm sensitive to human needs in that way."

44

Rannie was chatting casually as she got Honor to sign the release of liability for Dombey & Trouche, indorse the insurance check to be put in the trust account. "Well, they say humor is nothing more than thinly veiled aggression."

Honor thought about that, wondered if it was profound or just an observation. Said she guessed she agreed.

"In which case," added Rannie, "I always like the joke to be on the opposing side. And fuck 'em if they can't take it."

The trust account was used to make a record of the transaction and to separate out Rannie's hefty one-third fee. She tore Honor's check out of the big book and held it up to the light. "God I like money. There's an almost poetic fantasy about it."

Honor was surprised to observe she had gotten all of her lost investment plus a big whack more. Rannie pointed out that was the advantage of the punitive damages laid on top of the actuals. You can never overshoot the mark with those. Sure, you lose an appeal from time to time. But punitives keep the defense firms skittish—even terrified—especially when you've got a super plaintiff such as the seductive and unblemished Honor Revenue.

Honor said she wasn't totally unblemished. She had her catalog of bad experiences. Men were a big question mark to her. Like there was an impassable gulf between the sexes.

Rannie agreed it was a telling point. Sometimes she'd be giving a guy head, really getting into it, start moaning and groaning with her own excitement. And he'd panic. Wilt away to nothing. She'd realize they weren't singing off the same song sheet.

Honor didn't blink at the vulgarity. "They act so imperious when they want you. Cave man demanding blind devotion. I have trouble expressing my anger about it."

Rannie nixed that sentiment. Said resist all impulses to fatalism.

Honor said runway work, being under the hot lights and camera lens did that to you. You were extremely passive. Changing your guises according to the mood of a designer. The moves were standard repertoire. You could vamp or pout, but that was pretty much it. A lot of girls were on heroin because there was so much lethargy in the work, so much floating.

Rannie chimed in, "You're not alone. Sometimes I feel my career's like TV. A reality-based cop and lawyer show. I'm the young ingénue out of a method acting school. Been tapped to join the cast. You get my point? I feel like the whole thing is a put-up job. A performance. A simulated world."

Honor looked at her check. The money was truly there. Amazing. "You must get a lot of applause."

"Bullshit. Ever since I debuted as a lawyer, what I do,

I always face a mob of critics. You go head-to-head with men, they always cry foul. Charge you with general viciousness. 'Where are the last vestiges of femininity?' they huff. They bristle and mutter and whine. Can't take the torque of balls-to-the-wall litigation. If you ever stumble, lose the ice maiden composure and shed a tear, the bastards will cut you no slack. So you've got to deal in malice from time to time. Remind them you have claws."

In her mini-skirt and black stockings, blood red nails, Rannie looked like she had more than claws. She looked positively carnivorous.

"I tell you it's a wimpy world of hamster-dick guys out there," Rannie griped. "State attorney General's office has set up a hot-line to report school bullying. 888-NO-BULLY. Can you believe that? Where's the next generation of men to come from? Is there even a present generation? Real men who can do emphatic straight-on balling with precision in the details. Men with testosterone reservoirs too vast for an ordinary world. Has it all been culturally conditioned out of them by hordes of controlling mothers?"

She paused and looked out the window thoughtfully.

"You know, just about the time I hit puberty, my daddy took me to a race horse auction up in Camden. Huge, sleek, glistening stud racehorses being paraded in front of the select crowd. I watched a hard-jawed tycoon spend twelve million dollars in under ten minutes. He'd raise a big phallic unlit cigar to make his bid. Never hesitating. Absolutely certain of what he wanted from life. Money no object. There was an erotic intensity about it that got right to my vitals.

"In retrospect, I'm convinced it brought on my first period just at that moment. At the time I was mortified. Little teenager hustling out of the auction tent with blood dripping profusely down her leg. Stared at by high-tone ladies draped in sables and mink."

45

"Nobody tole me the road would be this hard!

I don't believe He brought me this far to leave me now!

Come on, Jesus, see me through!"

St. Ambrose was absolutely rocking to the massed voices of The Rock-a-delphia Brotherly Love Harmonizers; Deion Breazeale and the Blind Lemon Boys; Lottie, Hattie, Maybelle & Flo Quartet; and the Afrocentric Methodist Chorale. For a solid hour they had been sure enough laying down some righteous gospel.

Talisha ran the recording equipment, patient and stiff, very aware of her role, proud this would be a supreme hit for the ratings. Her momma had sent her off with the warning this strutting off to white churches, she had her nose so far up in the air she'd get drowned in a rain storm. Talisha just looked grumpy at her. Oneida glazed her eyes. Said she was going to go have an angina attack. Maybe a fatal one.

The Reverend Roscoe P. Morningstar in tomato red robes held out his hands like Moses dividing the Red Sea. The music fell to a steady humming. The basso profundo voice boomed.

"I've said it before."

"Un-huh."

"I say it now with greater impatience."

"Amen."

"Playing with sin is like unto routine handling of radio-active waste."

"Amen to that, brother."

"Radium will make you glow in the dark."

"You tell 'em."

Some of the whites had facial paralysis, but most of them were loving it like he was a local saint or something. Clapping their hands like the black folks. Getting into the amen saying. A couple of the charismatic white women fainted.

"Sin will light you up in the afterlife. Amen. Set you ablaze. Amen. Bring on that sulfur and brimstone. Unn-huh. Find you in a double slaying from fatal error. Yeh-man. For that's the kind of thing it does. Amen. For the Lord God on High will implement the letter of the law and the backward and behindhand will come to the mourners' bench in sorrow and in pain."

They were taking up so many collections, love offerings, special missions, insurance funds for churches burned out by KKK racists. Reverend Roscoe sweating like he had a fresh coat of varnish on him, egging them on. Urging them to give to the utmost. Don't just give on a Chevette level. Not just on a Mercury Grand Marquis. But move on up to Lincoln Mark VIII.

Meanwhile the massed choirs started doing their thing big time.

"I'm climb*in' up*
Onnn the rough side
Offff the moun-*tain.*
Doin' the best
That I can!"

That solid wall of sound just swelled and rumbled and echoed. It was so fine.

Just before the final benediction, Rusty Royall announced there would be a joint bank account of matching funds—WPST and St. Ambrose—for good deeds, good works and other goodliness.

As she bowed her head for that last prayer, Talisha thought—WPST had no money to contribute.

Then it went through her brain like a lightning bolt.

Holy Moses! It's the pigeon drop!

She couldn't begin to guess how far this would go and how bad it would turn out. All of those could be known if she saw the bank balance.

She edged her way up to Rusty Royall, said she thought it had come off just fine. She expected him to say it was a rousing success. Just gush all over her with praise.

Instead, he was very stiff. Accepting her tribute. She was now the nobody go-between for this important condescending white church and all the black rabble out there. Keeping a separate territory.

"I believe it went rather well," he said, looking over her head, greeting other people.

She thought high-tone asshole with the ghost flesh. The

contempt was writ-large across that sneer. What she said was, "You're making a mistake to allow Roscoe to get at that bank account."

"I think it is only . . . fitting," Rusty replied, carefully choosing the word. He used his obey me woman tone. I am the rector of St. Ambrose. Don't bother me with prattle.

This was the white man got thrown out on his ass from St. Memphis AME for talking about dick and pussy symbolism.

She saw Honor Revenue and wondered if she'd treat her like hired help too. Demand her million dollar commode back right in front of everybody.

Her voice just a little too bright, she told Honor that Reverend Roscoe was getting primed to run off with the money in the joint account. Honor shrugged, told her she had been fired by Rusty Royall.

Talisha got more insistent. "I don't want to be too stingy with the prurient details. But they're about to get fleeced by a thing called the pigeon drop. Pretend to find money. Get some old fool to put up an equal amount as good faith promising to divide the found cash. Take off with the fool's gold."

Honor seemed to think on the problem. She said she was trying to be sympathetic to St. Ambrose, but it was difficult. Rusty Royall kept getting between her and the church in her thoughts. It made for a fitful meditation.

Talisha went on saying she figured there were two choices. She could have a conniption. Or she could clam up. Realizing of course Roscoe was a missile she had aimed at the target even if it was Rusty Royall who pushed the button. Which tied her in with the guilt.

"You couldn't let the Reverend hide his light under a bushel," said Honor. "And, as I mentioned earlier, I've been fired."

■ ■ ■

"You low-grade moron," Rannie Ralston said flatly. Ordinarily, she would have been more expressively crude. Still, she had achieved the desired effect.

Browder Delamere seemed to shrink into his seat. "I was late for the golf course," he whined. "I told Rusty to do what he thought best."

What had happened was Reverend Roscoe had snookered Rusty into putting an "or" between the two names on the joint account instead of an "and." Which made it a cinch for him to return an hour later and withdraw all but $500 of the money.

"I guess he wanted to spare St. Ambrose having to pay service charges on the account," Honor suggested. "Minimum balance requirements."

Everyone turned her way.

"Hey, don't look at me. I was fired. Browder signed off on it." She proffered him the discharge letter. He looked at it like it had been fished out of a toilet.

"I think," said Rannie, "our Mister Delamere will be having some personal liablity on this one. I've never in my life seen such gross dereliction of fiduciary duty."

Delamere sqawked like a peacock with its tailfeathers yanked out. He couldn't believe the bank would permit such an obvious scam. There were other members of the board who had just as much responsibility as him. And what about Rusty Royall? He had actually done the deed. And it wasn't Broward's idea in the first place. Rusty had brought all this integration into the church.

"I'm not sure how we're supposed to respond," said Rannie. "Hallmark doesn't make a card that celebrates collective stupidity."

Rusty wandered in distracted like he had misplaced something and had come to fetch it. Delamere looked at his watch, frowned at the time.

Rusty hesitated as though seeing them all for the first time, addressed the group. "It's odd when you think about it. The Greek word *agapao*—love—used in the New Testament is actually a translation of the Hebrew word for 'seduce' or 'allure'. There would seem to be something a little more salacious there. Hmm? Wouldn't you agree?"

Browder spoke to him sharply. "Rusty, we're holding this meeting to deal with the purloined church treasury. You were expected, no, *required* to be here." He tapped his watch.

"Oh that. I seem to have an almost complete memory loss on the subject. I wasn't very helpful to the police, I'm afraid. Perhaps I'm suffering an adjustment disorder."

Browder said there were plenty of resources to help him refresh his memory. The *Post & Courier* and the two local TV stations were creating their own little media bandwagon. Because St. Ambrose was an Episcopal church, news of the scandal was expected to spread. Maybe make the national press.

Rusty kind of fluttered. "I've been tragically manipulated in so many ways. I really need to address these issues on Sunday."

"What I think you need," prescribed Rannie, "is a massive dose of horse tranquilizers. Afterwards, we'll vote you a profiles-in-asininity award."

He looked mildly shocked. "Oh my. I sense you're really exercised over this."

Rannie gave him a saturnine smile, knowing for sure he was doomed. This fact buoyed her up enormously. And that fool Browder with his portrait in heraldic armor. By the time she was finished he'd replace the entire sum out of his own pocket.

There were those weeks when she'd get discouraged with living South-of-Broad, think about moving over to Mt. Pleasant in one of those tract mansion subdivisions where the streets had names like Bay Rum Meander. At Halloween the Martha Stewart housewives would carve art deco jack o'lanterns. Fly orange flags with witches' cats on them.

No, she'd stay in the Broad Street office where her father's name was still stenciled on the door.

46

"The *title* of my sermon today is taken from a *headline* in the newspaper: 'Naked man throws head in dumpster.'"

Rusty Royall looked over his half glasses at the congregation, took a ministerial pause, then repeated it. Ministerial emphasis and oratory.

"*Naked* man . . . throws *head* . . . in dumpster. A severed head. Not his own."

He read the short blurb from Norman, Oklahoma about how somebody became suspicious when he saw a naked man throwing a bloody knapsack into a trash bin. So he looked inside and found a severed head. And the cops went to the perp's apartment and arrested him taking a bath. Rusty used the word 'perp'. Like a cop would.

"Events of this nature convince me for sure that Satan lives and walks among us. That he works often through the female in the form of a witch."

Pause to survey the congregation which sat in baffled silence.

"The star goddess rising. Ishtar. Isis. Astarte. Tanis."

Pause.

"I myself have had a personal experience of such a

fiendish creature. I knew her dark powers *immediately.* There was a *galvanic* skin response. Heightened heartbeat."

His words hung in the sanctuary. The rustling of feet stopped, everyone as still as mice.

He pulled off his glasses, sucked on them thoughtfully. "Perhaps I should have killed her," he mused at the ceiling. This was said lightly. Giving his citations. "Exodus 22:18; Deuteronomy 18:10."

His voice turned whining and self-serving. Making excuses. He was naive by nature. Busied himself with the rector's craft. Giving unselfishly. He had thought of introducing break dancing into the church. It had weighed heavily on his mind at the time.

"When the inevitable *seduction* occurred—mine of course—I'm an innocent victim here—but when it occurred, I flattered myself that I was serving the needs of a parish member crying out for help. I did not scatter my semen in the street among strangers."

The first gasp went through the congregation.

He shook his glasses at them, continued with steady emphasis, searching the faces as he spoke. "Oh sure, I could tell what was coming the moment her clothes were off. Before then it was problematic. She had moderately sized . . ." He held his hands before his chest as though cupping bosoms. "Would have preferred larger. They're a competitive advantage when you're a witch. *Anyhow*, I didn't relish the process of a fall from grace. But we live in a world with game show reruns of Tic Tac Dough. Do you follow me here? *Howsomever*, it worked out reasonably well. She was more than adequate at the Kama Sutra. Might have been sixty queens and eighty concubines.

That's a Biblical reference. What's my cite here? Hmm? Anyone?"

Old Elmer Wandsworth got up at that point and started trying to work his way down the aisle. He was notoriously incontinent and wore an adult diaper.

Rusty fixed him with a fierce glare. "Well ex-*cuse* me please for boring you."

Wandsworth mumbled an apology and sat down, the row shifting to give him space.

"Yes, I confess to *knowing* her. Our strokes were controlled *and* rhythmic. You groan when your flesh and body is *consumed*. I *panted* after her cave. I *accomplished* my desire in her thicket."

He paused. In the deafening silence, someone made a slight cough.

His rant became even more jumbled, almost incoherent. Later they would chatter all over town, repeating his biblical sounding homilies. The mouth of a loose woman is a deep pit. A harlot may be hired for a loaf of bread. Her house is the way to Sheol. And the most frequently quoted—Oral sex is not all peaches and cream.

Enrollment in the Bible classes rose.

But at the moment, everyone rigidly sat through it. He had dropped a little neutron bomb among them, and they were all corpses sitting there with the furniture and walls intact.

At last it reached a feverish crescendo. He realized his error. He was at fault and yet not at fault. She was a wanton harlot, an evil, malign, putrid seductress. He was ready to name names. Bring out the ducking stool, the stocks and the stake. These implements were all listed with relish. His eyes glared with an image of vengeance.

"The witch among us . . . a young woman whose appeal arises in *equal measure* from tits and ass . . . the dark sorceress among you . . . is . . ."

He gripped the edge of the pulpit readying himself for the last revelation. His eyes narrowed.

Honor shut her eyes and sank very low in the pew.

"Moira *Ralston!*"

A collective gasp went through the congregation. As one they turned and gaped at her.

"You are an evil, simpering little fuck!" Rusty thundered.

Moira was accustomed to a certain comfort level. Under ordinary conditions, palmetto bugs and silverfish would send her into a frenzy.

She began a high falsetto shrieking that seemed like it would never stop.

■ ■ ■

"I've always wondered why you don't find more avocado trees in Charleston," said Grace Revenue to no one in particular.

Honor was gaping at her mother. Grace standing there in the flesh outside St. Ambrose as everyone milled about, flower-decked hats everywhere, hats trailing chiffon. Rusty's sermon and Moira's attack of the screaming-meemies had them so preoccupied, they didn't really remark upon Grace's return from the grave.

"When you think about it," said Grace, "everyone takes

the big pit out of the avocado, suspends it on toothpicks on top of a glass of water. They get little green sprouts. But then what? What happens to all of them?"

Honor stared at this apparition. Grace was dressed for church in a salmon and white flowered dress, matching hat and white shoes. She had her bicycle although she normally walked to church without it. Had she retrieved it from the police?

"Let me ask the obvious," said Honor drily. "Where have you been?"

"Oh, that's not important. I just wanted a little rehearsal. Let you warm up to my being dead."

Honor rolled her eyes. "Sure. That's a plausible motive."

"You know, despite all the adverse publicity a whole bunch of cereal and cookie companies are still using coconut and palm oil. It will absolutely plug your arteries."

The ambulance came, its siren falling to a purr as it stopped. After a time, Rusty Royall was brought out in a straitjacket. "I'm willing to submit to a mediated discussion," he said in a brittle voice. "I would be remiss if I failed to propose it. But witchcraft is a fact. You have a right to redefine usage. True. Call a coven a goddess cult if you will. But the broomstick is a fertility pole. Let's face it. A phallic symbol. A dildo. The old religion—the worship of the horned one—survives among us. It's impossible to overstate the threat."

"You need to lie down, Rusty," ordered Browder Delamere. Authoritative. In charge. "Need a nice rest."

"Owww!" Rusty protested, struggling against them. Suddenly peevish. "My foot hurts me. It was run over by a golf cart when I was in college."

Moira had stopped her keening, now seemed perplexed by all the attention. Her voice was . . . well, warbling. She sounded a bit like a canary. "Oh my goodness it's sure bright out here in the light of midday. My eyes. I can barely see. Who are all these people? I swan you barely know anybody in church these days."

"This is nice seeing such a large crowd," said Grace. "Rusty Royall has certainly built up the congregation."

"Mental illness on your level should not go untreated," Honor said furiously.

47

A ruined and heartsick Chandler Lovelace sat in the cavernous Romneygate House staring at the *Post & Courier* sports section. Some gigantic negro with the bizarre name of Shaquille O'Neal had signed a seven-year $120 million contract with the LA Lakers.

One hundred twenty million dollars.

Chandler slurped down the last of his vodka tonic.

Because he had led the NBA in scoring.

About his move from the Orlando Magic the Shaq said, "Hey, change happens."

Chandler's teeth hurt him and his eyes were bloodshot. One hundred and twenty million dollars.

There used to be a strong sense of order, of the rightness of things. Now he felt displaced, vulnerable, solitary. Shuffling his way in carpet slippers towards an undeserved doom. A migraine headache resonated inside his skull like a funeral dirge.

Chandler longed for his old world of afternoon tea. Smoked salmon and water cress sandwiches. Drop scones smeared with strawberry jam and clotted Devonshire cream. Thick slices of Dundee cake. And then so quickly after, the sun sinking beneath the yardarm heralding the first drinks of the evening.

Lumbered by the dead weight of self-pity, he wanted to break down and blubber. And would have but for the entrance of Leone Jones who sat down and opened his own newspaper. Cocksure. His cap on in the house and turned sideways like some moron Step-n-fetchit.

"Man, you looking a right royal bunch of depression. And they say black folks are all sulky. You filling the room with gloom. And we got what here? Twenty foot ceiling?"

A sense of unreality clung to Leone. Those big grinning ivory teeth. A comic darkie made of Staffordshire china one would set upon the mantel alongside Toby mugs and pug dogs.

Leone folded the paper. "Being in broadcast medium, I'm a little out of touch with the print format. But here I happen to pick up the local rag and see some items of inter-est. Here's Charleston County paying a consultant dude $57,000 to figure out what kind of water-related recreation folks want. Ask about sailing regattas, power ski events, aquatic programs. Can you believe that sweet-heart deal shit? Get paid all that to ax'em what they want? You can fake any kind of answer you please. Anything would make sense. But that's the growth of big government for you. Nobody feels ashamed of stealing.

"Then I turn over the page and lookie here. WPST get-ting commodes of great value. I'm grateful for the media attention. Because it's brought right out in the open how you playing this whole greed thing close to the vest. You see what it is, the gossip among all the colored help down here in the big houses is them commodes worth a cool million apiece.

"Now Sierra Leone Jones show up with his patented just-in-time strategy. Upright like a wall. Sergeant Rock of Easy Company. Ever read them war comics when you a kid? No? I always liked him. 'Why do they call him the rock?' 'Cause a wall may fall, Mister, but not a rock.' Made me stay free of drugs growing up. Some dude offer me a blunt, I say no thank you."

"Did I miss the doorbell?" said Chandler, fixing him with a cold fishy stare. "You did ring didn't you?"

"No, man. The door was open. Didn't want to bother you none. You doing a social butterfly act all alone in this big place. Anyhow, it's time for direct action. We bust them suckers out of WPST by brute force. I tell you I'm custom-made for this purpose. It's a challenge and I accept it gladly. You see each of us got a arena where we the dominant player. Me with the muscle finesse, you in fencing the things in New York. We can capitalize on them differently-abled advantages. Did I mention I borrowed us a van type vehicle from some West Ashley fool had it just sitting there in his driveway? Chevy Silverado Suburban. Tinted glass. Captain's chairs. Custom running boards. Thing's like new. 35,000 miles. Still under factory warranty which we can't exactly use, but it'll replace that lost Oldsmobile of yours and it's much more practical for our needs."

Chandler sat rigid and silent. He was thinking this black African swine had just barged into the Romneygate House without so much as a by-your-leave. No doorbell ringing, no knocking for him. Giving him slow grins. Had actually winked at him.

Classic case of uppity nig-nog-itis. Always an error to delay the needed discipline. Give him the ol' heave-ho from a high place. Or perhaps a bit of gunplay. There had been something very satisfying about blasting Beau-Jack McCully. The startled look. The way he sprawled backwards.

Chandler's nostrils quivered with the excitement of the thought.

"Man, you got allergies? What's this nose wiggling? Look like a bunny rabbit. I tell you what. What say we cut a deal? We load up this furniture, drive north. Riding that van like a hot streak. Stop for fast food when we get hungry. Take a cooler with some brews. No tension. We're seemingly compatible. Good chemistry. Despite minor set-backs, we hit the Big Apple and scope out the antique scene. Get the feel of the street. Stress patience."

"You're being utterly obtuse," said Chandler, trying to focus on what this galoot was saying. Did he mean they could liberate the commode?

"What's that suppose to mean? Lemme guess. It's kind of a whole attitude thing. I'm trying to fend off discord, but you always talking down to me. Makes me wonder whether I do all this work I'll get my due."

"What I'm saying is I don't get your point."

"No double-crosses until we actually get our hands on the cash money. The purse. The ledger balance. Then it's every man for hisself. What do you say? Let's have a show of hands."

■ ■ ■

"You develop a customer base of scumbags," said Rannie Ralston. Explaining to this blue blazer little boy from the big law firm how she built her practice.

"There are no how-to articles to read. Do it by feel. You keep your prices up. No Blue-Light specials. Affordability's not the deciding factor in selecting a criminal lawyer. Dirt-bags want to be overawed by how expensive and important you are."

She knew the little twit. Reynolds Lanneau Smith-Darnelle. Two years out of law school. He had once given a speech at the Bar Association on the need for tort reform. That was code for stacking the civil litigation deck in the favor of the big insurance defense firms and effectively running people like Rannie out of business.

"It's, um, certainly a personality contrast . . . between you and your sister."

Rannie checked herself from saying Moira is the family equivalent of a root canal. Telling him she used to chop up Moira's Barbies with a meat cleaver. She was wondering why this earnest little shit had come to her office to waste her time. He told her.

"Noble Royall has a history of spiritual instability. He has spoken from the pulpit of a belief in psychic powers and reincarnation. In front of a hundred witnesses. The distress to your sister Moira was unconscionable. He . . . mauled her emotionally, I suppose you would say."

"Well, allow me to express shock at this point," Rannie said. He didn't catch the sarcasm in her voice. "It's definitely been a time of great stress for her. And she has come to me to repair her injuries."

"So what law would you say has been violated?"

"In the pulpit he is the agent of St. Ambrose. Under the common law, to impugn the chastity of a young woman is slander per se."

Rannie was completely taken aback when he proposed they join forces to sue St. Ambrose and Rusty jointly and severally. Thinking practically, the church's insurance policy had no experience-based premium. It would remain constant even if they took the carrier for a hefty sum. And Rusty probably had insurance of his own.

Rannie agreed it was an appropriate course of action in the situation. She admired the logic.

Reynolds cleared his throat nervously. "I hate to mar a professional relationship with sentimentality . . . but Moira . . ."

Rannie knitted her brows. "Yes?"

"I don't want to be too vague about our status. The current realities of the situation . . . are, um, we're communicating on an on-going basis . . . um . . . romantically. Which is why I need to associate you in this action. It might be otherwise unethical."

Rannie didn't make it easy for him. "Yes?"

"Moira and I have a clear consensus between us on most matters. Sometimes I feel rather like weeping from pure bliss." He was smiling stupidly at some idealized vision of southern womanhood.

Good God almighty, Rannie thought.

She had no direct precedents to draw on when it came

to matchmaking for little mint-tea Moira. But unless she missed her guess, this seemed about perfect.

Reynolds was a Citadel graduate. He'd have the sword mounted on his wall, the senior photo in the dress uniform with the brass buttons and white cross belts. Moira would come in her pants just looking at it.

University of South Carolina law school. Made the law review of course. Couldn't be in a big firm otherwise. He'd say things like the Citadel gave him the discipline to succeed in law school. This would be the part Moira would never quite plug into. The earning a living part. But he'd act all dominant and directive. Go off to work each day to pay for a big house South-of-Broad and let Moira water plants and plague servants with her endless demands.

He was the gold-plated bozo of her dreams.

Reality would pop up later. What did car dealers call it? Sticker shock? Wait'll he found out how expensive she was. And when the bubblyness turned to hysteria over lost small objects. But that was way off in the future where dreams die their sickly deaths.

Right now the burning June heat coming through the window, casting its vicious rectangle on the floor seemed mild and comforting. The dirty pigeons on the windowsill might have been nightingales from a magic garden of Kublai Khan.

Well. This was a boost to both profits and morale. Yes indeedy, the turnaround here was real. Maybe she'd have the three-chocolate mud pie for dessert at lunch. Not worry about her weight for once. Or the night cream she smeared on because there was no man in her bed with the deep green colored silk sheets.

"I'm looking forward to meeting your mother," said Reynolds. Voice holding a little quiver of humility. Hopeful of being accepted by the old Charleston *grande dame.*

Rannie smiled. Thinking he better do it before six in the evening when she passed out drunk.

On the return flight from Italy, Mary Canty had tried to bring fourteen coffee table books and a crate of Chianti onto the plane in carry-on luggage. The airline made her buy an extra seat.

48

Talisha looked at Honor Revenue real thoughtful, said, "You have any interest in an ownership share in a radio station? It's kind of a wild investment, but this is like the Wild West around here, all the folks what get shot up in this town.

"No need for an immediate decision. You could chill here for a couple weeks. See how you like Gospel Mainstream. Maybe even do a show. Help me get over sleep deprivation.

"What we do ultimately—once we get over the sophomore slump of low ratings—is put on gospel shows. We bring in class acts like Clarence Fountain and the Original Alabama Blind Boys. Get a preacher other than the thieving fat shit Roscoe Morningstar which was one serious fat mistake. Sell blessed one dollar bills for five dollars. You pick up eight maybe twelve dollars more a head than the gate. It's all in cash so the IRS has to guess the take."

She paused and used the remote control to flick on the ADT system downstairs, lock out the night and the wrong side of town. Talisha had let Honor through the front door around eleven p.m. You had to give the white girl points for integrity. She had come to talk about ownership. Not bringing that embodiment of badass lawyering, Rannie Ralston, with her.

Honor eyeballed the two commodes sitting side by side in the waiting room. "You really can't tell them apart," she said.

"I got me a genuine root doctor playing hanging-out cat each day. The man claim he can see behind the stars. He can't tell them apart."

It was about then that Leone climbed through the upstairs window looking like a gangsta cliché. Baggy pants and tennis shoes, black t-shirt with the sleeves cut out, cap turned backwards. And holding a short-barrel pistol. Said, "Is it lonely up here at the top? Hey, doing the schlockmeister Jesus late show are you? Lemme change the rhythm here."

He had put a ladder up against the side of the building. Chandler Lovelace came grunting and heaving through behind him. For a moment, it looked like he might get stuck. When he dropped his gun, they flinched back. He picked it up, shoved his shirttail in all around. He bent over, hands on his knees inhaling heavily like an asthmatic hippo.

"Look at the gun," said Leone, showing his own piece. "Be cool. Take your Thorazine."

He crossed to the open sound booth. They could hear him inside telling the microphone, "Lemme put you in touch with some emerging realities. New public stance. We're going to enjoy three straight, uninterrupted hours of the best jazz, boogie and blues. Starting out with, lemme see, Cassandra Wilson doing *Blue Light 'Til Dawn*. She will sure enough scorch you, un-huh."

"My inchoate desires are now made concrete," said Chandler, his voice atremble from either exhaustion or emotion, it wasn't clear which. "I believe in the gospel of prosperity." His gun waved from Talisha to Honor and back again. A little red laser dot bounced off them.

Talisha snapped at Leone when he came out to join them. "So you're more than a big mess of financial improprieties. You've come to arm rob me too."

He smiled big and ice-cold. "You got selective amnesia, girl friend. Living in a trance. I give up a big piece of my life to WPST. Toiling in the wings while you out on the stage taking bows like a star. Now I'm withdrawing my participation. Taking out my profit sharing so I can get me an annualized return."

Without visible sarcasm, Talisha said, "I guess I'm saying to myself, 'Why didn't I see the justice of that before?' Is this what they call an intervention? Bring everyone in and confront me with my addictions?"

"Well, I'm sorry to have to educate you on that point. Just think of it as tough love."

"I just couldn't take any more," said Chandler, his voice rising in excitement. He was talking directly at Honor now, pointing the gun at her. The little red laser button did a hip-hop beat on her chest. "Brutally castigated by everyone I knew. Mummy casting me out among the minimum-wagers. Tumbling into years of seedy decline and degradation. You openly flaunted our relationship, then turned your back on me when I was in need. My torment was transparent. Where was your compassion?" His eyes were misting up.

Leone told Talisha to hand them the remote control for the ADT system. She refused.

"Don't compound your problems. Hand it over."

"I don't think so."

"You know I've done some heavy cats in my time. Told them 'Death, be not proud.' Then blown their asses to kingdom-come."

Memories like an old black and white movie were going through Talisha's head. She remembered Leone's dorm room freshman year, him saying come on, shabazz, take them bra and panties off, drink some Tanqueray and get relaxed. When she refused, those two offensive-line mothers come out of the closet, hold her down. They all tell her lay back and enjoy the bone, bitch. We going in all the out-of-sight places. The hour that follow wasn't half so painful as the shit-eating white men from the Athletic Department talking about how three fine young men had "made some bad decisions."

Talisha stood stroking the side of her face with the remote. Looking contemplative. "You know I profess a belief in Jesus Christ. I believe in the Christian faith. Try to live it."

She gave it a deft underhand toss into the open stairway. It arched up over the electric beams and down with a crack of plastic on tile when it hit the floor. It lay beneath the criss-cross mesh of the electric beams.

A long pause followed. Leone and Chandler jointly stared at the remote, then at the window with the ladder, the reality slowly sinking in. They were trapped in the upper floor. The only way out without triggering the alarm was back through the window.

Talisha gave them a foolish smile. "I've got kind of a wealth of experience at throwing monkey wrenches into works."

■ ■ ■

"I'm trying to make a smooth transition here," Leone grunted. He was hefting the back end of one of the commodes upside down through the window, letting Chandler take the weight of it a fifth of the way down the ladder.

"You are nothing but a miscalculation of major proportions!" fumed Chandler. He took a step down. Grunting under the load. The whole operation precarious.

Leone said, "Good thing you don't smoke, man. All that weight you carry around. You must live offa fried pork rinds."

"Shut up, goddam you! Pull back! Pull back!"

Leone was pulling back hard on the commode legs, trying to keep some of its huge weight off Chandler. "I mean it. You really at risk for hypertension. They don't call it the silent killer for nothing. You got a family history of heart disease?"

"Stop. Hold it. I've got to catch my breath. I feel light-headed."

"There you have it. But it's cool. I'm looking past this little by-play. What I figure we do while we up in New York is get you on a physician supervised diet. Then put in some gym time. One of them high-end places with a personal trainer. It's like a whole lifestyle change. Get you shaped up and the chicks will dig you. Get a three-button velvet suit, maybe a cashmere turtleneck."

Chandler told him to shut up and do his bit. He was going to go down a step now. Careful. It was sliding.

"It suppose to slide," said Leone impatiently. "That's

how it get to the bottom. Now quit tampering with the focus. This'll work out. Trust me."

"You cause this to be damaged, get scratches on it . . ." Chandler left the threat hanging in midair. His double chin was flopping, drool running down his jaw.

Honor Revenue was thinking this well and truly sucks. Why did she come up here so late at night? Figured it would be less intrusive. Tell Talisha she's a Libra. Wanted a balanced outcome. Mediate the struggle. Make it a win-win situation. And what does she get? An offer to buy into WPST and then guns stuck in her face.

Leone looked back over his shoulder, getting a bead on where Talisha and Honor were. "You'll have to excuse me if I continue this dominance. But you two stand the fuck out of the way back against that wall."

"That seems like it's against safety regulations," said Talisha casually. "The way you're moving that thing."

Leone twisted his head around again, checking where they were. "What you saying? Safety? You want to co-write a study on it with OSHA?" He grunted and strained some. Said, son-of-a-mothafocka bitch this is one heavy mothafocker. Then back over his shoulder, "I mean what about my needs? Are they part of your safety equation?"

Talisha goes, "So your plan is you get away. Tool off into the sunset with a fortune in commodes. I'll be back here with a bankrupt radio station."

Sweat was running down his face. He was really straining. "Yeah, except I don't know about this back here thing. Letting you use the phone to get the cops on my ass. Well, it would create like a scheduling conflict."

"You're going to kill us aren't you?," said the black girl. Kind of nonchalent about it.

"It's like what the experts say about flying. You have a plane accident, there ain't a safest place to sit."

There it was thought Honor. The callous predator's voice. The song of the sociopath. She knew it so well, and she was freaked. But she had weird thoughts bouncing in her skull. She wanted to wash her hair. Use Finesse shampoo.

"I try to think of myself as more than a gun death statistic," said Talisha. That was when she took one step across the narrow room—nothing stealthy, just a quick darting move—and yanked the gun out of the back of his trousers.

Before Leone could even turn around, she had pulled the trigger and shot him in the back of the thigh.

BAM!

He let go of the commode, twisted around grabbing at the searing pain. Hunched over. Stared at the blood oozing through his fingers in disbelief. "You bitch!" he yelled. "You done shot me!"

She held the gun muzzle down at a forty-five degree angle, ready to give him another one. The leg gave way and he fell to his hands and knees.

Chandler's voice came through the window, kind of strangled and desperate with his strain. "What's happening? What's going on? Leone?"

"The bitch done shot me!" He was crying now, big tears running down his face. He collapsed onto the floor on one thigh in a slowly widening pool of blood.

Honor and Talisha stood at the window watching Chandler struggling under the full heft of the commode now. Grunting. Fighting the massive weight. He took a step down the ladder, the commode slid down behind him, threatening to run over him like a runaway freight train.

"We call the cops," said Talisha, "they'll pick him up in no time."

"True," agreed Honor. Thinking about it. This big teetering edifice on the ladder.

"What is that thing worth again?"

"One million, maybe a million five-hundred thousand dollars," said Honor.

"If it's the right one," said Talisha. "Otherwise what?"

"Maybe $50,000 for a high quality reproduction. If you sold it in New York or Chicago. And you'd have to pay the dealer's commission. Most of them want 40% now."

"And the million-five?"

"It'd go at auction at Christies. They take 15%."

They looked at each other thoughtfully.

"I was always taught that gambling was a godless thing to do," began Talisha. "But sometimes it do seem like fun."

"I'll do the honors," said Honor helpfully. She gave the ladder a strong push. It was planted at such a sharp angle that it moved quite easily.

Chandler couldn't see them. Nothing in his field of vision but ornately carved wood. And now the ground.

"What are you doing? Stop that I say! Stop that, goddamn you!"

As the ladder went into freefall, he peaked emotionally,

gave a piercing scream of pure terror. He hit the ground a split second before the crunch of the commode landing on him.

Together they walked downstairs and out the front door, breaking the electric beam and setting off the central station alarm that would bring the cop cars wailing.

Chandler lay under the Tiverton commode. He was making a gurgling noise and the color had gone out of his lips and cheeks. An urp of blood came out of his throat.

"I'm sure gone miss his cheerful smile," said Talisha.

Honor turned away in nausea from the gruesome spectacle.

Talisha gave her a hug. "You best believe it. That Old Testament eye-for-an-eye tradition was not a bad deal. Now we got what? Legal system tapping him on the wrist going there-there don't do that again now."

Through the upstairs window, Leone was still screaming, "You bitch! You ho'! I'm goin' numb! I'm goin' into shock! Fucking reckless homicide!"

49

"She takes the gun and goes into this attack mode," fumed Leone Jones sitting at the bolted down table in the tiny holding cell. "It's like she got an ego problem. Thinks she's the man. Trying to deal me a mortal blow."

Rannie interrupted and told Leone he needed $25,000 up front or she wouldn't take his case. Get one of those public defenders with the beards. When the judges see them coming they just roll their eyes and get out the maximum sentencing guidelines.

He shook his head in disgust. "Man, I know. Hiring one of them is like assisted suicide. But you gotta unnerstan'. I was borrowing a couple pieces of furniture, see? That's all. And she get all swept up in savagery. It's like collective madness on her part, losing control."

Rannie said borrowing it. That's why you went in with guns.

"It's a rough 'hood," Leone protested. "That's a mitigating circumstance. And anyhow the bitch was always coercing me. Just cause I ain't accustom to natural servility, she was, like, subjecting me to this forceful psychological duress behavior. It's like battered employee syndrome."

Rannie was nonchalant. "It should be an interesting case. Cops are tying Chandler's gun with the shooting deaths of a New York judge and his wife. I never thought of you as holding down a job as a big time hit man. Puts you on a level with Booger-T."

Leone gaped at her. Sweat popped out on his brow. "Say what?"

"Twenty-five thousand," quoted Rannie indifferently. "Up front."

He was whining now. "But what you quoting ain't a affordable cost. It's like a bill of infamy. I mean I gotta lament that big time."

She said if he couldn't raise the money to just come out and say it. She'd get on with her life. She had a hair appointment.

"You trying to belittle me? I think that's a disgrace. I know times have changed, but I got some rights as a client."

Rannie pointed out he wasn't a client yet and maybe he ought to evaluate prison as a permanent storage site for his sorry carcass.

He went, "Evaluate? You the one gotta warrant a re-evaluation of these charges."

Rannie stood up, banged on the door with the flat of her hand. Wham. Wham. "Well I can see you're a bit short of the mark. You'll have a few years to wallow in self-pity. Me? I'm a right and wrong kind of person. Not getting paid is wrong. Next case."

The bailiff opened the door, jammed Leone back in his chair while Rannie went out.

Leone yelled after her, "Ain't this supposed to be the Bible Belt? Where's your Christian charity?"

On the drive down to peninsula Charleston, Rannie was thinking what a jive turkey. They all want you to take their case for free. Say you'll get famous. Win headlines. And then everybody'll come to you. Reap a jobs bonanza.

It was pouring down rain outside, the heat wave finally broken. The wipers on her Cadillac swished. She remembered Leone from back when he was up for rape against Talisha Mackey. Him saying it was consensual group sex which was part of the college experience for the bitch. Anyhow he was the victim here. Being lied on by the ho'. And not having a student-athlete enrichment program outlining forbidden social behavior. What about that deprivation?

Well, what goes around comes around, even if it hits in ironic and unpredictable ways.

After the fashion of the corporate world, Browder Delamere had been blamed by the big conglomerate parent company for the entire debacle of Honor Revenue's disappeared mutual fund. Fired from Dombey & Trouche, he had set up what he called an "investment boutique" above a real estate agency on Broad Street. To date, he had no clients.

Recently separated from his wife, Browder was being sued for half his assets and both houses plus Bellefontaine Plantation. Rannie was representing the wife. When asked, she uncharacteristically declined to comment on the dispute.

Rannie parked on King Street near Elvita's where she always got her hair done. Stepped out of her car and opened an umbrella. In the window of a big wood-fronted jewelry store she saw her mother. Mary Canty was sprawled in a chair, drunk and pursuing a conversation with herself. She was back from Italy, had bought a pair of shoes every day she was there. Forty-five pairs of shoes.

And there was Moira and her fiancée Reynolds being manipulated by a shark of a jeweler who smelled blood in the water. Rannie poked her head in the store to catch a snatch of the action.

Moira said she wasn't about to have a platinum ring. Something that looked so space-age.

All suave, the salesman purred it had been enormously popular in the 1920s and 30s. It was banned from jewelry during WW II. That was why it went out of fashion. So there was a real history there. And it looked fluid and sensual.

Reynolds looked deeply troubled at the price tag, his worst fears confirmed. Stalling there, the temperature gauge on his motor moving into the danger zone.

Moira was doing a scavenger hunt in her purse, then started shrieking at him. "Honestly I had my handkerchief right here! I don't know what I did with it! It's just gone! And I've got something stuck in my eye and I can't see! I'm afraid I'm going to fall down! Take hold of me! Honestly I'm just such a klutz!"

To Rannie it was a scene worth a bit more than to the casual observer. Moira was well under way to driving him crazy with her perpetual victim routine. He was cuddling her kind of embarrassed. Neo-paternalism. Whatever it was called now.

"Hey, y'all two crazy kids pick something spectacular!" called Rannie, and then went back out on the street.

Despite the lawsuit, St. Ambrose was back to its boring somnolent self. The early service was cancelled due to lack of attendance. Pews only half filled at 11 o'clock. Admiral Pellegrin snoring through the sermon.

Rannie felt reasonably satisfied. Maybe even approaching serene. What was it Douglas MacArthur said? In war there is no substitute for victory?

Maybe she'd do something different with her hair this time.

■ ■ ■

Lying in the hospital bed, Beau-Jack said Chandler Lovelace was always up to some disruptive type behavior. It stood to reason he'd have furniture fall on him one day. Honor shouldn't feel bad at all about what happened.

Honor said oddly enough she didn't. There was no guilt to alleviate.

Suddenly, he got enthusiastic. "I do declare you got like this vivid and fluid body. What kind of rapturous terms would you like to hear? I swear I will do the heptathlon of love for you. Strain my hamstrings on the long-jumps. I'd like to believe I'm closing out a victory."

Honor shook her head no.

Taking this bad news he said he felt like he had been shit at and hit. Lying in there all day he had nothing to do but let music run through his head. He had composed a new song. "I'm your Mack Truck, baby. I'm semi-stuck on you."

"Kind of a man and his truck sort of song?" she said.

"Classic country theme for us unassimilated traditional rednecks. Aside from a few bullet holes, here I am in my stud prime. All Blue Ribbon beer and high octane. And you, you're like a sex symbol descended from a lavish penthouse on high. You're like irreality with a big-I. At least give me the impression I'm a strong contender."

"You were just trying to steal from me, right? At least at the beginning there was no infatuation."

"Well yeah. I mean no. It was more than a pure profit-making activity. Sure I got multifarious business deals going. I cash in the chips now and again. But the underlying attitude was pure-T romance."

"What I'm trying to tell you is I have a lot of trouble with *in extremis* love."

"You can't just give off intoxication without responsibility," he argued. "Reduce men to tears of desperation and refuse to marry one of them. There's got to be some kind of middle road into old age."

"Why not? I don't need furs, accessories. Eager neophyte boys forming fan clubs for me. A coterie of admirers. Maladroit young swains. Gloating old roués sipping their Sancerre. I'm used to a nomadic lifestyle. A world of primary colors."

"Well let's say I'm what? Hypothetically intense? For the sake of argument. Suppose despite this you just kept me around for routine pleasures. Let me claim your attention once in a while."

She said maybe during the transition period. Until he found a successor to go ape-shit over. He did have a decent chisel to his jaw. Kind of a cowboy rawhide look.

"I ain't intellectually formidable, but I got some surface smarts. I can feel something blossoming here. When I get all robust again, I see us going down to Edisto Island where they still have some beach the way it used to be. A light-suffused seascape. Pelicans cruising by. Me taking blackmail pictures of you swimming naked. Back here in Charleston we'll be the subject of lurid gossip and speculation."

Honor thought he may not be much of an improvement on previous men, but at least he's a formidable contrast.

50

Honor's mother ordered her to check the flesh of the red-fish. Worms and other parasites tended to bury themselves there. And you could never tell about industrial waste these days, even if it was cleaned thoroughly. She said this with her usual morbid gusto.

It had rained for 24-hours straight dumping two inches of water. Downtown flooded, water rising to the headlights of the cars. Grace Revenue said that was all very well, but the drought had them 6 to 8 inches behind for the season. The corn crop was already dead in most places. Bugs and birds had eaten it trying to get moisture. Squash had quit growing and the beans were just a desiccated mess. It didn't take a seer to pretty much see the future. World-wide crop blight. Starvation on a grand scale.

Honor brushed the pan with oil and shook a heavy dose of parsley on the redfish. Cut a lemon and squeezed it all over the fish. Life had changed in some ways in the dingy splendor of an empty house at the foot of Legendre Street in Charleston.

The Tiverton commode was being auctioned by Christies. With the guidance of Rannie Ralston, Grace had cleared her memory on the subject and decided she hadn't intended it to go to St. Ambrose in the first place. It wasn't exactly a godless moral lapse. She made Honor promise half the money would go to good works. The other half was being used to put Honor into the radio business with Talisha Mackey.

And Honor had a boyfriend she was quasi-serious about.

Beau-Jack was a real *cinema verité* bubba-boy. Kind of a Kid Creole on uppers. Burt Reynolds with real hair playing guitar against a backdrop of sawdust. He had played her a song he wrote called "Growing Up Redneck," then asked her to marry him. She said maybe. He said maybe when? She said just maybe.

At least he basically behaved himself. She didn't have to use kung-fu on him. She could always be confident about that state of things with him.

The day after she checked him out of the hospital, a surgeon and an anesthesiologist got into a berserk fistfight over her. It was preposterous really. She wasn't present. She didn't even know their names. They had operated on Beau-Jack, seen her while doing rounds. Some things stayed the same.

Grace said it was a mystery to her why the new government regulations for carcass beef were so stringent without the same standard being applied to poultry products. Fecal contamination was terrible in chicken. She couldn't count the number of E coli food poisoning outbreaks there'd been in recent years. It was absolutely virulent. Seventeen people had died in Japan this year.

■ ■ ■

Talisha's daddy Odis got so much attention for his performance art that he received a $245,000 genius grant from the MacArthur Foundation. He now called his opus work "Robert Kennedy—A death biography in black voices." All he had to do for the MacArthur money was sit around and be creative.

Her momma Oneida said she was glad of the money but she didn't know about the genius bit. It seemed like she had most of the family brains, managing to ward off the host of disease she kept getting. Her husband just made up stuff and her daughter with her fancy college degree did something at a radio station. She wasn't sure exactly what.

Talisha said that was her momma for you. Had no trouble hiding admiration for her daughter.

What Talisha was doing—with the help of her new partner Honor Revenue—was transforming WPST into a black voices station—gospel, jazz, R&B, soul—the whole musical scope of the African-American experience.

She was driving a Buick Park Avenue and had her hair in long cornrow braids with blue nylon string and brass beads. It rattled when she'd toss her head. She'd talk hip on the air now. Say, "They are just forever!" and "Oo-ee, don't they just throw down!"

The new gig was not totally original. The CD Leone had played during the robbery had gotten a whole bunch of favorable calls. With the cross-over format, the ratings were skyrocketing and ad sales slipstreamed right along behind them. She was suddenly making money for the first time in her life. Spent time thinking about dealing with the consequences of success. Maybe buy a beach house, paint the interior walls turquoise. Wear a python-print spandex bikini. Have folks saying that flower is in bloom.

The smell of money drew Alvin Teckler to the station like a symptom of blight. He still wore a neckbrace, said he hurt all over, was a mess of nagging injuries, felt like a man riding a bicycle home from a vasectomy. What he needed from her was a profit-sharing check for his hospital bills.

She told Alvin she was right familiar with his thieving ways and she had hired Rannie Ralston to handle a forced buy-out of his share. Honor Revenue was buying him out with some desperately needed cash that was about to come out of a certain commode.

He acted all puzzled and dismayed. "Do I need this verbal aggression? It's like a raging malignancy around here. Caustic attacks every way I turn."

She let a silence extend between them, then asked did he catch the name? Rannie Ralston? The watchword in brutal efficiency.

He grumped she's just a lawyer. Sure, there's some brazen audacity there. But he was pretty focused when it came to basic skills. He had the torque his clients needed. And as to WPST, he stood by the principles of absolute justice.

Talisha said what it was was he kept a daily calendar of self-interest.

He said bringing Rannie in was just externalizing the

source of the problem. Send everybody's blood pressure spiraling. Make them all chronically tense. Rannie was the worst divide-and-rule cunt he had ever met.

Talisha asked speaking of tense, did he ever watch the old monster-wrecks-Tokyo movies on TV? *Rodan? Godzilla?* Well Rannie could have written the screenplays. Take it as an act of faith. Or a self-evident proposition. Whatever.

Alvin was into gaze averting as he went out, muttering about how he was misunderstood. Talisha had distorted standards. Where was her moral touchstone? Rannie better have a dam' bazooka in her arsenal if she intended to take him on.

In the news, Clemson had its football team on campus for the summer practice and weight training, and the predictable scandals came in a rush. Armed robbery of a liquor store. Gang-rape of a stripper. Mugging of students. Cocaine distribution. Firing a pistol in a dorm room. The athletic department said it took great exception to this mode of behavior. It promised to re-intensify its student-athlete education program designed to help the players make good decisions on and off the field.

Talisha was musing on all this, thinking how far her life had come when the dude from ASCAP came in wearing a three-button Ralph Lauren suit and band-collar shirt. ASCAP was the middleman outfit you paid for the songs you played. With that long chin of his, the ASCAP dude looked kind of like Lionel Richie.

When he peeled off those killer shades, you could say that a hush settled over the room. He was riveting. No phony elastic smile. And from the way his eyes were playing over her, she met with his approval big time. The word mesmerized came to mind.

He said he was surprised to find she wasn't in designer duds. It tended to defy expectations.

Talisha told him she wasn't fruit of the narcississm tree. She had a strong sense of self. No need to keep time with a Rolex Oyster. Liked old jeans and consignment shop funky clothes. Earth-tones. If he was uncomfortable with it, he could give a fictionalized account when he went back to corporate headquarters.

He said he meant only critical raves. She must borrow her styling cues from, like, an off-duty Naomi Campbell. Look like *soigné* human nature parading its innate innocence. He liked the time-in-a-bottle office décor too. She must have firm ideas on most things. Was she a believer that love could endure?

She said there was sure nothing subdued about him either. It did attest to two powerful personalities encountering.

He proposed how about an interface over lunch at a stylish local restaurant? Maybe some mesquite broiled redfish drizzled with olive oil? And say yes to the wine.

She looked out the window and saw his car was a brand new Cadillac Catera, the model with the red duck in the wreath-and-crest hood badge. She liked the feel of temptation.

"Lunch in the right setting can be one of the journeys of life," he lured.

She said her surface mental state was deceptive. She

wasn't emotionally paralyzed. And she'd visibly revel in a young Beaujolais.

He said he figured maybe a short drink before lunch providing it didn't interfere with her moral code.

Talisha said, "It ain't exactly godless. Leastways not like things been around here lately."

About the Author

MARGOT SINCLAIR played front-row volleyball at Ashley Hall and studied ornithology at Cornell. She spends her winters in Barbour coats and Bean boots, owns her father's Purdey shotgun, and can pole a boat over a marsh at flood tide when the clapper rails can be seen among the Spartina grass.

Her grandparents were part of the Second Yankee Invasion of the South. Between roughly 1888 to 1940, Northern industrial wealth purchased vast tracts of worn-out cotton land, cut-over timberland, and abandoned rice fields. They restored old plantation houses or built new ones, and turned their estates into hunting preserves for duck, quail, turkey, and deer. The railroad brought resort towns to Pinehurst, Camden, Aiken, and Thomasville—golf, racehorses, polo, and quail.

Each winter, the Sinclairs migrated from Tuxedo Park, New York, to Run-a-Gate Hall on the banks of the Cooper River above Charleston. Margot's father was born there as she was much later. She is so much a part of the Lowcountry that she considers herself a valid "ben-ya."